Sisters and Lies

Bernice Barrington works in media and has been writing since she was a child. She lives in Dalkey, County Dublin, with her husband, Brian.

Sisters and Lies

BERNICE BARRINGTON

PENGUIN
IRELAND

PENGUIN IRELAND

UK | USA | Canada | Ireland | Australia
India | New Zealand | South Africa

Penguin Ireland is part of the Penguin Random House group of companies
whose addresses can be found at global.penguinrandomhouse.com.

First published 2016
001

Typeset in 12.5/14.75pt Garamond MT Std by Palimpsest Book Production Limited, Falkirk, Stirlingshire
Printed in Great Britain by Clays Ltd, St Ives plc

A CIP catalogue record for this book is available from the British Library

ISBN: 978–1–844–88371–4

www.greenpenguin.co.uk

Penguin Random House is committed to a
sustainable future for our business, our readers
and our planet. This book is made from Forest
Stewardship Council® certified paper.

For the beloved trio who made this happen:
Brian, Mum and Dad

And I say also this. I do not think the forest would be so bright, nor the water so warm, nor love so sweet, if there were no danger in the lakes.

C. S. Lewis

I.

Rachel: day one, 3.50 a.m.

Afterwards, everything she had done made sense. All those decisions I had questioned, those aspects of Evie that had seemed strange and contradictory, suddenly joined up, like dots on a page. And my own part in the drama seemed inevitable. Fated, even.

But when my mobile rang, deep into that warm August bank holiday, none of this had revealed itself yet. All I knew was that it was the middle of the night and that my phone was ringing and that such phone calls never spelled anything good.

'Rachel Darcy?'

'Yes.'

'This is Detective Inspector Daniel Ainsworth here, apologies for disturbing you like this.'

'What's wrong?'

'It's about Eve Durant. I'm sorry to be the one to inform you but she's been in a car accident. A single-vehicle collision in Lewisham about four hours ago.'

A noise erupted from my solar plexus. Somewhere between a whinny and a scream.

'She has survived,' he added hastily. 'However, she's badly injured, and currently in a coma. We found your number on her donor card. You're her ICE.'

'Her what?'

'Her "In Case of Emergency". Are you a family member?'

'Sister,' I whispered.

'And are there any other family members? A husband? Parents?'

'No,' I said truthfully. 'No, there aren't.'

Detective Inspector Ainsworth paused for a moment, coughed. 'The doctors have described her as serious but stable. May I ask where you're based?'

'Dublin,' I said, gathering breath. 'But I'll be on the next flight to London. Which hospital is she in?' I scrabbled for a piece of paper and a pen as he called out the details. The Queen Elizabeth in Woolwich, he seemed to be saying. Not far from Evie's flat.

'It's a terrible shock for you,' he continued. 'Take care if you're driving. Even better, get someone else to drive. Do you have someone else?'

'Yes,' I muttered. A lie.

'No point there being two accidents.'

'No.'

'I'll call you later in the day to arrange a meeting. Once again, I'm sorry for having to relay this bad news.'

I put down the phone and leaned against the nearest available wall. The clock over the kitchen arch read four minutes to four.

Evie. My artist. What have you done to yourself?

I leaned heavily against the wall, but it didn't seem solid any more – more of a blancmange texture that I could feel myself sinking into. A more logical woman would have grabbed onto something – a chair, a doorframe – to stop herself slipping.

But I didn't resist.

I allowed myself to fall.

When I came to, my cat, Erica Jong, was licking my face, bravely trying to resuscitate me. I held her furry body against me, attempting to catch hold of everything I'd just heard. Had I really understood that policeman correctly? Was Evie really in a coma?

I stumbled to the kitchen and forced down a cup of disgusting sweet tea. Then I tried to think logically about what I should do. First things first: the cat. With a calmness I didn't feel, I knocked on my elderly neighbour's door to ask her if she could mind Erica Jong for a couple of days. She agreed – kind of her, given that I didn't even know her name and it was the middle of the night – then took the writhing animal into her arms without further comment.

After that, I checked my handbag to make sure it still contained my passport and wallet (I'd just arrived back from a trip to Australia, so it did), then packed a tiny night-bag and switched on the security alarm. Ten minutes later I was speeding towards Dublin airport in a taxi, deserted streetscapes flickering past me as we drove.

The taxi driver didn't try to talk, which was good because I could barely breathe.

Evie. Light of my life. My sister.

The left-hand part of my brain reminded me again and again that she wasn't dead. She was serious but stable.

In a coma, though.

How could that be regarded as stable?

I twisted my wedding ring round and round my finger,

soothed by its solidity. I should ring Jacob. Let him know what was happening.

The first tear since the phone call collected in my eye, then fell, hitting my lip, like a salty snowball. But I wiped it away. There could be no tears. Not yet. Not when there was so much to be done.

'The first flight this morning is full,' said the woman at the Aer Lingus desk, her fingernails click-clacking across the keyboard. She had the heavily trowelled-on make-up of all women in that business, and her hair was styled in an immobile top-knot. 'But I can get you onto the seven twenty. Do you want to pay cash or credit card?'

I wanted to tell her about Evie, about the crash, because maybe then she would help me. But when I tried to enunciate the words, nothing would come out.

'Cash or credit card?' she asked again.

'Credit card,' I mumbled, handing over my Visa. She raised her face to mine, and I saw her taking in my appearance – my smattering of tattoos, my nose stud – before she processed the transaction and handed me back my card. 'Have a nice trip.'

The flight wasn't boarding for nearly two hours so I slumped into a metal seat, nauseous with exhaustion but unable to close my eyes. I thought of the book tour, the six-week trip around Australia and New Zealand I'd just arrived back from. Had that really been yesterday? It felt like a million years ago.

My mind drifted towards Jacob again – I hadn't seen him in nearly two months. We'd separated shortly before the trip – or, more specifically, I'd moved out of the home we'd shared. 'It's for the best, Jacob,' I'd told him, forcing

4

myself to believe it. But on the book tour I'd staggered around as if I were wounded – insomniac, drinking too much, incapable of taking off my ring.

I gazed at my phone now, desperate to talk to him. But it was only five o'clock – way too early. I stood up and returned to pacing.

At a certain point, I started to pray.

In London the skies were grey, clouds pregnant with rain. I waited in the taxi queue, smoking a cigarette. One of the few (very few) perks of not being with Jacob any more. No more busting my balls about lung cancer.

I gave the name of the hospital to the taxi driver and he nodded. Unfortunately, unlike my previous chauffeur, he seemed to want to talk.

'Lovely day, innit? Your first time here? Business or pleasure? Do you know Woolwich at all?'

He was young. Too young, maybe, to realize you didn't ask people going straight from a flight to a hospital if they were there for 'business or pleasure'.

'I'm going to see my sister.'

'She okay, is she?'

'She's in a coma.'

'I saw a documentary once. This bloke was in a coma for twenty-three years. Then one day he woke up. And he could speak German.' He was looking at me in his rearview mirror, almost jovial, awaiting my response.

For a moment I wanted to scream at him – call him out for being such an insensitive prick – but in the end I didn't have the will. 'I'm sorry, I'm tired. Do you mind if we don't talk any more?'

The driver glanced at me, a surprised, hurt look on his face. 'Fair enough,' he said, dropping his eyes. We drove in silence for the rest of the way.

In the hospital a heavy-set blonde woman was manning the reception desk, wearing a futuristic headset. As I approached, she held up her finger as if to say, 'One sec,' while she answered a call.

I stood there, inhaling the aroma of bleach and illness, wanting to scream at her, 'Hurry up! Hurry the fuck up!' until she finally glanced in my direction. 'Yes, madam? May I help you?'

'My sister Evie. Eveline Darcy. She was in a car accident earlier this morning. She was brought here – a garda rang me. I mean a policeman. A policeman rang me . . .' I stumbled to a halt, my breath ragged in my chest.

The woman ran a manicured nail down what I presumed was an admissions list, then tapped something into the computer. 'I'm sorry, but no one of that name has been admitted.'

'She could be under Eveline Darcy-Durant, or maybe just Eve Durant.'

'Can you spell that?'

I did.

'Oh, right, yes, Eve Durant. Here she is.' She looked up at me. 'Intensive Care. Second floor.'

'How is she doing?' I whispered, desperate for even the remotest hint that Evie had improved since DI Ainsworth's phone call.

'The ward sister will brief you on your sister's condition,' she boomed, as if we were in a veterinary surgery and she was talking about my cat. Then she looked over my shoulder and nodded at the next person.

I stomped off, muttering, 'Useless,' under my breath, only to find the lift was almost as ineffective as the receptionist.

'You'll have to take the stairs, love,' the electrician explained, as he fiddled about with a mish-mash of wires, so I did, jumping two steps at a time so I could get to Evie quicker.

And finally I found myself outside the ICU. The place where my baby sister was lying, somewhere between life and death.

Evie, my beautiful mixed-up Evie.

How the hell could this have happened?

But then it dawned on me. This day had been coming for a long time. Had, perhaps, always been coming. And I had done nothing to prevent it.

2.

I made my presence known to the ward sister, and shortly after that a consultant arrived through the swinging double doors to talk to me.

'Your sister has sustained injuries to the head, which have induced coma,' the petite brunette woman explained, in a voice somewhere between factual and empathetic. 'Dr Elizabeth Bartlett' was written on a name tag pinned to her chest. 'From CT scans we have ascertained that the cerebral cortex has been damaged – that's the grey matter, which covers the brain. It looks after perception, sensory input, all of the neurological functions, actually.'

'But she will wake up, won't she?' I said, hearing my voice rise to a level just under hysteria.

The consultant fixed me with her bright blue eyes. 'Ms Darcy, I'm sorry but I need to give you the full facts. The truth is, we don't know. She may wake up today, but it could be next week, next month, next year, even.'

'Yes, but people always wake up, don't they?'

'They don't always,' the doctor said, continuing to hold my gaze. 'But we'll do everything we possibly can for your sister.'

For a second we stood in silence. 'Can I see her?' I whispered.

'Of course,' she said gently. 'We'll just need you to wear a protective mask, and to clean your hands with the antibacterial liquid.' She pointed at a plastic container attached to the wall.

A few minutes later, when I was suitably attired, she guided me through the double doors and towards a single room where my sister lay. 'Please try not to be too upset by her appearance,' she said. 'Remember, she's getting the best possible care and any bruising or cuts you see are merely superficial.'

'Merely superficial'. That was ironic. Evie was the cleverest, most creative person I knew, but in the last few years she had become obsessed with her appearance. These days, she was all angles, highlights and expensive make-up.

'Her heart rate is stable, although we've had to ventilate her with a tube to help with breathing. And, as I said, her other injuries are minor: two fractured wrists, probably sustained on impact. Some bruising.'

I knew the doctor was trying to make me feel better but it wasn't working. 'Can I touch her?'

Dr Bartlett hesitated, then nodded. I edged towards the bedside and slowly reached out for Evie's hand. It felt surprisingly warm.

'I'll leave you alone for a few moments,' the doctor murmured, and the next sound was that of the door closing.

I didn't notice that I was crying until the tears ran into my mouth at a funny angle. I wiped them away with my sleeve. 'Evie. Sweetheart. What have you done to yourself? Why didn't you tell me?' I held her hand tighter, as the heart monitor pulsed in the background. Now that the initial shock was out of the way, I allowed myself to look at Evie's face more closely. She had a purple bruise above her right temple and numerous scratches across her face, but the doctor had been right: they would all heal. None seemed deep enough to leave a scar.

I reached out my other hand and touched her hair, half expecting her to jolt awake with surprise. But of course she didn't. She remained cadaver-still. I allowed my hand to explore her face, using one finger, as if searching for dust. I started with her forehead, tracing a slow vertical line between her eyes, moving downwards, along her nose. It still amazed me, that nose. Or should I say that new nose? (It was not the one she had been born with.) Finally, I ran my finger over her lips and finished at her chin, the road map of my sister's face complete.

'I'm sorry, Ms Darcy. Your time's up, I'm afraid.' The consultant was back in the room, still carrying her notes, her voice sympathetic but firm. 'You could sit in our waiting area, but my best advice would be to go to your hotel or wherever you're staying and get some rest. I imagine you need it.'

Reluctantly, I rose from my chair, hovered over Evie and kissed her forehead lightly. 'Fight, Evie,' I whispered. 'Promise me you'll fight.'

I was disappointed when she didn't respond.

Out in the corridor the doctor gave me some more information about the extent of Evie's injuries – something about a Glasgow Coma Scale; Evie rated quite badly – and told me she or a member of her team would ring me immediately if there was any change in my sister's condition. 'You're staying in London for the time being, I take it?'

'Yes,' I said. 'For as long as is necessary.'

The doctor nodded. 'As I said, we can't be certain of a time frame. There is a possibility she'll wake up in the next forty-eight hours. Many patients do. It would probably be as well if you could stay around here.'

'I will,' I said.

'Do you need help with accommodation? I can arrange to have our patient liaison officer help you find a hotel if that would —'

'That won't be necessary,' I said. 'I'm going to stay at Evie's.'

'Of course,' she said, adding, 'You seem close.'

'Yes,' I answered, although now that I thought about it, I wasn't sure. Why, for example, did I not know that Evie was driving again? That she had a car?

'Oh, it was her boyfriend's, I think,' Dr Bartlett said, when I voiced my confusion.

'Her boyfriend? Evie doesn't have a boyfriend.'

'Well, her friend, then. He was in here directly after the accident, but before you arrived. I think he said his name was . . .' She scrunched up her face. 'Doc-nah?'

Doe-nah? I'd never heard that name. Was it Middle Eastern? Asian? 'Where was he from?'

'Ireland, I think.' She paused for a moment as if double-checking her memory banks. 'Yes, definitely Ireland.'

It suddenly dawned on me. Donnagh. The Celtic name, meaning 'warrior'. Pronounced 'Dun-ah'. 'Do you have a number for him?'

Dr Bartlett tucked a rogue strand of hair behind her ear. 'I'm sorry, I don't, Ms Darcy. Although, no doubt, the police will have all that information for you.'

I sighed, annoyed at the lack of clarity. Who was this man? Why hadn't Evie told me about him?

Dr Bartlett turned to leave, giving my arm a quick squeeze. 'Stay strong,' she said. 'There's always hope.'

She reminded me of my mother then. The gentle look. The half-smile starting at the corners of her lips.

'Mammy,' I whispered, the name forming on my tongue before I was even conscious of it. I remembered the stories from the First World War. How the young boys had called for their mothers as they lay dying on the fields of Flanders. Had Evie called for our mother as she had crashed? I turned to the doctor again, knowing she wouldn't have the answer, but she had already walked away.

Another taxi driver, another streetscape, this time towards Evie's apartment.

Evie lived in Woolwich – quite near the hospital, in fact – in a tiny flat purchased with the proceeds from our mother's estate. It hadn't covered everything, but it had left Evie with a manageable mortgage, which was important since her day job, as a journalist for a business magazine, paid peanuts. All the same, I knew she felt guilty that she was in some way benefiting from our mother's death.

'Nobody thinks that,' I'd reassured her after visiting the place for the first time. 'In any case, you minded Mammy for that whole year she was sick. She wanted you to have something to fall back on.' I paused for a second, touching her lightly on the shoulder. 'She might be concerned about the cosmetic surgery, though.'

Evie drew away, casting me an angry look. 'Oh, fuck off, Rachel. That's none of your business.'

'Maybe not, but I'm worried about you. Since Mammy went, you seem to be overly concerned with –'

'With what?'

'With your appearance.'

'This from the prettiest girl in Leitrim. What right do you have to be lecturing me about what I do or don't do with my body? You've always had it easy!'

'I haven't,' I muttered.

'Yes, you have. Your little Audrey Hepburn features. Your tiny figure. And, by the way, the tattoos and blokey clothes are fooling nobody.'

I put my hand to my face, an attempt to stave off Evie's invisible blows. She was right, people did call me pretty – but only because I looked different from other Irish people: sallow skin, brown eyes, very dark hair. That didn't mean my life was perfect, though. Not the way Evie thought. 'I'm not trying to fool anybody,' I shouted. 'I dress the way I do because I like it. Same goes for the tattoos. And as for my figure, you know I've always been a beanpole. It's not a lifestyle choice.'

'Oh, how convenient!' Evie roared. 'Well, some of us aren't as genetically blessed as you, Rachel. The truth is, you feel threatened now I'm no longer the Ugly Duckling of the family. Now that I'm finally taking back some control.'

'Oh, for fuck sake! Would you listen to yourself?' Because I didn't feel threatened, I felt scared. Our mother had just died and now Evie was on some bizarre mission to reinvent herself. As if at some subconscious level she thought it would help somehow. As if it was going to bring Mammy back . . .

As the taxi sped towards Evie's place, I tried to ring her flatmate, Janet, to warn her of my arrival, but there was no answer, so I was forced to leave a message on her voice-mail. Did she know about the accident? About this Donnagh character? Would she mind me bedding down for a few nights – who knew how long? – while Evie was in hospital?

Once we got there, I buzzed the intercom a few times, but got no reply. Then I tried Janet's phone again. Still no answer. Finally, I rooted round in my handbag and withdrew a set of keys, which Evie had given me when she'd first bought the place.

'*Mi casa es tu casa,*' she'd said, attaching a fluffy pink key ring to them. That was the thing about Evie. She'd lash out one minute, and be the best of friends the next. 'An artistic temperament,' my mother had said. Exhausting, I'd secretly thought.

I pushed the key into the front door of the block, letting myself into the hallway, which was full of bicycles and junk mail scattered everywhere. There was no lift, so I took the large stairway, not quite able to jump them two at a time as I had done in the hospital.

I arrived at the front door of Evie's flat, staring at the canary yellow colour she'd painted it. Normally it made me laugh – Evie would rather die than be conventional – but today all I felt was sadness. How could my beautiful sister have wound up in this situation? How could things have gone so wrong?

I knocked once, to make sure that Janet wasn't there.

Then, when I got no response, I pushed the key into the lock and turned it.

I had just dropped my bag onto the floor when I felt a presence near me. I looked up to see a tall, dark-haired man standing directly opposite. 'Donnagh?' I said, feeling a knot tighten in my stomach.

'And you are?'

'Rachel, Evie's sister.'

'I suppose you'd better come in.'

3.

I couldn't figure out why Evie had told neither of us about the other. 'So you're saying Evie insisted she was an only child?' It made no sense.

'Well, she didn't insist exactly,' Donnagh explained, in a strange transatlantic accent. 'She just said she had no brothers or sisters. And I didn't question it.'

'Weird,' I muttered, clutching a mug of coffee. 'This is all so weird.'

'Yeah, it is,' he said, clasping his mug equally tightly. His forehead creased into a frown. 'How did the doctors say she was? Has there been any improvement since I was in there this morning?'

'No,' I said. Who the hell was he? Why had Evie been driving his car?

'I don't know,' he said, when I asked him that exact question. 'I was asleep in bed when she took it.'

'You were what?'

'It was late at night. I didn't even hear her leaving the flat. Honestly, Rachel, I haven't a clue why she would take my car. I didn't even know she could drive . . .'

I stared at him, his words swimming in my brain. He sounded plausible, but could I trust him? Why was he in my sister's apartment? Didn't he have his own place?

'I used to,' he said, in a subdued voice. 'But unfortunately it was flooded recently. Eve offered to let me stay here for a couple of weeks while it was being repaired. It wasn't like we were moving in as a couple or anything. It was just a temporary arrangement.'

'And what about Janet?' I butted in. 'What did she have to say about all this?'

'Janet?' Donnagh said, staring at me blankly. 'Sorry, I don't think I've heard of her.'

How could he not know who Janet was? Janet was Evie's best friend, the first pal she'd made when she'd arrived in London and by far her closest. She'd known about the nose job and about Mammy's death and had even called her 'Evie', just like me, not subscribing to this 'Eve' nonsense.

'I'm sorry, Rachel, I've never heard of her,' Donnagh repeated, leaning back in his chair. As he did so I noticed a small, surgical bandage on the underside of his neck.

'Hurt yourself?' I asked, pointing at it.

He shrugged. 'Just a shaving nick.'

'Must have been a pretty big razor,' I said, 'to inflict that kind of damage.'

'It was blunt and may have been used on a lady's legs shortly beforehand.' He smiled weakly. 'Not that I'd ever complain about such a thing.'

We were silent for a moment, the image of Evie defuzzing her legs with Donnagh's razor at once too frivolous and too intimate for this sombre environment.

After a few seconds, Donnagh looked at me again. 'I'm sorry, Rachel, I guess you must be confused as hell right now, given you didn't even know I existed until an hour or so ago. Do you want me to bring you up to speed? Start from the beginning, I mean.'

'The beginning?' I repeated. 'Yes, I suppose that makes sense.'

'Fine. Well, I suppose the obvious place to start is where we first met.'

'Go on.'

'Eve interviewed me for the business magazine she works for, *Business Matters*. She was profiling me.'

'Profiling you?'

'Yes. I'm the CEO of a construction company – well, of the European wing anyway.'

'So you're a high-flier?'

He shrugged. 'My uncle founded the main company, back in the States, so really I'm just the result of nepotism.' He attempted a smile but I couldn't bring myself to return it. 'Anyway, my job is to look after our European projects and drum up new business over here.'

'Right,' I said, taking in his large, smooth hands and his handsome face. He didn't look like a man who spent his days tramping round building sites. More like someone off a Calvin Klein ad.

'But back to Evie. How long have you known each other? I've been away in Australia and New Zealand for the last six weeks so I realize I'm out of the loop but, still, I'm surprised Evie didn't mention you.'

'Well, to be fair, it did all happen very quickly,' he said, reaching into his back pocket and pulling out his mobile phone. 'Let me see,' he said. 'Eve interviewed me on . . . Yes, here it is. The sixth of June, so that was what? Around eight weeks ago?'

'Yeah, about that.'

'And after that things went fast. We started dating within a week —'

'Living together within six,' I interrupted.

'Yes,' said Donnagh, meeting my gaze. 'I can see that might come across as a bit sudden.'

I nodded. 'Quite frankly, it does.'

'Okay, so here's what happened,' Donnagh said, lacing his fingers together and pushing himself forwards in his chair. 'We'd been seeing each other for about five weeks when, as I mentioned earlier, my apartment was flooded. I was informed renovations would take less than a month and, though I probably shouldn't have, I asked Eve if I could temporarily move in with her.'

'Why?'

'Well, on a practical level, this flat is quite near my office, plus I hated the idea of a soulless hotel.'

'So far, so handy for you.'

Donnagh glanced up, a wounded look on his face. 'It wasn't like that, Rachel. I was in shock. My home had been wrecked, along with most of my possessions. And I felt something with Eve.'

'Meaning what exactly?'

'There was a connection. An intensity. I felt quite vulnerable at the time. I know it sounds stupid but I think I wanted her to take care of me.'

Something welled up in my throat, making it difficult for me to speak. 'Fair enough,' I said quietly. I knew that feeling of vulnerability. Of needing love.

Donnagh straightened in his chair. 'Look, I know there can be no question of me staying here now. I'll move into a hotel, but please let me know if there's anything I can do – to help, I mean.' He pulled out a business card and thrust it into my hand.

'Um, okay,' I said, my head spinning. 'Will that be inconvenient for you? How long have you got left with the renovations?'

'Oh, it's run on, of course. It'll be another few weeks, but don't worry about that. I'll find a hotel.'

'I see.'

'I'll come back tonight and collect my stuff, if that's okay with you?'

'Sure,' I said, my mind whirring.

'I'm really sorry but I have to go now – I must put in an appearance at the office. They have no idea that any of this has happened.'

'Do your colleagues know Evie exists?'

'Some do. We've been at a few events together. But they have no idea she's been involved in a car crash.'

'Will you tell them?'

Donnagh's shoulders seemed to slump. 'I don't know,' he said quietly. 'I'm not sure I've told myself yet.'

At the door, Donnagh reminded me he would be back later in the evening. 'I'm so sorry about all of this, Rachel. I know you probably blame me, given that Eve was driving my car. But you must believe this: I cared deeply for your sister. I'm devastated this has happened.'

'Are you?' I snapped, raising my eyes to meet his.

'Yes,' he said. 'Yes, I am.'

I watched his retreating back as he made for the front door, my mind racing with questions: could I trust him? Had he been honest?

There seemed to be so much as yet unexplained, so many gaps in the picture he'd just painted. But then I thought of his sad eyes, the reference to Evie using his razor. I'd wanted to dislike him but, instinctively, I felt he was telling the truth.

As I walked out of the building's main entrance my phone rang.

'Rachel, it's Janet. I just got your message. Jesus Christ, is she okay?'

'Not really. She's in a coma. When did you move out?'

'A few months back. Didn't she tell you?'

'No.'

'Did you know she had a boyfriend?'

'No.'

Janet hesitated, then said, 'Can you make it as far as Greenwich High Road? I'm off today – we could meet for coffee.'

'That would be great.'

'Will we say that sandwich place Evie likes, the one with the pink wallpaper? Around half twelve?'

I looked at my watch – I had twenty minutes. 'I'll be there.'

4.

When I arrived, Janet was already standing in the queue. We embraced and she asked me what I wanted. 'Anything, I don't care,' I said.

She nodded, then gestured to two seats that had just become available in the far corner. 'Nab them.' A few minutes later she placed something wrapped in cellophane in front of me. 'How are you, hen?' she asked, gently touching my arm.

'I'm okay,' I said, and immediately disproved it by emitting a huge sob.

She pushed her chair back and came over to me. 'Come here,' she said, giving me a hug. 'Let it all out.'

I let some of it out, but it was a public place and I didn't want to make a complete show of myself. After a couple of seconds I withdrew and she handed me a packet of Kleenex from her handbag.

After I had mopped myself up, I explained what the doctor had told me about Evie's condition. And about the mysterious Donnagh.

'Who is he?' Janet said, between mouthfuls of her cheese and pickle sandwich.

'Haven't a clue, save what I've just told you.'

'Haven't you looked him up yet?'

'No,' I said, pointing to my ancient phone. 'No internet connection.'

'Jesus, Rachel. How do you survive without a smartphone?' Janet rustled in her handbag and withdrew a swishy mobile. 'Is it some writer thing? Afraid it'll interfere with the creative process?'

Actually, it was because Jacob had given me my phone – for my birthday years earlier – and I couldn't bear to part with it. But I didn't feel like going into all that.

'Okay, so how do you spell his name?' Janet continued.

I told her. For the next few minutes, she didn't say anything, just flipped through pages on the screen, deep in concentration. 'Right,' she said, looking up. 'As far as I can tell, he was born in Dublin but left Ireland for the US as a teenager.' She flicked the phone round so I could look at the screen. 'He's a partner in a company called Hibernian Constructions owned by his uncle Sean. He heads up the European division. I'll send you the link if you think you can find a computer to read it on.'

'Sure,' I said. Evie had a laptop in her bedroom. Not that the link sounded particularly useful – Donnagh had already given me most of this information during our chat.

'I can't believe Evie didn't tell you about him,' Janet continued, picking at her sandwich.

'I was about to say the same to you.'

Janet raised her head slowly, a deep blush spreading across her face.

'Jesus, Janet, what's going on? Donnagh said he'd never heard of you. Did something happen between you and Evie?'

'I suppose you could say that,' she said.

'So tell me.'

23

Janet coughed. 'Well, we had a falling-out about four months ago and we haven't spoken since.'

'Was it serious?'

She didn't meet my eye. 'Pretty serious.'

I wasn't sure how to respond. Should I press her for more details? In general, I'm a great believer in boundaries, respecting people's private lives, but not today. 'Janet, come on, you've got to tell me what's going on here. My sister is lying in a coma, and there's a stranger in her house who claims not to know who I am. Please, throw me a bone.'

'She'll kill me for saying anything. You know how much she looks up to you.'

Actually I didn't.

'There was this thing with my boyfriend.'

'You have a boyfriend?'

'Don't sound so surprised,' she said, but she smiled shyly. 'We met at work. He's a teacher too. Anyway, one night I walked in on Evie with her top off, trying to seduce him.'

'O-kay,' I said, thinking the most obvious thing: that it takes two to tango.

'It wasn't like that, Rach,' she said, intuiting my thought process. 'Patrick is useless around women. It took him ages to work up the courage to talk to me, and we work side by side. He couldn't seduce a dead cat, let alone a woman like Evie.'

'Go on.'

'Afterwards, I had it out with Evie but, of course, she denied everything. Said he'd come on to her, that it was borderline assault, and I'd be better off without him.'

'Christ almighty, why would she do such a thing?'

'Because she was jealous, I guess.'

'But that doesn't sound like the Evie I know. She'd never lie about something so serious.'

Janet played with her sandwich for a moment, then looked up at me. 'You haven't really seen much of Evie this past year, have you?' The way she phrased it didn't sound like an accusation, more a statement of fact.

'I suppose not,' I muttered.

'You've been busy. Evie told me. All your book success. Congratulations on that, by the way. She also said you and Jacob were trying for a baby.'

'Did she now?'

'Sorry, I wasn't supposed to know that, was I? Anyway, my point is, you've probably spoken on the phone more than seen each other in real life. Would I be right?'

'Yes.'

'Look, I'm not trying to be horrible. I know you're going through hell at the moment. But Evie was going through some stuff too.'

'Stuff?'

Janet coughed. 'Okay, I'm just going to say it. She was getting out of control, Rachel. Drugs, mood swings, sex with strange men.' She made the sign of the cross. 'May God forgive me for saying all this because Evie won't. She'll fucking kill me.'

I sat back in my chair, allowing myself to take in this new information. Well, new-ish information. I knew Evie had a wild side. It hadn't been evident during her teenage years – back then, I'd been the wild one – but since we'd lost Mammy, since she'd moved to London, I knew she'd changed.

I'd thought for the most part, though, it was under control. I mean, who in their right mind would move to the world's greatest capital and *not* take drugs and sleep around? Within reason. I don't mean injecting heroin into yourself in a squat in Stratford. I said as much to Janet.

'I thought that too for a long time. I'm not exactly a stranger to class-As myself. I'm from Glasgow, after all . . .'

We smiled grimly. Black humour. Always Janet's strong point.

'But she was changing as a person, Rachel. Becoming, I don't know . . .' She flung out her hands as if trying to grasp the right word. 'Self-destructive, I suppose you'd call it. Sometimes she seemed okay – exercising and eating well, going to her evening classes in art. But every so often there'd be these massive blow-outs, snorting a load of coke, picking up random men. And then there were the other times.'

'Other times?'

'When she wouldn't come out of her bedroom. When she'd just sleep all weekend . . .'

I shuddered. It sounded so depressing.

Janet drew a breath. 'When I got together with Patrick, things went from bad to worse.'

'How so?'

'She accused me of turning into, I quote, "a right boring cow". Mainly because I'd reined in my drinking a bit.'

'And she didn't like it?'

'To put it mildly. But I was nearly thirty and, for the first time in my life, in a good relationship that seemed to be headed somewhere. I wasn't going to risk all that by getting off my face with Evie every night.'

'And then she tried to sleep with your boyfriend.'

Janet nodded, her eyes suddenly teary. 'I was so angry with her, Rachel. I knew what she was trying to do. Destroy me and Patrick so she could have me back as her partner in crime. She didn't like the new clean-living me with a life, a future.'

'So what happened?'

'Well, first I tried to reason with her, tried to get her to seek help. But when she refused, I just lost it. I told her she was a lying two-faced bitch for even suggesting Patrick had come on to her, and that if she ever attempted to mess with me or him again that perfectly formed nose would be bashed into the back of her skull.' Janet sat back in her chair and took a deep breath.

'So did you move out or did she kick you out?'

'I moved out, bag and baggage, to Patrick's, and that was the last I heard of her until today. Until you . . .'

We sat in silence, looking at our half-eaten sandwiches.

'Janet, please don't think I don't believe you, but no one has mentioned anything about drink or drugs in connection with the crash. Not yet, at any rate.'

She nodded. 'Doesn't surprise me. The whole thing came in cycles. Sometimes Evie could be clean as a whistle. But when she went for it, I mean really went for it . . .' Janet slapped her palms together.

'Bang,' I whispered.

'Exactly.'

She stood up. 'I'm really sorry, Rach, but I've got to head off. I'm going on a bloody school tour to Belgium in the morning and haven't packed yet. But please text me if there are any developments. Otherwise I'll call you when I get home.'

I stood up and we hugged.

'The truth will come out, Rachel. It always does.'

'Hmm,' I said half-heartedly, as she headed for the door. To be perfectly honest, I'd never found that to be the case.

5.

As I made my way back to the hospital, mulling over what Janet had said, my phone rang. It was Detective Inspector Ainsworth, checking to see if I had arrived.

'I had to go to Evie's apartment briefly but I'm on my way back to the hospital.'

'I'll meet you there,' he said. 'Give you a run-down of the situation as we see it.'

The situation as we see it? What the hell did that mean? As I saw it, my sister was lying in a coma with no guarantee that she would ever come out of it. How many other ways were there to see it, exactly?

He was there when I arrived, a stocky man in plain clothes, sporting a paunch and a distinct air of superiority.

'Ms Darcy,' he said, extending his hand. 'Pleased to meet you.' Then he turned towards the nurse on Reception. 'Nurse, have you that spare room free?'

'Yes,' she said, coming out from behind the desk and padding towards us. 'Follow me.'

A few seconds later we were outside a door, with a sign, 'Family Room', on it. We went in, a sense of panic rising in me. I couldn't help feeling this was the place where doctors broke bad news: *Your father has died . . . Your son will never walk again.* Dr Bartlett hadn't brought me here when she'd explained Evie's condition, possibly with good reason. Rooms like this did not signal hope.

'I just wanted to go through a few things with you, Ms Darcy. The legal side . . .'

'Sure,' I said, as a wave of exhaustion washed over me. It was nearly four in the afternoon now. Almost twelve hours since I'd got the phone call. Thirty-six hours since I'd returned home from Australia. In the meantime I felt like I'd been through some sort of mangle.

'First, can I just clarify your sister's full name?'

'Eveline Darcy-Durant.'

'But she goes by Eve Durant generally?'

'Yes,' I said. As children we had made a pact to abandon the French part of our name, just as our father had abandoned us and fled back to France. But when Evie had moved to London she'd started using it again. All part of her self-reinvention.

DI Ainsworth nodded and wrote something in his notepad. Then he cleared his throat. 'Ms Durant was driving without a valid licence at the time of the accident, meaning she'll be formally charged when she wakes up.'

'She's in a fucking coma,' I spat, unable to help myself.

'I fully appreciate how difficult this is for you, but I need to clarify all aspects,' he replied, his jaw twitching. He seemed annoyed with me, which was fine because I was annoyed with him. Insensitive prat.

'Furthermore, the car she was driving was not her own. It belonged to one . . .' he glanced down at his notes '. . . one Donnagh Flood. We have spoken to Mr Flood and he says he doesn't want to press charges or recoup damages incurred. However, since Ms Durant does not appear to have any insurance, she will be required to foot all other bills, most especially those in relation to the wall.'

'The wall?'

'Ms Durant crashed into a wall, the property of Lewisham Borough Council, and will be billed accordingly.'

I stared at him, wondering if I'd been somehow transposed into a Kafka story: woman fights for her life as weird bureaucrat analyses how much she owes to the state. Was this some kind of joke?

'So have you people figured out what happened to my sister?' I said, trying to turn the tables a little. 'Evie can't have crashed for no reason. Somebody must have driven her off the road.'

Ainsworth eyed me coolly. 'Ms Darcy, I don't think you understand. There was no other driver. Ms Durant was alone on the road – well, save a few parked cars, which, luckily, she managed to avoid.'

'What?'

'It was quarter to midnight in a quiet suburb. She was the only one driving at the time, and there were no mitigating circumstances – no frost, no brake problems or otherwise with the car. Our mechanics have checked.'

'What are you saying?'

'I'm saying that the accident seems to have been the fault of the driver herself. She wasn't intoxicated but there are indications she was speeding. It could have been inexperience – as I said, she didn't have a valid driver's licence.'

'Okay.'

'Or maybe . . .'

'Maybe what, Inspector?'

'Single-vehicle collision, dead of night.'

I didn't like what he was implying. 'Are you trying to say it was attempted suicide?'

He had the good grace to blush. 'We can't rule it out,' he said, retrieving his coat from where he'd left it on a nearby seat. 'The hospital will let me know if there's any change in your sister's condition. I sincerely hope there is.'

'So you can formally charge her?' I muttered.

The policeman drew himself up to his full height. 'Ms Darcy, I accept that this situation is hard to come to terms with, but please bear in mind that I have a job to do. If your sister goes to court, she will most likely get a rap on the knuckles and a community-service order rather than a custodial sentence. But she has broken the law and this must be recognized.' He put on his coat, bade me good day and walked out of the room, leaving me alone.

'Wanker,' I whispered, at the still-swooshing door, not caring if he heard me.

I thought about all he had said. Jesus Christ, what had Evie got herself into? And why had she stolen her boyfriend's car?

And then I thought about the attempted-suicide comment, and his apologetic stance as he'd made it. What I'd failed to mention was that, if Evie had tried to kill herself, it wouldn't have been for the first time.

6.

Evie

So, to clear up that conundrum once and for all, can people in a coma hear? The answer is yes. Loud and clear, Captain.

Well, I can anyway. Maybe other people in this situation haven't a clue what's going on, and I'm the one-in-a-million freak show, but I doubt it. Human science really is a dark art, isn't it? No wonder I dropped out of medical school all those years ago. Might as well have been reading tea leaves.

I'm being facetious. Which shouldn't come as a surprise, seeing as I'm IN A COMA and my life has boiled down to this terrible nothingness. I'm exaggerating a bit when I say I hear 'everything' loud and clear. I hear fragments. I recognize voices. I already have my favourite nurse, whose name is Heather and who hums when she's alone with me. So far, I've recognized Beyoncé's 'Crazy In Love' and Snoop Dogg's 'Drop It Like It's Hot', although the latter needs a bit more work. Fair play to her for trying to hum hip-hop, though.

I'm pretty sure I've heard Rachel's voice. But only very briefly. Mostly I think I've just heard her crying. I don't know how to feel about Rachel being here. Relieved, I guess. But also mortified. She's going to bloody kill me.

I wish I could tell her I'm actually conscious in here, try to calm her down a bit, but unfortunately I'm incapable of movement, let alone speech, and I don't even have the luxury of Locked-in Syndrome, where at least I'd be able to do the blinky-eyelid thing.

It's ironic, really, because Locked-in Syndrome was always number one on my fantasy illness list. As in, when you're out at a party with friends and go, 'What's the worst illness you could imagine contracting? The absolute most disgusting, torturous thing?' And people start talking about flesh-eating tapeworms and the like. Well, mine was always that one: where you're totally functioning mentally, but completely paralysed, save maybe an eyelid, which you flap around wildly, trying to blink the alphabet.

What I wouldn't give to be able to blink the alphabet now. (My right tit, frankly.) Be careful what you (don't) wish for is the motto there, I guess . . .

But, Jesus, how did I get onto that? So much has happened that I don't know where to start.

I suppose most people would suggest the beginning – try to retrace my tracks a bit.

If only I could remember my tracks.

That's the problem, see.

Chronic amnesia.

Well, okay, maybe not chronic. I do remember certain things: memories from my childhood, going to secondary school, my twenty-eighth birthday party earlier this year. But recent events, as in what happened to me over the past forty-eight hours, for example . . .

Not a sausage.

The doctors say I crashed into a wall in Lewisham. Lost

34

control of the car. But even if that's true, there's got to be more to it. I don't own a car and I haven't driven in ages. Why would I have suddenly decided to take to the open road late on a Sunday evening? To bloody Lewisham! None of it makes any sense.

I can't help feeling somebody might have set me up – tried to make it look like I crashed. I wouldn't have thought I had many enemies, but then again, who knows? It's not like I've been a paragon of virtue since coming to live in London. Not by a long chalk.

So, now that I've got all this time on my hands, I've decided I'm going to go through my memories systematically, try to cobble together what happened out there. I've decided to start with two months ago, mainly because that's the point I can currently remember from, but also because it coincides with when I met Donnagh, and where I believe this story starts.

Donnagh Flood.

My boyfriend, I suppose you'd call him.

Did he hurt me? Did he put me in this coma? That's what I need to figure out.

I'm going to kick off my investigation with memory number one: my heinous boss Nigel sidling up to me eight weeks ago, in the middle of a sweltering heatwave, mouthing something I couldn't quite make out.

'Sorry, I didn't quite catch that, Nigel?' I said, taking out my earphones.

'I said, if you're not already hot and sticky, Durant, you're going to be. I've just put the wheels in motion for an interview with Donnagh Flood, rising star of Hibernian

Constructions and better in the sack than Colin Farrell, so the rumour goes.' Then, just in case I hadn't quite got the message, he looked at me and said, 'Major Irish shagger.'

I stared at Nigel and, not for the first time, wondered how my life had whittled down to this: poorly paid lackey for the world's most boring business magazine, not to mention the world's first human toad.

'We'll call the piece "Donnagh Deal",' Nigel continued, beaming at his own cleverness. 'Talk about how his uncle mentored him in America. How he feels about eventually taking over as worldwide CEO . . .'

'Where's he from?' I asked, trying to sound casual. The name had rung an alarming bell but it couldn't be . . . It just couldn't be!

'Ireland,' Nigel snapped. 'Or haven't you been listening to a word I've said?'

'I mean what part of Ireland?'

'Oh, right,' he said, pulling a face. 'Haven't a clue. I do have a photo, though.'

'Can I see it?'

He riffled through his desk and found the newspaper cutting that had obviously inspired the feature idea. He thrust it in my direction. 'You don't know him, do you?'

I stared at the piece of paper, my eyes riveted to it. No, it couldn't be. But when I looked down again, I knew it was him. It was definitely him.

'No, of c-course not,' I stammered. 'But, Nigel, um, would you mind if someone else did this one? I'm up to my tonsils and . . .'

My boss stared at me. 'Eve, I wasn't asking you, I was telling you. I want you to do it. Good-looking woman like you – bound to coax some secrets out of him that those two heffalumps wouldn't manage.' He pointed in the direction of my closest colleagues, George and Tom.

'Nigel, really, I'd prefer not to,' I said, trying to think of an excuse. 'I have to go to the dentist that day.'

'You don't even know what day you're interviewing him yet.' Nigel was staring at me, his bald head turning red with annoyance. It was not a good sign, that bald red head.

'But –'

'Eve. There are no buts. Set up the interview this week, and tell his people we'll use him for the front cover too – good-looking bastard that he is. You okay with that?'

Well, obviously not, I wanted to scream back. But I didn't. Mainly because my mortgage was due at the end of the week.

'Fine. I'm off for a fag,' he said, grinning at me.

Twat.

When he was gone I stared at the newspaper cutting once more. Donnagh Flood had lost the childish round-ness of youth but it was still recognizably him: the same almond-shaped brown eyes, the strong jaw, the slightly plump lips. Your average Mills & Boon hero, basically.

He and I had attended the same secondary school a decade and a half earlier after he'd joined my class in the second year. The teacher had introduced him as 'our new pupil from Dublin' – leaving out the fact that he was teen-dream gorgeous, all lips and shoulders and chocolate-brown eyes – then sat him with me at my desk. When he'd asked me my name, I could barely speak.

'Eveline Darcy,' I'd croaked, trying to smile.

'Evelyn?'

'No, Eve-leen,' I'd repeated, emphasizing the last syllable. 'After a short story by James Joyce, which my father loved. He's French, by the way.'

'Who, James Joyce?'

'No, my father. From a place called Calais.'

Donnagh looked at me as if I was an alien, then twisted his mouth into a smirk. 'Oh, Eve-*leeeen*, is it? Calais? Did he give you that humongous nose too? Is that also French?'

I could feel my smile falter as my hands rose towards my face. As a matter of fact, my father had given me my nose. I barely remembered him, but from the few pictures I'd seen, I could tell that his was the same as mine: Roman, with a hump at the bridge.

If Rachel had been there she'd have known what to say – something about Donnagh's stupid accent or the whiff of BO off him or his bacon breath – but Rachel was not there. She wasn't in the same school, even.

Back in the classroom, Donnagh Flood had garnered an audience. 'Big nose,' he whispered, as soon as the teacher's back was turned. He continued whispering it throughout the class, and then to my assembled classmates outside. And for the next five years.

Now I had to interview the bastard.

For the next few days, I weighed up my options. If I didn't do the interview I might lose my job. I had a mortgage to pay, and now that Janet had moved out – well, stomped off – there was no rental income to help subsidize it.

And it wasn't as if the world of journalism was exactly going through a golden age either: over the past year I'd sent out twenty applications and got precisely two face-to-face interviews for positions even worse than the one I was presently in – neither of which I got.

No, losing my job wasn't an option. But neither was interviewing Donnagh Flood. Just thinking about it reduced me to that fourteen-year-old girl again, biting the insides of her cheeks so she wouldn't cry and embarrass herself further. I'd have to think of a way out: feigning illness, death of non-existent family member, minor drug overdose.

If the worst came to the worst, I could pull out the menstrual card. Nigel's fear of women's problems was so great he couldn't even watch an ad for Tampax without gagging and making a face. Perhaps if I came in on the morning of the interview with a hot-water bottle, muttering about cramps, I'd somehow get out of it. It went against all my feminist principles, but it was worth a try.

However, any thoughts that I could dodge this particular bullet faded the next day when Nigel swaggered up to me. 'Good news. Donnagh Flood is on for the interview.'

'What?'

'I met him last night at that Builders Awards thing. Pure coincidence. Told him this sexy Frenchwoman wanted to interview him and he'd better be ready for her.'

'Nigel, I'm neither gorgeous nor French,' I said, when what I really wanted to say was, 'You fucking sexist moron. Some day I'm going to hit you with sexual harassment so hard it'll knock your balls off.'

'Anyway, he said he's looking forward to it. Wants you to ring his secretary and she'll fix up a time.' He pushed a business card in my direction. Donnagh's card. 'Think he said this week would suit best, something about going to Chicago next. So get on it.'

I stared at the card, taking in its blue logo: two unevenly sized skyscrapers.

'You all right?' said George, looking up from his computer screen. 'You're white as a sheet.'

'I'm fine,' I said, feeling my head sway a little. Then I ran to the Ladies to be sick.

7.

In the end I accepted my fate. I rang the secretary and arranged to meet Donnagh at a posh restaurant in Canary Wharf, near his office, no expense spared. Although I normally preferred interviews that didn't involve food, this time I was delighted to have the distraction of other diners. I was hoping it would make the whole thing less nightmarish. Maybe Donnagh wouldn't scare me so much once I knew there was back-up in the form of waiters and other people.

Maybe.

But I still needed a plan.

First off, I was going to look hot: smokin', as a matter of fact. That would mean getting my nails and tan done the night before, a trip to the hairdresser on the morning of the interview, and no carbohydrates for the rest of the week so I could fit into that knock-off Roland Mouret dress that looked discreet but was actually slutty as hell. I was going to make the guy think twice for having called me unattractive for five long years.

I also practised my affirmations in my bedroom mirror and a few cognitive-behavioural techniques I'd picked up here and there. 'You are a strong, beautiful woman,' I repeated, trying hard not to feel like a complete gobshite. Naturally I didn't believe it but that wasn't the point. What was important was that Donnagh believed it. Believed that I had changed.

And then there were the shoes – my *pièce de résistance*. Black-patent Jimmy Choo stilettos, bought as a treat for myself on my twenty-eighth birthday, with heels so spiky they could have been used for performing vasectomies. Once I was wearing those, I felt protected. Call it the footwear equivalent of Dumbo's feather. They would help keep me strong.

That and the half a Xanax I was intending to slip directly before the interview. Just enough to take the edge off, but not enough to have me slipping into the soup. I'd thought about a line of coke, but decided against it. I needed to be relaxed for this interview, not jumpy. And, anyway, I didn't do drugs during the week – certainly not class As. I mean, I did have some standards. After that, it was just a case of being my usual charming self.

How hard could it possibly be?

Easy, right?

I arrived at the restaurant early, my heart thumping so hard that I thought the manageress would comment on the sound. She didn't. Instead, having taken my coat, she guided me towards the table, her blonde ponytail swishing as we walked.

'Can I get you a drink while you're waiting?'

I wanted to ask for a large G&T, but I ordered a bottle of sparkling water instead. Mixing alcohol and prescription medication probably wouldn't be wise. In any case I needed to have my wits about me when that fucker showed up. Even as a teenager he'd been sharp, and I was sure time wouldn't have dented that.

I removed my recording device from my bag and placed

it on the table, checking for the umpteenth time that it was working. Then I took a sip of water. 'Some day this will be a funny story you'll tell your friends,' I told myself inwardly. 'The day you met the guy who bullied you half to death when you were a kid and you looked fabulous.'

I didn't feel fabulous, though. I could feel sweat patches developing under my arms (thank Christ, the dress was black) and a sinus headache beginning at the front of my forehead. 'Keep it together. Forty-five minutes, and it'll be over. You'll never have to see the bastard again.'

And then I spotted him. Hard to miss, really, given that he was over six foot and built like a rugby player. Yet somehow he seemed to glide among the tables – balletic, you might say.

I could feel sweat trickling down my back.

'Ms Durant. Donnagh Flood.' He proffered his hand. 'Please accept my apologies for running late. Something urgent came up at the office.'

'It's fine.' I was totally overwhelmed by the physicality of him. He seemed to have grown wider and taller since the last time I'd seen him. Not to mention even better-looking. It was like being in the presence of a movie star. The tan, the teeth, the perfect body under the expensive suit.

There was a second's pause, and then he pointed at my recording device. 'I suppose I'd better remember that's running so I don't give away too many of my trade secrets.' He flashed a smile in my direction.

'You don't mind, do you?' I spluttered. 'It's just so I can accurately quote you. I find it hard to take manual notes when I'm trying to eat.'

'Mind? Of course not. I just need to watch that I don't shoot my mouth off. I get the feeling you can be very persuasive.' He flashed that smile again, and something in my stomach flipped. Was he flirting? Already? Fucking hell, he'd barely taken off his coat.

But then again he was so manly you could practically smell the pheromones coming off him. Was that why my body was pinging to attention? Just like when I'd been fourteen. Sweet Jesus, had it learned nothing?

'So, *Durant*. That's French, yet you sound Irish. What's going on there?' More teeth. More smiling.

And then it dawned on me. Slowly. Very, very slowly.

He didn't recognize me.

He. Did. Not. Recognize. Me.

I began buttering a piece of bread, a delaying tactic while I considered what to say. It seemed indecent not to reveal who I was. And yet . . .

God, it was tempting not to. I mean, what did it matter anyway? It wasn't like I was going to see him again. And what harm could a little bit of deception do? A tiny lie of omission.

'My parents were French but I grew up in Ireland,' I said, avoiding eye contact.

'Where in Ireland?'

'Clare,' I replied, the first place that popped into my head.

'So you won't have to stop and ask me what I'm talking about when I say things like "feck", "arse" and "girls", then?' He was chomping a piece of bread now, like a lion tearing into flesh.

'Hardly. *Father Ted* is the greatest Irish TV show ever

44

made,' I babbled, still not looking at him properly. 'I can quote the Eurovision episode verbatim.'

'"My Lovely Horse"?'

'Exactly.'

'So you look French, but you've got an Irish sense of humour. Wow. You must be popular.'

I stared at him. Okay, he was definitely flirting now. But please, God, let him not ask me to speak French. I'd learned it at school but I was far from fluent.

We ordered some food, and then I got down to the business of interviewing him. My hand shook so badly as I pressed the Dictaphone button I was afraid he would comment on it. But if he noticed he didn't say anything.

We started at the beginning. The 'Tell me about your childhood' stuff.

'I spent most of my early years in Dublin,' he began. 'My father was a bricklayer, my mother a housewife. Happy enough childhood, I suppose. I was an only child.'

'Right. Sounds nice.'

'Yeah, it was, until I was fourteen, when my father died unexpectedly and me and my mam had to move to Leitrim.'

'Leitrim?' I said, my throat tightening. Three minutes in and we were already talking about my home county. There was no way I'd get through the interview undetected. No fucking way.

'Yeah, my mother had family there. Bit of a shock, needless to say, coming from the Liberties . . .'

'I can imagine.'

'Believe me, you really can't.'

'So were you popular at school? What kind of boy were you?'

Donnagh shrugged his shoulders. 'I don't know. The usual. Spotty. Arrogant. Full of hormones.'

'A nice boy?'

He looked at me, his eyebrows raised. 'Do you always spend so much time focusing on someone's childhood, Ms Durant?'

I coughed. 'Sorry, I didn't mean to make you uncomfortable. I just like to get a sense of a person's background.'

'It's not a problem,' he said, grinning a little. 'And to answer your question, no, I was definitely not a nice boy.' He paused. 'But, then, who wants a nice boy?' He caught my gaze and held it, causing my stomach to flip.

'Let's fast-forward a bit,' I said. 'You're now one of the most successful young Irish entrepreneurs operating in London. How did that happen?'

Just at that moment, our food arrived. An anaemic piece of salmon for me, rare steak for Donnagh. He dug into his food before answering, a stream of bloody juices erupting, lava-like, onto his plate. 'Do you want the long or the short version?'

'Um, whichever you prefer, I suppose.'

'Okay, the short version it is. After my dad died I went off the rails for a few years. Hated Leitrim, hated school. Barely passed the Leaving Cert – the final state exam . . . Well, of course you know what it is.'

I nodded. 'Yes.'

'Then I started getting into a bit of trouble with the law. Nothing huge. Nicked a car. Was caught with a small amount of drugs. But my mother saw the signs.'

'The signs?'

'That I was on course to do something really stupid with myself.'

I must have raised an eyebrow because he added, 'Ending up in prison. Or dead. She was probably right.'

'What did she do?'

'She got my uncle Sean involved. Out in Chicago. He's the man who founded Hibernian Constructions. We're in partnership. I head up the London operation. He's back in the States.'

'And am I right in saying you lived over there?'

'Yeah, for seven years, give or take. I was actually born there, before my parents moved back to Dublin. But Sean brought me into his business. Started as a labourer, worked my way up.'

'And according to my research you also got a management degree.'

He smiled. 'Someone's done her homework.'

I found myself blushing. 'It was all on the internet.'

'Well, yes, I did get a degree,' he continued. 'I realized that if I wanted to be taken seriously in this game I needed to know the fundamentals, so I did the course at night.'

'Impressive.'

He shrugged. 'Not really. Sean and his wife had no kids and they treated me like the son they never had. They were offering me the business on a plate. Would have been a schmuck not to take them up on it.'

'Schmuck? So you really have been Americanized.'

He grinned. 'I also say "trunk" for "boot" and "candy" for "sweets". It drives people crazy. But you'd know all about that, being bilingual, I presume.'

'Oh, yes,' I said, not contradicting him. A regular poly-glot, me.

The interview went on, and I picked at my food, barely able to swallow it. I was focusing so hard on not giving myself away, while at the same time asking credible questions, that I felt like I might pass out.

Finally, some ninety minutes later, and after I had declined dessert and coffee, the interview drew to a close.

'You never asked me about my love life,' he said, rising from his chair.

'Um, sorry. It's not that kind of interview.'

'Every interview is that kind of interview,' he said, taking my coat from the waitress and holding it open so I could slip my arms into the sleeves.

'And for the record, I'm free and single. No children. And not gay.'

'I was pretty sure you weren't gay,' I said, unable to stifle a smile.

He smiled back. 'Do you send me the article before it goes into your magazine or do I have to trust you?'

'The latter.'

'Lucky I'm the trusting sort, then,' he said, shaking my hand. 'Goodbye, Eve Durant. Or should I say *au revoir*?'

'*Au revoir*,' I said, to his back. Then, under my breath, 'May I never see you again.'

Okay, so why did he not recognize me? I wondered the same because, sitting opposite to him, I'd still felt like the terrified fourteen-year-old girl he'd taunted on the first day of second year. But while I still felt like her, I guess I didn't look like her any more.

The obvious thing was that I had lost weight. A *lot*. We're talking around five stone here. I was a fat little barrel when I was a kid, particularly once I'd hit puberty and had tossers like him telling me how unattractive I was. I comfort-ate and ballooned to about fifteen stone at my heaviest, which, even given that I'm five foot eight, was still pretty barrelly.

Also, I wore glasses and braces, and rocked an absolutely appalling haircut. And, of course, there was my nose. First you met my hooter, and then you met me. I've already described it — Roman, with a huge hump at the bridge — the kind of nose a rugged farmer couldn't pull off, let alone a young girl with otherwise delicate features. Not that I saw anything about myself as delicate. I used to look in the mirror at my eyes — which were green and some might say pretty — and curse God for playing such a cruel joke. Lovely, delicate eyes, all the better to observe the travesty of a honker I'd been born with. Needless to say, I learned the concept of irony early.

Anyway, I lost the weight at college and discovered contact lenses around the same time, which sorted out the glasses issue. Not to mention a good hairdresser who bestowed on me honey-blonde highlights instead of the mousy colour Nature had granted me. Which left my nose. That was the hardest thing to change. Not just because it required surgery and the means to pay for it but because it required me to become the kind of person who would have surgery.

I had been brought up to believe that cosmetic enhancement was the preserve of rich, mad Americans, not 'normal' down-to-earth people like me. My mother had encouraged me to love myself and embrace my difference, which was all very easy for her to say, given that she had a perfect snub nose, like Rachel. But when she was alive I had sort of believed her. Even though I'd hated myself then I'd trusted that at some point in the future I would grow out of it. With her help. With her guidance.

But then she died. It took nearly a year – ovarian cancer – and I nursed her through all of it. A week after the funeral, I booked the nose job.

Rachel and my boyfriend of the time, Artie, tried to talk me out of it, referring to the 'delirium of grief', but they might as well have been talking to a deaf person. They told me I should allow myself time to think about it when I was feeling better. But that was the problem. I couldn't feel anything. Nothing at all.

8.

Rachel: day three, 9 a.m.

Yesterday was hell. I spent hours sitting with Evie, talking to her, willing her to wake up. Nothing. She occasionally twitched and her eyelids fluttered, making me think that she was about to wake up. But then it was back to nothing again. On the doctors' advice I began speaking out loud, just in case Evie could hear me. I chatted about upbeat stuff: any celebrity gossip I could think of, what the staff were like, the things that had been going on in my life.

Well, some of the things. I didn't tell her about Jacob, about the fact that we were separated. She had no idea about that and I wasn't going to tell her now, when she was lying in a chronic vegetative state with no certainty she would ever come out of it.

The words Dr Bartlett spoke a few days earlier came back to taunt me: 'You seem close.'

I'd always thought so, and I'd been angry with Evie for not telling me about Donnagh. But who was I to talk? Jacob and I had been separated for over two months and I'd never breathed a word of it to my sister. Maybe it was because I knew she'd be so disappointed. She saw Jacob as the brother she'd never had.

'You okay in here?'

Dr Bartlett had joined me in the room. 'Fine, yes,' I

51

replied, trying to smile. My skin felt as if it might rip with the effort.

'Mind if I talk to you for a moment?'

'Sure.'

'I just wondered if you were coping okay. I know how traumatic this kind of thing is for relatives. We have a counsellor available if you wish to speak to someone.'

'No,' I said, shaking my head. 'That won't be necessary.'

'The thing is, Ms Darcy –'

'Rachel,' I interrupted.

'The thing is, Rachel, it's been more than forty-eight hours now and we still have no clear indication of when your sister will wake up. Many patients do so between two and four weeks after going into a comatose state. But some take longer.'

'And some never wake up.'

She held my gaze. 'Yes. That is true sometimes.'

I blinked, desperate to keep the tears at bay.

Dr Bartlett continued, 'I know you're based in Dublin so I just wanted to say that if you need to go home for any reason – to see family members, to collect belongings – you should do that. We'll keep you abreast of any developments.'

I stared at her, appalled.

Dr Bartlett sighed. 'Rachel, your sister is still heavily comatose. It could take several more days, weeks even, for this thing to play itself out.'

The tears I'd been holding back stung the corners of my eyes.

'I promise I'm not trying to panic you but if there are things you need to organize, work, children, family stuff...'

I shrugged weakly. 'Yes, some of those things.'

'. . . then go home and organize them. You'll feel better. If your sister wakes up we'll ring you immediately. If not, then at least you'll be sorted for the long haul.'

She touched my hand briefly. 'I wouldn't advise this if I didn't think it was for the best.'

I looked at my hand where she had touched it.

'I'll leave you to mull it over,' she said quietly, making for the exit.

Before she left, I called to her, 'You will ring me if she wakes up?'

'Of course, Rachel. That goes without saying.'

After she'd left, I stood beside Evie's bed for a second, barely moving. Then I was lunging for my jacket, reaching for my bag, and then I was kissing her. Over and over again. Telling her how much I loved her. That I would be back in no time, before she knew it.

Next thing I was running out of the door and into the corridor, nearly bumping into a group of nurses. It reminded me of something. A memory. A feeling.

Like I was a panther. Running all the way home.

I didn't even bother going back to Evie's flat. Instead I rang Donnagh and told him what my plan was. It seemed only polite now that we were flatmates. Crazy though it sounded, I hadn't actually kicked him out when he'd come round to pick up his stuff. I'd asked him to stay.

'Are you sure, Rachel?' he'd replied, clearly shocked. 'You don't even know me.'

'True, but I trust Evie's judgement,' I said, even though I wasn't sure I did. The truth was, I wanted to find out more about him, about his life with Evie. How could I do that if I booted him out onto the street? I might never see him again.

'If you're sure,' he said, putting his bags down on the carpet, looking at me doubtfully.

'I'm sure,' I said, and I meant it. Of course, it was a little risky to live with a stranger, but I'd had far more dubious flatmates in my time. In any case, I wanted the company. I couldn't bear the idea of wandering around London like I'd done in Australia: tormented, depressed, drinking too much. I needed someone to keep an eye on me. To remind me I wasn't entirely alone.

Once I had told Donnagh of my plan, I caught a taxi to the airport and booked myself onto the next available flight to Dublin, my mind racing. There was so much to organize: my cat, work, Jacob. I still hadn't rung him. And now that so much time had passed – nearly three days – it seemed wrong to blab out Evie's condition over the phone. I felt compelled to tell him in person.

He was going to be so mad with me. Actually, 'mad' was the wrong word. 'Chronically disappointed' was more like it. I could practically see his face falling, his eyes drooping. He would see this as yet another sign that I wanted our marriage to end and that it was all over bar the shouting.

The trouble was we still loved each other. But, as the cliché goes, we wanted different things.

To be specific, Jacob wanted a baby. He hadn't always wanted one. Before we'd got married I'd explained that I didn't want children and he'd been fine with that. 'You're all I'll ever want,' he'd said, and I'd believed him.

But then his little sister Grace had died, aged ten, from

leukaemia. For about six months Jacob had staggered through his grief, like a man flailing in a ditch of briars. One night he came home and started to cry. He didn't speak for a long time. Afterwards I understood why. It was because he was launching an atomic bomb at our relationship and was trying to put off the inevitable devastation for as long as he could.

'I want a child,' he whispered eventually, and I felt as if I had plunged off a precipice, the earth racing up to meet me.

He explained that grief had altered him, like when your skin is burned and you're left with a permanent scar. He talked about cycles. Lack of permanence. Wanting to have something 'real', though.

Until then I'd followed what he was saying. The grief stuff I understood. Mammy had been gone a few years longer than Gracie, but my loss was still a giant rent down the middle of my soul. Something real? 'Am I not real enough for you?'

He'd looked at me as if I was being obtuse, but then his eyes softened and he took my hands. 'I can't describe it, Rach. I just need something to begin again.'

He had saved himself with that line because I understood immediately what he meant. After Mammy had died, my new beginning had been him. Our relationship had been in its infancy, and he had dragged me across the line of grief into a world where things were possible again. Where *I* was possible again. But that had been six years ago. New love was not an option for Jacob. He needed a new life.

We tried. For a month I went off the pill, and we had

unprotected sex five times. Each time I felt as if I was floating above my body. I felt no pleasure at all. Only a sense that I was a vessel. It was the first time in our entire love-making history that I had felt disconnected from Jacob.

Maybe my body sensed my hostility because it didn't take. I got my period in a remote wood in Wicklow, to which I had driven when I should have been working on my third book. Nobody was around so I pulled down my jeans, stared at the rusty stain on my knickers and cried. I cried so hard my throat felt sore afterwards. But it wasn't out of disappointment. It was out of relief.

Later I told Jacob I loved him but I couldn't give him what he wanted and if he really needed to be a father the only sensible thing to do was to leave me.

'You know I'll never leave you,' he said. 'You're my life.'

But it's easy to say that. Over the next few months I watched as his eyes landed on kids when we were out in restaurants: the way he smiled unconsciously at something cute a toddler said or did, then tried to hide it when he realized I was looking at him. And the way his eyes dulled. I didn't want to be the reason his eyes dulled.

It was me who ended it.

'You want children,' I said, fighting to get the words out, 'and I don't want to deny you that.' Tears were trickling down both our faces. 'I think we should separate.'

'No,' Jacob said, grabbing me by the shoulders. 'Can't you see that this can't be it?'

I gently removed myself from his grasp. 'But if you want a family, you need to find someone willing to give you one. I know it's hard, but . . .'

He tried to hold me again, but I wriggled free.

'It's like ripping off a bandage,' I said, immediately regretting how flippant that sounded.

Something seemed to change in his eyes. 'You want this, don't you?'

I didn't say anything. But he was right.

Losing Jacob was like losing a limb. But if it had to happen I wanted it over with. Quickly. Also, I was tired of being the person who was denying him his 'real' life. I wanted to hand him back control.

9.

From Dublin airport I caught a taxi straight to my flat – the one I'd been living in since leaving Jacob. It was one of the soulless modern ones built near the docklands during the Celtic Tiger era, complete with paper-thin walls and beige everything. It wasn't beautiful but, in a strange way, it suited me: sterile, monochrome, the exact opposite of everything Jacob and I had shared.

I made myself a quick cup of coffee, then tapped on my neighbour's door. 'Hello, Mrs –'

'Oh, hello! Rachel, isn't it?' she said, extending her hand. 'I'm Mrs Flanagan. Well, call me Edith. Come in, come in.'

I entered her sitting room, and sat down at her behest. I could see Erica Jong in the kitchen and *pssh*ed at her to come over and join me. She ignored me. 'She's angry,' I said.

Edith Flanagan frowned. 'Cats can be like that. Don't take it personally. How is your sister? Better, I hope.'

I shook my head. 'That's why I'm here. She's still in a coma and the doctors have no idea when she'll come out of it. If she'll come out of it . . .'

'Oh dear,' she said, putting her hand to her mouth. 'I'm so sorry to hear that.'

'Thanks,' I said. 'Anyway, I'm just back for the day. Trying to sort things out . . .' I gestured at my non-responsive cat.

'Oh, goodness, don't be worrying about her. I can take care of her, if you want me to.'

'Mrs Flanagan – Edith, I couldn't possibly expect you to do that,' I said. 'A friend looked after her recently, when I went away travelling for a few weeks. I'm sure she'll help me out again.'

'Oh, no, please,' she said, quite forcefully. 'Please let me take care of her.'

'Are you sure?' I said, wondering why she was being so insistent.

'I'm sure,' she said. Then, in a quieter voice, she added, 'Ever since my daughter convinced me to move into this place I've felt like a fish out of water.' She waved in the direction of the kitchen. 'I know it's modern and that I should be grateful but . . .' She glanced at Erica Jong. 'Everyone is so young and so unfriendly. The cat is the only thing that's made me feel welcome since I moved in.'

For a moment we were silent as I looked down into my lap, feeling guilty that I was one of the unfriendly people she was talking about. 'Well, you must keep her,' I said. 'And, here, please take this.' I rooted around in my purse and withdrew a few fifty-euro notes. 'That should take care of her food and stuff for at least a month. After that, I can transfer more into your bank account if Evie still hasn't . . .' I was afraid I was going to start crying.

'Goodness, Rachel, it's okay. I don't need your money.'

I looked up at her, blinking hard. 'I want you to have it.'

'No,' she said softly, pushing my hand back towards my chest. 'You have enough to be worrying about. So please don't worry about your cat.' She took a biro out of her handbag and wrote something on a piece of paper. 'Here, take my number. You can ring me to check on her any-time.'

'Thank you,' I said softly, and then, without warning, we embraced.

Later I called my editor, Antonia, who was based in London. It would have made sense to call into her office when I'd been over with Evie at the hospital, but I hadn't been able to face her. Instead I did my explaining over the phone.

'My God, Rachel, I'm so sorry to hear that,' she said. 'To be frank, I'm amazed it hasn't reached the papers yet.'

'I don't think anyone in the hospital recognized me.'

'Well, let's hope it stays that way. Or do you want us to issue a statement?'

'No. I'd rather keep it under the radar for the moment, if you don't mind. Cross that bridge if and when we come to it.'

'Sure, if that's what you want.'

'It is.'

After that I told her the rest of the bad news: that, because of Evie's accident, I wouldn't be able to do any more speaking engagements, or have my third manuscript ready in time.

'Of course, Rachel,' she said, in a slightly tighter voice. She'd sounded concerned before, but now I couldn't shake the feeling that she was pissed off. Not with me necessarily, but with Evie. Or karma. Or whatever cosmic forces had caused this terrible misfortune to occur.

I couldn't blame her. Apparently I was 'hot right now' – I'd actually heard a publicist use the phrase – and they were eager to rush out my new book on the heels of *Sanc-*

tuary, my second, which had somehow made it onto the *New York Times* and *Sunday Times* bestsellers lists.

And now my silly comatose sister was derailing everything.

Well, fuck that and fuck them, I thought. I was going to stay by my sister's side as long as it took and they could stick their publishing deal up their –

'Rachel, are you okay?' Antonia said, sounding less pissed off now. 'Take as much time as you need. We all completely understand. Or if you want to send me what you've written and we'll see what can be done?'

'That's okay,' I said. 'I'll get it finished.'

What I didn't mention was that, as yet, I had failed to write one solitary word.

I had never intended to become a writer. I was the nomad of the family – Evie was the brainy one. After finishing my politics degree, I'd spent most of my twenties wandering around the globe, working in such varied jobs as tattoo assistant, cattle rancher and, briefly, receptionist in a Melbourne brothel. Finally bored of the peripatetic lifestyle I'd returned to Ireland, completed a master's and started working in a women's refuge. Then Mammy got sick.

Evie did the really hard work – the washing, accompanying her to chemo sessions – while I earned enough to cover the bills. Then, when I came home at weekends, it was my job to entertain. I would regale Evie and Mammy with stories from my travels, about the inspiring women I met through the refuge, my thoughts on politics, culture, feminism. At some point Mammy asked me to write them all down.

'And don't be censoring them. I know you've got up to all sorts. Tell me about it. I promise I won't be shocked. I'll be proud.'

I made an ironic face at her. 'Hmm.'

'I will. I love that I've raised such a feminist for a daughter. I love your tattoos and your Doc Martens and your fearlessness. I want to hear all about it.'

So that was what I did. I wrote her little vignettes, which seemed to spill out of me, then emailed them to her every week. Of course I edited them. I wasn't going to tell her about my 'summer of ketamine' in Budapest or that time in Chicago, when I'd had the lesbian fling.

Obviously.

But I gave her the gist.

And then one day, about four months after my mother died, I had a call from somebody called Antonia Lloyd, telling me she 'loved' my manuscript.

'What manuscript?'

'*The Restless Feminist*. The one you sent us six months ago.'

Mammy.

'It's so beautifully drawn: your travelling experiences, the underlying feminist message, your belief in the sanctity of human choice. Can we meet?'

I put down the phone and walked to my bedroom where a picture of my mother was framed beside my bed. 'What have you been up to, lady?'

A few days later I met Antonia, who was wildly enthusiastic about publishing my vignettes as a book. At the end of the meeting, she handed me an envelope. 'This came with the manuscript. Did you write it to yourself?'

She held out a thick cream envelope with the words: 'Only to be given to Rachel if you decide to publish her book. VERY IMPORTANT'.

'Um, yes,' I mumbled.

She was clearly confused, but didn't comment any further. At home, I opened a bottle of wine, locked the door and began to read.

Dear Rachel,

If you are reading this you have got a publishing deal or as near to one as makes no difference. I don't know anything about that world, but what I do know is that you have a remarkable story to tell and a remarkable talent. I want the whole world to know about it.

At this stage I am probably gone and you are probably sad. Don't be! Life is a river, it flows on. I will always be in your memory, I know that. What I want you to do now is to live fearlessly. Triumphantly. Carpe diem! Tell others how to do so.

Be brave, my darling girl. I love you so very much. I hope I am now looking down on you (I think I am), but the most important thing is that we had each other. For some time. And it was wonderful.

I know you will look after Evie. She is gifted beyond words also, but needs to recognize it. Please help her to.

Love you always,
Mammy

PS That boy you introduced me to, Jacob? Marry him.

I thought of Mammy's advice now as I sat in my freezing Dublin apartment in the half-light. I *had* married Jacob, on a sunny June Friday, wearing daisies in my hair and a long blue dress I'd found in a vintage shop. By then Mammy had passed away, but Evie had accompanied me down the 'aisle', the centre of a Victorian orangery, and Jacob's baby sister had read an extract from *The Little Prince*.

We had been so happy then. Jacob still had Gracie, with no inkling of what was to come, and I had started healing through him. Because of him.

Now, though . . .

'Live fearlessly'. The words Mammy had written in her letter came back to me. For so long that had been my motto, but now I just felt tired. As if I didn't have the energy to fight any more.

'Cop yourself on,' I muttered. I picked up my jacket and made my way to the DART. I was going to see Jacob. This was not the time to be falling to pieces. I had learned the hard way that fearless was the only option.

10.

On the DART I tried ringing Jacob's mobile to tell him I was on my way but it went straight to voicemail. Still, there was no backing out now. Whatever happened, there was no way I was going back to England without telling him what had happened to Evie. Not after I'd trekked all this way.

I tried to imagine how he would take the news. Shock? Sadness? Anger? He might insist on coming with me to England – convince me I couldn't do it on my own. But surely that would be an awful idea. We were separated. We couldn't resolve the children issue. Clearly, it was best all round if we just left things the way they were.

Although who was I trying to kid? I was dying to see Jacob. Sure I'd banged on about wanting to tell him in person, convincing myself it was because I wanted to do 'the decent thing', but in reality, I just wanted to be near him, to touch him. We hadn't seen each other in so long and I felt like an anorexic dying without nourishment. I'd been lying when I'd convinced myself about returning to Ireland: it hadn't been about my cat or my apartment or picking up clothes. I could have sorted all of that out from London. It had been about Jacob. It had been a pathetic excuse to see him again.

Over the past three days, as I'd watched Evie lying in a coma, something had clicked into place. I couldn't get through this without his love. Yes, I'd left our marriage because of my refusal to have kids – something which had seemed impossible to resolve at the time – but now, with all that had happened to Evie, maybe there was a way to put things back together. Jacob was my rock. My shelter. If I didn't have him, how could I find my way through this nightmare?

I continued thinking such thoughts all the way to Dun Laoghaire at which point I got off the DART and began to walk along the seafront. The day was sweltering so the place was thronged.

I removed my trusty leather jacket and, for once, cursed my jeans and Doc Martens. It was a uniform that stood me in good stead for ninety-nine per cent of the year in Ireland, but today I looked ridiculous. Like some kind of vampiric creature while everyone else was walking around in sundresses and cut-off shorts.

But I didn't care – soon I would be seeing Jacob and, though I knew I shouldn't, I started to imagine him slipping off my tank top, climbing on top of me and covering my mouth with the warm, salty tang of his own.

For a moment I allowed my mind to linger, imagining what it would feel like, but then I shook myself. 'For fuck sake, Rachel,' I heard my internal voice lecture. 'Things are already too confusing, plus your emotions are running high. Put your jacket on and stop thinking lascivious thoughts.' Reluctantly, annoyed at the logic of my own voice, that was exactly what I did.

And then, just a few minutes later, I was standing in front of it: the cottage I had once called home. It was small and ivy-clad, with sparkling views of the Irish Sea.

Every morning when I'd lived there, I'd risen and thanked the universe for giving me that life. For Jacob. For delivering him to me.

Now I stood in front of the familiar lilac door and tapped loudly on the brass knocker, pausing for an answer. Except no one came. I took out my phone and dialled Jacob's again but it was still off. He'd probably gone for a swim. If that was the case, he wouldn't be down at the nearby Forty Foot, like all the other sun-worshippers: he'd have cycled over to Killiney to his 'secret' beach, miles away. I could picture him there, his body strong and lithe – his arms piercing the water rhythmically with each stroke.

As I was thinking this, I heard a noise, somewhere between a crash and a thud, and, a few seconds later, Jacob emerged from behind the door, his hair on end, wearing only a pair of boxer shorts. 'Jesus Christ, Rachel,' he said, rubbing the back of his head, glancing towards the bedroom. 'What are you doing here? Ever heard of ringing?'

'I did,' I said. 'Several times. Your phone is dead.'

'Oh.'

'Can I come in?'

'Um, well, now's not a great time.'

'Oh, for God's sake,' I said, pushing past him. 'I really need to use the bathroom.'

'Rachel, you can't just barge in here like this.'

'Why not? It's my house too.' Out of nowhere I began to cry. 'Evie is in a coma. She may die!'

'*What?*'

'She was in a car crash in London. She was driving.' I

lifted my palms towards the ceiling as if to underscore my astonishment. 'Evie doesn't have a licence. You know that, right? And she's got this boyfriend . . .'

Suddenly there was another clatter, and then a voice.

A female voice.

'Jay, everything okay out there?'

Jay?

I watched as Jacob glanced towards the bedroom, then back at me – a flicker of dread passing across his face.

I couldn't move. It reminded me of the time, as a child, I'd watched a boy being knocked down but hadn't been able to shout out in time.

As if on cue, a young blonde woman appeared through the door, wearing just her bra and knickers. She had a body the very opposite of mine: large, pendulous breasts, flaring hips. She screamed as soon as she saw me. 'Who are you?' she said, reaching for the nearest thing she could find to cover herself up – a tiny red apron with the word 'saucy' emblazoned across the front.

'I'm Rachel,' I snarled at her. '*Jay's* wife.'

Minutes later, as I stomped down the road, Jacob appeared beside me, his breathing laboured. 'Rachel, please stop. Please let me explain this.' He grabbed my arm but I shrugged him off.

'Don't touch me,' I said, then chastised myself for the cliché. What right did I have to be angry? I had left my husband, against his will, so he could find someone to procreate with, and now he had.

'This wasn't the way . . .' He pushed his fingers through his hair. 'I love you, Rachel. I love you more than any-thing.'

'Funny way of showing it,' I muttered, refusing to look up at him.

'Yesterday was Gracie's anniversary. I thought you'd call me.'

I stood there, something exploding across my memory banks – Gracie? What the hell was he talking about Gracie for?

'She died a year ago yesterday, Rachel. The fifth of August.'

I stared at him, a sick feeling rising from the pit of my stomach.

'You forgot?'

'Oh, Jacob.' Shame overcame me. 'What with Evie and everything . . .'

'Fair enough,' he said. 'I understand about yesterday, but before that. Why did you refuse to talk to me? Why did you shut me out?'

'What?'

'I must have texted and called a hundred times when you were in Australia. Did you ever consider maybe picking up the phone? Letting me know you were okay?'

I dropped my eyes, trying to think of an excuse. But I had none. He was right – I had shut him out.

All of a sudden, Jacob grabbed my hand. 'Rachel, what you saw back there, it meant nothing. She meant nothing. We didn't even have full sex. I've been drinking. For days, actually.'

He stepped closer, as if to embrace me. For a moment I wavered – the desire for him to draw me in to him almost overwhelming. But something inside me clicked into action: something instinctive and familiar. 'Just leave it,

Jacob. Don't you understand? I can't do this any more . . . We can't do this.'

I wobbled away from him. Bit down hard on my lip so I wouldn't cry.

'Rachel, please listen to me. I need you. We need each other. Especially after what you've just told me about Evie.' He was crying now, big man tears plopping down his cheeks – tiny rivulets of pain.

'I need nothing of the sort,' I snapped, causing passers-by to glance up from their ice-cream cones. 'What I need now is for you to go back to your big-breasted friend, whatever her name is. Accept our relationship is over.'

Jacob raised his eyes to meet mine. 'Rachel, come on.'

Something inside me hardened. 'Jacob, get it into your head. Our relationship is finished. We're through.'

For a second he stood there, as if rendered mute. Then, before I could stop him, he bent down and kissed me. There was no trace of the girl: just a hint of his deodorant. And something else. A smell only I knew.

'I love you so much,' he murmured. 'Please come back to me.' Then he turned and walked away and I was left standing there. A vampire in the sun.

11.

Evie

I'm still in a coma. I have no idea how much time has passed because I have no concept of time. And it's not like I can open my eyes and look at a clock. But I can definitely hear voices. Rachel is still here, or at least she was. She's gone back to Ireland briefly, something about picking up clothes and sorting out her cat, but she has reassured me she's coming back. In the meantime I'm trying to figure out ways to communicate with her, let her know I'm awake. Not that anything has worked so far, mind you. When she squeezes my hand, I try my hardest to squeeze back but she never seems to notice. Or when she kisses my forehead I try to open my eyes, make my eyelashes brush against her cheek. But as of yet . . . *nada*.

The only noteworthy thing I've learned so far is that she's living with Donnagh. I overheard her telling Dr Bartlett yesterday: 'I moved into Evie's apartment in the end. I'm sharing with that boyfriend you mentioned, Donnagh Flood.'

I wanted to scream at her then, tell her he was number one on my suspect list and that she needed to get away from him, very far away. But I couldn't. No matter how hard I tried.

'It's going okay. He's seldom there. Seems to travel a lot.'

Dr Bartlett muttered something I didn't quite catch, then Rachel said, 'Yes, I was a bit shocked to find him there initially. But I've adjusted now. To be honest, I've had worse flatmates.'

'He could be a maniac!' I wanted to shout. 'An axe-murderer!' But, of course, I remained silent.

I'm thinking very hard at the moment. Trying to form a coherent timeline. The last few days before the coma remain a mystery. But the previous two months are all there, quite clear in fact. The months prior to that, though, go back to being a jumble, riddled with gaps and lacunae. I remember some things – my interactions with Janet, the arguments we had – but other stuff, what my life was like pre-Donnagh? To be honest, it's all over the place.

But returning to events I can actually remember . . .

The morning after Donnagh's interview an enormous bouquet of flowers arrived on my desk. George handed them to me, having picked them up from a courier. 'Somebody's popular,' he said, winking at me.

I plucked the card from the cellophane wrapper: 'Enjoyed lunch. Can we make it dinner next? DFx' My breath caught. DF – Donnagh Flood. Jesus Christ, why was he sending me flowers? And what was all this about wanting to meet me again?

As if on cue my phone rang and before I could stop myself I'd answered it.

'You are going to come, aren't you?' It was him.

'I, um, well . . .'

'Too late. If you haven't thought of an excuse by now, then on some level you want to come out with me.'

'Who are you – Sigmund Freud?'

'I dabble,' he said. There was a pause. 'Come on, you can teach me the words of "My Lovely Horse". I'm not sure I know them all.'

'I can't, I have to go to –'

Donnagh began to sing the lyrics loudly down the phone.

'Please stop,' I said, into my handset. 'Did anyone tell you you sound like a foghorn?'

'I admit singing isn't my strong point. Although my main talent *does* involve my mouth . . .'

I laughed, despite myself. In terms of flirting, he was a fucking pro.

'Come on, Durant. You'll come. What's the problem? Very least you'll get a nice meal out of me. Possibly some champagne if you're being really good. What's not to like?'

'Okay, okay,' I said, relenting. No wonder this man worked in construction. He was like a battering ram.

'I'll get someone to pick you up. What's your address?'

'No, please. That's unnecessary. I'd prefer to make my own way there.'

'Fine. I'll get my secretary to email you directions. Seven o'clock tomorrow evening suit you?'

'Sure,' I said, hoping he couldn't hear the terror in my voice. Why the hell was I agreeing to this? What was I getting myself into?

As I put down my phone, Tom turned to me. 'You okay, Eve? You look a little startled.'

'I've somehow agreed to go on a date with Donnagh Flood,' I blurted out.

'What – the Irish guy you interviewed yesterday? I thought you said he was an arsehole.'

73

'Did I?' I mumbled. 'I'm not sure he's an arsehole, exactly. Just incredibly persistent.'

'Do you want me to ring him back? Cancel for you?'

'Thanks, sweetie,' I said, 'but I'm a big girl now – I think I'll just have to go through with it.'

Tom tutted. 'Sounds like a bully, if you ask me. Just remember to take care of yourself. Don't take any shit from him.'

I was tempted to laugh, though of course I didn't. If only Tom knew – his advice was coming about fifteen years too late.

I tried to tell myself it was another 'one-off'. Except now it was a two-off. Was Donnagh right? At some subconscious level did I want to see him again? After all, I couldn't help noticing that, amid all the fear and panic I felt, there was a frisson of something else. Excitement, perhaps?

The guy who'd been repulsed by my physical appearance all those years ago was now sending me flowers, ringing me up, cajoling me into dating him. Maybe I could have some fun with this. Play with him a little.

So it was on with my tight black Karen Millen cocktail dress, my hair piled high on my head, and dangly diamanté earrings that caught the light when I walked.

People said I looked nice, these days, but I still mainly focused on the flaws, just as I had as a teenager. My skin was dull. I needed to lose ten pounds. Was that more cellulite on my arse? When it came to my body, I felt like a lion tamer, daily cracking my whip to prevent this wild beast – my flesh – from overpowering me. Controlling Donnagh Flood was an even scarier proposition.

There wasn't a big enough whip in the world for this guy.

'You look beautiful,' he said, kissing my cheek – an old-fashioned gesture, at odds with the flirty playboy I'd interviewed. 'No tape recorder with you this time?'

I shook my head. I was suddenly so nervous I thought I was going to choke. I guzzled the glass of champagne the waitress presented to me.

'Far from champagne I was reared,' said Donnagh. 'Is it just me or does it taste a bit like puppy breath?'

'You've obviously been drinking the wrong kind of champagne . . .'

'Or hanging around with the wrong sort of puppies.' He smiled at me.

I continued to drink. It was Friday night, after all. Every Friday night was the same for me. It was like an internal switch went off and I changed from puritanical health freak to hedonistic party girl.

For a long time Janet had been my partner in crime. 'We'll be a long time dead,' she'd say, as we looked at each other every Sunday morning, the fear taking hold of us like a vice. 'You didn't do anything that bad,' she'd reassure me. 'Sure everyone has sex in a cupboard at some point in their lives.'

'Have you?'

'Of course! Once I did it in a fridge.'

'Fuck off.'

'When I was a waitress. The cooling system had broken down and me and one of the chefs got jiggy over the Baileys ice-cream.'

'Ew.'

'You've got to remember I'm from Glasgow.'

Every anecdote Janet ever told always ended with that.

But that had been a long time ago. Well, it seemed a long time ago. Janet no longer reassured me about the fear. Now I had to handle my hung-over 'alco-noia' all on my own.

By dessert, I knew I was hammered. I knew it because of one thing. I wanted to snog Donnagh. The alcohol was numbing me, making me forget things. And all I could think of was how beautiful his top lip was, how it curled. What it would feel like to touch it. Or the way the top two buttons of his shirt were open, revealing a hint of chest hair underneath.

I shook myself, trying to dispel those feelings. I hated this man, so why was I feeling ... lust, I suppose you could call it? If I didn't get out of there it would over-whelm me. He would overwhelm me.

'Thank you for a lovely evening,' I said, wobbling unsteadily to my feet.

Donnagh looked at me in confusion. 'But we haven't even had coffee yet.'

I grabbed my coat and bag and, without further ado, made my way towards the exit.

It was blindingly rude, of course. But not as rude as what would happen if I didn't get away. I couldn't trust my own libido. It didn't remember the things Donnagh had done. But my brain did. The waitress near the door raised her eyebrow as I rushed past, but she didn't under-stand. No one understood. That man looked nice. Beautiful, even. But he could destroy you if he wanted to. I'd learned that the hard way.

I rushed down the high steps outside the restaurant, still feeling wobbly. Something caught and I felt myself come loose, unravel. I spun, like a drunken ballerina, but managed to remain on my feet. My left shoe, however, had come off, and lay on a higher step. My black Jimmy Choo stiletto. My lucky feather.

'Eve.' Donnagh was standing at the top of the steps. 'What's the story?'

I stared at him, then at my shoe. There was but a milli-second to make a decision. If I went back for the shoe, I went back for him. *On some level you want to come out with me.* His words reverberated inside my head. No, I don't, I thought. This was a mistake and I want to stay as far away from you as possible.

That was when I ran. I whisked off my other shoe, held it in my hand, and ran in my bare feet on streets no one should run barefoot through.

The taxi was only metres away. 'Christ, love, what you trying to do? Cut your feet to ribbons?' The driver was staring at my bare feet in horror. 'Could be glass or nee-dles or all sorts out there.'

I gave him my address, tempted to say, 'Step on it,' but resisting because, you know, it wasn't *Cagney & Lacey*.

I didn't look back because I knew what I would see. Donnagh, staring at me. Wondering how he would retaliate.

I heard nothing that weekend. In fact, by Monday even-ing, I thought I'd got away with it. That we'd never see each other again.

But that evening, as I walked up to the door of my apartment building, I saw a familiar figure sitting on the steps outside, holding a bag. I froze. 'How did you find out where I live?' I asked, hearing the terror in my voice.

'I have my sources,' he said, smiling up at me. His body was so long it spanned almost all of the steps. For a second, he reminded me of a piece of sculpture. 'Just wanted to give you something,' he said, holding out a bag in front of him. It was one of the posh ones with ropes. 'That shoe you lost – the heel was broken, so I bought you some new ones.' He withdrew a pristine box from the bag, the same brand as my old ones, Jimmy Choo.

'Sit down there, please,' he directed, pointing to a step. 'We're going to have to make sure they fit.'

I did as I was told. For some reason, I couldn't bring myself to speak.

It was late and the street was empty. All that could be heard was a faint rustling of trees and some cars in the distant background. He knelt in front of me and gently prised off the shoes I was already wearing – a pair of black pumps with a ribbon on the front. I worried that my feet would smell: I wasn't wearing any tights. But they didn't appear to. All that was in the air was a faint waft of Donnagh's aftershave, something musky, of course, with the faintest tinge of orange.

Then he made a great show of removing the new Jimmy Choos from their box – withdrawing the stuffing from the toe, pushing out the leather with his fingertips – then finally sliding them onto my feet. 'They fit,' he whispered, delicately holding my ankles. I looked at him, unable to say anything. My heart was thumpety-thumping in my chest.

Slowly he traced his finger up one of my bare legs,

stopping at the inside of my knee. I heard myself moan, and wanted to cut out my voice box.

He stared at me for a second and then, with a sudden movement, he wrapped his hands around my waist and pulled me towards him. 'You didn't say goodbye properly on Friday night,' he said, his mouth inches from mine.

I focused on his top lip again. The way it jutted out slightly. 'Goodnight,' I said, the first word I had spoken for ages.

'You can't run away from me, you know.'

'I know,' I said, looking directly into his eyes.

And then I kissed him.

I 2.

Rachel: day three, 5 p.m.

I went back to the flat, still in shock, threw a few things into a suitcase, then caught a flight straight back to London, tears obscuring my view the whole way. However, on the aeroplane I gave myself a stern talking-to. I had been the one to walk out on Jacob; I had encouraged him to find someone else. So, now he had, why was I bawling and sniffling?

I needed to be strong. In my experience, the only thing for it was to bite down and push through the pain. That was what I had done after Mammy had died, when I'd left Jacob the first time. And after the abortion. When I was seventeen.

Back in London, I went directly to the hospital to check on Evie. Still nothing. The tears threatened to start flowing again but I hurriedly wiped them away when a young nurse entered the room.

'Any improvement?'

The nurse, Heather, smiled weakly at me. 'Well, she's no worse,' she said. 'Her blood pressure and her heart rate are good.' She fiddled around with some wires and wrote something on a chart.

Evie was never going to wake up, was she? This was it. How it would go on. Day after day after day of endless hoping, waiting, expectation.

At least when I'd thought Jacob and I might get back

together, the uncertainty had seemed bearable, manage-able. But now . . . now that I knew that wasn't going to happen, how would I survive this horror?

'Let me know if you need anything,' the nurse said kindly, as she made her way towards the door.

I nodded, and soon all was still.

After that I sat holding Evie's hand and cried till my throat hurt. 'Please wake up,' I whispered, as I laid my head on her arm. 'Come on, Evie. You can't do this to me any more.'

But nothing happened. Not to Evie, anyway. All I noticed was evening setting in, a darkening of the light and, at some point, another nurse popping her head through the door to tell me that visiting hours were over, that it was time to go home.

When I reached Evie's apartment, Donnagh was back from his business trip, cooking something in the kitchen.

'Hey, Rachel, would you like to join me for dinner? I've made some pasta,' he said, nodding towards a saucepan. But I declined the invitation. First off I was wrecked after everything that had happened with Jacob, plus I was in no humour for making small-talk with a stranger. 'Okay, suit yourself,' said Donnagh, but he looked hurt. Then, in a quieter voice, he said, 'I don't bite, you know.'

'It's not you, it's –' I was suddenly afraid I was going to start bawling again, so I ran to my room, mortified at my childish behaviour but knowing I had no alternative. How could I explain to a man I had only just met everything that had happened? Where would I even start?

*

During the night I dreamed about Jacob – that he was drowning and I was trying to rescue him. Except every time I came within touching distance of him, a wave crashed over me, dragging me further and further away. In the final frame all I could see was Jacob sinking as I bobbed in the water, paralysed, unable to do anything except scream.

I woke up a shivering, shaking mess, got out of bed and padded to the living room. There, I sank into the couch and just sat for a while, staring at the grey London dawn.

'You okay?'

I turned to see Donnagh in the doorway, wearing just a pair of boxer shorts and a T-shirt. 'Jesus Christ, you scared me.'

'Sorry.' He downed a glass of water, then went towards his coat. He held up a packet of Benson & Hedges and rattled it. 'You want one?'

I looked at it for a second, every inch of me craving a cigarette, but gave a terse shake of my head.

'Fair enough,' he said. 'I'll be out on the balcony if you change your mind.'

He didn't comment when I slunk up beside him a few minutes later, dragging a plastic chair behind me. 'Here,' he said, proffering the packet in my direction. He flicked his lighter and I bent my head towards it, took a long drag inward.

'Jesus, that feels good,' I said, inhaling the smoke deep into my lungs.

'Spoken like a true nicotine addict,' Donnagh said wryly. 'Been trying to give up?'

'Kind of.' I shrugged, not wanting to get into it. Jacob

had hated me smoking and had waged a constant battle against it, but it seemed pointless now to fight the urge. To fight anything, really.

'So how's Eve? Any change since I've been away?'

'You mean you haven't been to see her yet?'

'Jesus, give me a chance. I only got in the door a few hours ago.'

'Oh, right. Well, she's the same. Still hasn't woken up.'

'Oh.'

For a while we said nothing more, the cigarette smoke twirling through our fingers, like snakes.

At some point Donnagh looked at me and nodded in the direction of my left hand. 'You'll wear a hole in your finger if you keep doing that.'

'Doing what?'

'Fiddling with that wedding ring of yours. Missing your husband, I take it.'

'I . . . um . . .' A huge lump had formed in my throat, and for the life of me I couldn't speak.

'Hey, none of my beeswax,' Donnagh said quickly, clearly realizing he had put his foot in it. 'Forget I mentioned it.'

I took another drag from my cigarette. 'About my husband,' I whispered. 'That's the reason I was so rude earlier.'

'Sorry?' Donnagh said, flicking ash onto a nearby saucer.

'When you asked if I wanted dinner . . .'

'Oh, that. Jesus, don't worry. It wasn't exactly *haute cuisine.*'

'Maybe not, but you were nice to offer, and I owe you an apology. The truth is, my husband and I split up recently.

83

Well, today, in fact. I went back to see him in Ireland, to tell him about Evie and everything.' Here I paused for a moment, drew a quick breath. 'Anyway, it didn't work out, so I decided to end things. That was why I was acting so weird tonight. Licking my wounds and all that.'

Donnagh shook his head. 'You didn't need to explain,' he said softly.

'I felt I did.'

We returned to stillness once more, the smoke continuing to curl through our fingers. Beneath us, faint echoes of sirens and car horns rose from the city.

'For what it's worth, it does get easier,' Donnagh said, moving his head a fraction, so that he was now looking at me properly.

'What does?'

'That feeling. After a marriage ends.'

'How could you possibly know?'

Donnagh shrugged. 'Because it happened to me too. A long time ago when I was living in the States.' He paused, as if lost in thought. 'We were just kids and had no business getting married. But when it ended, it still, you know . . .'

'. . . hurt like hell,' I said, finishing the sentence for him.

'Something like that. Yes.'

A few moments later he stood up and stubbed out his cigarette in the saucer. 'Christ, I'm tired,' he said, stretching his arms above his head, revealing a taut six-pack. 'It's been good talking to you, Rachel, and I'm really sorry to hear about what happened today.'

'Thanks,' I mumbled, diverting my gaze from his stomach. 'Oh, and thanks for the cigarette.'

'No problem,' he said, then turned to face me. 'I find

that's one of the benefits of being single – you can smoke as much as you want, when you want.'

'Hmm,' I muttered half-heartedly.

'Or fall in love with someone who smokes,' he said, holding my gaze for a second. Then he slid the balcony door open and returned to the living room. Away from me. Not looking back.

13.

The next morning, Janet rang. 'Hi, hen. How have you been bearing up? Any updates on Evie?'

'No,' I said, desolate. 'She's exactly the same.'

'Right. Well, I've discovered something I think you'll find interesting.'

'Really?'

'Yes. Did you know that Donnagh Flood went to secondary school in Leitrim?'

I assumed I must have misheard her. 'Say that again.'

'I know – unbelievable, right? I was in WHSmith in St Pancras last night. Just back from that school trip to Belgium I was telling you about.'

'Go on.'

'Anyway, I came across the magazine Evie writes for, *Business Matters*. It comes out quarterly so the edition with Evie's interview of Donnagh Flood was still on the newsstand.'

'And it mentions Leitrim?'

'There's a whole paragraph on it. Apparently he moved there from Dublin as a fourteen-year-old after his father died. Settled in some place called Mohill. I missed the piece when we checked the internet the other day because it's subscription-only.'

'Jesus,' I said, forcing myself to breathe properly. 'Mohill is where Evie went to school.'

'And Donnagh didn't tell you any of this?'

'No.' I felt a dark fury pass through me. 'No, he fucking well didn't.'

Janet took a deep breath. 'Do you think he might have known Evie from childhood?'

'I haven't a clue.' I'd never before contemplated the possibility. Not when I'd thought we'd all grown up in completely different places. But now that I knew he'd lived just down the road from us ... What the fuck was going on?

I tried him on his mobile but couldn't get an answer, so I rang his office.

'I'm sorry, Mr Flood is in meetings all day,' his secretary said unhelpfully. 'Do you want to leave a message?'

'Forget it,' I said, hanging up, but that evening, as soon as I heard the key in the door, I pounced on him. 'You never said you lived in Leitrim,' I snarled, before he had even taken off his jacket.

'Hello to you too,' he said, throwing me a confused look. Then: 'Why, may I ask, is Leitrim relevant all of a sudden?'

'Oh, Jesus, Donnagh, don't act the innocent. You know that's where Evie and I grew up too.'

Donnagh swung round. 'Sorry, but did you just say you grew up in Leitrim?'

'Yes.'

'I thought you came from Clare.'

'Whatever gave you that idea?'

'Eve told me. She said your parents were French but that she'd grown up in Lisdoonvarna.'

'My father is French, but we have no connection with

Clare. Not that I know of, anyway.' I sank onto the couch, my mind whirring. Why would she say that?

'Which school did you go to?' I continued.

'The community school in Mohill,' he replied. 'Why?'

'That's where Evie went. You must have known her.'

Donnagh's eyes widened. 'Eve went to my school?'

'Looks like it, yes.'

He shook his head. 'I have absolutely no memory of her. I'm a year older so we were probably in a different class but still . . .' He removed a box of cigarettes from his pocket, took one out and began fiddling with it. 'She's so pretty, though. It's hard to believe I would have missed her.'

Actually, it wasn't hard to believe. With the weight loss and the nose job, Evie looked nothing like her teenage self, but surely her name should join up the dots for him. Eve Darcy. Eveline Darcy. Come on, how hard could it be?

'There was no Eve Durant in my school,' Donnagh continued. 'Everyone was either Reynolds or Brennan or McKeon. There was a kid from Cork called Mackey but that was about it.'

'Eve Durant,' I repeated. Had I misheard him? Did he honestly not know my sister's real name was Eveline Darcy? That my surname was Darcy?

'And shouldn't I remember you?' Donnagh interrupted, his voice cutting across my whirring thoughts. 'If we all grew up so close together?'

'Evie and I went to different secondary schools,' I said, a sad memory coming back of Evie telling Mammy she couldn't go to the same school as I was in. That she didn't want to be 'compared'. 'Just forget I mentioned it,' I snapped, irritated now. 'You clearly don't remember her. She clearly didn't want to mention her background to you.'

'Why the hell not?' Donnagh spluttered. 'What was she? A spy for the Russians?'

'I don't know,' I shouted. 'That's something we'll both have to ask Evie when she wakes up.' *If she wakes up*, I added silently.

'So is the interrogation over? Am I dismissed?' Donnagh was staring at me, his face flushed with annoyance.

'Oh, Jesus, Donnagh. I'm just trying to figure out what the hell is going on here.'

'And you think I'm not? The girl I was dating has a sister she never told me about. Now I've found out she went to my school. You don't think I might be confused? Scared, even?' For a second he did look quite scared.

'Oh, calm down. Evie obviously had her reasons for keeping some things to herself. Maybe she didn't want to talk about her past. Our father abandoned us when we were kids. Our mother died of cancer. It wasn't exactly a barrel of laughs, you know.'

'Your mother had cancer?' Donnagh exclaimed. 'She never mentioned that either.'

Another ripple of shock passed through me. Why would Evie keep this information from him – the single biggest tragedy ever to befall her? 'She never really got over it,' I said. 'I think that's probably why she lied about her background. She just wanted to forget about it. Start over.'

'Funny way of starting over,' Donnagh muttered, walking towards the sliding balcony doors. He stayed there for a few seconds, as if mulling something over, then turned back to me. 'Rachel, maybe this was a mistake – me staying here. Especially now I know Eve was concealing so much.'

I held his gaze as I shrugged my shoulders. 'You're probably right.'

Donnagh made to walk off, but then a thought occurred to me. If Evie had lied about her identity, what other things was she hiding? And could Donnagh help me figure it all out?

'Actually, Donnagh, now that I think about it, I'd prefer you to stick around for a while.'

'What? Why?'

'Because you're the last one to see my sister conscious. You're the only one who can help me.'

'Help you? Rachel, I've told you and the police everything I know.'

'I'm sure you have,' I said. 'But there are still things I don't understand, that I want to figure out.'

'Hmm.' He frowned. 'I'll think about it.' A few moments later, he walked towards his bedroom and closed the door. He didn't come out again for the rest of the night.

I sat on the couch, nursing a beer. Why had Evie lied to Donnagh? And why had I failed to tell him my sister's real surname or that she'd had cosmetic surgery? Was I becoming part of the subterfuge? As I continued to drink, I played with my wedding ring, my thoughts returning to Jacob. I wanted desperately to talk to him, to fill him in on everything that had just happened, but there could be no talking now. Not after the girl. A streak of pain passed through me with such force that my body buckled. Had I really lost him for ever? My beloved Jacob?

I was tempted to knock on Donnagh's door and offer him a beer – just to distract myself from all these toxic thoughts. But I couldn't summon the energy even to do that. Instead I dragged myself off to bed, pulling the bed-clothes high around me, like I used to do as a little child.

I stared at the ceiling for ages, watching the moonlight cast shadows over its surface, until my focus dimmed and eventually I crossed the line into sleep.

14.

Evie

So now Donnagh and I were kissing. I'd wondered what it would be like and suddenly it was actually happening. He tasted good.

Very gently, very quietly, he murmured, 'Let's go inside.'

I nodded, pulled out my key and opened the door before I had time to second-guess myself. Next thing I knew, I was guiding Donnagh through the messy communal space, up the staircase and towards my flat.

Inside, he closed the door quietly, then spun me around to face him and kissed me hard. 'You're so beautiful, do you know that?' he murmured. He directed me towards my couch, where we half sat, half lay, still kissing.

He took his time. There were no grubby attempts at removing my top, at putting his hand between my legs. For ages it was just his lips on mine, one hand gently brushing against my shirt.

At some point, though, he began upping the ante: hands tracing the outline of my breasts, then slowly unbuttoning my top.

I let him. I felt like I was in a dream. Or, if not a dream, a trance, something from which I would eventually wake. But not now, not yet.

'Your breasts,' he said quietly, but with the faintest

touch of wonder. He was staring at them as if they were precious jewels, encased within the lace and cotton of my bra.

'Mmm,' I said.

He cupped one, pulled the bra down ever so slightly, so that the nipple was revealed. 'Let me taste . . .' Suddenly he had my nipple in his mouth and he was sucking. The feeling was exquisite: pain and pleasure perfectly mixed.

That was when I jolted.

A memory.

'No,' I heard myself say, pushing his head back with my hands.

'Okay,' he said, and removed his mouth. He attempted to steer it back towards my lips.

'No,' I said, out of the trance now. I pushed myself into an upright position and began rebuttoning my top.

'Eve, are you okay?' Donnagh had sat up too and was staring at me.

'Yes, yes, I'm fine,' I said. 'But I have an early start tomorrow.' I let the implication hang.

Donnagh stood up.

I got to my feet to face him.

Carefully, he took my hands in his. 'I've scared you, I think. I'm sorry, I didn't mean to go so far. It's just that I'm so attracted to you.'

I felt my gaze drop, but Donnagh reached his hand under my chin and lifted it. 'You know I really like you, Eve, don't you?'

I didn't say anything. I could barely move.

'Well, I do. And I want to get to know you better. Will you allow me to do that?'

I tried to speak, but it was as if I'd been struck dumb.

'Eve, I'm sorry. Was it too fast? Is that the problem? Did I go too fast?'

'Yes,' I whispered.

'I apologize,' he said, pressing hard on my hands. 'I shouldn't have done that. Come out with me on Saturday night, and I'll make it up to you, I promise.'

His eyes were shining, whether out of adrenalin or contrition, I didn't know. He looked so tall and beautiful and earnest, standing there.

'Okay,' I said. 'I'll come.'

After he had gone I sat on the couch, hugging my knees close to my chest. I felt as if I was dreaming because surely that couldn't have been real. I couldn't have just made out with the boy who'd tortured me at secondary school.

I gazed down at my breasts, then cupped the left one with my hand. The way Donnagh had looked at them, like stolen treasure. If only he had known that they were reconstructions, not the ones I'd been born with. In my defence, I hadn't had a boob job in the traditional page-three sense: no implants had been inserted. Instead I'd had a breast reduction and lift. But it had still involved a scalpel. It had still involved being cut open.

It had taken me two years of solid saving to afford it. After the rhinoplasty I'd briefly toyed with the idea of not getting my boobs done. I'd dreamed of breast reduction since I was fifteen, but the reality of surgery had hit home. It wasn't like popping to the dentist for a filling. It was a big deal. Did I really want to be sliced open like that? Filleted like a fish?

94

Yet something continued to pull me towards it. A memory. A trauma.

I'd gone to the best surgeon I could find, an old Etonian type, who practised in London's Harley Street and was reputed to do all the top celebrities. He'd taken one look at my saggy 34Gs, and said that, yes, I was an ideal candidate. All I needed to do was sign on the dotted line and pay. We agreed that a nice natural D cup would work best. They would be perky but wouldn't swamp my frame; they'd be in keeping with my personality, rather than being vulgar.

I had checked myself into the hospital, telling nobody, not even Rachel. Especially not Rachel. She would have been apoplectic. She already thought the nose job was insane and would never admit that it had realigned my face. Instead she'd bandied around phrases like 'inner confidence', 'knowing your own worth', and 'not giving into patriarchal concepts of beauty'.

I had wanted to hit her. She was so full of shit sometimes. What would she know about the torment of being born ugly? Of having a nose that people pointed and laughed at? What would she know of a body that oozed over the edges of your clothes, like an overstuffed pie?

Nothing. That's what. Absolutely nothing.

So I had kept it to myself. All the fear and loathing and stress, I had locked it inside me and refused to let it out. All would be well. I trusted the surgeon. Things would be fine. I would be fine.

When I woke up, though, I feared I had made a terrible mistake. The pain was like nothing I had ever felt before. Shooting stars of agony exploded across my chest, making me gasp. I could barely hold down a cup of water as nausea swept through me, while the pain in my arms and shoulders meant I could do nothing for myself.

I stayed in the hospital for a few days, paying through the nose for the pleasure, and cried when I looked down at my bandages and saw that they were filled with blood.

'All perfectly normal,' said the surgeon, as if he had just taken my temperature, not sliced me open.

'But I feel like I'm dying,' I mumbled.

'Don't worry,' he said, smiling. 'Everyone feels like that when they come round. We'll up your pain relief and soon you'll feel like a different woman.'

'Okay,' I said, deciding to trust him.

After he left, I allowed myself to cry, the pain and fear mingling. I wanted someone to say it would get better. Mammy, Rachel, Artie.

But Mammy was gone. So was Artie. And even if they weren't, would they even recognize me now? Was I the same person I had always been? Or was I an imposter?

The truth was, I honestly didn't know.

15.

The next day, the day after I'd kissed Donnagh, I felt as if I'd downed ten bottles of vodka and snorted ten grams of coke. Everything around me felt blurry, unreal. I was practically holding my hands out in front of me to feel my way through the mist. Had Donnagh and I nearly had sex?

Even the lads at work noticed.

'Earth to Eve?' George shouted in my ear, and I jumped a little in my chair, whereupon they all started laughing.

'What?' I snapped.

'Do you want to come to the pub tonight? It's Bob's birthday.'

'Oh, right,' I replied, thinking it over. 'Fine, yes. That sounds good.'

'Fair enough. We're going to head off around half five. In the meantime, sign this, and if you have a few quid handy, stick it inside.' George shoved a large card in front of me.

'Will do.' I smiled apologetically, trying to say sorry for being so tetchy. I found a tenner in my purse and shoved it into the envelope, then wrote some anodyne message in the card, something about sixty being the new forty. Or the new thirty. Or maybe even the new twenty. I handed it to George.

'Five thirty. Don't be late,' he said, mock-sternly. 'I don't want to be waiting outside in the cold while you do your face.'

'Of course, Sergeant Major,' I said, and gave him a little salute. 'My face will remain exactly as it is.'

During the day a text arrived from Donnagh: *Sorry again if what I did last night was too full on. You must realize it was only because I like you.*

When I didn't reply, he sent me another.

I meant it when I said I wanted to take you to dinner. Does Saturday night suit? Around 7 p.m.?

I stared at the texts for ages, the words eventually swimming in front of me.

'Eve, are you sure you're okay? You've been staring at your phone for the past fifteen minutes.' This time it was my shyer colleague, Tom, looking over at me, his forehead bunched up in concern.

'Oh,' I said, feeling my cheeks redden with embarrassment. 'It's nothing.' Then I snapped my mobile shut and buried it in my handbag, making a big show of getting back to work, click-clacking really loudly on my keyboard.

A few hours later we moved on to the pub. Bob, whose birthday we were celebrating, was the quietest man on the planet so I knew it wasn't going to be a raucous affair. I just hoped it was lively enough to keep my mind off what had happened the previous night, and the two texts waiting to detonate in my handbag.

But, sadly, it was even duller than I'd expected. Bob drank his bitter and stayed mostly silent, while the rest of us desperately grabbed onto the legs of any conversation we could think of. At some point, after we'd discussed how evil Nigel was for the third time, I made my excuses and fled to the Ladies. The messages were still there, unanswered, blinking at me.

What was I going to do? I had told Donnagh I was going to meet him on Saturday, but how could I possibly do that? Not after what had happened in my flat. I applied a bit of lipstick and stared at my face. To the outside observer I probably looked normal. But inside I felt as if everything had turned to quicksand. As if *I* was turning to quicksand.

I walked out of the loo, and took a deep breath. I didn't know how long I could go on making polite conversation. I'd thought the company would distract me from everything but somehow it was making me feel even more jittery.

'Oh, my God, I'm sorry.' Without realizing it, I had walked straight into the arms of a man carrying two pints of lager.

'You're fine, don't worry,' he said, and something in his accent registered with me. It was only when I looked up that I saw why.

'Jesus Christ, Artie,' I said, feeling as if I had been winded.

Artie Columb. My former boyfriend. My soulmate.

'Evie,' he said, looking equally shocked.

'I'm so sorry. Did I spill beer on you? Here, let me get you another drink.'

'No, don't be worrying, you're fine.'

'Really, seriously, let me get you another.'

'Evie, honestly, you didn't spill anything.' He was staring at me as if he couldn't quite believe I was real. 'Is that actually you?'

'It is,' I said quietly. 'What are you doing here?'

'I'm just having a pint with some lads from work.'

'From work? You mean you live around here?'

'Well, yes, just down the road in Lewisham, actually. But I work in Greenwich.'

'Jesus,' I whispered, hardly able to take in this new information. 'And there I was, thinking you were still back in Leitrim. You know I work in Greenwich too? And live very near here – in Woolwich.'

'Go on out of that!' Artie said, his eyes widening. 'Talk about a small world.'

'I know,' I said, smiling. 'Are you an engineer here – same as back home?'

'Yes,' Artie said. 'Except at least here there's work. The recession wiped us out in Ireland. We were about as much use as –'

'Tits on a bull,' I finished, recalling the phrase. One of Artie's favourites.

'Exactly,' he said, and we both laughed. 'Look, let me leave these drinks down, and then I'll come back over so we can chat properly.'

He made to walk off but I stopped him. 'Listen, tell me if I'm being cheeky or whatever, but would you like to get out of this place? Have a proper chat, I mean.'

I watched a flicker of uncertainty pass across his face. 'Well, I was just about to head home after this drink . . .'

'Okay,' I said, shrugging. 'It was just a thought.'

He paused, as if weighing something up. Then: 'But if you give me a minute or two, I'm sure I could find some-one to take this pint off my hands.'

'Are you sure?'

'Yes, why not? It's been six years after all.'

My mouth curled itself into a smile.

'Listen, will we meet out the front in two minutes? Give us both time to grab our jackets.'

I looked over in the direction of my work colleagues. Bob was gazing silently into his pint, while Tom was surreptitiously picking his nose. 'Sure,' I said, positively beaming.

A short time later we were off.

16.

Rachel: day five, 7.30 a.m.

That morning I didn't go immediately to the hospital. Didn't even check the papers as I usually did for any sign of a 'leak'. Instead I walked around the nearby park for a bit, trying to get everything straight in my head.

So Donnagh hadn't known who Evie was. She had kept her identity hidden from him. But why? In what part of Evie's fucked-up mind had that seemed like a good idea?

I walked on and on, my brain beginning to hurt with the exertion of trying to figure it all out. Was it something to do with Donnagh being from Leitrim? The fact that they'd gone to the same school together? Did Evie feel he would judge her if she revealed her cosmetic surgery to him?

In a bizarre way, that made a strange sort of sense. Anyone who really knew Evie (which wasn't many people) was aware of how secretive she could be. For most people, hiding your true identity because you're afraid your boyfriend will remember and dislike you sounds insane. For someone like Evie, it sounded borderline reasonable.

I grabbed a large black coffee off a street vendor and kept on walking, imagining how this would have played out in Evie's head. She'd have recognized Donnagh, of course, from their schooldays. Then she'd have been shocked and probably flattered when she realized he fancied her. I wondered when she'd clocked the fact that Donnagh hadn't recognized her. When it had dawned on her she could get away with not revealing who she really was.

I knew how she would have justified it. She'd have convinced herself that if she told Donnagh the truth – that she'd had surgery, changed her name – he would be disgusted. He'd think she was a freak. Better to wait a while, see if he really liked her. If he did, he'd understand. If he was an idiot, she'd find out soon enough, and no harm would have been done either way.

Well, she'd been wrong about that. Very fucking wrong.

The problem wasn't so much Donnagh thinking Evie was a freak, more that that was what she thought of herself. It was where all her problems stemmed from. As a kid, she'd been so creative, brilliant at anything to do with writing or art. But after puberty, when she'd gained a lot of weight, something fundamental had shifted. She'd still loved art – studied it all the way through secondary school – but somewhere along the line she'd begun to hate herself. She dealt with it by retreating into exams, into perfectionism, suddenly obsessed with gaining maximum points in the Leaving Cert so she could become a doctor.

It seemed an odd choice to Mammy and me. Yes, Evie was good at science – she was good at all subjects – but she'd never shown any particular interest in medicine. Art was her real passion.

But she couldn't be dissuaded. Every evening she'd study for hours on end, ignoring me or telling me to feck off when I'd come asking for outfit advice for whatever guy I was trying to impress at the time. 'Oh, Rachel, you'd look good in a sack. Wear whatever you like.'

But the truth was, I didn't care about getting fashion advice – I just wanted to bring Evie out of herself a bit, make her see she could be smart and have fun too. It didn't seem healthy, all the studying she did.

Mammy didn't think so either. 'Rachel, maybe you could take her to one of those discos you go to. Find her a nice boy . . .'

And I'd feigned outrage, because Mammy had never encouraged me to find a nice boy – probably because she knew I only liked the bad ones.

But, of course, nothing we did made a blind bit of difference. Instead Evie continued with her manic schedule of studying, going on to achieve a perfect score in the Leaving Cert, and gaining a place in medical school at Trinity College Dublin, just like she'd hoped. Except that was where the fairytale came crashing to an end. A year and a half in, having lost half her body weight, Evie attempted suicide, forcing her to drop out of the course and return to Leitrim to get better. The psychiatrist in charge had diagnosed chronic depression and anxiety, which she linked back to Evie's being bullied as a teenager.

We were aware, of course, that Evie had experienced some problems through school, knew there were a few jealous arseholes determined to bring her down. We'd even tried to intervene – me by going to her school one day and offering to beat them up; Mammy by making an appointment with the school principal, determined to sort it out. But on both occasions Evie had accused us of interfering – no one liked a snitch and could we please just stay out of it, she'd handle it herself. Which, very reluctantly, we did. And as the months passed, Evie appeared to grow happier, even going as far as to say that the bullying had 'settled itself down'.

It was only after the suicide attempt at Trinity that Mammy and I discovered she'd been lying to us. The bullies had never gone away, as Evie had implied. Far from it. They'd found even more ways to bring Evie down.

Just thinking about it, all these years later, still made me feel sick with guilt. Sure, I'd tried to help Evie at the start, with my macho 'beat 'em up' talk. But shortly afterwards I'd fallen pregnant and had my own troubles to contend with – which meant I hadn't been there for my sister. Not properly. Perhaps if things had been different, I could have stopped her trying to take her own life. Saved her from the coma, even . . .

I thought again of me and Evie as teenagers, of me appearing at her school one hometime, demanding she tell me the names of her tormentors so I could confront them. And her turning to me, her entire body shaking, and whispering, 'Rachel, can't you see that that will only make it a hundred times worse? Please just leave it. Please just let it go.'

And I could still see myself staring at her in confusion. Didn't she want to pay them back for what they'd done to her?

But when I looked at my sister again, I realized that revenge was not Evie's aim. Invisibility was. She didn't want to confront the bullies, she wanted to disappear from them. So that she could be at peace. So they couldn't hurt her any more.

17.

Back in the flat that night, I slumped onto the couch and watched Donnagh cook in the kitchen. I noticed that his shoulders were almost as wide as the archway that separated us. For some reason his physicality seemed ludicrous set against the tiny scale of Evie's flat.

'You know Evie went by Darcy when she was a kid, not Durant?' I said in the direction of the kitchen, attempting to feign nonchalance. I knew I couldn't put off revealing this vital detail to him any longer, despite some part of me wanting to protect my sister's identity. But who knew how he would react? Viewed from most angles, the whole thing seemed pretty sordid.

'Sorry?' he said, draining something in a colander. 'Can't hear you. I'll be with you in a minute.'

A couple of seconds later Donnagh poked his head through the archway into the living room. 'You were saying?'

'Um, just that Evie went by the name Darcy in secondary school, not Durant. She'd have been known as Eveline Darcy.'

Donnagh stood there, colander still in hand. 'Eveline Darcy,' he said quietly. 'I remember a girl of that name. But she looked nothing like Eve. Not even remotely.'

'It's the same person,' I said, without flinching. 'She's lost a lot of weight, got her nose straightened and changed the colour of her hair. But, yeah, that's Evie. Or Eve, as you call her.'

Donnagh sank onto the couch beside me. 'It can't be.'

'It is.'

'But how is that even possible?'

'Donnagh, I've just explained.'

'Right, okay,' he said, pushing his fingers through his hair. His right leg was jiggling, like he'd got an electric shock. 'We *were* in the same class,' he said eventually. 'She hated me.'

I jerked my face up, surprised. 'What? Why?'

'I was a bollocks to her. That's why.'

I felt the blood drain from my face. Had he been one of the faceless, nameless bullies who had driven Evie to despair? I asked him.

He nodded. 'I'm afraid I probably was.'

For a while I didn't say anything, trying to take in this new information. 'What did you do to her?' I asked eventually, trying to keep my voice steady.

'The usual,' he said. 'Called her names. Made reference to her nose. To her body in general, really.'

'Stupid prick,' I mumbled incoherently. And then louder: 'You stupid fucking prick.'

For a long time neither of us spoke.

'So, this was what?' Donnagh said eventually. 'Some kind of bizarre revenge fantasy?'

I shrugged. It all sounded so crazy. Like a bad made-for-TV movie. 'Why did you do it?' I asked, in a tight voice. 'Whatever it was you did to her.'

Donnagh dropped his eyes and laced his fingers together, as if in prayer. 'I don't really know,' he said.

'You don't know,' I repeated, a sneer creeping into my voice. 'Well, think, for Christ's sake.' I slammed the palm of my hand hard against the coffee-table. 'Try to fucking remember.'

'I'm sorry, Rachel. I don't think there was much of a reason, aside from the fact that she was so clever and perfect at everything.'

'And you wanted to take her down a peg or two.'

'Something like that,' Donnagh muttered.

The silence stretched out again in front of us. I wanted to hate him. I did hate him. And yet he was also my only real link to Evie . . .

'Look, if you really want to know the truth, it was because my father had just died. Plus I'd moved to a new county. I was all over the place.'

'So how did bullying Evie fix that? She had no father either, you know.'

'I didn't know that. For years, actually, I didn't have a clue.'

'Oh, come on.'

'It's the truth. The first time we sat together in class she'd said something about her dad being French. Mine had recently passed away, and for some reason it was like a red rag to a bull. I was angry with her for having a father, for boasting about it.'

'She wasn't boasting.'

'I found that out later. But for most of my secondary school career I was under the illusion that Eveline had some exotic French dad who used to cook her onion soup and wear stripy Breton tops.'

'You moron.' I couldn't look at him.

We sat there in silence. At some point, without me even realizing it, Donnagh pulled out two whiskey glasses.

'You think I'm going to drink with you? The man who bullied my sister to a pulp?'

'Rachel, please,' Donnagh said. 'I want to explain to you.'

'Explain what?'

'I don't know. Whatever it is you want to know.'

'I want to know if you're responsible for the fact that my sister is currently lying in a coma.' I was crying now: I could feel the hot flow of tears and snot sliding down my face.

'Jesus, Rachel, of course I'm not. If you'd just sit down and have a drink with me, I'll explain things to you. What I know about your sister –'

'What you know? You know nothing, you ignorant prick. Nothing about the sensitive girl she was – the loving daughter. You were too busy taunting her. Destroying her.' I was growing hysterical, I knew that. I wasn't even making sense.

'Rachel, come on, let's talk about this.'

'Fuck you!' I shouted. 'Don't you understand what you did to her? The pain you caused?'

'Look, I know I was a jerk but –'

'A jerk? You fucking ruined her.' I was beyond reason now – flecks of spittle leaving my mouth and landing on Donnagh's face. 'You can take your whiskey and shove it up your arse, you horrible bastard.' And with that I stomped off to Evie's bedroom, banging the door so hard the whole flat shook.

*

Hours later, after I'd sobbed myself into oblivion, I got up and made for the living room. When I entered, Donnagh was still sitting at the table, a tumbler of whiskey in front of him.

'Rachel,' he said, straightening himself. 'Are you okay?'

I shrugged.

'Please sit down and talk to me.'

'What's the point?' I said. 'I feel I know all I need to.'

'Please?' he said, pulling out a chair and gesturing towards it. Reluctantly I sat down. 'I'm so sorry about what I told you earlier.'

'You mean you're sorry I found out or sorry for what you did to Evie?'

'To be honest, probably a bit of both,' he said. I tutted and made to stand up. He touched my arm lightly. 'Don't go. Please let me explain. Let me apologize.'

I shook his hand off me, but sat down again. 'Go on.'

'Look, I really am sorry about what a creep I was to Eve as a kid.'

'Sure you are.'

'I am,' he said, and when I studied his face he appeared contrite.

'Is that it? Is that all you've got to say?'

Donnagh remained silent, but when he looked up again, he seemed almost nervous. 'Actually, I did want to ask you something, about what you said earlier.'

I looked at him, my eyes narrowing. 'Go on.'

'You said I destroyed Eve. What did you mean by that?'

I snorted. 'Like you don't know.'

'I don't, Rachel, I swear to God. Last thing I knew Eveline Darcy had got straight As in her Leaving Cert and was off to study medicine in Trinity. I, by contrast, was being hauled off to the copshop for stealing a car. It seemed pretty clear who had emerged victorious – at that point in our lives anyway.'

'Shows how much you know.'

'Tell me, then.'

A sudden wave of exhaustion flooded me. Why was this man in my life? 'Okay, if you're that interested. Evie went on to suffer a serious nervous collapse at university and tried to commit suicide. The doctors at the time blamed stress, brought on by being severely bullied at secondary school.' I wiped something off my face and found I was crying again.

Donnagh seemed to be on the point of crying himself. 'Jesus, Rachel. I had no idea. I would have been in Chicago by then.'

I stared at him. 'She must have really hated you to put herself through this nightmare.'

'You mean dating me? I guess she must have,' Donnagh said quietly. 'Although, to be honest, I thought we were getting on really well together.'

I continued to stare at him, wondering how he could be so deluded. 'She despised you, Donnagh. You destroyed her life. This fiasco can only have been about getting back at you.'

'You think?' There was the merest hint of challenge in his voice.

'What else could it have been?'

'Maybe she liked me too. She might have been afraid to come clean to me in case she ruined what we had together.'

'And what had you?'

Donnagh rose. 'I thought you didn't care about any of that. I thought I was just a stupid prick.'

I took a deep breath. Then I stood up, went over to my leather jacket and pulled out a packet of cigarettes I'd bought earlier. 'I'm sorry for that. Do you want to go out to the balcony? Talk properly this time?'

Briefly Donnagh seemed to hesitate.

'You owe me that much at least,' I added.

'Okay,' he said, getting up and walking towards the balcony door.

A few minutes later we were sitting on the plastic chairs, our cigarettes lit. The evening was balmy, with a light breeze.

After a few moments of silence, Donnagh turned to me. 'So, what is it you want to know, Rachel?'

I looked at him – at the beauty of him – trying to understand the power he wielded over my sister. 'Everything, Donnagh. I want to know everything.'

He nodded, and took a long, deep drag of his cigarette.

Then he spoke.

18.

Slowly, painfully, Donnagh delineated all the horrible details of his teenage torture of Evie: the name-calling, the rabble-rousing. Other, more physical, things. Then, when I couldn't take it any longer, he fast-forwarded to the present day, recounting again how he had met Evie through the magazine she worked for. How he had fancied her from the moment he first saw her when she interviewed him.

'She was so gorgeous that I decided immediately to pursue her. But it wasn't just that she was beautiful. It was her sense of humour. Her slightly dark slant on things. After years of living in America it was refreshing.'

'Yeah, yeah. You shared a sense of humour. But what else?'

He talked about the eight weeks they'd spent together. The initial hedonistic phase, which had quietly turned into something more. 'It all culminated with a trip to Paris.'

'What trip?'

'The weekend before her crash, I brought Eve there. It was a thank-you for letting me stay here.'

'And you didn't think to mention this earlier?'

'Sorry, Rachel,' he said. 'But up until very recently we were barely talking. And, anyway, it didn't seem particularly relevant.'

Suddenly he got up and disappeared into the hall. A few seconds later he was back, with a digital camera in his hand. 'Here are a few pictures we took.' I flicked through the photos, some of Donnagh and Evie beaming into the lens, a few of Evie on her own, looking chic and glamorous. It took every fibre of my being not to cry. 'Okay, I believe you. You went to Paris. So why, the night you get back, is Evie discovered four miles away, slammed up against a stone wall driving your car?'

Donnagh let out a deep sigh. 'I know. It's impossible to make sense of.'

'Had you had a row?'

'No. We'd had a lovely romantic time in Paris. I thought everything had gone really well.'

'It makes no fucking sense.'

'I know,' said Donnagh, tiredly.

'The obvious explanation is that you know something and you're keeping it from me.'

'Why is that the obvious explanation?' he shot back. 'I've been open and transparent about everything, both with you and the police. It's your sister who was keeping secrets.'

I was unable to contradict him on that one. Eventually I said, 'Are you trying to lay the blame at Evie's door?'

'No,' said Donnagh, exhaling again. 'No, I'm not.' He took another drag on his cigarette. 'Look, Rachel, I know you want someone to blame and I know, given what I did to her as a kid, I must seem the obvious candidate . . .'

'You can say that again.'

He reached out his hand suddenly, making brief contact with my arm again. 'But please understand I would never have done anything to hurt Eve. I'm not the enemy here.'

'You're not?'

114

Donnagh dipped his head. 'I know what you think of me. I know I don't deserve impartiality.'

I remained silent.

'But, please, I'm asking for one thing.'

'What's that?'

'The benefit of the doubt.'

19.

Evie

Artie and I walked the short distance to another pub — well, more a wine bar, really. But it was quiet, and I knew we'd be able to talk.

'So I guess a pint is probably out of the question here.'

I smiled at him. 'I imagine so, yes.'

'Well, then, I'll go for the Chilean Sauvignon Blanc with top notes of plum,' he said. 'See, Evie? I've become refined since we last met.'

'I'll believe that when I see it.'

'What can I get you to drink?'

'A glass of pinot grigio would be lovely, thanks.'

As Artie ordered the drinks from the bar, I found myself staring at him, at the body concealed under the brown woollen jumper and worn jeans. Back when we'd first started going out, Artie had weighed about nine stone, which, given his six foot four frame, was a tad on the malnourished side. Since then he'd filled out nicely. His shoulders were broader, his arms bigger and more muscular. I wondered if he'd known I worked in Greenwich, if that was why he'd found a job there too. He could have found my details online — on the *Business Matters* website — he'd have known to search for the surname Durant as well as Darcy.

But I dismissed the thought, lovely though it was, almost immediately. What Artie and I had experienced together had been so long ago. Light years ago. Some things were just a matter of coincidence. Like this. Now.

'Here you go.' Artie set my wine in front of me. 'It's so good to see you, Evie.'

'Yes,' I said, returning his smile.

'So, tell me, what have you been up to since we last met?'

I told him, then made a face. 'Pretty crap, huh?'

'Are you joking? High-flying journalist, owner of your own apartment. Sounds like you're doing pretty well for yourself.'

'I wouldn't go that far.'

'Well, I would. Although, if I'm honest, the journalist thing does surprise me a little bit. For some reason, I thought you'd end up doing something visual.'

'How do you mean?'

'Ah, I just had a notion you might become an artist or work in a gallery or something.'

I shook my head. 'No money in art, Artie.'

We both smiled at the alliteration.

A few seconds later, probably to fill the growing silence, Artie headed off on a different tack. 'So, apart from work, are you married? Living with someone?'

'Jesus, no,' I replied. 'Sure, who'd have me?'

'Who indeed?' he said, tossing his eyes dramatically to Heaven.

We both grinned.

'And you? Any significant other in your life?'

'You mean, apart from Leonard Cohen and Bruce Springsteen?'

'Yeah, apart from those two.'

'Well, actually there is someone,' Artie said, shifting ever so slightly in his chair. 'My fiancée, Shannon. We got engaged a few weeks ago, actually.'

'Oh, wow,' I said, a fluttery sensation passing through my chest. Despite myself, I insisted he fill me in.

'Well, she's American, a lecturer in psychology. She has strong Irish roots.'

'As in literally, like a tree?'

'Yeah,' Artie said. 'Her lower half is one hundred per cent wood.' He cast me a sardonic smile. 'Glad to see you haven't lost your surreal sense of humour, anyway.'

I shrugged. 'That'll be the final thing to go.' After a few seconds I added, in a softer voice, 'Jesus, Artie. Engaged.'

'I know. Very grown-up, isn't it?'

'Do you think she'll mind us meeting up like this?'

'How do you mean?'

'Ah, I don't know,' I said. 'The fact that we dated, that we've seen each other's wobbly bits . . .'

Artie shook his head. 'As I said, Shannon's a psychologist. She's very level-headed about stuff like that.'

'So she knows about me.'

Artie looked up. 'Of course she knows about you.'

I reached for my wine glass, took a large slug. My hands seemed to be trembling – in fact, my whole body was.

'Anyway, enough about my love life, back to yours,' Artie said brightly. 'I'm not buying this whole single-girl act. There must be *someone* on the scene.'

I attempted to feign nonchalance. 'Okay, now that you mention it, I suppose I am seeing someone. It's early days but things seem to be going pretty well.'

I had no idea why I was lying. Or perhaps I did. How could I admit I was alone, given Artie's near-married status and his horrifically right-on fiancée? On a secondary note, she sounded like a right dose.

'So, is it serious?'

'I wouldn't go that far, but there's definitely great chemistry.'

'Thanks for sharing,' Artie said, kicking my leg.

'You're welcome.' I smiled, kicking him back. 'The only problem is, he's terribly handsome and successful.'

'God, that's an awful problem, all right.'

'No, really,' I muttered. 'I'm not sure I can measure up.'

For a moment, Artie's face lost its playful expression. 'Jesus, Evie, are you still going on with that aul' nonsense?' He sounded annoyed.

'What's that supposed to mean?'

'The self-loathing thing. I thought you might have grown out of it.'

I was too taken aback to answer.

But then, quick as a shot, he reached over and gently placed a hand on mine. 'Christ, Evie, that was a terrible thing to say. I've obviously had too much to drink.'

For a moment we just stared at each other and in that instant a surge of electricity ripped through me, nearly knocking me off my chair. But if Artie felt it too, he didn't show it. Instead he silently removed his hand and averted his gaze.

Soon after, he stood up and said, 'I should probably get going.'

'Oh, come on,' I pleaded. 'We haven't seen each other in six years. Plus you just mortally offended me back there.'

He looked at me, his eyes unsure. Unsettled.

'Just one more drink,' I said. 'Then I promise to release you back to your fiancée unharmed, and with a full pardon.' To defuse the tension, I cast him a big goofy grin.

Still he stood there.

'Artie, seriously, relax! I'm not mortally offended, I promise. I'm just glad to have bumped into an old friend.'

It was only then that Artie's face appeared to soften, the word 'friend' seeming to have clinched things. He sat down again and, as he did so, he cast me a smile – so small and beautiful it made me ache. It reminded me of when we'd been together, young and in love. It reminded me of hope. Of beauty.

It reminded me of dawn rising over the Leitrim hills.

I had been a virgin the first time with Artie.

Obviously.

We'd met on an evening course in Leitrim, painting with watercolours, a subject in which Artie had approximately zero interest but reckoned he'd meet loads of women through. He did, except that all the women were about fifty-five, and then there was me. Just gone twenty-one and recovering from a botched suicide attempt. I'd lost most of the weight by that stage and got rid of the glasses and mousy hair, but the old nose still loomed, large as ever.

Not that Artie was a perfect specimen himself. In fact, I'd go as far as to say he was the dorkiest man I'd ever seen: all limbs and angles and curly hair.

'What the hell is evening primrose oil?' he'd whispered, during the second class, as we'd stood mixing colours.

'What?' I said, trying to ignore him.

'All the women keep talking about it. They're all on it. Is it E for old people?'

I couldn't help laughing. 'No, you madzer. It's for the menopause. E for old people! You're such an eejit.'

This was how it went with Artie. I laughed about ninety per cent of the time I was with him, which was ninety per cent more than I'd laughed in my previous existence.

He kissed me one night after he'd cajoled me to go for a coffee with him and I nearly jumped out of my skin. 'Christ alive, what was that for?'

'It wasn't *for* anything,' he said. 'I like you.'

'Oh,' I said, and promptly ran away from him up the road, like he'd attempted to remove my chastity belt.

I stuck with the watercolours class, though, and by the tenth session I'd even managed to stand still while we kissed. I didn't have a clue what I was supposed to be doing and, to be honest, I don't think Artie did either. We just made it up as we went along.

It took us ages even to contemplate the possibility of sex, and fair play to Artie, he never pushed me. But sometimes I could feel his frustration that I was so slow-moving.

'Did you have a bad experience?' he asked, after I'd slapped his hand away from 'down there' for the fortieth time.

'No, not really. Kind of,' I mumbled, thinking of Donnagh – of what he'd said and done. In particular, of what he'd done.

'You know I don't want to hurt you, Evie,' Artie had murmured, and I'd dropped my head onto his shoulder, breathing in the warm smell of his skin. 'And there are people you can talk to if it was, you know, assault or abuse or anything.'

I looked up at him and shook my head. 'It wasn't like that,' I said. Because it wasn't. 'It was just unpleasant. Nasty. It left me feeling ashamed of myself.'

Artie had tilted my face up very gently. 'Evie, I never want you to feel shame when you're with me. Can't you see that I love you?'

I'd smiled at him then, a huge throb of happiness bursting in my brain and in my heart. It still took me ages to open myself up to him fully. And ages again before I could finally enjoy sex. But when I eventually did, oh, my.

We shared a very beautiful year together. There was a lot of sex but also a lot of other things. Dog-walking (Artie had a dog called Mutt), sitting by lakes, driving lessons in Artie's battered Toyota Corolla as he attempted to teach me the rudiments of motoring.

My mother adored him. 'Artie, you'll take a piece of my apple tart home with you.'

'Ah, now, Mrs Darcy, I can't be robbing your baking every time I come here.' Then he'd drop his voice: 'Even if it is the best cake this side of the Shannon.'

And she'd smile and give him the entire cake and say, 'I'll bake another one. It's for you, Artie. Take it. Take it.'

It was all very sweet, really.

Even when she got sick he was amazing: making sure I passed my driving test, so I could bring Mammy to her hospital appointments; cutting the lawn; fixing taps. All the practical things. He was even there at the end, when it was just me and Rachel. Mammy had called him in on his own, and when he came back out he was crying, big child-tears.

He wouldn't tell me what she'd said, claimed it was a 'secret between Kay and me'. But I partly guessed. Something about taking care of me, I imagined.

She needn't have worried. I knew Artie would always take care of me. I knew it in my bones.

We had now finished the second drink and I was well up for more but Artie insisted he had to get home. 'No, really, Evie. I told Shannon I'd be back by half nine. I genuinely have to go.'

'Fair enough,' I said, disappointment surging through me. The longer I spent with Artie, the less time I spent thinking about Donnagh.

But it was more than that. Being with Artie was like a homecoming. We talked about Leitrim; we talked about people we knew and what they were doing now.

'Tommy the Whale got married to a girl from Thailand,' Artie said. 'Sheena Reilly built a new house overlooking the Dolmen – you know, that lovely patch of land we used to go and pick blackberries in, remember?'

Of course I did. And how we fed them to each other and gave each other big black mouths. I missed it all so much.

'It's been so great seeing you,' he said, giving me a careful hug, handing over his business card. 'Sure, maybe we could do this again some time. I'll bring Shannon and you can meet her. Or you could come over to ours for dinner.'

'Hmm,' I said, looking down at the card. We both knew I was never meeting Shannon.

We stood in silence, the London throngs surging past us on the pavement.

'Well, sure, I'll be off, then,' Artie said, giving me one final kiss on the cheek. Then he dug his hands into his jacket and marched off.

'Have a nice life,' I whispered after him, as I watched him walk away. It wasn't long before he was just a speck among the crowd, and soon he had vanished completely.

20.

Rachel: day six, 7.30 a.m.

In the end I allowed Donnagh to stay. Yes, he was my sister's bully, but he was also her boyfriend. The relationship between them was clearly a lot more complex than I'd previously imagined. And, in any case, having him in the apartment suited my own ends. I wanted to find out more about Evie. About her movements in the lead-up to the crash.

Even though DI Ainsworth seemed convinced Evie had been trying to commit suicide, I wasn't so sure. The pictures Donnagh had taken in Paris showed a happy, smiling woman. If she was so ecstatic why would she want to end her life? Why would she be in a relationship at all?

'Are you absolutely sure?' Donnagh said, as if surprised by my about-turn. 'I really don't want to stay here if there's going to be bad blood between us.'

'No, I want you to stay,' I said, meaning it. 'But you have to promise me one thing – that when Evie gets through all this, you won't blame her for concealing her identity. That you'll apologize for what you did to her as a teenager . . .'

'Of course,' he said, bowing his head.

Neither of us dared bring up the elephant in the room: *if she gets through this.*

Before he left for work, I questioned him on the one

thing that had been on my mind for ages: Evie's relation-ship with drugs.

Between spoonfuls of granola, Donnagh confirmed that, yes, she had used drugs, but he didn't seem to think it was a major problem. 'We smoked weed together at the weekend, and maybe I saw her doing coke once or twice, but I didn't think she was out of control. She was just let-ting off steam.'

'Hmm,' I muttered. 'Her best friend – well, her former best friend – Janet, thinks she had a serious problem.'

Donnagh glanced at me. 'Not that I could see. She didn't seem so much different from any other young woman in London. She held down a job, she did a bit of class As. But everyone does. I'm sure you have.'

'Of course,' I muttered. I'd taken everything under the sun at one stage in my life. 'But I didn't crash into a wall and land in a coma.'

'True,' said Donnagh. 'But who said the two things were linked? Didn't the policeman say she was sober at the time of the accident?'

'He did, yes.'

'Well, then.'

I wanted to believe him. I desperately, desperately did. Because the guilt I felt for neglecting Evie was eating away at me. Corroding me like acid.

To distract myself, I decided to swerve off my normal route to the hospital and buy a new mobile. Janet was right: my current phone was a complete relic, plus this way I could check my emails without feeling pressured to write long, complicated responses.

'Apple, Samsung. Or I can offer you one with a Windows operating system . . .' the salesman – more salesboy – said, as he reeled off my options.

'Yeah, anything that's easy to operate. Plus I need to be able to use my Irish SIM card.'

'Okay,' he said. 'For that you're going to need an unlocked phone, which we can do. It's going to cost you a lot in roaming charges, though.'

'Doesn't matter.'

'Fair enough,' he said. Next, he guided me towards a swish display. 'Your best bet is the iPhone 6. It's simple to use. Totally idiot-proof.'

'Are you saying I'm an idiot?' I said, trying to make a joke. And failing.

'Um, well, er . . .' he stammered, colour flooding his cheeks.

'Oh, listen, I didn't mean . . . Look, I'll take it,' I babbled, thrusting my credit card in his direction.

An hour later, ensconced in the corner of a café, I fiddled with my new gadget, relieved that the idiot-proof description seemed accurate. The man-boy in the mobile-phone shop had set up my gmail account, and for the first time since Evie's crash, I clicked into my email. It was mostly junk – erectile dysfunction ads and numerous Groupon deals – plus some fan emails, too, redirected from my website. Normally I loved getting reader messages – the sense of connection I felt to people I'd never met still astonished me – but today I combed each message forensically for any mention of Evie's accident. It could be only a matter of time before somebody heard something about it on the grapevine and leaked it to the press. Not that I was particularly famous – I was a writer, after all, not Beyoncé – but I had appeared on TV a couple of times, and I frequently wrote columns for some of the broadsheets. Frankly, it felt like a minor miracle that nobody at the hospital had blabbed.

As I continued to scroll through, I spotted the link Janet had sent me about Donnagh, plus an email from Jacob, apologizing profusely for what I'd seen in Sandycove, begging me to return his calls. I stared at it for ages, my fingers hovering over the keypad. It would be so easy to type a few lines and re-establish contact. Forget everything that had gone before. But then I thought about the half-naked woman, about Jacob desperately wanting a child, and reached the same conclusion: we needed to end it. For good.

As I was thinking about this, my eyes fell on another email, just arrived, with the words 'So sad!' in the title box. Something about it unsettled me, but I clicked into it anyway, curious to know what it was all about.

Dear Rachel,

Such a shame, what happened to your sister. So beautiful. So much to live for. I'll be watching over you, just to make sure you're okay. Watching your lovely body.

TBM

I read it a few times, confused. Who was this? And what did TBM stand for? Unable to resist, I clicked a link at the bottom of the page, and found myself redirected to a new website – something called The Better Misogynist. The homepage was slick and monochrome, featuring what I could only presume was our eponymous hero, a handsome, dark-haired man in profile smoking a cigar. The tagline was short and to the point: 'For the discerning woman-hater'.

I scanned the page quickly, trying to find out the real name of this TBM guy, but when nothing was forthcoming, I homed in on his blog posts. The most recent one was entitled 'Fuck you, Feminazi', and when I read it, I was shocked to discover it was about me: a long, bitter piece referencing Evie's accident and claiming karma was getting its own back for my 'anti-man' stance. To top it off, TBM had created some kind of meme: my head superimposed on the body of a porn star, getting shagged from behind by a guy in Nazi uniform.

For a moment I felt overcome with nausea, a sudden desire to smash my new phone against the wall. But I forced myself to breathe, to catch hold of my anger. So much for keeping Evie's accident under the radar, this bastard would put paid to that. But who the hell was he? And, more importantly, what did he want?

A few minutes later, as I packed up my things to leave, I noticed that my hands were trembling. 'For fuck sake, Rachel, cop yourself on.'

It wasn't the first time something like this had happened. In the past I'd received lots of sexually explicit stuff from men – it went with the territory, if you were a writer who wrote about feminist issues, as I did.

But something about this seemed different.

Thoughts of Jacob came back to me again. If only we were still together, he'd reassure me about this nut-job.

Tell me he'd protect me. I looked at my phone again, tempted to reopen gmail and contact him. Then logic swooped in. Jacob and I had ended things. It was done. There was no point in breaking the scab. It would just be more painful next time round.

'Keep moving forward,' I whispered, as the noise and din of the café swirled around me. Wasn't that my golden rule? The rule I lived my life by? Do not dwell, Rachel. That way madness lies. All you have is the moment. The current moment. Everything else is gone.

21.

That night, at Janet's insistence, I went around to her house for the evening.

'Hey, hen,' she said, hugging me and taking my coat. 'You okay? You look pale.'

'I'm fine.' I nodded. 'Just tired.'

The truth was, I'd found it hard to get that stupid email out of my head. But there was no way I was going to tell Janet about it. She'd blow it out of proportion, think it meant more than it did. I just needed to forget about it. Forget I'd ever seen it.

A tall West Indian man came up behind Janet, and introduced himself. 'Nice to meet you, Rachel,' he said. 'I'm Patrick. I was so sorry to hear about Evie.'

'Thanks,' I said, choosing not to bring up Evie's attempted seduction of him just a few months previously.

'Any change?' Janet said quietly.

'No,' I said, shaking my head.

Janet had gone to the trouble of cooking dinner ('Mince and tatties, sweetheart, don't get too excited'), and though my appetite had shrunk to almost non-existent, I did my best to get through some of it.

Sensing my low mood, the two did their best to cheer me up – Janet by telling me outrageous stories from the secondary school where she taught, and Patrick explaining what it was like being of West Indian origin in England

— 'They think I should be able to play cricket. Personally I like darts.'

At the end of the night, when I'd said goodbye to Patrick, and Janet was walking me towards the door, she finally brought the conversation around to Evie again. 'Have the doctors said anything positive?'

'Not really,' I said. 'Just that most people wake up between two weeks and a month.'

'Well, it's only been, what, less than a week?'

'Yeah.' I shrugged. 'There's still time.'

'And what about Donnagh? Have you seen him again?'

'I'm living with him.'

Janet rocked back a little. 'You're what?'

'We're sharing Evie's flat. I told you, didn't I?'

'No, you damn well didn't,' she said. 'Are you out of your mind?'

'It's fine,' I said, placing my hand on her shoulder. 'Stop freaking out.'

'He's a stranger, Rachel. He could be a psychopath.'

'Don't be so melodramatic! He's my sister's boyfriend. He's from Leitrim.'

'A fact he didn't tell you,' she put in.

'No, but then again he thought Evie was from Clare.'

Janet's eyes widened. 'What?'

'It's a long story. It doesn't matter.'

'I don't know, Rachel. You hear such horror stories.'

'Janet, it's not like you to be such a wuss.' And I whispered, 'When we first met, you were bringing home strange men every night of the week.'

Janet flicked her eyes towards the kitchen, where Patrick was tidying up. 'That's all in the past now, Rachel. I'm a completely different person. And, anyway, my point is you could have stayed here with us. In the spare bedroom, I mean.'

'Thanks,' I said, a huge wave of guilt hitting me. 'Look, I'm sorry I said that just now. I don't know what came over me.'

Janet shrugged. 'It's okay. You're under a lot of pressure.'

Suddenly a thought occurred to me. 'Do you remember Evie saying anything about a college course before she crashed? You mentioned something that day in the sandwich bar and it triggered a memory.'

'What kind of memory?' Janet said, her forehead creasing a little.

'Well, before I went on the book tour she told me she'd started a new art course. Trouble is, the telephone line was really bad and I was completely distracted, about to get on a flight. I can barely remember a word of what she said.'

'It's quite possible,' Janet replied. 'When the mood was good, Evie often did evening courses – upholstery, oil painting, anything art-related.'

'And this new one?'

'Sorry, Rachel, I don't have a clue. Remember, I hadn't spoken to Evie for a few months before the crash.'

'You're sure?' I said, barely concealing my disappointment.

'Yes, I'm sure,' she said, then drew me in for a hug. 'I have a friend who's a policeman if you want to do any background checks,' she said, into my hair.

I looked at her in confusion. 'You mean to find out about Evie's art course?'

'No, you eejit. To find out more about Donnagh. Make sure he's clean.'

I couldn't stifle a laugh. 'You've been watching too many Nordic *noirs*, missus.'

'Fair enough. But I just want to make sure you're safe. After everything that's happened.'

'Thanks,' I said, withdrawing from her embrace and reaching for the door handle. 'But I promise this guy is so clean he's squeaky. He puts the toilet seat down and everything.'

'Wow, he really is one in a million, then, isn't he?' She was smiling, but I could see faint traces of worry in her eyes. 'Just promise me you won't get too close to him. We don't know anything about him.'

'I have no intention of getting close to him.' Or to any man, I thought. If I couldn't have Jacob, I didn't want any of them. I would get by perfectly fine on my own.

22.

Evie

The coma continues. I have still no idea what happened to me – except what I mentioned earlier about crashing into a wall in Lewisham. And it still sounds ludicrous. I mean, I haven't driven since Artie first taught me years ago – and I don't own a car. Why would I have decided to take up driving now? Why Lewisham? None of it adds up.

I'm trying really hard to think, to collect my memories in a bundle and sift through them. But it's like holding onto snowflakes. As soon as I touch them, they melt away, right there in my hands.

On the physical front, I'm still unresponsive. Well, externally at any rate. Internally, I'm a bloody riot.

I've been experiencing really bad panic lately, when my heart thumps and my skin prickles and I feel all clammy and terrified. Then at night I have these ... well, delusions, I suppose you'd call them, where I'm convinced I'm up and walking around, with no end in sight. During these episodes, the world seems very dark and very cold and I don't know where I am or where I'm going. But at least I'm walking. I'm moving. I'm me again.

That's when I jolt 'awake' and reality kicks in: I'm not walking. I'm in a coma. My legs don't work. None of me works.

I may never get out of here.

Cue another panic attack.

This is literally how I pass my days.

But even with all of that I'm still determined to get to the truth of how I wound up in here – I'm still determined to trace my tracks.

I believe I'm up to the point now where Artie and I said goodbye at the wine bar: I remember walking slowly to my flat afterwards, my head full of him – the way he smelt, the way he moved – wondering how I could possibly have let him walk away.

And my obsessing didn't get any better the next day. I mean, what were the chances of us having bumped into one another like that? It was almost as if Fate was intervening. Serendipity.

I'd left him the previous night, positive I'd never see him again, but what if I'd been wrong? What if this was the universe's way of telling me to grab that opportunity by the horns and run with it?

'Bollix,' I could practically hear Janet say. 'He's getting married, Evie. He's moved on.'

But that was all very well for Janet to say. She was loved up and content in her life. I was nearly thirty and alone.

Now I had the chance to rectify that. Who could possibly blame me for what I was about to do? No jury in the land would convict me. I dug out Artie's card from my handbag, flooded with relief that I hadn't thrown it away. I'd just send him a quick email, thanking him for the wonderful evening. Then maybe suggest a casual drink one night after work. It was hardly *Fatal Attraction* territory. I mean, I wasn't going to start boiling Shannon's pet bunny or anything.

Not yet, at any rate.

So that was what I did: I sent off a jaunty email to Artie's work address, telling him how much I'd loved bumping into him, and would he like to do it again sometime? Possibly this week. Then I'd practically sat on the computer, like a hen with an egg, waiting for an answer.

Eventually, five long hours after I'd sent the original email, I got a reply.

Eveline, it was so good to run into you the other night too. And, yes, Shannon and I would love to meet up with you. How about dinner this Thursday night at our place? Would that suit?

I stared in horror at the invitation. What was he talking about? I had obviously meant it to be just the two of us, not him, me and his bloody perfect-sounding girlfriend. Quite frankly, I couldn't think of anything more nightmarish. But what was I going to do? Ask him if we could keep her out of it? Tell him I wanted a quiet tête-à-tête, just me and him? Why didn't I just ask him to call the wedding off and be done with it?

Confused, I spent the rest of the evening mulling over what to do, trying to find a way to see Artie but cut out the annoying fiancée without appearing rude.

As I did so, another text landed in from Donnagh.

Hey, gorgeous, hope you're well. I'm back from Chicago next week. Are you still up for dinner on Saturday? DF

I sighed. This man didn't give up, did he? It was like one of those David Attenborough programmes on the telly:

hungry lion pursues unsuspecting, slightly stupid wilde-beest. Well, I was damned if he was going to devour me, like he did every other woman. I wasn't that bloody thick.

For a second, my thoughts skidded back to that night outside my flat when Donnagh had shown up with the new pair of shoes. I felt flooded with shame just thinking about it. How could I have let him do that to me? All those intimate things. What had I been thinking?

I closed my eyes and turned my thoughts back to Artie. He was everything Donnagh was not: kind, gentle, humane. Being around him had made me feel good about myself for the first time in half a decade. I needed to see him again. I didn't think I could go on if I didn't. Anyway, maybe having dinner with him and Shannon wouldn't be so bad. In terms of lions, Shannon seemed like the less dangerous option.

The minute I got into work, I typed Artie a reply:

Sorry, only seeing your email now. What a lovely idea! What time should I come round to your place?

I wanted to make myself sound casual. Like I did this kind of thing all the time. Like it was no big deal.

About twenty minutes later, my inbox pinged.

Great! Shannon is dying to meet you. Shall we say 7.30 p.m.? I'm attaching my address and a map below. By the way, S wants to know if you have any special dietary requirements.

I looked at the email, not knowing whether to laugh or cry. Dietary requirements? Did the desire to consume Artie whole count? I suspected not.

I could almost hear Janet adding the punchline: 'She adores men's hearts.'

I arrived at Artie and Shannon's door at 7.28 p.m., feeling as if someone had pulled my innards out and wrapped them around my waist. I thought meeting Donnagh had been terrifying, but this seemed to be on another level altogether.

I'd spent hours and hours preparing for that moment, ransacking my wardrobe so I would look 'just right'. I suspected Shannon, a psychologist, wouldn't be so naive as to enter a 'who's the more glamorous' competition. And if I went over the top it would come across as needy and insecure. I had to judge this one perfectly.

In the end I went for a floral tea-dress with a pair of Chelsea boots: feminine enough to show off my (fake) tanned legs but not so try-hard that I looked as if I wanted to steal Shannon's fiancé.

Which, of course, was exactly what I wanted to do.

But I wasn't going to show my cards just yet.

I rang the buzzer, and a woman's voice came on the line. 'Eveline, is that you? This is Shannon. Just press the door. We're number twenty-one, on the second floor.'

I did as I was told, and made for the stairs, feeling my legs turn to jelly. Suddenly everything felt wrong. My make-up; my dress; the bottle of Merlot I had thought would be perfect but now felt cheap and unoriginal. I took deep breaths as I walked slowly up the stairs. Why did I keep landing myself in these excruciating reunions with people I should long since have forgotten?

'And you must be Eveline!'

A tall, remarkably blonde woman was standing in front of me, smiling widely. She was wearing a pair of jeans and a tight white T-shirt, the only blast of colour a slim turquoise necklace that appeared to be made from shells.

'Yes,' I said, panting from the stairs exercise. 'You're Shannon.'

'That's me,' she said, holding open the door, then taking my coat and the bottle of wine. 'Come inside. Artie's cooking up a storm.'

'Artie can cook?'

'Kind of,' Shannon said, half smiling. 'He's definitely enthusiastic.'

As we walked into the sitting room, Artie popped his head out from between two sliding glass doors. 'Evie, you made it. Sorry, just at a slightly delicate moment with the barbecue.' I could see smoke billowing behind his head.

'Jesus, are you okay out there?'

'I'm grand. This always happens. Shannon will look after you for a few minutes. I'll be there in five.'

'Okay,' I said, and when I turned around, Shannon was holding a glass of prosecco in my direction.

'Don't worry about the smoke. That always happens,' she said, handing me the glass. 'You do drink alcohol, don't you?'

'God, no,' I said. 'Never touch the stuff.'

Shannon's smile wobbled. 'Would you prefer some fruit juice? Or maybe some sparkling water?'

'No, no, I was just . . .'

For a second Shannon didn't say anything, then all of a sudden she slapped her palm against her forehead. 'You were joking, weren't you?' she said, with another wide smile. 'Sorry. I'm still struggling with the Irish sense of humour.'

'It's a tricky thing, I suppose.'

'Yes. All the irony and euphemism. Everyone saying the exact opposite of what they mean. And I'm the big thick Yank who takes it all literally.'

I smiled. At least she knew how to do self-deprecation. That was something.

She grinned and linked my arm. 'Come sit down on the couch and tell me all about yourself. I'm dying to hear.'

Obeying, I plonked myself beside her, sneaking a look at her tanned profile when she turned her head.

She wasn't beautiful exactly, her chin was a bit 'chinny' and her nose a little too long, but something about her radiated attractiveness. Her smile was infectious, her movements were open and inviting, as if she was comfortable in her own skin, and wanted me to be too. I had a brief desire to lay my head on her shoulder and ask her to rub my hair.

'So, I want to know everything. Artie has only told me snippets.'

I bet he has, I felt like saying. *Extremely small snippets.*

'Um, not much to tell,' I lied, my mind suddenly blank. For some reason all I could think of was a sign I'd seen earlier on a colleague's desk: *Keep your friends close and your enemies closer.* From *The Art of War*, Tom had informed me, when I'd asked him about the quote's provenance. Sun Tzu.

'Well, I work for a business magazine in Greenwich. I live in slightly less glamorous Woolwich.' I paused for a second. 'My favourite colour is purple.'

Shannon laughed. 'You're hilarious.'

'Okay, the barbecue has been rescued.' Artie was standing in the living room, wearing a red pinny and an even redder face. 'Now for the next important question. Eveline, how do you like your steak cooked?'

'Um, I don't mind. Medium, I guess.'

'I can do it well, if you'd prefer?'

'No medium's fine,' I said. 'Unlike most Irish people I don't require my meat to be incinerated before eating it.' I smiled at Shannon to demonstrate that this was yet another example of my biting Irish wit but she wasn't looking at me. Instead, she was gazing at her fiancé adoringly.

'Wait till you see this one's version,' Artie said, pointing his thumb in the direction of his girlfriend. 'She likes it practically mooing on the plate.'

Shannon smiled and gestured, as if to say, 'Who – me?'

'Don't deny it,' he said, fluffing her hair as he walked back out onto the balcony.

'Oh, I won't,' she said, with a huge grin. 'I have a great taste for blood.'

23.

Possibly because Shannon seemed like a decent human being, despite the slightly scary blood comment, the dinner was even more excruciating than I'd anticipated.

'Artie tells me you guys dated as kids.' She was ladling more potato salad onto my plate and I was trying to stop her.

I flicked a glance at Artie, and for a second, the merest second, he looked away. 'Um, well, we were twenty-one and twenty-three respectively, so I wouldn't say we were kids exactly . . .' Had I just used 'respectively'? At eight o'clock on a Thursday? At a barbecue?

'Yeah, but even so it wasn't serious, was it?'

'Um . . .' I wanted to say it had been deadly serious, that we'd talked about marriage, children, spending our whole lives together '. . . no, I suppose it wasn't,' I mumbled. I noticed Artie was still refusing to look at me, and that he had barely touched his food.

'So what happened? How did you wind up in London?'

'Er, Shannon, I'm not sure Eveline wants to go into all of that.'

'Oh, my God, sorry. Feel free to ignore me.' Shannon was looking genuinely contrite. 'I'm just being a nosy old psychologist as usual.'

'No, no, it's fine,' I said. 'The truth is my mother died and I needed to get away. I couldn't cope with Leitrim, all the memories it held.' I was looking at Shannon but really I was addressing Artie now. I wanted him to understand that I'd been totally fucked up after Mammy's death. Obviously. Or I would never have let him go.

'I'm so sorry to hear that,' Shannon said softly. 'How awful. I take it she was young?'

'Forty-nine,' I said, hearing a tiny wobble in my voice. We were all silent for a second.

'Eveline, tell Shannon about your job. She's really interested in journalism.'

Shannon looked quizzically at him but I knew he was trying to lighten the mood, deflect the talk from the past, from Leitrim.

And so I told her about my dead-end job and my awful boss Nigel, hamming it up for comedy purposes. Then I told her about my flat, and finally about Rachel.

'OhmiGod! Rachel Darcy is your sister?'

'Yes,' I said. I hadn't meant to play the famous-sister card so soon. Once people knew about her, they tended to lose all interest in me.

'She's fantastic,' Shannon said, as if she meant it. 'I've actually recommended her books to my clients. Especially *Sanctuary*, the one dealing with the aftermath of her abortion. It's incredibly moving.'

'Yes, it is,' I said, accidentally pushing my chair back so that it made a violent screeching sound. I was proud of what Rachel had achieved but, frankly, I had enough to deal with, never mind her teenage termination. I didn't have the stomach for any more 'woe is me' family history.

'Who's for dessert?' Artie said, as if he had read my mind.

'Is it tiramisu?' Shannon said, gazing up at him with doe eyes.

'Yes, it is. Specially made today, using the finest Italian espresso.'

Shannon groaned.

'I'll take that as a no, then,' he said, and she slapped him playfully on the hand.

'You'll bring me an extra large portion or you'll face the consequences.' She was beaming at him now, like he was some kind of god.

I had lost my appetite. *Keep your friends close and your enemies closer.* It suddenly dawned on me why Shannon and Artie had invited me round for dinner. And it had nothing to do with war or enemies. The truth was, they were happy. They were in love. This wasn't a sepia-toned memory of a love shared back when Artie and I were kids. This was real. This was now.

'You'll stay for coffee at least?' Shannon said, when I told her it was time for me to leave.

'No, no, you're so kind, but I have to be up early. I'd better go.'

At the door both of them kissed me, talked about doing it all again.

'Yeah, sure,' I said, desperate to get out of there.

I looked at Shannon then, at her even teeth and her wide smile. I had seriously misjudged the situation. I had thought she was going to be the enemy, but it turned out to be even worse than that. She could have been a friend.

24.

Rachel: day seven, 11 a.m.

Evie's story had found its way into the newspapers and everything exploded. There were several slightly hysterical voicemails on my phone from my publisher and agent, as well as a good clutch of emails from readers asking me if I was okay. A quick Google search confirmed that three red-tops and a few broadsheets were carrying the story, 'Author's sister in horror smash', with some insinuating it might have been a suicide attempt. All of them, without exception, had spelled Evie's name wrongly.

My publisher and agent naturally sounded the most agitated – both wanted me to get back to them as quickly as possible so they could issue a statement.

Jacob had also sent a message. He was coming over. 'If you're not going to answer any of my messages or my phone calls I'm going to have to fly over in person. I should have done it days ago.' But I'd clamped down on that immediately. It was too soon. Too confusing. And I still felt sick about the girl I'd found in our home. I tried not to think about it but when I did I wanted to retch.

Please don't, Jacob. I'm sorry I haven't been in contact sooner but I needed time to think. I'll keep you updated on any developments with Evie, I promise. And maybe in a few days we can talk properly. When everything's calmed down a bit.

Rachel, are you sure? he'd replied, and I'd pinged back, *Yes. I'm sure.*

Miraculously he'd left it at that.

Eventually I rang my publicist back. 'I don't think it was suicide,' I said, rubbing the skin on my finger where my wedding band had recently sat. 'Evie wasn't trying to kill herself.'

'We won't mention anything about suicide,' she said matter-of-factly. 'We'll say your sister was involved in a car accident on Sunday night and is currently in a coma, but with every hope she'll recover. Keep it short and sweet.'

'Anne, I don't know if there is hope she'll recover. Some coma patients never regain consciousness.'

'And some do, don't they?'

'Yes, I suppose so.'

'Well, then, that's what we'll say.'

I knew what she was trying to do. Keep my spirits up. Remain positive. But it was easy for her to be positive, sitting in her cushy office in Covent Garden with a skinny latte. All she had to do was write a press release. She wasn't dealing with the reality. She wasn't dealing with a fucking life.

I paced around the apartment, like a caged animal. The emails were flooding in, mostly from nice people wishing my sister well, but also from a few crazies, telling me this was my fault because I was an atheist. Because of what I'd done to my unborn child.

The TBM email of the previous night seemed like small

147

fry in comparison to that lot. The things they wanted to do to me: torture, flaying, an eternity damned to Hell and back. If only they'd known I'd just chucked in my marriage as well. They'd have had a field day.

They had no idea, of course, of the actual story of my abortion – how I'd got pregnant by the first man I'd loved, the first man I'd had sex with. And sometimes I wished I could explain to them how hard it had been to make that decision; how alone and scared and powerless I'd felt. But I couldn't, because people like that never listened, didn't want to listen. They would never understand that there had been no choice. Only necessity.

I had taken that option because it was the only option. By terminating the pregnancy I had allowed myself to survive.

I had no desire to rake over the details again, reopen the wound. But in the stillness of Evie's flat, the memories came flooding back.

And so did he: Luke Spain. The one-time love of my life.

We'd met one night, when I had just turned seventeen, in a bar several miles from where I lived, and I'd almost passed out with attraction to him: his dirty-blond hair; his motorbike leathers; the way his eyes crinkled when he smiled.

He'd wooed me with cheap alcohol and vinyl – sharing his love of rockabilly, his obsession with Elvis. When we talked, I felt understood in a way I never had previously; during sex I bucked like an animal – alive and wild.

Until I found out I was pregnant, and he decided not to answer my calls any longer. Finally, I tracked him down to where he lived – he'd always been alarmingly vague about it – and when I arrived at the door, it was not Luke who answered but a tiny, fragile four-year-old.

'Is Luke Spain here?' I stammered, taken aback, but she just stood there smiling at me, twirling a strand of white-blonde hair round one finger.

A moment later, a pretty brunette woman appeared. 'Hello? Can I help you?'

'I'm sorry,' I said. 'I'm looking for Luke.'

'Well, he's at work at the moment. Maybe I can help you. I'm his wife.'

And that was when the ground had fallen from under me. I mumbled something about being a Jehovah's Witness. That I had got Luke's name from the phone book. And then I had slithered home to repeat the word over and over and over.

Married.

With a daughter.

Everything we'd shared had meant nothing.

It had been a lie.

I didn't decide on the abortion immediately. For a week or so, I spun it round in my head – all the while thinking, *I love him, I can't live without him.* And I tried calling him endlessly – until my fingers were weary from pressing the buttons on the public telephone.

On the seventh day, he eventually showed up outside my school and yanked me into his car, drove me to a secluded lake, then turned off the engine. 'Don't you *ever* go near my home again, do you understand me?'

'But I'm pregnant, and you wouldn't answer my calls. What was I supposed to do?'

He stared at me then, a strange, demented look coming over his features. 'Christ, Rachel, don't you understand? This was just a bit of fun. I'm married. I have a kid. I don't want another.'

'But –'

'You need to get rid of it,' he said quietly.

I reached for his hand. 'Please, come on . . .'

But he pulled away. 'Rachel, just be sensible, for fuck sake. I don't love you. I don't want anything to do with you. I love my wife.'

Tears ran down my cheeks. 'Luke, what we had –'

'What we had was fun, but it's over now. Don't be selfish. Do the right thing. Have an abortion and pretend this never happened.' He drove me back to school in silence.

Two weeks later, when I had figured out the logistics and the money, that was exactly what I did.

My mind stayed in that place. After the abortion I had been like a zombie – all feelings suppressed so I could just get through life without Mammy or Evie suspecting what had happened to me. But it had had a ripple effect. I'd become colder and more distant, which Evie had interpreted as rejection, with the result that she no longer confided in me about the bullying, no longer told me what was going on in her head.

I wanted her to open up. I wanted us to be close again. But I couldn't summon the energy to make it happen. How could I console her when I could barely drag myself out of bed each morning? Most of the time I just wanted to be dead.

Looking back, I was suffering from depression and possibly post-traumatic shock, but I didn't realize it, and by the time I did, it was too late. The damage had been done and Evie had lost faith in me. By that stage the wound was too deep to heal.

I thought now of all the horrible emails I'd just received – from the Bible-bashers; from TBM. How censorious they sounded; how they wanted to make me feel bad for my abortion. But the truth was, I didn't regret it. Not remotely. What I did regret was how I'd lost my connection to Evie during that year, how I hadn't been able to tell her what was wrong with me and, as a result, she didn't tell me what was going on with her.

Sure, she'd found out about the termination eventually and, no doubt, worked out why I'd been so distant that year, but I'd never said the words to her face: 'I'm sorry I abandoned you when you needed me most, Evie. I'm sorry I was so caught up in my own pain that I didn't recognize yours.'

I stared at my phone, unable to ignore the vile emails and horrible tweets clogging up my inbox. The reality was, I didn't care about those people. I'd take them on a million times if it meant Evie would wake up. If it meant I could hold her in my arms and say sorry for what I'd done.

But as the bile and vitriol continued to stream in, I realized that that was not how life worked. I couldn't trade my suffering for Evie's recovery – no matter how much I wished it.

Nor could I undo the past. Even though I wished, from the bottom of my heart, that I could.

25.

For a long time, I stayed like that, lost in time, thinking about Evie, about the termination, about Luke. But eventually I got up from the couch and shook my body loose. I shouldn't be doing this, I thought, losing myself in pointless, maudlin thoughts. I'd got over the Luke thing years earlier – that was what *Sanctuary* had been about – and while it was true that I could never change what had happened, I could certainly influence my present, my future.

I went towards the coat-stand, grabbed my leather jacket, then found my boots and pushed my feet into them. I needed to stop moping and do something productive. I needed to find a new way of helping Evie.

I thought of DI Ainsworth – how stuffy and unhelpful he'd been. Maybe it was worth paying him another visit to give him the new information I'd gleaned since our last chat. He might start taking me seriously if I relayed to him what Donnagh had told me. That Evie had been hiding things. That she'd been living a lie.

When I arrived, Ainsworth did not seem particularly excited to see me. Before I'd even had a chance to sit down, he launched into the reasons why Evie's 'accident' was not under criminal investigation.

'I don't understand,' I said, even though I was pretty sure I did.

'Because, as I explained to you initially, Ms Darcy, it was a single-car collision, dead of night. No mitigating factors, no other car.'

'I have new information, which may change your mind about all that.'

'Do you now?'

'Yes.' I ignored his condescending air. 'It will change everything.'

Ainsworth emitted a heavy sigh. 'Well, I suppose you'd better take a seat.'

'So you're saying your sister was living a double life?' DI Ainsworth was fiddling with a pen, peering at me through his spectacles.

'That's exactly what I'm saying,' I replied. 'She was hiding her true identity from Donnagh, her supposed boyfriend.'

'Why do you say "supposed"?'

'Well, it turns out, he used to bully her at school. Badly. And yet as adults they were in a relationship and living together. Even though he claims he didn't know who she was. Doesn't that strike you as odd?'

Ainsworth continued to peer at me. 'Many things appear odd to me, Ms Darcy, but this does not change the facts. Eve was alone in the car when she crashed. Mr Flood wasn't with her. He wasn't chasing her. There were no old bruises or scars on her body that would suggest he had been physically violent towards her.'

'I know,' I said, exasperated. 'I'm not even saying Donnagh was the one responsible for Evie's crash. I've also received this strange email from someone who goes by the title "The Better Misogynist". I've been wondering if the crash could be linked to him.'

Ainsworth summoned what appeared to be the bare minimum of interest. 'What did this email say?'

I repeated it verbatim.

'Hmm,' he said. 'It was just one email, though, was it?'

'Yes, but –'

'And you're a well-known author, am I correct?'

I shrugged.

'That email is probably just trolling, then.'

I couldn't believe how quickly he was dismissing this new evidence. 'I don't think so. It sounded like he knew Evie. Like he knew me too, actually.'

'Unlikely,' Ainsworth said, picking something from his nose. 'I'd say keep an eye on it, but I'd be very surprised if there was any link.'

'For fuck sake,' I muttered under my breath. Then, in a normal voice, I said, 'Won't you even report it to your cyber-crime unit – see if they can find who might have sent it?'

Ainsworth seemed to chuckle. 'Our cybercrime unit,' he repeated, as if he found the idea very amusing. 'Because we have one of those.' He paused, breathing heavily. 'Ms Darcy, I'm sorry to have to bring this up again, but all the evidence points to this being an attempted suicide.'

'You say that but –'

Ainsworth held up his hand as if to halt me. 'Given your concerns about a possible motive, I took it upon myself to ring Ms Durant's local GP. The details were in her wallet, which we found at the scene of the crash. He confirmed that she had come to him suffering with anxi-ety and that he had prescribed Xanax and antidepressants.

154

He also said she had told him about a previous suicide attempt when she was a student, back in Ireland.'

I flushed, embarrassed.

'It would have been helpful,' he went on, 'if you'd mentioned that during our earlier discussions.'

'It was years ago. She was only a kid.'

'She was twenty-one,' Ainsworth said. 'Ms Darcy, I'm sorry to break it to you but it looks extremely likely that your sister crashed her car, well, Mr Flood's car, intentionally. All the evidence would suggest that.' He laced his hands together, and tilted his head, as if to say, 'Please, you silly woman. Just accept the obvious.'

Something exploded inside me. 'For fuck sake, Ainsworth, why don't you, for just one second, stop talking about Evie trying to commit suicide as if it's fact and do something proactive for a change? Why aren't you out there trying to find the person who did this to her? Why aren't you looking for the fucking perpetrator?' I broke down in a stream of sobs so loud that people in the corridor could probably hear me.

For a second there was complete silence. Then I heard the squeak of a chair leg and the loud thud of a door shutting.

A few moments later Ainsworth was back in the room. 'Here,' he said, handing me some tissues and a glass of water. I took them.

He sat down again and took off his glasses, rubbing at his temples. 'Ms Darcy, I'm going to ignore that little outburst and try to make you understand things from my side.'

I nodded. Even I knew cursing blue murder in front of a policeman wasn't the greatest idea in the world.

'In my line of business, we operate on this thing called evidence. And so far the evidence regarding your sister is as follows. Some time between eleven and midnight on the third of August, your sister, Eveline Durant, took her boyfriend Donnagh Flood's car and drove four miles into the borough of Lewisham. At some point she lost control of the vehicle, a 2015 Porsche Carrera. It was a mild night with no ground frost or rain so we can rule out weather as a factor. There was no other vehicle involved, no blood on the front bumper to suggest she'd hit an animal or even a human. Following the accident, we interviewed Mr Flood, who said he had been seeing Ms Durant for roughly eight weeks, and that they had just returned from Paris. As a precaution, I contacted the Irish police, who carried out a background check on Mr Flood. He committed a few minor offences as a teenager – possession of a small amount of drugs, one count of stealing a car as a minor – but since the age of seventeen there have been no further infractions. And his record in the UK is also clean.' Ainsworth took a gulp from a plastic cup that he had brought in at the same time as the one for me. 'Are you following all this?' he said in my direction.

'Yes,' I said quietly, conscious now that I must do nothing more to piss him off.

'I also discussed the case with a number of colleagues and as of now we can find no reason why we would regard it as suspicious.'

'Even with this new information – the fact that she was concealing her identity from her boyfriend? The email I got from TBM?'

Ainsworth sighed. 'None of it changes the facts, Ms Darcy. The ones I have just enunciated.'

'At length,' I replied sarcastically.

He narrowed his eyes. 'Ms Darcy, I'm a busy man and, though I sympathize with your situation, I can't allow this case to take up any more of my time.'

'But what about the email? Won't you at least follow it up?'

'Ms Darcy, as you said yourself, it was one email. Fair enough if a few more come in, I'll see what I can do, but for the moment I just don't have the resources to spend on something as minor as this.'

'Minor? You think Evie's coma is minor?'

'Oh, for pity's sake,' he said, in a semi-growl. 'How many more times do I need to explain?'

'Can't you at least try to pretend you care about Evie? About what happened to her?'

'Ms Darcy, I do care, but as I said, I'm a very busy man. Your sister had mental-health issues and all the evidence points to the fact that she tried to kill herself – that's the nuts and bolts of it, I'm afraid. What more do you want me to say?'

I stared at him, open-mouthed, at a complete loss for words. I'd come here seeking help and all I'd got was total apathy.

No, it was much worse than that.

It was total disdain.

I wasn't just shocked at Ainsworth's attitude, I was incensed. As I stood outside the station, dragging hard on a fag, I wanted to kick the bastard's head in. How could he have been so dismissive? So inhumane. Yes, maybe it looked like every other suicide crash he'd ever investigated, but didn't he owe it to me at least to talk to Donnagh and look into the TBM email? To pretend he cared?

True, I didn't have any hard evidence, but I had the beginning of something: leads, suspects, potential motives. All I needed was somebody to help me, a bit of genuine support.

A dart of pain passed through my heart, causing me to drop my cigarette. There it was again. Guilt. Rolling, crashing waves of it. I hadn't been strong enough for Evie when we'd been teenagers, when I'd left her to rot among the bullies at her school. But I was damned if I was going to let it happen again and allow history to repeat itself.

Back in the flat, I sat down on Evie's sofa. 'Think logically,' I told myself, taking out a notebook and a pen, jotting down my thoughts on Evie's 'accident': the date, the time, other facts Ainsworth had mentioned about the case.

I'd never been the biggest fan of the police, always assuming people who got off on throwing their weight around couldn't be much better than the criminals they purported to catch. And, frankly, my dealings with Ainsworth over the past few days hadn't done anything to assuage that feeling.

But one thing had become very clear. If he and his lot were not going to get to the bottom of why Evie had crashed, if they were going to treat it like some botched suicide attempt, somebody else was going to have to take charge and lead the investigation.

Me.

26.

Evie

It was only the next morning when I was getting ready for work that I realized I had left my jacket in Artie and Shannon's flat.

'Subconscious desire to see Artie again,' I could practically hear Janet say, giving me her Freudian take on the whole thing. 'Leave him alone, Evie. He's getting married. It's not fair.'

She was right, of course. But what was I going to do? Leave my favourite coat in his flat? It had cost me nearly three hundred quid. I sent Artie a quick text, explaining the situation. *No problem, do you want to call round for it this evening?* he replied. *I'll be back around seven.*

Sure, I said, and left it at that, but for the rest of the day I got practically no work done, obsessing about whether Shannon would be there and what I should wear. In general, being a neurotic maniac. So humongous was my anxiety that I nipped out during my lunch break and went back to my flat to change into a very tight dress and drop a Xanax to calm me down.

Fuck the floral tea-dress. I needed to bring out the big guns now. I'd remembered how much Artie had loved my body (even the pre-surgery one). How he would drop his head into the crevice between my breasts, and just lie there as if I was his own personal piece of Heaven. Maybe if I reminded him of that time, he'd want it back. Dump Shannon – nicely, of course – and rekindle what we'd had together. Rediscover us. Rediscover all that love.

When I arrived at Artie's flat, luck seemed to be on my side. Shannon was out.

'She said to pass on her love, and that she hopes to see you soon,' Artie said, giving me the briefest peck on the cheek.

Yeah, right, I thought. Sure, we'd got on well the night before, and in a parallel universe we might even have been friends, but she'd be a saint if she wanted to see me again, knowing my history with Artie. Even Mother Teresa wouldn't be that generous.

'So here's the coat.' Artie was holding out my jacket. Was it me or did he seem a little jumpy?

I took it and just stood there, refusing to budge. Finally, after a rather excruciating wait, Artie asked me if I wanted a coffee.

'Sure,' I said, flashing him a smile, then followed him into the kitchen, adjusting my cleavage behind his back.

'Is Americano okay?' he asked, taking two white cups out of the cupboard and lining them up in front of what looked like a brand-new Nespresso coffee machine.

'Jesus, Artie, 'twas far from Americanos you were reared.'

'It sure was,' he said, a reluctant smile forming on his lips for the first time since my arrival. 'Tay with a reused taybag. That was as much as you could expect in our house.'

'Well, there were about twenty of you.'

'Twenty-five,' he said. 'If you counted the cousins from Tipperary.'

We both grinned.

'So, back to the coffee question, is Americano okay? Or would you prefer something else?'

'Americano is fine,' I said, relieved Artie seemed to be coming out of his dour mood.

A few minutes later, at his suggestion, we were carrying our cups and saucers in the direction of the lounge, which he said would be 'more comfortable'. He was right: it was, but not just because of the squishy couch or the light streaming through the window. It was mainly because Shannon wasn't there. Without her presence, it felt like old times again. Just me and Artie. Together at last.

'Shannon really likes you,' Artie began, taking a slurp of his coffee.

'Oh, go on out of that,' I mumbled, not wanting to ruin this perfect moment by talking about Shannon.

'She thinks you're hilarious. She reckons you should go into stand-up comedy.'

'Really?' I said, unsure whether to take that as a compliment or not. Why hadn't she mentioned that I was pretty? Was she trying to take the piss? 'Um, well, I thought she was nice too. Very upbeat.'

Artie nodded. 'Oh, yes, she really is. An incredibly positive person.'

He looked at me rather pointedly, and I couldn't help feeling uncomfortable. Did he mean in comparison to me? His former miserable girlfriend? It certainly seemed that way.

'The coffee's nice,' I said, rather limply.

'Thanks,' Artie said, shrugging. 'Shannon gave me the

Nespresso machine for my birthday, and I've been trying to get into using it.'

'You seem to like sophisticated things, these days,' I observed quietly.

'I wouldn't go that far.'

'I would.'

We sat in silence for a minute, both of us seeming a bit lost for words. Well, that wasn't entirely true: I knew what I wanted to say. How sorry I was. How much I'd missed him. And other things. That I felt an emptiness inside me every day. That I felt cocooned in loss.

'Actually, Eveline, I'm glad you came over. There was something Shannon and I meant to tell you last night but we couldn't because of a timing issue.'

Suddenly there was the jiggling of keys in the lock and we both looked towards the door.

'That must be her now,' Artie said, getting up quickly, smoothing his trousers. 'Hi, sweetheart,' he said as she came in, and went to kiss her cheek.

'Hi, Eveline,' Shannon said, walking over, and giving me a quick hug. 'You got your jacket, I see.'

'I did,' I said, holding it up to show her.

'You're back early,' Artie said. 'Did something happen with your class?'

'Oh, that,' Shannon replied, slipping off her coat. 'The instructor came down with food poisoning and it was called off at the last minute.'

'What was the class?' I asked, feeling a sense of foreboding overwhelm me.

'Oh, didn't Artie tell you?' Shannon said, looking at her fiancé, who shook his head.

'Didn't get the chance,' I heard him whisper tersely.

For a second I saw something glimmer in Shannon's eyes. 'It was pregnancy yoga, Evie,' she said, taking her boyfriend's hand. 'Artie and I are expecting a baby.'

It was one of the worst fifteen minutes of my life. As I struggled to keep my coffee down, Shannon delineated in excruciating detail everything connected with the pregnancy.

'We wanted to tell you last night, but we didn't hit the twelve-week mark officially until today.' Shannon beamed at Artie, who was acting a lot more subdued than she was.

'We had our scan earlier this morning.' She went over to her handbag and produced a black-and-white image of her womb. 'See?' she said, pointing at the centre of the picture. 'That's our little munchkin. See how she's waving her little hand at everyone.'

'You know it's a girl?' I said, feeling nauseous. I'd always thought Artie and I would have a girl. A perfect, beautiful little girl.

'Well, I don't for sure. It's too early to tell, but I have a feeling. You know how it is . . .'

Actually, I didn't. And at the rate I was going I was never going to find out either.

'Shannon, I'm sure Eveline doesn't want to be bored senseless with our baby talk. You probably need to get going, don't you, Eveline?'

Artie, I noticed, had turned extremely pale.

'Arthur, don't be so rude. Of course she doesn't want to go. Do you, Evie?'

'No,' I said, shaking my head, although I was desperate to flee.

'And did he tell you our other great news?'

Christ, there was more?

'We're moving back to the States. I've been offered a teaching position in Vermont.'

'Huh?' My legs turned to jelly.

'Yes, I know. It's hard to believe, right?' She laughed as I remained statue-still.

'But how is that even possible?' I said, swivelling to look at Artie. 'How will you even be allowed into the country?'

'We're going to get married beforehand. Back in Ireland.'

'So there'll be no immigration issues. No visa problems.' I knew I was saying all this with disappointment in my voice but I didn't care. I'd just found Artie, and Shannon was taking him away from me. No wonder she'd had no qualms about meeting me. About inviting me to her home. She hadn't been intimidated because she hadn't needed to be.

She held the jewel in the crown.

Artie's baby.

'In a way it's such a shame you and Artie only ran into each other now. We would have so loved to get to know you better.'

Artie already knows me, I felt like saying to her. And, by the way, why was she already talking about me in the past tense?

'But I suppose there's always Facebook and Twitter.' She was walking towards the kitchen. 'WhatsApp, Instagram, Skype . . .'

Once she had left, I turned to Artie. 'When do you leave?'

'Not for another few months. I still have to serve out

some notice. Shannon has to do the same and, of course, we have the wedding in Ireland to plan.'

We looked at each other then, not saying anything. It felt as if a chasm had opened up between us, so wide now it was impossible to cross.

'Artie,' I began, trembling with emotion. I needed to say this stuff now before I lost my nerve. 'I'm so sorry about everything that happened between us. If I could turn back time I would. It was a mistake – the biggest mistake of my life.'

For a moment Artie looked startled. Then he held up his hand. 'Evie, stop. There's no need to apologize. It's all water under the bridge. Another lifetime. Another planet.'

I made to speak again, but then it dawned on me: there was nothing left to say. 'Goodbye, Artie,' I said, kissing him lightly on the cheek. 'Good luck with everything.'

'Goodbye, Eveline,' he said.

Shannon walked back into the living room, just as I turned to leave. 'Hey, don't you have a kiss for me too?' she said.

'Of course.' I moved to peck her cheek.

'You must come to our leaving do. I'm not sure where we're going to have it yet, but I'll send you an email.'

'Sure,' I said, needing to escape now. To make all of this stop.

'Or maybe visit us in Vermont. When the little one comes along.' She patted her non-existent belly, and reached for Artie's hand.

'Yeah,' I said, feeling something break inside me. 'Perhaps I will.'

27.

I felt as if my heart had splintered into a million tiny pieces, which was stupid because Artie and I had broken up years ago. So why did I feel like I'd just lost him today? I'd been such a fool. Shannon hadn't been nice to me because she'd liked me, it was because she was pregnant. All the time she'd been fucking pregnant.

I began to cry. I'd always thought it would be me and Artie having a child together. I could almost picture it: his curly head bent low, kissing my damp forehead after I'd given birth, beaming with love for me and the little one.

I kicked a rogue Coke can, which bounced off a street-lamp. Why was I so fucking angry all of a sudden?

'You left me,' I could hear Artie whisper. 'I wanted you for ever and you just let me go.'

'But now I want you back,' I heard myself say aloud. 'I need you back.'

A homeless woman looked up at me, her eyebrows raised.

Soon Artie would be jetting off to get married in Ireland, then to America. And in six months' time he would be a father – to a child that wasn't mine. It seemed so final. So unstoppable. Like a giant avalanche rolling down a mountain.

I stopped walking, threw some change into the woman's coffee cup.

'Thank you, dear,' she mumbled. 'Any chance of a bit more? For a hostel like . . .'

I looked at her, the anger gone now, just resignation in its place. 'Sorry,' I said sadly. 'I've nothing left to give.'

For the rest of the week I found it hard to sleep. I kept dreaming about my mother. In one dream she was making apple tarts but had no eyes. In another she was in London, shaking hands with Donnagh, but as soon as their skin touched, her body disintegrated, leaving nothing but a pile of dust. Each time I woke up, writhing and shaking, my entire body lathered in sweat.

Donnagh had texted me yet again about meeting up on his return from Chicago, and I was still trying to work up the courage to tell him it couldn't happen. Yet something stopped me. Something I couldn't put my finger on.

I wandered into the city on the Thursday evening, utterly confused, my heart racing. I wanted nothing more than to get off my head, but I had no drugs. And, second, no drinking companion. A woman in a tight bustier handed me a flyer. 'La Petite Mort,' it read. 'For adventurers, for provocateurs, for lovers.'

'A sex shop?' I muttered out loud.

'Yes, but a very beautiful one,' she replied. Her face looked as if it had been sculpted from porcelain. 'You have a boyfriend?' she asked, and I nodded even though I most certainly didn't. 'They do some incredibly sexy lingerie, if you want to give him a bit of a thrill tonight.'

'Hmm,' I said noncommittally, but I found myself walking in the direction of the shop anyway.

Inside, it was clear that the place was aimed at middle-class women, not men in macs. The carpet was thick and champagne-coloured and the assistants were dressed like models on the cover of *Vogue*.

'Can I help you?' one said. The name 'Lola' was written on a heart-shaped badge pinned to her chest.

'I don't know,' I said truthfully. 'I'm not really feeling myself at the moment.'

The woman lowered her voice. 'Can you give me a bit more detail?'

'It's complicated. There's this man . . .'

'Isn't there always?' She smiled at me and took my hand. 'Don't tell me. He's gorgeous, the relationship's new, and you need a bit of a confidence boost in the bed-room . . .'

I shrugged, not exactly contradicting her. Should I tell her about Artie? About bumping into him? About the fact that an American earth-mama was, at this very moment, carrying his child?

Lola didn't appear to need any of this extra informa-tion. Instead she began riffling through the rails, selecting tiny pieces of underwear as she went. 'Come with me.' Unlike most changing rooms, this one wasn't stark and unflattering: the lighting was low and high heels were pro-vided. There was also a small hole in one of the walls, which I pointed out to Lola.

'Oh, that's a voyeur hole,' she explained, as she ducked her head between the curtains. 'Sometimes partners like to watch their girlfriends getting undressed.'

A tiny shock ran through me. Women brought their partners here? To ogle them? Bloody hell!

I peeled off my boring old non-sexy underwear, and proceeded to try on some of Lola's offerings. The dim lighting was a godsend. Normally in regular changing rooms I try not to look at my naked body. It's not fat but there are stretch-marks from gaining and losing so much weight. There are scars. But in that semi-dimmed cubby-hole of erotica, I felt okay. Good, even. And the pure silk creations adorning me were definitely helping.

Lola peeped in at me, and I couldn't help but feel that must be part of the sales pitch. The vaguely Sapphic energy. 'My God, you look incredible.'

I was wearing a black balconette bra, extremely low cut, with tiny pink ribbons running around the edging. The knickers were the same design, thong shaped, with suspenders attached.

'The thing is, you have to fake it till you make it,' she said solemnly.

'What?' I said, turning round.

'You're feeling intimidated because your new partner is sexually experienced. Am I right?'

I dropped my head. Actually, I was feeling shit because my old partner didn't love me. But I was pretty sure G-string knickers weren't the answer – not where Artie was concerned.

'So you need to pretend to be confident. Men are simple creatures. If you turn up looking hot, and like you know what you're doing, the rest will follow.' She gave a sly smile as if she had plenty of direct experience in that area.

I pirouetted slowly in front of the mirror, turning this way and that. In the selective lighting the overall look was impressive. Not perfect, of course, but good enough for a normal person. In any case it wasn't even the look that mattered as much as how the outfit, the shop, made me feel. In this get-up, I was as far removed from Artie, Shannon and baby bumps as I could possibly imagine. No more thinking about the past. No more dreaming about my mother.

'I'll take them,' I said, and Lola nodded, as if she'd known all along that I would.

At the till I handed over the money and bit down the guilt at spending so much on underwear when my electricity bill was overdue. As Lola ran my credit card through the machine my phone pinged with a message from Donnagh: *Okay last chance. Do you want to see me or don't you?*

He sounded pissed off. Aggressive, even.

Fake it till you make it. Lola's voice rang in my ears as I thought of what to do next.

I want to see you, I replied, then paused and typed in something else.

Book a room.

28.

Rachel: day eight, 1.30 p.m.

I was determined to solve the mystery of Evie's crash, except there was one small problem: I had no idea how to go about it. But then it occurred to me that I did know someone who could help me. Someone who knew that business inside out.

I retrieved my battered green Filofax from my bag and began skimming through it. It was where I kept all my contacts, going back decades.

'Lorelei Dixon speaking, PI.'

Years earlier, when I'd been travelling around the States, I'd made friends with Lorelei, who at the time was a cop, and had a brief fling with her. We'd both realized very quickly I wasn't girlfriend material.

'I'm your "experimental phase",' she'd said, over one too many beers, and I'd had to admit she was probably right. Though I adored her, and found her sexy, some-thing about what we were doing didn't feel entirely real. More like a reaction to something else.

'Lorelei, it's Rachel. Rachel Darcy. I know it's been a long time. How are you?'

For a second there was silence, and then a huge rush of words. 'Jesus Christ, Rachel Darcy, how the fuck are you? How are you doing? How's the writing? I saw your new book in the store last week.' I removed the phone from my ear for a second, Lorelei's delivery delightful but over-powering on the eardrums.

For a couple of minutes we strolled down Memory Lane. She told me she was married now, to a woman called Mary-Beth, and they had two children, Mike and Alice. Her private-detective business was doing well, though her mom had passed away the previous winter so she was still coming to terms with it. 'And you know all about that kind of loss.'

'I do,' I said quietly, and we moved on. Eventually Lorelei stopped and asked about my life. 'That's kind of why I'm calling,' I said. 'I need your help.'

After that she listened as I explained about Evie and the crash. About Donnagh. I was tempted to tell her about the TBM email but at the last minute I decided against it. It was just one email from some sex-starved wack-job. It would just confuse things. Muddy the waters.

'What's your gut telling you about the guy?' Lorelei finally said.

'He seems okay. He's certainly very charming. But the thing is, I know nothing about him, save what I can find on the internet.'

Lorelei snorted. 'Fuck the internet. You were right to come to me. You say he lived in America for seven or eight years?'

'Yes.'

'Okay, I can do some proper background checks. Police data. College records. That kind of thing.'

'Look, I'm sure he's fine. And I don't want to put you to any trouble if you're busy.'

'Rachel, are you kidding me? This is my job.'

'I'll pay you, obviously.'

'Would you quit it? Give me a few hours, maximum a day, and I'll find out as much as I can.'

'You're a star, Lor.'

'Huh, too bad you didn't think that when we were sleeping together.'

There was a chuckle in her voice and, despite myself, I laughed too. 'That was a long time ago,' I said.

'Yeah. Speaking of which, I read that you got married.'

'Yeah,' I said, the smile leaving my voice. I didn't want to think about Jacob. Not now, when I was trying to remain focused.

'Well, I hope he knows how lucky he is,' Lorelei said, giggling. 'A million lesbians would happily replace him.'

I tried to laugh in response, but it was a fake, empty sound.

'So I'll let you know, hon, about this Donnagh character.'

'Sure,' I said, and we parted.

That was the other thing I remembered about Lorelei: her sense of timing. It was what made her such a good private detective. She had an uncanny ability to know when to keep digging and when to leave well enough alone.

A few hours later, good as her word, she rang back. 'Well, he's certainly a looker, isn't he?' she said, then proceeded to fill me in about his life in America: the college he'd attended; the name of his ex-wife; when he'd got divorced.

'But so far, legally speaking, he's coming up clean as a whistle,' she said, almost as if she was disappointed. 'All I can find are a few speeding fines.'

'Hey, Lor, don't sound so down. This is good news. It means I'm not living with a psychopath.'

'You're living with this guy?'

'Yeah, didn't I mention that?'

'No, you didn't. I don't need to say that's a fairly stupid idea, Rachel, given the situation your sister is in.'

'Yeah, well . . .'

'Look, hon, he's coming up clean for now. And you're right, that is good. Just be careful, is all I'm saying. People aren't always what they seem.'

'Sure,' I said, and thanked Lorelei for her concern.

'I'll do some more work on him. See if I can find anything else on the guy.'

'Okay,' I agreed. 'But don't kill yourself. Not if you're busy. You've already given me the basic information I need.'

'Fine,' said Lorelei. 'And, Rachel?'

'Yes?'

'You'll come through this.'

'Will I?'

'Yes. Just keep strong.'

29.

Before we hung up, Lorelei gave me some basic tips on how to go about investigating Evie's crash on my own.

'Talk to her neighbours – see if they can tell you anything. Then get your hands on her cell. Failing that, try to access her emails. Anything that will show you who she's been in contact with.'

'Evie's laptop is password-protected. Plus I have no idea where her phone is.'

'It could have been retrieved from the scene of the crime. Talk to the police and see if they'll hand it over. They might, seeing as you're next of kin.'

'Anything else?'

Lorelei paused. 'Trust your instincts, Rachel. Most detective work is about listening to your gut. If something feels off, it probably is. And, Rachel?'

'Yes?'

'Be careful, okay? I'm just at the end of a phone if you need to contact me.'

'Sure,' I said, then hung up. In a world of complete chaos, speaking to Lorelei had been like swimming in a sea of reassurance. She seemed so confident; so in control. That's how I needed to be if I was going to get through this. If I was going to get to the truth of how Evie had crashed.

*

I started with the neighbours, but none of them seemed to know anything or, if they did, they were not inclined to tell me. The only one who had offered an opinion was an elderly lady with a blue rinse, who clicked her teeth on hearing Evie's name, muttered something about 'loose moral standards', then slammed the door in my face. After that I abandoned interviewing the neighbours, and rang around a few local art colleges, hoping to find out more about the evening course Evie had told me about. Unfortunately, though, none would release any information, claiming it was confidential. I got off the phone, buzzing with annoyance, but then again, who wound up in a coma from doing watercolours? The art course was irrelevant. I needed to focus on more substantial clues – like who Evie had been in contact with. Like TBM.

Lorelei had mentioned the police report so I went back down to the police station and managed to get a copy of it. Ainsworth wasn't around and I was grateful for that. If I ran into him, I wasn't sure I'd be able to control myself. I was genuinely afraid I might try to smash his smug face in.

Instead I focused on the report. According to that, a number of items had been found at the scene of the crash, most significantly Evie's wallet and handbag. The bag contained all the usual things: her phone, some make-up, a notebook. What gems did the phone and that notebook contain? Details about the person who had hurt my sister? Details of her former life?

I scanned the rest of the list. Apparently, the police had

also retrieved other items: a silver locket, now broken, which had slid off Evie's neck as she'd been hauled from the wreckage of the car; a photograph, slightly ripped, referred to as 'Man and Child'.

I tried to steady my breathing. The silver locket had been my mother's, a family heirloom passed down through generations of Darcy women. She'd given it to Evie shortly before she died, and I knew Evie never took it off. I wished that I could retrieve it now and wrap it around my sister's neck again. Even if I didn't believe in God, I still believed in my mother. In the power of her love.

The photograph, 'Man and Child', was another matter entirely. It was a snap of Evie and our father, taken on Evie's third birthday – just a couple of months before he had abandoned us and fled back to France. Evie had found it at the back of a cupboard when she was eight and had insisted on holding on to it. Why she'd bothered, I would never understand.

I'd long since accepted that, while he was technically related to us, my father wasn't really my father. He was just a DNA link. A biological memory. To be honest, the whole thing wasn't even painful now. It was just reality. Like the fact that the earth is round or the sky is blue. But Evie had never been as pragmatic as I was. She had always nurtured a secret dream that one day we would all be reunited. Past hurts washed away – that kind of thing. It was sweet but it was also a delusion.

Our father was a scumbag, who had abandoned a wife and two small children to a life of near poverty. Whatever about Evie, I never wanted anything to do with him. As far as I was concerned, he was as good as dead.

Back in the apartment, I moped around a bit – pissed off I hadn't got my hands on Evie's phone or wallet. Without her phone, how was I supposed to find out who her contacts were? And while her computer was promising, there was a major problem because I didn't know her password. All in all, it looked as if my 'investigation' was over before it had even begun.

I'd walked downstairs to get some fresh air, and come up with a new plan, when I spotted a postman in the lobby just about to drop a bundle of letters into Evie's postbox. Without thinking, I called out to him, and he turned. 'Hey, are those for me?'

'Are you Eve Durant?'

'Ye-es . . .' I mumbled.

He handed me the bundle, clearly taking me at my (flimsy) word.

Back in the apartment I placed it on Evie's kitchen table and stared at it. Was I really going to go through Evie's personal correspondence?

Was I that desperate?

The truth will set you free. John 8:32. I had passed a preacher on the street earlier bearing a placard with that message.

Would the truth set Evie free?

Set me free?

But for some reason I couldn't do it. Sure, I'd appointed myself lead detective on the investigation into my sister's life but when it came to it, did I have the nerve to pull her secrets apart? To pull her apart?

I took the letters and, without looking, pushed them into a drawer. Maybe it was best to forget about this whole stupid conspiracy theory. It wasn't like I had proof of anything. Perhaps Ainsworth had been right: Evie had been trying to commit suicide. Simple as that. And I just needed to accept the truth.

That night I didn't eat dinner. Instead I went to bed early, tying myself in knots about Evie and what I should be doing to help her. After hours of insomnia, I found a bottle of Calpol and downed several large spoonfuls, desperate to escape from my horribly mixed-up mind.

Later, deep in sleep, I dreamed I saw my mother. She was dressed in white and wearing Evie's locket. She was mouthing something but I couldn't hear what she was saying. The closer I got, the further away she moved. We were in the desert and I kept falling in the sand, my feet weighed down by something I could feel but could not see.

At some point, she began tracing something on the ground, beckoning me to join her. I did so, but as I got close she became fainter and fainter, until finally she had disappeared.

'No!' I screamed. I began crying and, suddenly, I was back in Leitrim with my father who, bizarrely, was holding a fishing rod and some bait.

'Here, Rachel, come to Daddy,' he was saying, as if I was a cat. 'Will we go fishing?'

I was embarrassed by him, and wanted him to go away, but he caught my hand and held me tight. I screamed at him to let me go, but he wouldn't. I was standing on the same sand that had been in the desert when I'd been with my mother. I looked down and saw the letters my mother had traced. She had written just two words, huge and overpowering. Impossible to ignore.

Save Evie.

30.

Evie

I had a plan. Or, at least, I thought I did. Armed with this knowledge, I was prepared to take on the might of Donnagh Flood. I was prepared to do battle with him.

Having said that, I had never felt more nervous in my life. As I tried to do up my bra, which I had bought in La Petite Mort, my hand kept slipping. 'Fuck it,' I whispered into the air. *Just keep it together, Eveline. For one night only. Keep your shit together.*

With the bra and suspenders finally on, I squeezed into a tiny bandage dress, then added a pair of towering stilettos. I touched Mammy's locket for luck, but forced myself to remove it, placing it carefully in a drawer and putting on some costume jewellery instead. I couldn't sully her memory by wearing it tonight. Not given what was ahead of me; the sordid things I had planned . . .

When I reached the hotel, Donnagh was already at the bar, looking like something out of an ad for a male perfume: lean body, chiselled cheekbones and hard jaw. 'Eve,' he said, raising his hand.

I walked over, feeling my hips move to the rhythm of my very tight dress.

'You look . . .' he paused '. . . you're more stunning each time I see you.'

'Thanks,' I said, not trusting myself to say more. I noticed my hands were shaking.

'What would you like to drink?'

'A glass of white wine, please.'

'Why not make it champagne?'

'Sure,' I said. 'If you're paying . . .'

'I'm paying,' he said, and for the briefest second he placed his hand on my arm.

I felt my breath catch.

'Eve, are you okay?'

'Yes,' I said, in a tiny, trembly voice.

'There is no need to be scared of me,' he said quietly. 'I don't want to hurt you.'

I didn't say anything.

'Eve,' he said, 'I'm sorry about the other night. I'm not expecting you to do anything you're not comfortable with.'

'I asked you to book a room,' I whispered.

'I know,' he said, smiling a little. 'But you don't have to feel under pressure to use it. This is just a drink and some dinner. To get to know each other better. Okay?' He squeezed my hand.

My champagne had arrived and Donnagh passed it to me, then reached for his own drink, a pint of Guinness. 'To dinner with no strings,' he said, raising his glass aloft, encouraging me to do the same.

I clinked. I tried to smile but I couldn't, finding it impossible to shake the suspicion that, when it came to free dinners, there was really no such thing.

There were many ironies that night. The first was that

Donnagh seemed to think I was a puritanical virgin, terri-fied of a man's touch. I'm not saying I'm a slapper or anything (though others might) but I wasn't quite the innocent he seemed to think.

I tried to relax. This was only going to work if I got into the atmosphere of the night. If I allowed myself to be in control. Over dinner I switched into journalistic mode: I asked Donnagh to tell me more about his time in Chicago. His business. His favourite music, films, art . . .

'Art?' he exclaimed. 'I'm not really an art man.'

'Why not?' I demanded.

'I don't know. Because I don't really understand it, and it seems poncey and overpriced.'

'A lot of it is,' I agreed.

'And you?'

'What about me?'

'Do you like art?'

'Yes,' I said simply, not wanting to tell him the truth. That art was the oxygen I breathed, the only thing that, during the tough times, had got me through. In fact, recently, I'd even enrolled in a new evening class, hoping it would help me deal with the depression I'd been feeling lately. Not that Donnagh needed to know that. Not that he'd want to.

'I'm really sorry, Eve, but I'm absolutely gasping for a cigarette,' he said all of a sudden, flinging his napkin down on the table and pushing back his chair. 'Would you mind if I stepped outside for a moment?'

'Sure,' I said, nodding. The break suited me perfectly. When Donnagh had gone I made for the Ladies and did a quick line – an essential ingredient for the job that lay ahead. Then, jacked up on my coke high, I wandered into the smokers' area and found him.

'Hang on a second,' he said, dumping his cigarette in a bin and producing a packet of Fisherman's Friend. He downed one, then offered the pack to me.

'Do I need one?' I said, pretending to be offended.

'God, no,' he said. 'You smell like something out of a rose garden. It's just so I'm not the only one who stinks of throat lozenges.'

We were standing close to each other now, and suddenly I felt Donnagh's arm wrap itself around my waist. I flinched.

'I'm sorry, Eve. I didn't mean . . .' He let his hand fall.

'It's okay,' I said, swallowing hard. 'You can put it back.'

'Are you sure?'

I nodded.

'Tell me,' he said, 'are you usually this nervous around men?'

I looked at him then and wanted to blurt out everything. That he was the reason I was flinching. His ability to bully. What he'd done to me as a kid. Except that would have ruined everything. I would have been a victim. As I always had been with Donnagh.

Tonight was about rectifying that.

Be brave, Eveline, a voice whispered inside me. *Soon this will be over. And then you can forget about Donnagh Flood. Forget he ever existed.*

'I just want you to tell me if . . .'

If what? I felt like saying. Why this sudden interest in my well-being? Where had that been when he was a teenager? When he'd tortured me like an insect. 'The truth is,

I'm not long out of a massive relationship,' I lied. 'I'm not used to being with another man.'

Donnagh's eyes were soft and understanding. 'Eve, we don't have to do anything.'

He sounded so sincere.

'That room you booked . . .' I whispered, the tremor in my voice audible. Donnagh didn't respond, so I asked again: 'Donnagh, the room. Did you book it here – in this hotel, I mean?'

Slowly he lifted his eyes to meet mine. 'Yes.'

'Okay,' I said, breathing deeply. 'Shall we go, then?'

'Are you sure, Eve? I don't want you to feel pressured.'

Oh, for God's sake, I wanted to scream. *Quit the fake concern. I know what you're like. What you're really like.*

But, of course, I didn't say any of that. Instead I said, 'I'll be fine.'

3 1.

The room Donnagh had booked was a five-star wonder – all chrome lighting, deep-pile carpets and a huge, cushion-strewn bed. But I barely had time to register any of it. My heart was beating so rapidly, it felt like it might explode.

'Is it okay if I do this?'

Carefully, Donnagh slid my jacket off my shoulders and threw it onto a chair. Then he took my face in his hands and planted the lightest of kisses on my lips.

'Yes,' I murmured.

The next embrace was longer, more searching. There was no denying he was a skilled seducer.

As we kissed, harder and deeper, I felt his erection against my leg. 'Can you give me a minute?' I said. 'I just want to freshen up.'

'Sure,' he said, breathing deeply.

In the marbled bathroom, I bent my arms over the washbasin and took deep breaths. This was it. Now.

This was the moment.

I'd had a plan all along, you see. Pretend to Donnagh that I was some delicate, damaged thing. Next get him into the room, bamboozle him with my sexy underwear.

Then . . .

Well, that was the surprise bit.

That was when the fireworks were really going to happen.

I began to remove my dress. The cocaine was wearing

off far too soon and I realized with despair that I didn't have any more. I'd just have to get through without it.

'Be strong, Evie,' I whispered into the air. 'You can do this.'

And so, finally, I stood there. In my new sexy suspenders and towering stilettos. I noticed there was a ladder in my stocking. But there was nothing I could do about that. I'd just have to get on with it.

Wing it.

I should be going now. Yet I remained in front of the mirror, transfixed by my own image. Who was this woman? The one with the fake tan and the fake boobs and the fake nose.

'Eve, you okay in there?'

Donnagh was calling, and I knew I had to go out there.

There was just this one last thing to do and then I would be free of him. Free of him and all he represented to me.

'Coming,' I said, in the breeziest voice I could muster.

It was show-time.

'Holy Mother,' Donnagh said, when I stepped out, wearing nothing but my underwear.

'You like?'

'I certainly do,' he said, easing himself onto his side for a better look. 'Here, let me touch.'

'Not yet,' I said, shaking my head. 'You'll have to do what I say first.'

'Okay, whatever you want.'

'Take off your clothes.'

'If that's what you want.'

'It is.'

He took off everything, including his boxer shorts,

revealing a huge hard-on. 'That's for you,' he said, nodding at it. 'Does it frighten you?'

'No,' I lied. 'I've seen bigger.'

Donnagh smiled. 'Have you now?'

'Yes.'

To be honest, I hadn't. I was overcome with sheer panic. His nakedness. His penis. The stupid ladder in my stocking.

The thought *I can't do this* streaked through my mind.

It was too frightening.

Too huge.

But another voice encouraged me onward. *Do this for the Evie of twelve years ago. Do this for her.*

I thought back to that Evie. To my teenage self.

The reality was that, even though I had hated Donnagh, I had also kind of loved him. Well, certainly lusted after him. I would have done anything back then to have him desire me like this. Validate me.

'Let me touch you,' he said, reaching out his hand, trying to draw near to me, his face taut with desire.

'How much do you want me?' I whispered.

'Very much,' he said. The smirk had gone off his face and now he looked like a man who'd stumbled across an oasis in the desert but was not allowed to drink from it.

I inched closer to him, bending down so my right breast was within touching distance. He placed his hand on the soft silk of my bra, sighing as he did so. 'Please, Eve. Let me . . .'

He didn't say what he wanted me to let him do. Now was the time. Now was the do or die.

I'd prepared a speech.

The cunning surprise.

In it I would reveal who I was. Who I *really* was. Remind him of the things he had done to me as a kid. How he'd hurt me. Humiliated me. But look at me now, how pretty I'd become, and, more importantly, look at him. Pathetically begging me to have sex, drooling over me like some sex-starved teenager. Who was the victor now? Who was the real winner?

In my fantasy, this was the point at which I would put my dress back on, cast him one final lingering look, say, 'Never call me again,' then leave him, with his wilting erection, staring after me.

It was going to be perfect.

'Eve.' Donnagh was straining towards me. 'Please.'

This was it, my moment. I looked at his face and tried to remember my lines. But nothing came out. There was a pause, which seemed to last for ever. The silence in the room stretched out, like a dark winter's evening.

'Eve?'

Still nothing.

'Okay then,' Donnagh said suddenly. 'If you're going to be like that about it . . .'

Quick as a flash he grabbed me around the waist, then flipped me down on the bed. He leaned over me, smiling because he was back in control.

My breathing accelerated. This was not how it was supposed to be. What about my speech? What about escaping out of the room?

Donnagh was staring down at me, running a finger along my collarbone. 'Do you think you can tease me like that without repercussions?'

I didn't say anything. He carefully unhooked my bra – a

skill he'd clearly mastered through practice – and cast it to one side.

I was naked on top and so was he. I could feel my nipples harden as they brushed against his chest hair. Now was the time to go. Forget the speech. Forget my victory. I just needed to get out. To escape. Before this got really serious.

Except, for some reason, I couldn't.

Something was stopping me. And it wasn't just that I was pinned to the bed. It was something else. Something more visceral. The truth was, I liked how Donnagh was watching me, how I could sense his desire. It made me feel powerful and in control and sexy – almost as if I wanted him too.

'Donnagh . . .' I made one last effort to extricate myself, but he silenced me with a kiss.

A vision of my teenage self floated into my brain once more. It had been so long ago and I was so different now. Could this be another type of victory?

Donnagh looked down at me, his face serious. 'Do you want this, Eve?' he said, forcing my chin up with his hand. I tried to wriggle free but he held firm. 'Do you?'

Plan A had failed. And now we were on to Plan B. Could I go through with it?

'Yes,' I said, a surge of desire coursing through me.

He pushed me back against the bed, smiling. 'That was all you needed to say.'

32.

Rachel: day nine, 6.30 a.m.

I scrabbled for a knife in the cutlery drawer and found one. The steel glinted in the sunlight and I found myself thinking strange things — that it looked sharp enough to kill a man, that it would be easy to use as a weapon.

Seconds later I was using it to cut my way through each envelope, the blade slicing through the paper like an oar through water. I found myself trembling. A part of me felt sick that I was invading Evie's personal space. Yes, it seemed important to know as much about my sister as I could in the lead-up to the crash, but at the same time this was loathsome: I was about to read correspondence that had never been meant for me.

Another voice told me to keep going, though, that I must harden myself against feelings like this and get to the truth of my sister's life. Of her double-life.

Disappointingly, most of it was junk — with a few bank statements thrown in for good measure. It seemed Evie was overdrawn: between credit cards and her current account she owed about two thousand pounds to the bank. But was that enough to make her want to drive her car into a wall? It seemed unlikely. And nothing about her payments seemed odd. There was a standing order to a gym, a few transactions with high-street retailers.

Only one thing caught my eye: a £160 payment to a shop called La Petite Mort. Wasn't that the French term for 'orgasm'? The little death. I thought of Evie lying in hospital now, caught in her own little death. Had her crash been connected with this payment? With kinky sex?

I took out my new phone and googled shops in the London area with the same title. One result immediately jumped out – a shop in Soho describing itself as a 'provocateur's emporium'. A sex shop.

My heart was racing. Did Evie really frequent places like that? And, if so, what was she buying and for whom? There'd been a lot in the media recently about the rise in BDSM practices but I'd never thought Evie might be into any of that. She seemed far too fragile and body-conscious. But then again, what did I know? Perhaps those were the very traits that drew a person to that world.

I walked to the sink to get a glass of water, noticing that my hands were quivering. I should stop this whole stupid enterprise right now. Where did I think it was going to get me?

I walked back to the table, ready to put the bundle of letters away, when I spotted something I'd previously overlooked: a small colourful postcard jutting out slightly from the side. I picked it up and examined it – taking in the painting of two little girls wearing bonnets on the front – then read the blurb on the reverse: Two Children, *Auvers-sur-Oise, 1890, Vincent Van Gogh.*

I stared at it for a second, my curiosity rising. Van Gogh was Evie's favourite painter. She absolutely worshipped him.

The sender had kept the message short, and had

addressed it to Eveline Darcy not Eve Durant: *Eveline, do you still love me? Dx*

I flipped the postcard back and forth a few times, confused by its contents.

D: was that short for Donnagh? And, if so, how did he know Evie's real name? Why was he asking her if she loved him? Had the bastard been lying to me all along?

I pounced on him before he left for work. 'Did you send this from Paris?' I said, waving the postcard in front of his face.

Donnagh flicked it over a few times. 'Never seen it before in my life.'

'Come on, Donnagh, I'm not thick. It's signed D.'

'So?'

'So you're called Donnagh. You and Evie went to Paris on a mini-break.'

'Um, okay, Poirot. But, on a point of information, why would I be sending a postcard to someone I was already in the company of? Plus, my handwriting looks nothing like that.' To prove his point, he grabbed a pen off the table and copied the line onto a piece of paper in front of me. I examined it carefully, but had to admit the two scripts bore no similarity.

'In any case, Evie and I weren't at that point yet.'

'What point?'

'The love point.'

'Oh,' I said.

He peered closer at the card. 'And I don't know if you've noticed but this postcard was posted from Calais. I've never even been to Calais.'

It was like someone had poked me with a cattle prod. 'Calais?'

'Yeah, why? Does that address mean something to you?'

'No,' I lied. 'No, it doesn't.'

'As for the D, I've no idea who that could be.'

Except I did.

Dad.

Our father had abandoned us when I was five and Evie was three. We'd been too young for it to register as a major trauma – although Evie possibly felt differently. All I knew was that, for a while, he was there and then he wasn't. At some point Mammy explained he wasn't coming back.

We'd been so young we'd hardly questioned it, and in any case, our mother's love seemed large enough to cover both roles. As long as we had her, nothing else mattered.

As we grew older, she didn't talk very much about him. We knew he was a fisherman from Calais, that he'd had to go home for reasons too complicated to go into, and that, no, we couldn't contact him. He wouldn't want it.

I was okay with that. You couldn't force someone to love you. If he didn't want anything to do with us, fine. I didn't want anything to do with him either.

But Evie had never been quite as willing as me to give up on the dream. As a teenager, she'd won a scholarship to France as part of her Junior Cert exam and had hatched a plan to track him down. She'd unearthed an ancient address for him, purloined from our mother's diary, and had begged me to be part of her grand excursion.

Naturally I thought the whole thing was ludicrous – for a start the address was years out of date and I doubted her host family would allow her to go. But a week into her scholarship, she'd rung me to say her family were fine about letting her out for the day as long as she had an adult, meaning me, with her. So, really, what choice did I have? Off we went.

Of course, I'd never expected to find our father, and was really just going along with things to humour Evie. It might finally help her to heal a little, help her to let him go.

However, when we got to the appointed place, a man answering to the name of Jean Durant opened the front door. He didn't recognize us immediately and for a few seconds we just stood there, waiting for the penny to drop.

'*Merde!*' he exclaimed, when it dawned on him who we were. He threw a panicked look in the direction of his sitting room, then banged the door shut and bundled us off to a bar.

'It is better if things stay the way they are,' he said, as he sat nursing a small beer. His face was deeply lined, and there were streaks of silver running through his black hair.

'But we're your daughters,' Evie whispered, over her glass of orange juice. 'You have an obligation to us.'

Our dad dropped his head. 'Yes, but . . .'

'But what?' I snapped. 'Too much bother, are we?'

Evie threw me a filthy look. I could tell she was still clinging to the notion that our father loved us and was afraid that my snarling might somehow scare him off.

'Perhaps we could get to know each other. Catch up on all the time we've missed out on.' She was leaning across the table now, towards our father, the words coming out in a tumble.

A look of mounting panic spread across his face. 'Eve-line, you don't understand. It is not as easy as that.'

Evie was openly crying. 'Why not?'

He looked at her then, with a tortured, almost animalistic stare, and in that moment I noticed his eyes were the exact same colour as mine, deepest brown.

I stood up, dragging Evie with me. 'Come on, Evie. This is a waste of time.'

'Please, Rachel. One more minute. This can't be it.'

I pulled harder on her sleeve, irritated. What had she been expecting? That our father would dramatically declare how much he loved us? That he'd been wrong to leave us? That it would end in a fluffy group hug?

'All I want to know is why you left us,' Evie continued. 'If you just tell me that, then I promise I'll leave you in peace and never contact you again.'

'Eveline,' he began, 'I wish I could explain it. There is no . . .' Then he stopped completely and just stared at us for a while. 'It is better if we do not talk about these things.'

'Better for whom?' Evie shouted, her voice loud now. 'Don't we deserve to know the truth of why you abandoned us? The real reason?'

The owner of the bar was scowling at us now.

'Evie,' I whispered, 'come on, sweetheart. He's not worth it. Let's just go home.'

But she shook me off and moved closer to him. 'Stop being a coward for once in your life and tell us the truth. The secret.'

'There is no secret,' he muttered.

'There is!' she shouted. 'I know there is!'

196

The owner was walking towards us now, all gesticulating hands and a torrent of loud, aggressive French.

'Come on, hon. Leave it. We're not getting anywhere.'

I finally got Evie to move, but somewhere between the clamour of moving chairs and bodies and the tirade of outraged French, our father disappeared. No goodbye. No 'I'm sorry'. Almost like a magic trick, as if he'd been whisked away in a puff of black smoke.

'What was all that about a secret?' I asked Evie on the walk back to the railway station, but she remained silent and shook her head – her way of saying, 'Leave it.'

So I did, and I tried not to think about our father any more, encouraging Evie to do likewise.

'We have Mammy,' I said, 'and she's better than two parents.'

'She is,' Evie agreed. 'I don't know what I'd do if I lost her.'

'You won't lose her,' I said, and at the time I truly believed it. We had paid our dues to the gods in the form of one parent. There was no way they were going to take another from us.

But I was wrong.

Cataclysmically wrong.

Because they did.

Back in the apartment, a defiant Donnagh was still holding the postcard, staring at me. 'Look, Rachel, at this stage, I don't really care if you believe me or not. And, by the way, you haven't exactly been one hundred per cent honest yourself, Miss Famous Writer.'

'How did you . . .?'

'Well, there's this thing called the internet, see. You happen to be all over it.'

I remained quiet for a second, embarrassed that he had found me out. Then I said, 'I believe you about the postcard. And I'm sorry if I jumped to conclusions.'

'It's okay,' he said, his voice softening a little. 'Apology accepted. Now, if you don't mind, I need to get to work.'

'Donnagh,' I said, as he turned for the door.

'Yes?'

'I really am sorry. I'm not thinking straight, these days.'

He sighed and laid a hand on my shoulder. 'I understand, Rachel, but please try to remember we're on the same side here.'

For a second neither of us said anything, a strange new energy occupying the air.

I withdrew my shoulder and hastened towards the kitchen.

By the time I returned to the hallway, Donnagh had gone.

33.

Evie

I didn't remain with Donnagh in the hotel all night. I slipped out as he lay sleeping and caught a taxi home. After my alcohol and cocaine high had worn off, all I felt was revulsion. *That* should never have happened. *That* had been a terrible mistake.

The obvious thing would have been to go to bed and sleep it off, but for some reason I knew that was not a good idea – and anyway, my body was still too stoked with tension. Instead I pulled on my runners and went for a walk in the semi-light, hoping the fresh air would help clear my head. It was very early on a Sunday morning and London looked beautiful – wrapped in the kind of pink-red haze that made me think of a Turner painting.

Here and there stragglers from the previous night's revelries wobbled into my pathway – drunken lads swigging out of open cans, girls carrying their sandals, mascara and eyeliner running down their faces.

I found a tiny coffee shop that was open, went in and ordered a double espresso. Anything that might keep me awake – anything that might stop me falling . . .

The siren call of home was summoning me – Xanax, my bed. Oblivion.

But I needed to avoid that scenario. The last time I'd

taken to my bed like that, after Janet had moved out, I'd spent nearly a week there and had nearly lost my job. I couldn't risk that. Not this time.

When we were still friends, Janet had called those episodes 'depression' and had urged me to seek help. 'Evie, hen, this can't be right. The way you're either out caning it or shut up here in your room. Don't you think maybe a little therapy might help?'

Janet had been a one-woman promotional package for psychotherapy ever since she'd attended a shrink herself about a year earlier. She'd attributed to it all kinds of wonderful things that had happened in her life: becoming a trainee teacher, meeting Patrick, getting over issues she'd had with her mother.

But I was having none of it. 'It's not depression,' I'd snapped back. And even if it was, I couldn't understand how 'getting help' was going to actually help me. What could it do? Bring back my mother? Make my father care for me? I had melancholia of the soul. The condition of being human. I was pretty sure there was no doctor who could cure that.

I continued walking, feeling the drugs and alcohol sweat themselves out of my system.

Sunday morning. Coming down.

Christ. When had I become such a cliché?

Ironically, that song had been playing in the taxi as I'd made my way back from the hotel a few hours earlier. The perfect score to my stupidity. I'd never listened to the words before, always thought there was something a little irritating about the tune, but now, as I pounded the London streets in the pink and red half-light, snippets of Kris Kristofferson's words came back to me.

His talk of sleeping city sidewalks; fading dreams; wanting to get stoned . . .

My sidewalk wasn't sleeping as such. It was more populated with zombie people: the homeless; the immigrant workers; the still-drunk brigade from the night before.

But I knew now what Kris Kristofferson had been getting at.

The loneliness.

The sheer unadulterated emotional pain of it being just you and your hangover and nobody around to love you. To care for you.

I would have done anything at that moment to have Mammy around: 'There, there, darling, this will make you better.' I had a sudden blinding memory of being eight, sick and feverish, and Mammy feeding me broth, flying it into my mouth, like an aeroplane. 'You'll be fixed soon,' she'd soothed, laying a cool flannel on my head. 'Soon you'll be right as rain.'

I continued walking, the desire to go home and take a load of sedatives now virtually overwhelming. Who cared if I lost my stupid job? Everyone knew I hated it.

I could sell my flat, take the money and go on a big trip around the world, visit all those places I'd intended to see but had never got round to. It would be brilliant – I could go to an ashram, meet a dashing foreigner, like Julia Roberts does in *Eat Pray Love*, and come back all spiritually cleansed and loved up. For a moment or two, I actually convinced myself that that was a real option.

But, as I continued to walk, reality kicked in. I had panic attacks in railway stations. I had no sense of direction. And, in any case, what did it matter what country I was in?

At the end of the day nothing would have changed. I would still be me. Mammy would still be gone. For a second the pain of her loss caused me to stop and bend over. Why did it still hurt so fucking much?

I continued to pound the pavement, trying to block out all thoughts of my mother. Of Donnagh. But it was proving impossible. What the fuck had I done?

Back there, in the hotel bedroom, I'd thought what I was doing was empowering – some kind of post-modern take on revenge. So why did I feel so dirty and ashamed?

Images from the previous night skittered across my brain. Donnagh's tongue all over my body, the top of his head bobbing as he sucked on my breasts. I touched them protectively. He hadn't said anything about the scars – the silvery-grey lines that circumnavigated the edges from the surgery. Perhaps he hadn't noticed them – it had been dark. Or perhaps he hadn't wanted to ruin the mood.

He'd seen my breasts without scars too, when we were younger, though he probably wouldn't remember that. It had been a long time ago, twelve years to be precise. At a PE class in the local pool when he'd yanked down my swimming costume in front of the whole class for a dare. He'd called me 'Saggy Tits', then told me I was a 'disgusting fat cow'. I wondered what he'd say if he found out the breasts he'd been sucking on last night were those same saggy ones. That I was the same fat cow.

'How did you feel at that moment?' The psychiatrist's voice came back to me suddenly – the only therapist I'd ever gone to see, following my suicide attempt at college. She'd somehow managed to coax the swimming-pool story out of me, and I'd been forced to unpick it. Slowly. Like a knot.

I'd felt humiliated. Exposed. Like I might die a little death from the shame. But I didn't say any of that. Instead I shrugged. Told her I preferred not to dwell on it.

She'd frowned at me, as if I'd said something wrong, then proceeded to probe me with questions. Had it made me ashamed of my body? Of my sexuality?

'I was already ashamed of my body,' I told her. 'And my sexuality.'

'But this cemented things for you. This assault.'

'It wasn't an assault,' I said, and she'd just stared at me, then started scribbling frantically in her notepad.

'How would you describe it then, Eveline?' she had asked.

And I hadn't been able to respond to that. Because I hadn't been able to think of a word for what Donnagh had done to me. Did such a word even exist?

I thought about all of this now, as I walked through a dawn-lit London, my feet moving quickly across the grey slabs of pavement.

If what Donnagh had done to me was so bad, if it was assault, why had I gone to bed with him the previous night? Why had I allowed him to stick his dick into me? What did that make me? A slut? A victim?

I sat down on a nearby bench and started to cry. I had betrayed her – that childhood Eveline. I had let her down. I was a coward. No, worse than that. I was a hypocrite. I had served myself on a plate to Donnagh, then complained when he'd eaten his fill. I wasn't a victim. I was an accomplice. Yes, he had fucked me. Treated me like a slab of meat. But the ugly truth was, I had wanted it.

I had wanted to come undone.

34.

I walked around for as long as I could, trying to stave it off, but eventually I had no choice but to return to the flat. The walls seemed unbearably close and the rooms cramped, like jail cells with no windows. I longed to talk to someone, anyone, but of course Janet and I weren't speaking and Rachel was on a book tour in New Zealand.

Jesus, she really was becoming famous. I'd attended one of her events about six months earlier and had seen for myself the kind of zealot-like adoration she attracted. I joked that if she wanted to start a cult she'd definitely have the numbers. 'I could design your logos. Maybe something involving a tattoo or a Doc Marten . . .'

Rachel had laughed and said she'd stick to writing, though she did enquire if I was 'doing anything artistic, these days' in a fake it-doesn't-really-matter-if-you're-not voice. Even though I knew it did.

But she needn't have worried. I'd been attending a local art college for the past few months, doing a 'foundation art course' in the evenings. If I passed, there was a chance I might be accepted onto their part-time degree programme, possibly escape the hell-hole that was *Business Matters*.

'Sounds great, Evie,' Rachel said, after I'd filled her in. 'What exactly does it involve?'

'Oh, lots of things – design, fine art, photography, film. I'm going to have to submit a project in a few months' time.'

'You mean like Tracey Emin's bed or something?'

'Yeah, exactly like that,' I said, and we both laughed. 'Actually I was thinking more along the lines of a video installation. I've got a friend who's good with AV stuff. He's going to help me choose a camera.'

'Evie, I'm so sorry – you're breaking up on me, what did you say?'

'I said I've got a . . .'

But then a booming announcement interrupted me, and Rachel said, 'I'm really sorry but I have to get on this flight, sweetie.'

'It's fine. Go. Enjoy yourself on the tour.'

And she'd said goodbye then, telling me she'd call when she got there and that she loved me, asking me to take care of myself.

'Bye,' I'd said, staring at the phone, feeling empty. In comparison to her dazzling career, my silly little art course sounded ridiculous. My tutor was a pretentious git who thought he was Damien Hirst, and I was deluding myself if I thought it could lead to greater things, like a career. In reality, it was nothing more than a tether, something to stop me floating away . . .

When I got home after my dawn walk, I succumbed, inevitably, to an all-out Xanax and bed binge. My front-door buzzer went a number of times, but I ignored it. I had a horrible feeling it was Donnagh and I couldn't face him. What would I say? I never wanted to see him again.

Monday morning loomed and I tried to drag myself out of bed but I was so zonked from all the drugs I didn't have the energy. I called in sick, knowing Nigel would lose his mind. But I didn't care. I just took more Xanax and went back to bed. This continued for two more days until I finally accepted I had to face the firing squad.

As I got dressed on the Thursday morning, crippled with a dread I couldn't even put a name to, Janet's voice sounded in my head again: *Evie, they can fix this. It's not the eighteenth century. People can help you get through it.*

I had ignored her advice, said she needed to stop watching *Dr Phil*.

But now as I looked in the mirror her words haunted me, and I wanted to yell at her and say she was wrong: that there was no fixing me.

I was broken.

Always had been.

Always would be.

Didn't she understand that?

That was just the way it was.

35.

Rachel: day nine, 11.30 a.m.

It was preposterously stupid, but after finding the post-card, I decided to try to contact my father. I rang International Directory Enquiries, remembering the ancient address Evie had used to track him down, then nearly fell over with shock when I heard that, yes, a Jean Durant was still listed for that address and would I like to be put through?

'Um, okay,' I mumbled, but in the end all I got was a voicemail. I left a tongue-tied, garbled message, nearly forgetting my own number, then hung up.

I had thought it would be impossible to re-establish communication with him after so many years, but it had taken me less than five minutes. If I could do it so easily, had Evie been able to do likewise? Feeling shaky I walked into the kitchen to retrieve a glass of water only to find Donnagh standing there. 'I thought you'd gone to work,' I said.

'I did go, but then I couldn't concentrate so I came back here. I was worried I'd upset you. I was thinking we could go to the hospital together to see Eve.'

I stared at him, a little surprised by the offer. It had occurred to me a few days earlier that I'd never actually seen him at the hospital at the same time as me, and assumed he was operating to a different schedule. Recently, though, I had suspected he wasn't going at all.

'Donnagh, are you sure? You don't need to do this for my sake, you know.'

'I know that, Rachel. I want to. And I also wanted to apologize for being such a prick earlier – about the post-card. It was only natural you would think I sent it.'

'It's forgotten,' I said, trying hard to sound like I meant it. Maybe I had.

We travelled in Donnagh's hire car (a top-of-the-range Audi) and for a moment I was reminded of how wealthy he was, how strange it was that he had chosen to live in my sister's tiny flat. But then I gave myself a stern talking-to. What was all that about us being on the same side now? I really needed to stop second-guessing him. I needed to start giving him the benefit of the doubt.

'A penny for them,' Donnagh said, almost as if he could intuit what I was thinking.

I glanced in his direction, and was caught off-guard by his profile – the hard beauty of it, the perfect sweep and curve of his face. 'Oh, nothing. Just thinking about Evie.'

'Of course,' he said, changing gear. 'And I bet you're wondering why I haven't been to see her.'

'You haven't?'

'Oh, come on, Rachel, you know I haven't.'

I shrugged my shoulders, trying to feign nonchalance. 'I just thought you were busy at work.'

'You think I'm an arsehole, more like.'

'I didn't say that.'

'Didn't need to.' Donnagh sighed. 'The thing is I *have*

been busy at work. Manic, as it happens. But that's not the reason I haven't visited Eve. Nor is it because I couldn't be bothered.'

'Why then?' I snapped, realizing that I *was* angry with him. Angry for his neglect of my sister.

He paused, then looked in my direction. 'If you want to know the truth, it's guilt. She was driving my car. I was the one who pursued her.'

'Pursued her?'

'Romantically, I mean. I asked her out on a date. I kept asking her out on dates. If it wasn't for me, she probably wouldn't be in this mess.'

'Oh,' I said, breathing deeply. For a second back there, I'd thought he meant he'd pursued her in a car.

'And there's something else I haven't told you.'

I turned to him.

'You remember when you asked me about the postcard, and I said we weren't at that stage yet. The love stage.'

'Yes.'

'Well, I lied about that. We were. I was.'

'Why would you lie about it?'

Now it was Donnagh's turn to shrug. 'Because I wanted you to believe me about the postcard. That I didn't send it.' He stopped for a moment, took a deep breath. 'And because it was too painful,' he said quietly. 'Better to pretend Evie didn't mean anything to me. Keep working. Pretend all of this wasn't actually happening.'

'So why the change of heart?'

'You,' he said. 'You love your sister so much. And you're facing the pain head-on. Like I should be doing. Instead of being such a fucking coward.' He seemed to wipe something off his cheek.

'But you'd only known her a little while. How could you love her? It was too soon.'

Donnagh glanced at me, taking his eyes off the road for the merest second. 'I don't know why,' he said, 'but I did.'

Later I watched through the glass of the intensive-care unit as Donnagh stroked Evie's hair, and whispered to her words I couldn't hear. Donnagh loved Evie? Was he for real? Or was he just bullshitting me? It occurred to me that I'd forgotten to ask him if he felt the love was mutual. If Evie had harboured similar feelings . . .

Finally, about thirty minutes later, he emerged, red-eyed and exhausted-looking.

'You heading back to work?'

He nodded grimly.

'Time for a quick coffee first?' I said, trying to sound friendly. I was damned if I was going to let him walk away without getting to the bottom of his latest admission.

'Sure,' he said. 'Why not?'

In the canteen, I poured coffee into two polystyrene cups, paid for them, then brought them over to where Donnagh was sitting. 'It probably tastes like piss,' I said, 'but I wasn't sure if you drank tea.'

Donnagh smiled wanly. 'Thanks.'

'How are you holding up?' I asked.

'I'm okay,' he said. 'Just a little shocked, I guess. All the wires and tubes and that . . . I didn't expect her to look so frail.'

'Yeah. It takes a bit of getting used to, all right.'

We both took slurps of our coffee, then made gagging faces simultaneously.

'Even worse than anticipated,' Donnagh said.

'Piss would probably taste better.'

Donnagh held my gaze. 'I want to apologize again for how I've acted, Rachel. I'm not usually so spineless.'

'It's fine,' I muttered, trying to play it down. 'It's the shock. It does weird things to people.'

He nodded. 'One minute everything's going great, the next . . .' He took another slurp of his coffee, winced.

'Donnagh, you know what you were saying back there in the car, about being in love with Evie . . .'

'Yes?'

'I know this is probably a stupid question, but do you think Evie felt the same way about you, despite your history?'

For a while, he didn't say anything. Then, 'I don't know, Rachel,' he finally replied. 'Of course I hoped the feeling was mutual. We certainly seemed to get on well. But then the crash happened, and I found out her real identity, and I didn't know what to believe any more.'

'Sure,' I said. 'It must be very confusing.'

'I brought it on myself, I guess. The way I treated her as a teenager. The awful things I did . . .'

We lapsed into silence again, me picking away the polystyrene from the edge of my cup.

'I'm really sorry, but I'd better be going,' he said, glancing at his watch. He reached for his jacket, then stalled, as if he was deciding whether to say something or not.

'Donnagh, are you okay? Is something wrong?'

'Yeah ... No. I mean, everything's fine. It's probably nothing.' He stopped, picked up his jacket.

'Donnagh, tell me.'

'Look, forget it, Rachel. I'm being ridiculous ...'

'Tell me,' I said, my voice louder now, causing a couple of nurses to turn and look at us.

'To be honest, I don't even know what I'm trying to say.' Donnagh sat back in his seat, exhaling. 'I fell hard for Eve. I already told you that. And for most of the two months we were together I thought she felt the same way. But there were times when she seemed distant. Not quite herself.'

'Not quite herself?'

'It all made sense when I found out she was hiding her past from me. That's why I didn't say anything before this, why it seemed irrelevant.'

'What are you trying to say now, Donnagh?'

He let out a low sigh. 'I don't really know, Rachel. It's just I've had time to think. And even given that she was hiding her identity from me, some things still don't add up.'

'Such as?'

'Okay, it's going to sound mad. So be prepared for that. But I think Eve might have been seeing someone else at the same time as me.'

'What?' I said. 'You think she might have been having an affair?'

'Is it even an affair if you've just been going out for a couple of months?'

'Have you any proof?'

'No,' he said, shaking his head. 'Not really.'

'Not really?'

'The only thing I'm going on was this one night. She came back kind of flustered and there was this smell off her. Like a man's aftershave or something. I could smell it on her hair.'

'So maybe somebody stood too near her on the Tube. That proves nothing, Donnagh.'

'I know. That's why I didn't say anything. It was stupid. Just something about it reminded me of my ex-wife.'

'Your ex-wife?'

'Remember I told you about her? Well, she cheated on me. And Eve's behaviour brought it all back. But then again, it was just an instinct. A gut feeling.'

'And do you find your gut lies to you much?' I said, looking at Donnagh directly now, a prickling sensation breaking out across my skin.

'Not really,' he said quietly.

'Didn't think so,' I said, getting up. Then I ran.

36.

I got to Evie's apartment, not even sure what I was looking for. All I was going on was adrenalin, and a feeling that
Donnagh was right. That Evie had been seeing somebody
else. Perhaps he had sent the postcard. Perhaps he held
the key to my sister's crash . . . To her life.

But how did you track down a person you didn't even
know existed?

A name. I needed to find a name.

I started in the living area, pulling open cupboards, ransacking drawers, looking for anything to suggest Evie was
in a relationship with somebody else.

I found no evidence of that, but what I did notice was
how carefully Evie had concealed her identity from Donnagh. She'd hidden all of her books, paintings and letters
– anything with the surname 'Darcy' on it. Even her
favourite mug was missing, the one with 'Eveline' emblazoned in swirly pink letters across the front. I had to hand
it to my sister: she'd been ruthless. She'd destroyed all
traces of her real self.

I understood why: she hadn't wanted Donnagh to figure out who she was, not yet, at any rate. But where had
she stashed those items? She couldn't have just thrown
them away. I walked into the hallway, my eyes scanning
upwards for an attic. But there was no sign of one. And
the airing cupboard didn't hold any clues either – it just

featured the usual stuff: towels and sheets, a few tattered old clothes.

Now, much as it sickened me, I had no choice but to ransack Evie's bedroom. It felt sordid and wrong, picking through my sister's intimate space, like some kind of pervert. But I had no choice.

I pushed open the door and just stood there, as if I was entering that room for the first time. True, I'd been sleeping there since I'd arrived – Donnagh had taken up residence in the spare room – but I'd been super-careful not to disturb anything, to respect Evie's space.

Not any more, though.

I started with her wardrobe, digging deep into the back for any hidden boxes or files. I knew Evie kept a diary and that she was never without a photo of Mammy, so I figured they must be in there somewhere. But after ten minutes of searching, I had turned up nothing.

The only noteworthy thing about Evie's wardrobe was the sheer volume of clothes and shoes it housed, many of them high-end. I knew Evie made a pittance in her day job, so perhaps somebody else was bankrolling all this flash fashion. Donnagh? Or the mysterious other man?

I moved towards the chest of drawers and pulled open the first drawer. Disappointingly, it was nothing but a jumble: mounds of underwear mixed up together, like an explosion in a knicker factory. I opened the second, expecting to find more of the same, but this one was a wholly different prospect: tiny wisps of fabric lay next to a packet of condoms, a pair of black suspenders, a bottle of lube . . . I slammed it shut.

Evie's sex drawer.

Jesus Christ, did I really want to go there? Was I that desperate? But then I took a deep breath, recalling the payment to La Petite Mort. I needed to know about this side of Evie's personality. This was the one place I *must* look.

Slowly, I opened the drawer again, and began unpacking its contents. Most of it was lingerie. Carefully, I lifted out a pair of black-and-pink silk knickers and a matching bra. For a few seconds, I held them, staring at them in confusion. Were they trying to tell me something?

The obvious answer was that Evie enjoyed a healthy sex life. But with whom? Donnagh or the mystery guy? And what about all those one-night stands Janet had told me about?

I riffled through the drawer again, hoping to find something more helpful – a diary, a camera, a secret phone. But there was nothing. Nothing even remotely useful.

I slumped on the bed, staring up at the ceiling in defeat. This apartment revealed nothing about Evie. Not the Evie I knew, anyway.

My phone buzzed and I jumped. Could my father be getting back to me? Or maybe it was Donnagh, with more secrets to divulge. But it was nothing – just a text message from my service provider about roaming charges.

I threw the phone onto the bed in disgust. My father was a useless waste of space. I knew that. And as for Donnagh – I still hadn't made up my mind about him.

But Evie? Her family – we'd been so important to her. Why had she removed every last trace of us?

I understood that she didn't want Donnagh to find out who she was. But that alone didn't explain what was going on. And neither did a potential affair. It was almost as if Evie had been trying to wipe me and Mammy from her life. Just like our father. Extinguish us. As if we had never existed.

37.

Evie

So, where were we? Ah, yes: me cowering in my apartment after having sex with Donnagh, unable to face the world. Although by Thursday I had managed to haul my arse back into work.

When I got there, Nigel was standing at my desk, not looking like a happy camper. 'Well, well, well! So you've deigned to grace us with your presence, have you?' he said, arms folded across his chest. 'I presume you have a doctor's note?'

'Yes,' I whimpered, handing it to him. I'd gone to a dodgy guy in Peckham, who'd given me one, no questions asked, once I'd forked out a hundred quid.

'This is the second time you've been off sick in three months,' Nigel continued.

'I'm sorry, Nigel. I've just been a bit unlucky with my health recently. I'm feeling much better now, though.' I smiled as brightly as I could, but Nigel wasn't even looking at me.

'And what about those?' he said, pointing at something I couldn't see. I bent down, following the slant of Nigel's finger, until my eyes fell on the offending items: three bunches of flowers, expensive, still sitting in their water-filled plastic bubbles.

'They've been arriving every day since Monday morning,' Nigel said, emitting an accusatory sneeze. 'If you don't get Donnagh Flood to stop sending them, I swear to God, Eve . . .'

Donnagh was sending them? Sweet Jesus. Was there no end to the man's persistence?

'Ring him now and tell him to stop it.'

'But, Nigel!'

'Now, Eve. That's if you want to keep your job.'

Very reluctantly I opened my handbag and pulled out my mobile.

'Fine, fine,' I muttered. 'I'm doing it.' Then I stomped off to an empty corridor so that Nigel wouldn't get the opportunity to eavesdrop.

A few moments later I heard Donnagh's voice answer at the other end of the line.

'Hi, Donnagh,' I said, trying to keep the quiver out of my voice. 'It's Eve here.'

'Hi, stranger,' he said. 'You've been keeping a low profile. Did you get my flowers?'

'Look, that's what I'm ringing to talk about. Nigel isn't happy. He's got chronic hay fever and the flowers are affecting his allergies.'

'Ah, God love him,' Donnagh said *faux*-sympathetically. 'You did make it clear the flowers aren't actually for him, though, right?'

'Donnagh,' I said, not wanting to make a joke out of this, 'you've got to stop. Seriously. He's going to fire me.'

'No, he's not.' Donnagh laughed. 'That would be illegal.'

'Well, okay, maybe not fire. But he's going to make my life a misery. Or even more of a misery . . .'

'I suppose I'd better stop sending them, then.'

'Yes, Donnagh,' I said, sighing with relief. 'That would be great.'

'Fair enough, but only if you come on another date with me.'

'What? No way,' I spluttered.

'Jesus, Eve, I'm not proposing marriage. I just want to take you out for dinner. I thought we had a good time the other night. In fact, I was under the impression you rather enjoyed yourself.'

I forced myself to concentrate on my breathing. *Stay calm, Eveline. Just stay calm.*

'Come on, one more time. Then, if you decide I'm not for you, that's it. No more flowers, no more texts or emails. I promise I won't contact you again.'

For a second I wanted to scream at him. Why was he holding me over a barrel like this? But then I thought of Nigel and his face of thunder. The fact that my mortgage repayment was due at the end of the week.

'Eve?'

'Do you absolutely promise, Donnagh?'

'Yes,' he said. 'Scout's honour. So how's about we meet tomorrow? Say, half six in front of Covent Garden Tube station.'

I paused for a second, barely able to breathe. 'Okay,' I said. 'But you promise no more bouquets, right?'

'Right,' Donnagh said. 'Can't wait to see you.' Then he hung up.

'Christ on a bike, that took you long enough,' Nigel said, when I eventually got back to my desk.

'Sorry,' I said blankly. 'We got slightly side-tracked.'

'Of course you did. Now kindly get to work. And keep those bloody weeds out of my face.'

I watched him stalk off, feeling my heart go ninety to the dozen in my chest.

Had I just agreed to meet Donnagh again? What the fuck had I done?

38.

I got ready to face Donnagh. As I dressed, I consoled myself with the fact that it would be the last time I ever had to see him. All thoughts of revenge had been thrown out the window. All I cared about was getting through tonight unscathed and drawing a line in the sand under this entire incident. Lesson learned: do not date the boy who bullied you as a kid. It will not end well.

I pulled on an extremely boring shift dress and flats, not bothering with much make-up and rolling my hair into a bun. Who cared if Donnagh didn't find me attractive? Who cared if he never found out who I really was? The most important thing was that I got away from him as soon as possible – with my sanity intact.

'Hey, gorgeous,' he said, as I arrived at our preordained meeting spot. 'Loving the sexy librarian look.'

I glanced up at him, and saw that he was smirking.

'Am I allowed to pull your bun out later in the evening?'

When I didn't respond he caught my arm, and said, 'Come on, I need to swing by a party briefly. I want to introduce you to some people.'

'Party?' I mumbled, my insides clenching. 'You didn't mention anything about a party.'

'Oh, it's nothing, just a leaving do for an employee.'

'Donnagh, this wasn't part of the deal.'

'I'm sorry, sweetheart, I should have mentioned it

earlier, but I promise you it'll take twenty minutes max. I just want to pop my head in and say hello, and, of course, show off my new girlfriend.' He gave me a wink.

'I am not your girlfriend.'

'We'll see about that,' he said, kissing me suddenly on the mouth.

I wanted to say that, yes, we would see. That there was no way I would ever go out with him, not if he was the last man on earth, etc., etc. But I didn't say anything. Instead I followed him, like an obedient lamb, not shrugging him off when he took my hand in his.

The party was in a bar in Covent Garden, and Donnagh squeezed my palm as we walked through the doors. 'No need to be nervous,' he whispered into my ear. 'They'll love you.'

'Hmm.' I was conscious that my hands were slippery with perspiration. In the back of my mind I had a vague plan about escaping through a toilet window. I was hoping it wouldn't come to that, but the plan was there in case of an emergency.

'This is Eve,' Donnagh said, introducing me around the room. I noticed that, unlike a few minutes ago, he didn't use the term 'girlfriend' and felt a little disappointed.

When Donnagh was in the loo Anja, the girl whose leaving party it was, took me to one side. 'So, you guys been seeing each other long?'

'God, no,' I said, shaking my head. 'We barely know each other.'

Anja flicked her swishy blonde hair off her shoulder. 'Well, word of advice, darling. Don't push him too hard. I did, and that's why I'm going back to Sweden single.' She laughed heartily, a deep smoker's laugh that made me warm to her.

'You and Donnagh were a couple?'

'In so far as you can ever be in a couple with Donnagh, yes, we were.'

'What do you mean?'

'Oh, come on, you must know?'

I shook my head.

Anja placed a hand on my shoulder, and leaned in towards my ear. 'Donnagh is used to possessing things. He loves the chase, he loves the woman to put up a fight, but then he gets bored and, well, he eventually sells her off at a profit.'

'Huh?'

'Sorry, I was trying to make a property analogy but it didn't quite work.' She laughed her throaty laugh again. 'Actually, don't mind me. I'm completely pissed.'

I watched as she reached for a glass of champagne from a passing waiter's tray.

'You seem nice. What did you say your name was?'

'Eve.'

'Well, Eve, all I'm saying is have a good time, enjoy it for what it is, but don't expect miracles.' She drank a mouthful of champagne, squeezed my shoulder, then made off, her long, tanned legs wobbling unsteadily as she went.

'Whatever she said, don't listen to any of it.' Donnagh was back at my side, grinning. 'She's mad as a box of frogs.'

'To be honest, I have no idea what she was saying. I think it was something about you being a commitment-phobe but I can't be sure.'

'I'm just waiting for the right girl,' Donnagh said, winking and grabbing my hand. 'Come on, let me introduce you to some more people.'

And off we went.

We were chatting to a beautiful American couple, whom Donnagh knew from Chicago, when I spotted him out of the corner of my eye.

Michael Flaherty.

Or 'Big Mick', as he'd been known back in the day.

Jesus Christ, what was he doing here? He'd been Donnagh's right-hand man when we'd all been in secondary school together: the Laurel to his Hardy; the *yin* to his *yang*. A vivid memory came back to me, of Mick laughing as I'd stood at the side of the swimming-pool, my breasts hanging out.

'Mick, come over here, my man. There's someone I want to introduce you to.'

Mick joined us.

'This is Eve Durant. And, Eve, this is Mick Flaherty. We went to school together many moons ago and he's now my head foreman in London.'

'Hello,' said Mick, in the same thick accent I remembered, holding out his hand for me to shake. I had a violent urge to smash it back against his chest.

'Hello,' I muttered.

'So how did you meet this bollix?' he said, jerking his head in the direction of Donnagh.

'Hey, language, please,' Donnagh chided, but I could tell he was loving the banter.

'Through work.' I took an enormous gulp of champagne. It would be so easy to slip up here. One wrong word, one inappropriate reference, and he could twig who I was.

'But sure Donnagh doesn't *do* any work. He leaves that to his lackeys.' Mick was smiling widely and so was Donnagh, reminding me of the old days when they'd been teenagers. When they'd ruled the roost.

'Fair enough,' I demurred. 'The truth is, he's been stalking me for weeks now and I've basically just given in.' I held up my hands in a what-are-you-going-to-do? gesture.

Mick and Donnagh laughed simultaneously.

'Sorry, guys. If you'll excuse me I just have to pop to the . . .'

'Oh, sure, sure,' Mick said, moving slightly so I could slide past him. 'And while you're there, could you see if you can find my wife? I think she might have fallen down one of the toilets.'

'Of course,' I said, with no idea who his wife might be. Someone who was deaf, dumb and blind, perhaps.

The only other person in the loo was a tall, dark-haired woman, who had her back to me. It was only when she turned around that I recognized her: Gemma Brady. Miss Leitrim 2005 and Donnagh's on-off girlfriend when we'd been kids.

She couldn't possibly be married to Mick Flaherty, could she?

'Gemma,' I said, forgetting myself just for a moment.

'Sorry?' She looked up. 'Do I know you?'

'Um,' I stammered. 'I'm Donnagh's . . . Well, I'm with Donnagh. He mentioned I might run into you.'

'Did he now?' she said, frowning. 'What did he say exactly?'

'Oh, God, nothing bad. Just that you were an old flame.

Or have I got that wrong? It seems like Donnagh's dated everybody at this party.'

Gemma snorted. 'No, you haven't got that wrong,' she said, making the finishing touches with her lipstick, then placing it back in her bag. 'He's a complete and utter man-slut. I'm sorry, what did you say your name was?'

'Eve,' I replied, taken aback by Gemma's aggressive tone. She seemed pissed off about something. Very, very pissed off.

She let out a long sigh. 'So, you're his latest conquest, are you?'

'Pardon?'

'You and Donnagh. I take it you're an item.'

'Well, I wouldn't say that exactly.' I was flustered. 'We've only been out together a few times. We're not a couple or anything.'

'Oh, you will be,' she said, in a bored manner. 'If Donnagh brought you here tonight it means he wants you. And, believe me, what Donnagh wants, Donnagh gets.'

I stared at her, not sure how to respond.

'Look, I'm not trying to freak you out,' she continued, as if sensing my unease. 'It's just I've known Donnagh a very long time. I know what he's like. You were right earlier, I did go out with him – when we were kids.'

'You did?'

'Oh, yes, many moons ago. But now I'm married to Mick Flaherty, his foreman.' Her face hardened as she said this, and if I'd been a betting woman I'd have put money on theirs not being among the happiest of unions.

'I met Mick a few minutes ago,' I said, trying to smile.

'He asked me to check if, um . . .' I stalled, unsure whether to quote Mick verbatim.

'To check if I'd fallen down the toilet?' she said, with another snort, and I nodded. 'Gobshite,' she added, under her breath.

As Gemma's face toughened up once more, I forced myself to breathe. Perhaps she hadn't noticed my gaffe earlier when I'd said her name. Perhaps everything was going to be okay . . .

'What did you say you were called again?' she said, turning back towards me, giving me the once-over.

'Eve,' I repeated, feeling myself tremble. Christ, could this be it – the big reveal? Had Gemma figured out who I was?

'Eve,' she repeated slowly, holding her gaze. 'That's a pretty name. But then again, you're a pretty girl, aren't you? And Donnagh always chooses pretty girls.'

'Does he?'

'Oh, yes,' she said, flinging a paper towel into the bin and giving me a last lingering look before heading for the stairwell. 'He does.'

Once she was gone, I stumbled into a cubicle and slumped onto the toilet seat. My hands were shaking, and I couldn't get control of my breath. I felt like I was lost at sea, sinking and drowning in waves of panic.

All these people, these reminders of my past. Surely they would sniff me out. Unmask me. Not to mention all the women Donnagh had fucked. He didn't fall in love. He collected people. I could see that now.

Finally, after what seemed an age, I exited the cubicle and walked back towards where Donnagh was standing.

'Hey, there you are. What's the story?'

'I'm not feeling well, Donnagh. I think I need to get home.'

'What's the matter?'

'It's my tummy,' I lied. 'I think I might have eaten something dodgy.'

'Oh, God,' he said. 'That's not good. Do you want me to call a cab or shall I take you home?'

'No, please, Donnagh, you stay. I just need to get back to the flat, lie down. And if it is a bug, I'm probably contagious. I don't want you picking up anything off me.'

'Are you sure?' Donnagh said, looking vaguely relieved. 'Have you been sick?'

'No, but I feel like I'm going to be. Honestly, you can't do anything for me. I just need to get home. I need some privacy.'

He nodded. 'Fair enough, but at least let me call you a taxi.'

'No, Donnagh, honestly it's fine. I can do that myself.'

He stared at me. 'You sure?'

'Yes, I'm sure. Now please go back and join your friends at the party.'

He caught my hand and pulled me towards him, kissing my hair. 'Get well soon, gorgeous, I'll call you tomorrow. And, by the way, this does not count as a full date, just in case you thought it did.' He was smiling now, mischief in his eyes.

'We'll see about that,' I muttered.

He was crazy if he thought I was ever going to meet him again. This thing was over. Finished. Dead in the water.

I had paid my debt in full.

And, more importantly, I had made it out alive.

39.

Rachel: day nine, 4.30 p.m.

And then there was a breakthrough. I was in the loo, cleaning myself up after searching the apartment, when I flicked open Evie's tiny bathroom bin and saw it there – a small cream business card lying among some discarded cosmetic pads. I picked it out of the rubbish and turned it over carefully: *Arthur Columb, Civil Engineer, Conlon & Forsythe Engineering.* The office was in Greenwich; there was a telephone number and an email address.

I stared at the card, not quite sure whether to trust it. Could this be Artie, whom Evie had dated back in Leitrim? The one she'd been madly in love with? Was he the mystery man Donnagh had mentioned in the hospital?

I ran into the sitting room, grabbed my mobile from my bag and stabbed in Artie's number so fast I messed up and had to do it again. I was practically panting by the time I got through to him.

'Hello, Arthur Columb speaking.'

'Artie? Is that you?'

'Um. Sorry, who is this?'

'It's Rachel Darcy. Evie Darcy's sister. Hopefully you remember me.'

'My God, Rachel, of course I do. Long time no hear. How are you keeping?'

'I'm okay, Artie. Listen, Evie's been in a car accident. I heard you were working around these parts, so I was just wondering if you might be able to meet up for a coffee and a chat. If you were free, that is.'

'Evie's been in a car crash? Is she okay?'

'She's alive but in a coma.'

'Jesus Christ,' he said, and for a moment, it was as if the line had gone dead.

'Artie, are you still there?'

'I'm still here,' he responded.

'Where do you live?'

'In Lewisham,' he replied. 'But I'm at work in Greenwich at the moment.'

My breath snagged. Lewisham was where Evie had crashed. 'So, do you think we could meet up?' I continued, recovering myself. 'There's a pub just off the Old Woolwich Road – I think it's called the White Horse or Hound, something like that.'

'I know it,' he said. 'I actually work right beside it. Can you give me an hour?'

'Of course,' I said.

'I'll see you there.'

Artie looked much more haggard than when I'd last seen him, six years earlier. True, he'd always had a wild, slightly unkempt air about him. But today he looked practically homeless. 'Rachel,' he said, pulling me immediately into a hug. 'How is she? Will she be okay?'

'I don't know,' I said, unfolding myself from his grasp and sitting down. 'The experts say there's hope, that most people wake up after two weeks to a month.'

'How long has it actually been?'

'Nine days.'

'So, not that long, then. There's still a good chance?'

'I guess so. I hope so.'

When Artie went off to the bar to order drinks I tried to get my plan straight in my head. I needed to ask him why Evie had his business card in her flat, whether he was having an affair with her. But I couldn't just blurt it out as soon as he sat down. I needed to bide my time, draw him out a bit.

'So what brought you to this area?' I asked, trying to sound nice and casual.

Artie was doing a good job of looking upset. 'What? Sorry, Rachel. I just can't believe it – about Evie, I mean.'

'I know,' I said. 'It's hard to take in, all right.'

For a minute or two, Artie remained completely silent. But after a few slugs from his pint, he came to a little. 'I moved here with my fiancée,' he said eventually. 'I lost my job back in Ireland, and around the same time she got offered a position at Goldsmiths College. We decided to make the move – seemed like the only solution, given the state Ireland was in.'

'Your fiancée?'

'Yes. Shannon. Shannon Curtis.'

'American, by any chance?' I asked, taking a punt.

He nodded. 'From Boston originally, but with Irish heritage. That's how we met. She was visiting her home-place in Leitrim, tracing her roots, when we bumped into each other one night. Got talking . . .'

'. . . and love blossomed?' I finished, watching his reaction.

'Yes,' Artie said, seeming to blush a little. 'I suppose it did.'

For a moment I just sat there, taken aback. I hadn't expected Artie to be engaged – hadn't pinned him as the unfaithful type at all, in fact. But a lot of time had passed since we'd last seen each other. A lot had changed. And there was something about his demeanour now that seemed jumpy. He looked like a man with a secret. A secret I was determined to find out.

'So, you and Evie,' I continued, 'you'd obviously been in recent contact.'

'Sorry?'

'Your business card. I found it in her apartment. I just assumed you'd met up.'

'Oh, that, yeah,' he said, reaching for his pint again. 'We bumped into each other about two months ago. Had a few drinks together.'

'And was that all you saw of each other?'

'About a week later she came round to our flat for a barbecue.'

'The flat you and Shannon live in?'

'Yes,' Artie said, shifting a little in his seat. 'If you don't mind me asking, Rachel, were you hoping to find out something in particular from me?'

'Sorry, sorry,' I said, trying to hide my agitation. 'It's just I've been away on a book tour so I wasn't in much contact with Evie before the accident.'

'And you're trying to figure out what exactly?'

'I don't really know,' I said, terrified he was on to me. 'I suppose what she'd been doing, who her friends were . . .'

'Oh,' said Artie, unhunching a little. 'Well, if I can help you with anything I will.'

'Thanks,' I said, attempting to steady my breathing. 'Tell me, how did Evie seem on those two occasions you met her? Was she in any way upset? Did she seem distracted?'

'Distracted?' Artie repeated. 'I'm not sure that's the word I'd use. She talked about some new relationship she was in. Said it was going really well, actually.'

'She said that?'

'Yes. She said there was "great chemistry" between the two of them. Though she did seem worried he was out of her league.' Artie raised his eyes to Heaven.

'Typical Evie,' I said, nodding. 'Always doing herself down.'

'Yeah,' Artie agreed. 'To be honest, I was hoping she'd have grown out of it by now.' He leaned across the table. 'Did you know him, Rachel, this new boyfriend?'

'Kind of,' I replied, noting Artie's curiosity. 'His name's Donnagh Flood. He's from Dublin originally but he lived in Leitrim as a teenager.'

'Jesus, not Donnagh Flood from Mohill, by any chance?' Artie said, his eyes widening.

'Yes, why? Do you know him?'

'Know him? I used to play football against him. Dirty player, so he was.'

'Sometimes I wonder if he still is.'

'What makes you say that?'

'I don't know,' I said. 'Paranoia, maybe? All I know is he's very cocky and very successful.'

'Sounds like Donnagh, all right.'

'You're not a fan, I take it.'

Artie shrugged. 'I just can't picture him and Evie together, that's all. He's not exactly her type.'

'Unlike you,' I said, before I could stop myself.

Artie stared at me. 'That was a long time ago, Rachel, a very long time.' He pointed at my glass. 'Do you want another?'

'Sure,' I said. I needed to take this slower, get him on my side. Maybe if he dropped his guard a bit, he might say something. But not if I went at him like a battering ram. I'd get absolutely nowhere with that strategy.

When he came back with the drinks, I guided the conversation into safer water. We talked a little about my career as a writer, and also about old times. About Leitrim. About Mammy.

'She was such a lovely woman,' Artie said, seeming to have calmed down a bit now. 'How was Evie coping with her loss?'

I emitted a deep sigh. What I wanted to say was 'by taking drugs and shagging lots of unsuitable men' but I didn't. Instead I said, 'Not brilliantly,' which was also accurate.

'She looks so different now,' Artie continued. 'So sophisticated.'

'Yeah, all the weight gone, and the new nose. I didn't think you'd recognize her with it. Most people don't.'

'I'd recognize Evie anywhere,' Artie said quietly. 'In any case I'd seen the new nose. Briefly. Before we broke up.'

'Oh, of course. You were dead set against it, weren't you?'

'Of course I was. It was madness. Her mother not cold in her grave and there she was haring off to a plastic surgeon to get her face ripped open.' Even now Artie sounded angry. 'It was just so unnecessary, Rachel, you know? She was lovely as she was.' He coughed, as if he'd said something he shouldn't have.

I nodded. 'She couldn't be talked out of it. I think it was her way of dealing with the grief.'

'Maybe so.' He took another swig of his Guinness, lapsing back into silence.

Afraid I was losing him, I tried to manoeuvre the conversation in a different direction. 'Artie, do you mind if I ask why you and Evie broke up? I never really got to the bottom of it.'

'I'm not sure there's any point in raking over all that again.'

'I know,' I said, trying to sound coaxing. 'But it's just that Evie changed after she left Ireland. Became . . .' I searched for the right word '. . . wilder, I suppose you might call it. I was hoping you might be able to shed some light on that.'

Artie looked at me as if I'd laid a trap for him, but then he said, 'Okay. If you want to know the truth, we broke up because of that stupid nose job.'

'How do you mean?'

'I didn't collect her from the hospital after the operation. Didn't visit her for about a week.'

'Why not?'

'Because I was fucking angry with her, that's why. I felt she was being selfish, taking herself off to have surgery when you'd both already lost your mother. What if something had happened to her, too, on the operating table? You hear about things like that occurring sometimes.'

'Yes,' I agreed. 'You do.'

'But it was all an act. I caved after about a week and

went around to see her, but she'd decided she didn't want us to be boyfriend and girlfriend any more and was refusing to have anything to do with me. Next thing I knew she had moved to London.'

'God, Artie, I'm sorry I didn't help you out. I barely registered any of it at the time.'

'Ah, you had your own troubles, Rachel, coming to terms with your mum's death and everything. And I got over it eventually.' He reached for his pint.

Without thinking, I put my hand on his arm, causing him to look up. 'Did you, Artie? Get over it, I mean?'

For the tiniest moment I thought I saw something flicker across his face (guilt, perhaps?), but then he jerked away. 'Jesus, Rachel, what are you trying to say here?'

'Artie, tell me truthfully, was there something going on between you and my sister?'

For a second, he remained statue still. Then, 'What did you say?'

'You claim to have only met up once – just you and Evie, I mean. But what I want to know is, was there more to it than that?'

'More to it?' I could see Artie's eyes darken. 'Is that the reason you got me to come here today? To find out if I was sleeping with Evie?'

'Were you?'

'Jesus Christ, Rachel,' he said, standing up so quickly that his chair gave a sharp squeak. 'Didn't you hear me when I said I was engaged?' He reached for his jacket. 'Christ almighty, what do you take me for?'

'Artie, wait, I didn't mean –' I got up too, attempting to block him.

'Rachel, get out of the way,' he said, staring down at me. 'I've had enough of this.'

'I know,' I said, still standing sentinel. 'But you must understand that I've had enough of things too. Watching Evie in that coma day in, day out, with no idea what happened to her, who might have put her there.'

'And you think I might have had something to do with it? You think I could have hurt Evie?' Artie gave a dry, bitter laugh.

'Of course not,' I spluttered. 'I'm just trying to piece everything together. Get to the truth of the matter.'

'Well, here's the truth for you, Rachel. I wasn't sleeping with Evie and I wasn't involved with her crash. Do you think you can comprehend that?'

Around us, other drinkers were staring. I stood there, too mortified to argue.

'Let me know if there's any change in her condition but otherwise . . .'

Otherwise, go fuck yourself, was what he was saying. Don't worry, I got the message.

I moved myself a fraction so he could get past me, then watched him walk away.

40.

I walked home from the pub, cursing myself. So much for taking it slowly, getting him to open up and reveal all to me. I'd learned nothing new. Nothing helpful, at any rate. All I'd done was insult Artie, and suggest he'd been indecent with my sister. Way to go, Rachel. Way to fucking go . . .

What was I going to do now? On the one hand, a tiny part of me couldn't help thinking there was more to the story than Artie was admitting to. He'd looked so wrecked – his eyes bloodshot, as if he'd been crying – and he'd been so twitchy. Maybe he'd just had a rough day at the office or maybe . . .

Maybe something else was going on.

A memory floated into my mind, from years earlier, when Mammy had been in the final throes of her illness. She'd wanted to see our apple tree one last time but had been too weak to walk, so Artie had carried her in his arms into the garden. There, he'd plucked a pink blossom from the tree and gently held it against her face.

'We'll have apples soon, Mrs Darcy, for all those wonderful apple tarts of yours,' he'd said.

She'd turned her watery eyes to meet his and whispered, so quietly I could barely hear her, 'You'll have to make them without me this year, Artie, darling. I'll give you the recipe.'

Even now, six years on, I could still recall how Artie had averted his eyes then, so that Mammy wouldn't see him crying. So that his tears wouldn't spill over her soft brown hair . . .

Back in the apartment I had a shower, desperate to clear my head after the horrible altercation with Artie, then lay down, exhausted, on the bed. I gazed at the ceiling for a while, trying to make sense of everything.

Was I losing my mind, accusing someone as nice as Artie of doing . . . What exactly? And even if he and Evie had slept together, how did that implicate him in her crash?

I picked up my phone, hoping the internet might shed some light on Artie's life in England, but before I could do that, I noticed I had two new emails. When I clicked in, I saw that the first was from Jacob, apologizing once again for 'the girl', asking my permission to come and see Evie. Until now, I'd been adamant that his visiting would be a terrible idea. I'd told him to keep his distance until I'd got my head straight. But now I felt desperate to talk to him, share what had happened with Artie. Hear his voice.

Afraid I might type something to him along those lines, I clicked into the second email, which had come via my author website.

Rachel, I really hope your sister is making a swift recovery. By the way, you look beautiful tonight. I love watching you naked. And, just so you know, I am watching you.

TBM

What the fuck?

I looked down at myself – naked, as the email stated – and instinctively reached for a nearby towel to cover myself up. It was that stupid fucker again: The Better Misogynist.

Who the hell was this guy? And how did he know I wasn't wearing any clothes? I tried to calm myself. So, somebody was trying to scare me. But who? And, more importantly, why?

I shuffled through my memory banks, attempting to recall people I'd recently pissed off. There'd been that Catholic guy on the TV panel who'd called me a Nazi for 'exterminating' my unborn child as a teenager. But he'd been about eighty. Did he even know how to use email? A few 'men's rights' representatives popped into my head. They all hated me or, at least, hated what I stood for. But were they really stupid enough to send threatening emails of a sexual nature? They were misogynists but they weren't idiots. If they were uncovered, the PR blowback would be disastrous.

Briefly, my mind went to Artie. Had I pissed him off so much that he'd wanted to counter-attack? But that was ludicrous. He hadn't known about Evie's crash until this afternoon, and I was pretty convinced he wasn't lying about that. There was no way he could have sent the initial TBM email. I was just being paranoid.

The sound of a key clicking in the lock alerted me to the fact that Donnagh was home.

Donnagh.

I am watching you.

Could he be trying to rattle me? Had he sent that email? Was there a peephole through which he could see me?

I got off the bed and began walking around Evie's bed-room, searching for a hole — some place Donnagh could spy on me. But after five minutes, cold and on my knees, I stopped. Was I losing my mind? Donnagh had just arrived home: unless he was capable of being in two places simultaneously, he hadn't been looking into my bedroom. And, anyway, he was a man who could have any woman in London.

I got off the carpet, threw on a dressing-gown and flopped down on the bed.

That email had been designed to freak me out. And it had succeeded. But I was damned if I was going to waste any more time thinking about it.

It had been sent by some internet nerd who'd seen the news about me and Evie in the papers — some pimply youth who'd never had sex. Or, alternatively, some obese middle-aged guy, whose only bit of action was a blow-up doll. It was pure coincidence about the naked thing. He just wanted to scare me.

Well, he could fuck right off if he thought he was going to succeed. He was underestimating just how hard I was to scare.

41.

Evie

After leaving Donnagh and the party, I stumbled outside in a daze. I'd come so close to getting caught. I had no idea what to do. If I went home I would spend the night in inexorable terror, going over every word Gemma had said. For about the thousandth time, I wished I still lived with Janet. If she were around, she would talk me down, convince me it was all one big, hilarious misunderstanding, which we would laugh about in years to come.

I stood there, staring at my phone, my fingers hovering over the buttons. There was so much I needed to apologize for: being such a bitch to her, such an awful flatmate; the whole horrible incident with Patrick. Just thinking about it made me wince with shame.

There'd been no terrible assault, as I'd insinuated. In fact, it was the other way round: I'd come on to Patrick while I'd been off my head on coke at a party in the flat. Patrick, ever the gentleman, had pushed me gently aside, explaining that while he thought I was a 'very nice girl', he was in love with Janet, and could I please put my top back on because I might catch a cold. He'd even retrieved my blouse from the floor and tried to encourage me to put my arms through it, allowing me to hold onto him for balance because I was so high I couldn't do it on my own.

That was when Janet had walked in, me half in, half out of my blouse, Patrick standing in front of me, one hand on my arm, looking mortified. For a second I froze, sick with shame, but then some dark, evil bit of me saw an opportunity and I grabbed it, too embarrassed to admit the truth.

Of course, Janet didn't believe a word of my story. She clocked what had happened in an instant and sided with Patrick before I'd even had time to put my top back on.

'Fuck sake, Evie. Is this what you've been reduced to?' she spat, her cheeks flaming.

I didn't respond, just held my arms defiantly across my chest. She turned to Patrick then: 'In case you were wondering, Evie is shit-faced on coke. That's why she's behaving like this.'

'Fuck off,' I said. 'That's none of your business.'

'Well, actually, it is my business when you bring your druggie friends back to our apartment on a whim, without even telling me, then try to shag my boyfriend behind my back.'

'Sorry, Janet, but in case you hadn't noticed, I own this apartment. You're my lodger. I can do what I fucking well please.'

She didn't speak for a good few seconds. Then: 'You know you have a problem, Eveline, don't you?'

I tutted. 'Oh, of course, silly me. I'm a drug addict.' I hit my forehead with the palm of my hand, and threw her a sarcastic scowl.

'Well, yes, you do have a problem with drugs, but there's a lot more to it than that. You're also chronically depressed – borderline suicidal, I would say – and your self-esteem is so low you have to sleep with strangers to fill the empti-ness ... You even have to come on to my boyfriend because you can't bear to see me happy. That's how low you've sunk.'

I felt my mouth fall open. She'd hit the nail on the head so accurately I felt dizzy.

'Evie,' she said, a little softer now, 'I know you're wor-ried you're losing me and you're jealous of Patrick, which is why you did what you did back there. But you've got to understand you're unwell.' She glanced at her boyfriend, who nodded. 'You've got to know you need help, sweet-heart.'

I stared at her, rendered mute. A trembly feeling had started to envelop my limbs.

'Come on,' she said, really soft now. 'We'll kick every-one out. I'll put you to bed and then, in the morning, we'll go to the GP together. Get you referred to a rehab centre. I can call Rachel. We can all do this together.'

Still, I remained unmoving.

'Evie,' she said, moving closer to me, reaching out her hand, 'come on, hen. I know it'll be hard but you can do it. You know you haven't been yourself in a long time now, and if this continues much longer, well, God knows what'll happen. Come on,' she said. 'Just allow yourself to surrender.'

I continued to stare at her, at her hand, knowing I was just centimetres away from help, from salvation. But then I thought of all the implications if I took Janet up on her offer: no more drugs; no more sleeping with random strangers or locking myself into my room. I'd have to face the reality of my unbearably shitty existence. Accept that

I had psychological and addiction problems. Accept that Mammy was gone.

'Go fuck yourself,' I whispered, from a place inside me I hadn't even known existed.

'What?' she said, clearly thinking she had misheard.

'I said, fuck you and your *faux*-piety and your great Saviour of the World act.'

'Evie . . . I'm trying to help you. I'm trying to make you see reason here.'

'No, you're not. You're trying to feel superior to me.'

She threw me a hurt look. 'Why would I want to do that?'

'I don't know,' I said. 'Because you're unhappy in yourself. Because you're jealous now that Patrick has forced you to become a boring cow.'

'Patrick hasn't forced me to become anything.'

'Are you sure? You used to be fun, and then you met him, and now you think anyone who drinks three beers has addiction problems.'

'Evie, come on, be reasonable. You know how much I care for you but I can't keep overlooking your behaviour. I'm trying to be your friend but there's only so far you can push me.'

'Well, then, don't bother,' I shouted, the trembling in my limbs really bad now.

'What?'

'Don't be my fucking friend. I don't want you to be anyway. Not now you're dating a thug.'

'What did you say?'

'I said, why don't you and your sexual predator of a boyfriend just fuck off and leave me alone?'

'Evie, I didn't go near you. Please stop lying.' Patrick looked distraught, as if he was about to cry, and I felt terrible, but I needed Janet to leave me alone, to stop antagonizing me about getting help.

'Evie, I'm going to ask you one more time, really slowly. Please kick these loser druggies out of your apartment and let me help you get the treatment you need.'

She stared at me, and I stared back. This was my last chance.

'Leave me alone,' I said again. 'I don't need or want your help, thank you very much.'

Janet stood there, as if thinking something over, then she came right up into my face. 'Fine. Don't say I didn't try. I'm leaving now, Evie, and I don't intend coming back. And just so you know, if I ever hear you defaming Patrick's character again, I will break that perfect nose into the back of your face, got it?'

I didn't respond, just waited as she grabbed Patrick's hand, and said to him, 'Come on, babe, let's get out of here.'

Next thing I knew suitcases were being thrown on the floor and doors were being slammed. And after a few hours, when all the drugs and booze were gone, everyone else left, too, until it was just me, alone in the darkness.

And, true to her word, Janet never came back.

That had been months ago. Now I was standing in the street, still shaking from my encounter with Gemma and Mick at that awful party. Right now a few lines of coke would have been wonderful to take the edge off. But my mate Chaz, my dealer, if you wanted to be pedantic about it, was out of the country, and I really wasn't a drug addict. I could cope with life's ups and downs.

I walked around for a few minutes, wondering what to do. I could ring Pandora, one of the people Chaz had introduced me to. She was bound to have something doing. But when I called her number, her mobile was switched off. I tried a few more of the gang: Will and Saffie and Megan. But it was the same thing: either their phones were off or they rang out. They were probably in a pub somewhere, getting pissed.

A feeling like a raging thirst ran through me. I wanted to be with them. But then I thought of Janet, and heard her patronizing voice again: 'You've got to get to the bottom of your problems, Evie, not self-medicate with booze or cocaine every time something goes wrong.'

Well, tonight I was going to prove her wrong. Even though something very frightening had happened, I was going to be the essence of virtue and restraint.

And, anyway, she wasn't technically correct. Sometimes when things went wrong, I slept. In fact, taking drugs was usually a sign I was in good form. Full of energy, bursting to do things. It was the sleepy periods I dreaded.

I walked on for a while. Ate a McDonald's. I wasn't even hungry, but I figured it might help quench the need inside me.

It didn't.

I walked past a guy, and I knew, just knew, he'd be able to score me some drugs. I stopped and looked back. He was still there, staring at me. A couple of words with him, a few minutes, and I'd be on a highway to oblivion, all thoughts of Donnagh and my terrifying schoolmates left behind.

Then reason intervened. What was I thinking, buying drugs off a stranger in the middle of central London?

You see, Janet had been wrong. Yes, I liked the odd toke, the odd class A on a Saturday night. But the fundamental difference between me and a junkie on the street was quite simple: I knew when to stop.

42.

In the end I rang Artie. 'I'm sorry to disturb you like this. I don't suppose you're out and about?'

'I'm in Mayfair, actually, just out of a meeting,' he explained. 'Are you okay?'

'Oh, yeah, yeah, I'm fine,' I said. 'I'm fairly close by, in Covent Garden. Would it be weird for us to meet up?'

There was a pause down the line. 'Are you in trouble, Eveline?'

'No. I mean yes. I mean, I don't know.'

Again, there was a pause.

'Look, I don't want to cause any problems between you and Shannon. It's just I could do with a friend and –'

Artie sighed. 'Evie, you're not causing any problems with me and Shannon. Listen, of course we can meet up. I'll ring home and explain, and maybe we can go for a drink or something.'

'Would you do that?'

'Of course.'

'Thanks,' I said, finding myself suddenly tearful. It was the kindness that was making me so emotional. I wasn't used to it, these days.

About twenty minutes later, Artie arrived and gave me a quick hug. 'Did something happen to you? You look very pale.'

'No, I'm fine,' I said, just relieved to be in his presence, far away from the party, Donnagh and all those frightening people from my secondary-school days.

'So what do you want to do? Do you want to go for a drink?'

I shook my head. For some reason, now that Artie was there, I didn't feel like drinking. Or getting off my head. 'Would you mind if we just walked for a while?'

'Sounds good. I could do with getting some air into my lungs after the week I've had.'

So we walked. Along the way, Artie stopped and bought each of us an ice-cream, getting my flavour right without even having to ask. 'Pistachio. You remembered.'

'Of course I did,' said Artie. 'Although, of course, pistachio is easier to acquire in modern London than in rural Leitrim of the mid-noughties.' He smiled at me. 'But you did always have very obscure taste.'

'So did you,' I said, smiling shyly back.

We stopped outside the National Portrait Gallery and saw that it was open late – there was a special Lucien Freud retrospective taking place.

'Have you ever been inside?'

'No,' Artie said, shaking his head.

'And I take it you've never seen Lucien Freud's work either?'

'Is he the guy who paints people all queer, with the big thighs and fallen chins and all that?'

I laughed. 'God, Artie, sometimes you're so Leitrim. But, yes, he's the guy.'

'Nope, I've never had the pleasure and clearly you think I've been missing out. Will we go in?'

I pointed at my ice-cream, which was only half eaten. 'What am I supposed to do with this?'

'Oh, come on, Darcy, don't pretend to be dainty. Horse it into you.'

I did as I was told, gobbling the last of my cone in two bites. 'All gone.'

'Not quite,' he said, laughing. 'It's all over your face.'

'Oh.' I began dabbing furiously. 'Have I got it?'

'No, go again.'

I did.

'There's still some on your . . . Oh, here, let me.' He rubbed his finger against my cheek. 'Gone now.'

We found ourselves staring at each other, and I had a sudden urge to grab Artie's hand and put it back on my face.

'Come on so,' Artie said, and turned away. I could see he was blushing.

We went into the gallery, where I handed in my coat and bag. Artie waited for me a few feet away. Had he always been so tall? Had his hair always been so curly?

To me, Artie was as much a part of the Leitrim landscape as the glacial lakes or the rolling drumlins. To see him in urban London was weird. Not bad, just odd. I wondered if he ever felt homesick for Ireland, like I did.

I asked him as we walked along the galleries, taking in the 'quare' paintings of Mr Freud.

'Homesick?' Artie repeated. 'Well, I'm here with Shannon now, so obviously that helps a lot. But, yes, I suppose, sometimes, a little.'

'It must have been hard to leave Leitrim, given you were so attached to the place. What did you do with Mutt?'

'He died a few years ago, and I didn't replace him.'

'And your parents must have been really sad to see you leave.'

'Dad passed away last year, and my mother moved to Spain to live with her sister. So . . .'

'God, Artie, I'm so sorry.' I found myself placing my right hand on his arm and rubbing his jumper.

Artie looked down, then back up at me. 'Thanks, Evie. It's okay. I'm okay.'

I dropped my hand.

We wandered around for over an hour, studying the paintings.

'Do you like the way he depicts people?' I asked Artie, after a while.

'I don't know if "like" is the word,' he said. 'But there seems to be an honesty to it.' We were staring at a picture of a huge woman reclining on a couch, her thighs and breasts colossal.

We moved on to another: a man splayed on a bed, revealing his testicles and penis in an almost obscene gesture.

'That's the way the human body is, isn't it?' he said quietly. 'Fleshy, sagging, but also compelling. Beautiful, even.'

'Shannon isn't exactly saggy.'

'Well, no,' he said, beginning to walk in the opposite direction.

Why had I mentioned Shannon? What the fuck was wrong with me?

A few minutes later, the tannoy announced that the gallery was closing and that all visitors should make their way towards the exit.

'Will we go for that drink now?' I asked, hoping he would say yes.

Artie looked at his watch. 'I really should get home, Evie. I told Shannon I'd be back by half ten.'

'Oh,' I said, sure the disappointment was written all over my face. There was an awkward pause.

'Oh, Jesus, now you're making me feel guilty,' he said. 'Okay, let's go for one, but then I really need to be making tracks.'

'Of course,' I said. 'Just the one.'

In the bar, we drank our one drink, then, while Artie was in the loo, I ordered a second for both of us.

'Ah, Jesus, Evie,' Artie said. 'What did I say to you?' But he sat down again and took a slurp anyway.

Over our pints we reminisced about the past, the characters we knew, the evenings in Leitrim by the lake.

'I really do need to get going now,' Artie said eventually, putting on his jacket and checking to see if he'd left anything behind. 'You want to come with me? Walk to the Tube together?'

'I think I'll stay out a little longer,' I said, not meeting his eye. While I'd been in the loo, Saffie had texted. She and Pandora were going clubbing and wanted to know if I'd join them. They had coke.

'Are you sure?' Artie asked. 'It's getting pretty late.'

'Don't worry, Grandad, I'm a big girl now,' I said, squeezing his elbow gently. 'But I'll walk with you to the station, if that's okay?'

A crooked smile formed on his lips. 'Of course it's okay. Just don't call me "Grandad" ever again.'

'Understood,' I said, grinning.

As we strolled along, I realized the weather had turned a lot cooler, and I had a sudden urge to link arms with Artie, to feel the heat of him. I moved in closer, ready to take his hand, but at the last minute I drew back, suddenly afraid.

'Well, that's me now,' he said, at the station. 'It was great to see you again, Evie.' He pecked me on the cheek, but just as he did so, somebody tumbled against us, pushing our bodies tightly together.

'Sorry, mate,' the guy shouted, but neither of us responded. For a second we just stayed there, our faces touching, eyes locked.

'Artie,' I whispered. He didn't move.

He'd never looked more beautiful to me than he did then. A group of Friday-night revellers swirled around us but all I wanted to do was lose myself in Artie's face, the lines of it, the contours. I lifted my hand, and brushed his hair away from his eyes. 'I've missed you so much.'

He didn't say anything – just continued to stare at me.

Around us people were still swirling; in the background there was the far-off din of trains.

I moved my head just a fraction, near enough so I could feel his breath. 'Artie . . . My darling Artie.'

And then, as if by magic, we kissed.

43.

Rachel: day ten, 10 a.m.

I debated ringing Lorelei about the second TBM email, but
I figured she was doing enough unpaid work for me already,
so I kept it to myself. I thought back to the creepy email.

I am watching you.

Was he? Or was it all just one monumental bluff?

I'd give it another few days. See if the little fucker got
back in contact. If he did, maybe I'd consider mentioning
it to Lorelei. If not, I'd keep shtum.

I still had one final destination to check out: Evie's
office. It had dawned on me that this building held a
potential mine of information: her computer for one, her
emails, not to mention any thoughts her colleagues might
want to share about Evie's recent behaviour.

All in all I had high hopes.

But when I reached the *Business Matters* headquarters –
a higgledy-piggledy collection of offices wedged above a
tanning shop in Greenwich – something about the place
made my heart sink.

As did Evie's boss, Nigel.

'So sad,' he said, shaking his head when I introduced
myself to him. 'Eve was on top of the world. Everything
to live for . . .'

'She's not dead,' I snapped.

'I never said she was.'

'You used the past tense.'

'Well, Jesus, she *is* in a coma,' Nigel said, his face changing from fake concern to annoyance. 'Was there something you wanted?'

'Yes, actually, there is. I need to check Eveline's emails.'

'You what?'

'I'm trying to find out what led my sister to crash and I need to read her emails. I need access to her files.'

'I'm sorry, Ms Durant –'

'Ms Darcy,' I interrupted.

'I'm sorry, *Ms Darcy*,' Nigel repeated. 'But there's hyper-sensitive information on Eve's desktop. It's absolutely out of the question.'

'Hyper-sensitive? You make it sound like she was working for the CIA.'

'I'm sorry, but there's nothing I can do. My hands are tied.'

If only, I wanted to add. And your legs and arms too. Then I'd drop you down a large manhole. How had Evie managed to work with this Neanderthal?

Nigel stood up, flicked something off his shoulder. 'So if that's all, Ms Durant – sorry, I mean Ms Darcy . . .' He smirked.

'Can you at least show me Evie's desk, so that I can take home a few of her mementoes? I promise I won't look at anything sensitive, if that's what you're worried about.'

He was clearly dubious. 'Fine,' he muttered, then stomped out of the office, without saying anything, forcing me to scamper after him, like a puppy. A few seconds later he stopped in front of a tiny work-station.

Two men raised their heads briefly to see what all the fuss was about, although no formal introductions were offered. I could only assume they were George and Tom, Evie's closest colleagues.

'Take what you want,' Nigel said, flinging one arm in the direction of Evie's belongings. He seemed delighted that I had scuttled after him.

'Not much, is there?' I was surprised that Evie's desk was so bare. The only non-work-related thing I could see was a small poster with Van Gogh's *Starry Night* on the front and a packet of mints. Not exactly a huge selection.

'Do you mind giving me a few minutes?' I said, trying to sound coaxing. 'It's just I'd like to remember Evie quietly . . .'

'I thought you said she wasn't dead.'

'She isn't,' I growled, feeling my right arm twitch. Lorelei had taught me how to throw a mean right hook and I was tempted to use it.

'Ah, Mr Lytham, so that's where you are. They're waiting for you in the boardroom.' A tiny blonde girl, presumably a secretary, had appeared in front of Nigel, holding a clipboard.

'You go on, Nigel. I'll help her out if there are any issues.' One of the two men was speaking now but I had no idea if it was George or Tom.

'All right, then,' Nigel said, sniffing. 'But remember what I said about all files being confidential.'

I nodded deferentially. 'Of course.'

After Nigel had fucked off, the kind man stuck out his hand. 'I'm George, by the way. So nice to meet you. You must be Rachel.'

'Yes, I am. Evie told you about me, then?'

'Of course. Famous author. We're honoured.'

'I don't think he is.' I nodded in the direction of Nigel's retreating back.

'Oh, pay no attention to him,' George said, grinning. Under his breath, he added, 'Bit of an arse.'

I sat at Evie's desk, and drummed my fingers. 'Don't suppose there's any way I could get into Evie's emails, is there?'

George raised an eyebrow. 'After what Ivan the Terrible just said on that subject?'

'I know, but . . .'

'Don't think so,' George said, writing something quickly, then dropping it casually on Evie's keyboard.

'Well, I'm just off for a coffee,' he declared loudly. 'You coming, Tom?'

The other man, who had yet to introduce himself, glanced up at his colleague, then over at me. 'Oh, right, sure,' he said, the penny dropping. As they were leaving, George whispered, 'I'd say you have about a quarter of an hour.'

When they were gone, I grabbed the piece of paper and read it. Good boy, I thought. George had supplied me with the password to get into Evie's computer, as well as her username. I powered it up, quick as I could, then logged in. Instantly dozens of emails swam in front of my eyes and, without wasting any time, I began searching for my three main suspects: my father, Donnagh and Artie.

Much to my dismay, each name drew a blank. Evie clearly didn't mix work correspondence with play. Although, given that she had a boss like Nigel, it was hardly surprising.

After giving up on the emails, I began flicking through some of the folders on Evie's desktop, hoping to find a Word document or jpeg that might give me some clues. But pretty soon I realized it was a hopeless task. Going through all Evie's files would take ages and I reckoned I had only a few more minutes before Nigel reappeared.

I threw a pen at the dividing wall of Evie's cubicle and sighed. Why was it that nothing I did seemed to work out? Why was everything so bloody hard?

All of a sudden, I heard somebody cough beside me and I glanced up.

'Jesus Christ,' I stuttered, putting my hand to my heart. 'I thought you were Nigel.'

'Don't worry. Nigel's still in that meeting. I'm Tom.' He stuck out his hand and I shook it, taking in his appearance as I did so.

He was short and balding, dressed in the uniform of all men in the creative sector: jeans, with runners and a hoodie. The slogan on his top read: 'Have you switched it off and on again?'

'So, let me guess,' I said. 'You're the IT guy, right?'

'Yeah,' Tom said. 'As well as the graphic-design guy, the audio-visual guy, the content-marketing guy . . .'

'Nigel's quite the slave-driver, I take it?'

Tom tossed his eyes to Heaven. 'You could say that, yes.'

For a moment, neither of us spoke.

Then: 'So how's she doing? Eve, I mean.'

'The same,' I replied. 'Still in a coma.'

'I'm really sorry to hear that, Rachel,' he replied, looking genuinely forlorn.

'Everything okay back here?' George said, arriving at

his desk with a takeaway coffee, glancing from side to side.

'Fine,' I said, switching off Evie's computer. I didn't want to admit the whole thing had been a fiasco. Not after George had been so lovely.

The three of us stood there for a few seconds in awkward silence. Everything seemed so confusing right now.

'Did either of you think Eveline was a bit off before the accident? Was she acting strangely or out of character?' I asked.

'Not really,' said George, scratching his head and looking vaguely uncomfortable. Tom just shook his head.

'And this Donnagh guy. Did you meet him? Did they seem happy?'

Tom cleared his throat. 'He popped into the office once or twice but that was it. She didn't seem unhappy.'

'Okay,' I said, crestfallen. Yet another blind alley. Where did my sister actually reveal herself, if not at work or at home?

'Do you know if she was depressed? Or took a lot of drugs?' I couldn't believe I'd just asked that question, but now that it was out I was relieved. I couldn't keep tiptoeing around the situation.

George glanced nervously at Tom. 'Maybe a bit,' he said, still scratching his head. 'As for being depressed, who isn't? Especially if you work in this place.' He attempted a smile but it didn't quite reach his eyes.

'Please, George, please tell me anything you think would be helpful. I'm working almost entirely in the dark here. I feel as if I don't know who my sister was.' The last few words were wobbly, and I could see panic descend over George's face for fear I might start blubbing.

'Look, Rachel,' he lowered his voice, 'Eve struck me as the kind of person who had her demons, but she never opened up about that kind of thing. We had a laugh here, occasionally went for a pint after work, but that was it. We didn't do deep and meaningful with each other.'

'Okay,' I said, thankful he'd told me that much at least.

Then, as an afterthought, he added, 'I did think it strange she was in a relationship with Donnagh Flood, though. When she was originally asked to interview him she refused. Looked like she was going to vomit at the thought, actually.'

'Really?'

'Yes. But obviously something must have changed — I'm not sure what.'

I looked at Tom, who was nodding. 'Tom, do you know anything? Anything at all that could help me.'

He pushed his glasses back against his forehead. 'I'm sorry, Rachel, I wish I did, but I can't add anything to what George just said. Honestly, I can't.'

'Shit! Nigel's coming back,' George whispered. Both men immediately retreated to their desks and put on their headphones.

'Collect your mementoes, Ms Darcy?' Nigel boomed, casting me a look so smarmy I felt an instant desire to shower. When I looked down, I had nothing in my hands.

'I couldn't find one worthwhile thing to take from this office,' I said, returning Nigel's hostile look. 'Funny that.'

'You'll probably want to leave,' he said, 'if we've proved to be such a waste of space.'

'Oh, don't worry, I'm going,' I said, mouthing a silent thanks to George and Tom.

'Don't let the door hit you on the way out,' I heard Nigel say, as I made my way to the lift. But I knew he was watching my arse as I went.

It was an hour later and I was back in the flat, curled up in an armchair. I'd been so distracted I'd barely noticed it, but now, for the first time, I realized how beautiful it was – antique, with a pastel blue finish – and I wondered if Evie had reupholstered it. It was the kind of thing she might have done at one of her evening classes.

The trip to the office had been such a massive waste of time. That numbskull, Nigel, had made me want to hit him, and even though George and Tom had been lovely, they'd offered no new information. Nothing that could help me, at any rate.

As I was thinking this, my phone started ringing, and my heart missed a beat. Could it be TBM? Had he somehow figured out my phone number now too? But when I glanced down I saw it was Jacob.

For a moment I wavered, a part of me desperate to speak to him, but in the end I let it go to voicemail. About a minute later, my phone pinged, alerting me to a new text message: *Rachel, I need to talk to you urgently. Ring me back.*

I gazed at my phone, my fingers hovering over the dial button. It made me shake just to contemplate it, but I knew I should do as he asked – I should talk to Jacob. However, at that moment I heard a key in the lock – Donnagh's – and then his voice booming into the silence: 'Rachel, you home?'

I didn't answer, didn't move a muscle.

'Rachel?' he called again.

'Yeah, I'm here,' I said, throwing down my mobile onto the bed and opening the bedroom door.

'Oh, there you are. Listen, I picked up a few beers on the way home and was wondering if you'd like one.'

'Oh,' I said. 'Well, okay. Give me a second and I'll be there.'

A few minutes later, when I reached the living room, Donnagh was already pouring me a glass of pale ale. We didn't talk much – just smoked and drank – but I was grateful for the window of respite. It meant I didn't have to think about Jacob. About the 'urgent' text message I should be replying to. About the fact that our marriage was dissolving right before my eyes.

And it also meant I didn't have to dwell on my failed detective work – the pointless time spent down at *Business Matters*. The fact that I had made no progress whatsoever.

In fact, it was almost as if Donnagh had given me permission, for one night, to stop thinking completely. Just to sit quietly and sup beer and be a normal human being. As if I really was normal. As if nothing bad had happened at all.

44.

Evie

So I am *still* in a coma, and I am still having panic attacks and delusions. And though there is no sign of any recent memories resurfacing, a really old one has come back to me: a flashback from years ago, of me as a little girl, standing outside our cottage in Leitrim, half frozen and with no shoes on, wearing just a flimsy nightdress.

In the flashback, I'm sleepwalking – something I used to do quite regularly as a kid. And I can still remember that night, my teeth chattering, hearing Mammy and Granny talking – well, fighting, really. Saying stuff I knew they wouldn't want me to hear.

I feel a rip of adrenaline pass through me. Could that explain things – the sleepwalking, I mean? Could it explain this coma? Why I drove a car without a licence? Could it explain why I crashed Donnagh's Porsche into a ten-foot wall?

I have no recollection of recent sleepwalking incidents, but then again I have no recollection of most things. But let's just say it's true, does that mean I've been barking up the wrong tree, accusing people unfairly . . . accusing Donnagh unfairly?

Jesus, is it possible that he's actually innocent? That it was just a case of me caught in stage-three non-REM sleep, walking out of my bedroom, out of my flat, getting into his car and losing control?

Could it really be as simple as that?

When I think about it, this explanation seems such a good one. So neat. But then again, is it a bit too neat? And why would I have started doing it now, twenty years later, without any warning?

Okay, maybe there had been some warning. I know I was under a lot of stress before the crash and I'd probably been taking a few more drugs than normal. But then again, I was under a lot of stress when Mammy died and when my relationship with Artie broke down, and I didn't sleepwalk then. At least, I don't think I did.

And thinking about it further, would I really have been able to find Donnagh's keys, walk down the stairs, get into his Porsche and turn on the ignition – all while fast asleep? It seems so unlikely. The worst Rachel ever reported was finding me in the kitchen trying to put bread in the toaster. Surely I couldn't have stretched to a fifteen-minute drive to Lewisham in a car I was unfamiliar with?

Could I?

Speaking of Rachel, she seems very down. I know my being in a coma can't be helping, but it seems more than that – like she is broken somehow. When she speaks, she sounds exhausted and there is something else: a type of sadness I've never heard before. There is no sign of Jacob and I can't understand why he hasn't been to see me. It's odd. Until very recently, he and I were best of pals.

Even though he's the polar opposite of me – logical, tidy, good with money – Jacob and I are surprisingly close. He's a sociology lecturer. He and Rachel met when she

266

was doing her MA in Social Studies – and I wish he was here now, so he could tell me how my coma is just an ideological construct and I am no less human now than I ever was. On that point I would agree with him. Ironically, I've never felt more conscious or more real than I do right now.

Other people have been to visit too. Donnagh, for example. He's been to see me at least once, and spent the whole time stroking my hair and saying my name over and over again. I should have felt scared. At the time he was my chief suspect, and, quite frankly, he still is. But, much to my surprise, I held my nerve. I've come to realize that if I am ever to get out of here, I need to stop panicking and think logically. Much as I hate to admit it, Janet was right: I need to put my neuroses to one side. I need to start believing in myself.

Astonishingly, Artie also dropped by. I thought I'd never see him again. Not after the last time. For ages he said nothing. And next thing all I felt were these wet splodges on my chest: he was crying. He didn't say much – barely touched me. Just at the end, he squeezed my hand and said, 'Get better, Evie.' Then he left. No kiss on the cheek. Nothing.

I never felt as impotent as I did then. Every part of me wanted to rip all the IV lines off, swing my legs out of the bed, run after him and beg him to stay.

But, of course, I didn't because I was in a chronic vegetative state and couldn't move one finger, let alone all the muscles in my body.

Fucking coma.

There was another visitor too. Very strange.

That person didn't touch or talk to me at all. Just stood over the bed – I could detect their toxic 'energy' – and breathed down on top of me in a strange, creepy way. For a while I began to think I was imagining it. That my brain was starting to play tricks on me and that I was suddenly conjuring up strangers. But then a nurse bustled in and said, 'I'm sorry, visiting hours are over.'

And the stranger grunted something and walked off. For a second, I thought I recognized the grunt. It sounded kind of familiar. But in the end I couldn't attribute it to anyone I knew.

Should I be suspicious of this person? This grunter? Are they in some way linked to the crash? I wish I could say yes, but the truth is I don't have a bloody clue.

I lie here in this coma, thinking it all over, and for some reason my mind lurches back to that earlier memory – of me standing on the porch at our cottage, wearing only a flimsy nightdress. Even now, all these years later, it's as if I could still hear the voices of Mammy and my grandmother Eilish, clear as crystal, and the extraordinary things coming out of their mouths.

'I take it you never hear from him.'

This one from Granny, who didn't visit us very often. She and Mammy didn't get along too well.

'No,' Mammy snapped back. 'Of course I don't. You know I don't.'

'I always told you he was a waster. That you should never have had anything to do with him.'

Mammy harrumphed. 'Oh, yes, you were very clear on that.'

'And yet you never listened,' Granny said, and I could

practically see her lips purse into a cat's bottom. 'You always were a very stubborn girl.'

'You got two beautiful grandchildren out of it, didn't you?' Mammy retaliated, her voice high and squeaky now – a sure sign she was about to blow it.

Granny didn't say anything for a bit. Then: 'Sometimes I think you should contact him. He owes you a fortune in maintenance.'

'No,' Mammy barked, and I noticed her voice had changed. It was harder, colder now. 'That man can never come near my children again.'

Granny tutted. 'In an ideal situation, no, but you work as a barmaid and there's a recession on. You need the money.'

'Mother, didn't you hear me?' Mammy said, not shouting exactly but angry. I could hear it in her voice. The power of it suffused the air.

'Katherine, I know he did a terrible thing.'

'Stop,' Mammy shouted, and Granny did just that. Finally, in a lower tone, Mammy said, 'Mother, don't you understand? He could do it all again, without a second's thought. There's no way I'll ever take that risk.'

I moved closer to the window now, desperate to hear more.

'The children must never know about what happened,' she continued. 'They have enough baggage to be dealing with, without knowing about him, about what he did to them.'

'Well, they won't hear anything from me,' Granny said huffily. 'In case that's what you were implying.'

Mammy stayed silent. I suspected that was exactly what she was implying.

A minute or two passed before Granny declared, 'Well, seeing as you refuse to see reason, I'll head for my bed.' I heard her stand up and make for the doorway. I nearly puked – she might see me. Luckily she disappeared down the hallway and into her bedroom without incident. Once the coast was clear, I crept back inside and scampered to my own bedroom, waking Rachel as I ran in.

'Feckin' hell, Evie, what's all the commotion?' she said, sitting up and rubbing her eyes. 'Have you been sleep-walking again?'

'Yes,' I said, about to explain what I'd stumbled across. But then I stopped myself. How could I explain every-thing to Rachel when I didn't even know what I was describing? When I hadn't even processed it myself.

Later that night, as I lay in bed, I sifted through the words spoken by Mammy and my grandmother, trying to make sense of them.

'I know he did a terrible thing.'

What the heck had Granny meant by that? What terr-ible thing had my father done?

I asked Mammy about it eventually, though I'm not sure when. All I really recall was her reaction: how her face had turned pale and ghost-like; how she'd dropped the mug she was holding on the hard kitchen tiles beneath us, where it had smashed. 'I'm so sorry, Evie, I don't feel well all of a sudden. I need some air.' She'd staggered out of the room, swaying from side to side, almost as if she was drunk.

A few minutes later, after I'd cleared up the cup, I'd walked out to find her. She was sitting on the big granite step at the back of our house, a cigarette in her hand, gazing at the roll-ing fields beyond. 'Mammy, I didn't mean to upset you.'

'You didn't upset me, darling,' she said, smiling wanly and patting the ground, encouraging me to sit down.

I did.

'I'm sorry if I gave you a fright there. I think I might be coming down with something – a bug or the flu or that.'

I ignored the lie, just kept my eyes focused on the earth beneath me, tracing a line on the ground with my finger.

After a few moments, Mammy shifted her body so she was facing me. 'Evie, look at me for a second. You were asking about your father and there's something I want to tell you.'

I raised my eyes just as my mother had asked – my pulse racing at the thought of finally getting a proper answer.

'Evie, the thing you need to know is that you are not to blame for your father leaving us.' Mammy was facing me full on now, holding my hand in hers.

'I know that, Mammy. But I just want to know *why* he left us. The terrible thing Granny said he did to us. To me and Rachel.'

'Don't mind Granny,' Mammy said, trying to sound dismissive. But I could see that her cigarette was trembling in her hand as she spoke, causing ash to spill all over her faded yellow skirt.

'You agreed with her, Mammy. You said you would never risk it happening to us again.'

For a moment she didn't say a word, just took a long drag of her cigarette and looked off into the hills. I didn't realize it at the time and I still can't know for sure but, at that moment, I think she was on the verge of telling me something.

The truth, maybe.

271

However, almost as soon as I felt that, the moment was gone.

'Evie, you were sleepwalking again, weren't you? You might have become confused, darling.'

I stared at her. I hadn't been confused. I'd been perfectly lucid.

'The thing is, your father wasn't capable of being a parent. Can you understand that?'

I shook my head. 'Not really.'

Mammy sighed. 'I know it's hard to grasp.' She flicked ash off her cigarette. 'But the truth is, not everyone has the temperament for it. Some people just aren't cut out to be parents.'

'But I thought he loved us?' I asked, genuinely baffled.

Mammy stared straight ahead. Very quietly she whispered, 'So did I.'

For a minute we stayed there, locked in silence. 'Maybe we should contact him. Maybe he's better now and he'll be able to take care of us properly.'

'No.' Mammy took my hand again. 'Evie, there are some things I will never be able to explain to you about your father. But you must trust me when I say it's better the way things are. And, anyway, we're doing perfectly well as we are, aren't we? We lead a grand life.'

'Yes,' I whispered, snuggling into her shoulder. I didn't want to tell her the truth. That sometimes I felt so lonely I could hardly breathe . . . as if I was a stranger in my own life.

Mammy kissed my forehead and leaned her weight against me. 'So are we okay now, darling? Will you promise me you'll forget about what you *think* you heard?'

I nodded, ignoring the word 'think', even though it was irritating. 'Yes, Mammy,' I said, because what else could I say? Then we got up off the step and made our way back towards the house, leaving Mammy's cigarette butt smouldering on the step.

Things got back to normal pretty quickly after that, and I never again asked questions about our father or what he had purportedly done to us. But I couldn't forget it. That whispered conversation between Mammy and my grandmother lodged in my soul, like a bullet, and I knew I wouldn't rest until I'd found Daddy and asked him about it. I'd studied like a lunatic in French class, convinced, somehow, that this would be my ticket to finding him. Sure enough it had garnered me a scholarship to Normandy, which, when I looked on the map, was only a train ride away from Calais. His hometown.

I had hoped for so much from that meeting, but it had been a dismal failure. An utter, abject disaster.

Recently, I had taken to writing him endless letters. Reams of paper, asking him every question under the sun.

For ages I didn't have the guts to send any – I'd just allowed them to build and build in my bedside locker. But then one morning when, frankly, I was so pissed from the night before that I could barely see straight, I'd got one out, attached a stamp and sent it off – as easy as that.

Of course I hadn't heard back. And now, when I thought of it, all I felt was mortification. There should be rules against that: drinking and posting. What had I been thinking? As if my father would want to hear from me. As if, after all this time, he could ever love me back.

You may think it strange I never told Rachel any of

this. Not when we confronted our father in France. Not even when I demanded that he reveal his secret. But the thing was, I knew the conclusion she would jump to: that he had abused us. Or was violent towards us.

I know he did a terrible thing . . .

Sure, what else could she be expected to think?

But the thing was, I was willing to give our father the benefit of the doubt. Allow him to explain himself. Rachel wouldn't have done that. It would have been more grist to her mill: that he was a coward. A waste of space. Maybe even a paedophile.

I did not think he was a paedophile.

Sometimes, as a little kid, I used to imagine that my father and I were cut from the same cloth. Artistic, temperamental, sensitive. It had to be so, because I had so little in common with my mother or even with Rachel. Don't get me wrong, I would have loved to resemble Mammy: to have her kindness and gentleness and grace, but it was pretty obvious I had none of those qualities. As for Rachel, she and I were like chalk and cheese. Not just looks-wise, but also in terms of pragmatism, confidence, self-worth. No, I was nothing like her either.

Which left my father.

Okay, so maybe he *had* tried to hurt us. Maybe he was a bit mad. Who cared? I was a bit mad too. Sometimes, as I lay in bed, the weirdest stuff would go through my head and I would wonder, does he think like this too? Is this why he couldn't be a parent, why he couldn't lead a normal life? I thought if I met him, got to know him, we could share our madness. Make peace with it. That was why I had travelled over to Calais, and why I had posted the letter.

Mammy had tried to deny it, but I knew there was a story. A secret. I knew that.

And there was something else I knew.

That I wouldn't rest until I had found it out.

45.

I was beginning to lose faith now. I'd followed every lead I could find, checked and rechecked Evie's apartment for clues, but nothing was forthcoming. I hadn't even cracked something as basic as the password to Evie's laptop. It seemed like the whole venture had been utterly pointless.

I headed into the hospital, feeling a sense of utter defeat. I had failed in my role to unlock Evie's last days and, as a consequence, I had failed Evie. Without that knowledge, I felt convinced she would never wake up.

Head bowed, I approached the corridor where her room was located, a sick feeling in the pit of my stomach. I'd convinced myself that if I unpicked Evie's secrets, the shackles of her coma would spring open and she would be released to the world, alive and conscious. But it wasn't working out that way. Not even remotely.

'Rachel.'

I looked up and could hardly believe my eyes. Jacob was standing in front of me, his eyes puffy and bloodshot. 'Jesus Christ. What are you doing here?'

'I'm here to talk, Rachel, plus I wanted to see Evie – I tried calling you yesterday evening to tell you I was coming over.'

'Did you?' I said unconvincingly. 'I must have missed it. In any case, I thought I told you to stay away.'

'You did, but I decided to ignore you. We need to talk, Rachel. You know we do.'

I sighed, trying to feign irritation. But the truth was, I wasn't really angry at seeing Jacob there – the only emotion I felt was relief. 'Come on so, if you want to see Evie. She's in here.'

Tentatively Jacob followed me, and soon we were in Evie's room. I watched closely as he took in my sister's figure – the tiny unmoving creature she had become. 'Christ,' he breathed softly, when he saw she was wired up to all the tubes and monitors. 'Can I touch her?'

'If you want.'

Jacob took Evie's hand and began to stroke it. 'Evie,' he said gently, and when I looked again I could see he was crying.

A few minutes later, he turned to me, and though I knew I shouldn't, I made a semi-circle with my arms and beckoned him to enter it. Silently we hugged, long and deep. It felt so good to touch him. To feel the warmth of his skin on mine.

A little while later, we drew apart and sat down.

'What have the doctors said?' he asked quietly, turning a little in his chair so he could face me.

'That she's stable, though still heavily comatose. It's been eleven days now. Not necessarily a long time in coma terms.'

'But a lifetime for you, right?'

I nodded. Eventually I found my voice. 'All is not entirely lost, though. If she wakes up within the next two to three weeks, there's a strong chance she could make a full recovery. Or certainly a significant one.'

'And after a month?' Jacob said, without flinching.

I allowed my eyes to drop towards the floor. 'I prefer not to dwell on that, to be honest.'

After that we just sat there, not saying much, just taking turns to stroke Evie's hand, to wipe her brow. Occasionally Jacob would offer a conversational titbit: how warm the sea was at the moment, the new ice-cream place that had opened down the road in Dun Laoghaire, what he was doing at work. He didn't mention that girl again and I didn't ask. It was hard enough to block her from my mind's eye as it was. I could still picture her standing there in her underwear. The memory made me feel sick.

After a while, Jacob asked me did I want to grab a coffee and maybe go for a little walk.

'A walk?' I said, as if he had said 'safari'.

'I thought it might be nice to get some fresh air.'

I knew I should refuse so that he'd realize how angry I still was – but I didn't have the energy for anger. And, in any case, had he really done such a bad thing? I'd been the one to walk out on him, not the other way round. To my surprise, I found myself nodding.

And so we walked.

Jacob didn't try to take my hand and I was grateful for that. He didn't try to talk to me about our relationship either, even though I knew he wanted to. Not that I was complaining or anything. For the moment, I was just happy to keep walking, not saying much, just gazing at the sky, feeling the blissfully cool air on my skin.

At some point I began telling him about my detective

work, and he listened as I explained my attempts to under-stand Evie's last moments before the accident – to figure out why she'd been driving the car, if she'd been having an affair and whether there was any basis to the rumour that she'd been a drug addict.

'A drug addict?' Jacob said, sounding shocked. 'I mean, I know Evie had her difficulties but I didn't see that one coming. She seemed okay in February.'

Jacob and I had flown over to London earlier in the year – I was being filmed for a British TV show – and we had gone out to dinner with Evie on two separate occasions.

'Yes, but both of us were so distracted, Jacob. What with our work, and the fact that our marriage was falling apart, I don't think we were capable of noticing if any-thing was wrong with her.'

Jacob paled – it was probably the 'marriage falling apart' comment. 'I noticed how much she looked up to you, admired you,' he said.

'Did you?'

'Evie always thought you were brilliant.'

I felt a lump form in my throat. 'Sometimes I thought she hated me.'

Jacob touched me lightly on the sleeve. 'She didn't hate you, Rachel, she adored you. The problem was, she felt she could never match up.'

We had been walking for about forty-five minutes when out of nowhere the heavens opened. 'Run towards that tree,' I said, pointing at a big horse-chestnut in the dis-tance, but it was too late: we were in a particularly open part of the park and within seconds we were drenched straight through.

We ran to the tree anyway, cowering under its branches as we waited for the rain to abate. Fifteen minutes later, it was still pouring down, monsoon-like. 'Fuck this,' I said, shivering and annoyed that I'd brought no proper raingear. Jacob was even worse. His light shirt provided absolutely no protection whatsoever. 'Come on, let's make a run for it.'

'A run? Where to?' Jacob said, hair sticking to his forehead.

'To Evie's apartment. It's a mile or so away.'

Jacob nodded, and we withdrew from under the tree.

Twenty minutes later we stumbled into Evie's apartment, rain-sodden and panting.

'Here,' I said, throwing him a towel from Evie's hot press. 'Have a shower, before you catch your death. I'll throw your jeans into the tumble-dryer.'

'Thanks,' he said, and did just that. When he came out of the bathroom, I directed him into Evie's room where he could wait until his jeans were dried. Then I had a quick shower myself.

About a quarter of an hour later, I tapped on the door, wearing a robe, holding Jacob's now dry jeans. 'Here you go,' I said, bending down to give them to him. He was lying on top of the bed flicking through one of Evie's books, wearing just his boxers and a T-shirt.

He took the jeans and our hands touched. At the same time, I felt the front of my robe gape open, exposing part of my left breast.

'Rachel,' he said, and in that instant time stood still, neither of us speaking. Then he tugged me towards him using the cord of my robe.

'Jacob,' I whispered in what was supposed to be a warning tone. But it was no such thing. I could already hear the desire, thick and heavy, in my breath.

I allowed him to remove my robe, and then I just stood naked in front of him, as he ran a hand over my breasts. 'I've missed you so much,' he murmured.

I didn't reply, didn't move a muscle, but when he pulled me closer, I allowed my head to fall into the crook of his neck so I could breathe him in.

There was no girl now: just me and Jacob and the tiny universe we occupied, everything at once so familiar and so foreign – the smell of Jacob's skin, the weight of his arms. It had been so long and I'd missed him. I'd missed him so much.

Jacob put his hand under my chin and lifted my face to meet his, looking deep into my eyes, breathing in my breath. Then we kissed, for what felt like hours, and everything became sense and touch: our own private paradise.

Finally, he entered me, whispering, 'I love you,' over and over, and so did I, tears building at the corners of my eyes before trickling down my cheeks and running into my mouth.

Afterwards, we just lay there, wrapped in each other's arms, staring at the ceiling.

'I mean it, Rachel. I do love you. I can't do this any more. I want you back.'

I turned to face him, traced a finger down his cheek. I knew what he meant. The only thing that made sense any more was the love I felt for him. But how could we get back together when I knew he wanted children? When I knew I wasn't enough.

'Do you mind if I get a cigarette?' I said, throwing back the duvet cover, touching his arm to reassure him I wouldn't be long. I was hoping a quick smoke might give me a chance to make sense of what had just happened. Everything was propelling me towards saying yes to Jacob, agreeing to get back together. But I needed a moment to catch my breath and make sure I was doing the right thing.

I threw my robe back on and headed for the kitchen where my bag lay.

'Hello, there.'

I nearly jumped out of my skin to find Donnagh sitting at the dining-room table, cutting an apple with a knife. 'Fucking hell, when did you come in?'

'About five minutes ago. Didn't you hear me?'

'No, I didn't,' I muttered. 'What time is it anyway?'

'Six o'clock.'

Six o'clock! Jacob and I must have nodded off for over an hour after we'd made love.

Donnagh continued to look at me, a quizzical expression on his face. 'Are you okay, Rachel? What's with the bathrobe? Are you sick or something?'

'Not sick, no.' I looked back towards the bedroom.

'Listen, I was thinking. Do you fancy grabbing a bite to eat? I'm fed up of cooking and I'd like a steak. Do you want to go to the bistro down the road – my treat?'

I stared at him, trying to quell a rising panic. Why was it that I didn't want Jacob and Donnagh to bump into each other?

A moment later there was a bang, then the creak of a door opening. In an instant Jacob appeared wearing nothing but his boxers, scratching the back of his head. 'Rach, are you okay out here? I thought I heard voices.'

I froze.

'Rachel,' he said again, and advanced further, past the half-wall that separated the dining room from the living space.

'Jesus, who are you?' he said, jolting upon spotting Donnagh.

'I might ask you the same thing,' Donnagh said, getting up from the table and putting down his apple but not, I noticed, the knife.

'Donnagh, this is my, um, husband, Jacob. He was just over visiting Evie.'

'Was he now?' Donnagh said, in a strange, unfriendly voice. He looked at me then, an accusing glare, and I felt like asking what his problem was. Jacob was my husband, for fuck sake, even if we were separated. I didn't have to explain my sex life to him. How dare he pretend to be outraged?

'And you are?' Jacob challenged, not seeming the least bit intimidated.

'I'm Donnagh, Eve's partner,' he said, and I nearly laughed. *Eve's partner* indeed. The two of them had only been going out with each other for five minutes.

'What are you doing here?' Jacob asked, in a similarly hostile tone. 'Why are you in Evie's flat?'

'I live here, or didn't your wife tell you?' Donnagh said, his jaw twitching.

Jacob looked at me as if Donnagh had punched him. 'Is this true?'

'Yes,' I said, unable to meet his eye. 'Yes, it is.'

Back in Evie's room, Jacob was furiously throwing on his clothes, his face contorted with anger. 'Who the fuck is that clown? And what were you thinking, moving in with him?'

'He's Evie's boyfriend. I told you about him.'

'When?'

'That day in Dublin.' I paused. 'That day with the girl.'

Now it was Jacob's turn to drop his eyes. 'Rachel. What the hell is he doing here? He could be a madman.'

I shrugged. 'He and Evie had moved in together temporarily. He was here before I was. How was I supposed to kick him out?'

'Oh, for fuck s-sake!' Jacob stuttered. 'This is a farce. You don't know him from Adam.'

'I've been living with him for nearly two weeks, actually. I'll admit I had my own suspicions at the beginning, but he's turned out to be okay.'

Jacob sighed. 'Rachel, I really don't like the vibe off that guy. I'm going to get rid of him.'

He made a beeline for the door, but I ran in front of him and blocked it. 'You'll do no such thing!' I exploded. 'You're not going to come in here now, like John fucking Wayne, and cause a huge fight with someone you don't even know. Who I have to live with.'

'Rachel, you've got to admit there's something dodgy about him.'

I clicked my tongue. 'Jacob, how would you know? You've only just met him. And, quite frankly, how dare you? You were asked to stay in Ireland. You came here anyway. Now you want to throw out Donnagh, even though he's Evie's boyfriend. Even though she wanted him to be here.'

'I'm just worried about you, Rach. He seems creepy.'

'Worried about your ego, more like. You don't like the idea of me living with a tall, dark, handsome man.'

'Fucking handsome,' Jacob spat. 'Did you see the way he kept holding that knife? What was that about?'

'Oh, just quit it, Jacob. Not so nice now, is it? Getting a dose of your own medicine?'

'What's that supposed to mean?'

'It means it was fine for you to be caught in bed with someone else. But when you find I'm living with a gorgeous man, you can't handle it.'

'You think he's gorgeous?'

'No,' I said, feeling my cheeks flame. 'I'm just saying you're jealous. And you want to wreck things.'

'I don't want to wreck anything,' he said, a little softer now. 'I just want to help you by kicking that arsehole out.'

'Oh, for fuck sake, Jacob,' I said, slamming the palm of my hand back against the wall. 'Just go, will you? Go back to Dublin and stop causing all this hassle.'

Jacob looked at me as if I had forty heads. 'Rachel, what are you talking about? What about what we just did back there?' He pointed towards the bed.

'What about it?'

'We made love. For the first time in three months. It was amazing.'

'It was just sex,' I said, the words tumbling out.

'*Just sex*,' Jacob said. 'Rachel, who do you think you're talking to? This is me, Jacob, not some stranger. Please speak to me normally, for Chrissake.'

A deep sadness enveloped me, but the toxic words continued to tumble from my mouth. 'Jacob, I am speaking to you normally. I was lonely. We shagged. Now you need to leave.'

I had no idea what was making me say these things.

Jacob took a step towards me, grabbed my shoulders. 'Rachel, you can't mean that. I love you. You love me. Whatever has happened, we can get through it together. You know we can.'

His eyes were shimmering now, and I could feel the heat of his body at the point where we touched. Slowly, I removed myself from his grasp. 'Jacob, I'm sorry, I can't deal with this now. Please go back to Dublin.'

'Rachel, come on. This is madness.'

'Jacob. Please.'

Tears were running down his cheeks. 'Rachel, I know there's the kids issue but –'

'Jacob!' I shouted, loud enough to stop him in his tracks. 'Don't you understand? I can't deal with this right now. Have some fucking compassion and just leave me in peace.'

He looked as if I had slapped him hard across the face. For a second he remained completely still. Then, all of a sudden, he swung into action, picking up his jacket from the bedroom floor. 'Fine, if that's what you want, I'll go.'

'Good,' I said, my mouth screwed up in anger.

'Are you sure this is what you want? Because I won't be coming back a second time.'

'I'm sure,' I said. 'Now go.'

46.

Evie

I suppose I'd better get back to Artie, mortifying though it is to think about him. Let's just say it didn't work out. In fact it went badly, badly wrong.

The kiss lasted all of about half a second before Artie pulled back, a look of horror on his face. 'Christ, Evie, I'm so sorry. I shouldn't have done that.' He struggled to get the words out.

'Artie, it's okay,' I said, trying to rub his arm – but he had moved away from me.

'Evie, I'm sorry,' he said again. 'I honestly don't know what came over me.'

'It's okay, it was my fault too. I kissed you first. I know it was wrong but . . .' I stopped. If I'd known it was wrong, why had I done it? Normally I harboured nothing but revulsion for adulterers, for people who tore apart families.

'Evie,' Artie said quietly, trying to gather himself, 'look, we had a bit to drink. We're both tired and emotional.'

I shrugged.

'And we never got to say goodbye all those years ago, not properly, I mean.'

I hung my head in shame. That had been my fault – I had skulked off to London without telling him. I hadn't even left a note.

'So let's chalk up what happened back there to a final goodbye. Closure, if you want to call it that.'

I stared at him, trying to figure out if he was being serious or not. Back when I'd known him, he'd never used words like 'closure'. But he was different now that he was with Shannon.

'Evie,' Artie said. 'We have a lot of history together. We loved each other once upon a time. So maybe that was all those long-lost feelings coming to the surface.'

I felt my heart leap.

But my hopes were dashed.

'I'm in love with Shannon now, Evie. We have a little baby on the way.' He dropped his head, then looked up again. 'So I want to apologize – I was completely out of order. And now, for both our sakes, I think we should say goodbye.'

'Goodbye?' I squeaked.

'Yes. I don't think we should meet up again. It's not fair on any of us, most especially Shannon, and we need to move on with our lives. Agreed?'

His wild curly hair was even wilder and curlier than usual – and in that instant I felt such a surge of pain that I thought I would faint with the power of it. I realized how much I loved him – how much I had always loved him. But I had cast him away and now it was too late. He was right: the only decent thing to do was to let him go. His place was with Shannon and his child now. And I would never be so callous as to break up a family. After all, I had come from a broken home. I knew what the reality of that was like.

'Okay,' I whispered, unable to look at him.

'Evie,' he said, not daring to touch me again. 'Please promise me you'll take care of yourself.'

'I will.'

'Will you?'

'Yes,' I repeated, more forcefully. 'I will. And you mind yourself too – good luck with the wedding and the baby and all that.'

'Thanks,' Artie said, casting me one final sorrowful look, then turned on his heel and walked into the Tube station. By the time I'd wiped the tears from my eyes, he was gone.

For days afterwards, I couldn't sleep. I paced around my flat, wide-eyed and wild, unable to cope with the loss. I felt as if someone had flayed me alive so that every nerve was now raw and exposed to the world. My whole body was tingling.

At some point during that mad period, Donnagh texted me, asking if I wanted to meet up. The words barely made sense to me. I was almost delirious from crying and lack of sleep – but somewhere in the back of my mind an idea formed: perhaps Donnagh could be the answer to all of this. How else was I going to stop thinking about Artie? I figured I needed something extreme to snap me out of the morass into which I'd fallen: some kind of shock therapy. And Donnagh was nothing if not shocking. Maybe he'd help me cope with these feelings.

Of course it was madness. But it seemed like the lesser of the two evils because, one thing was for sure, if I didn't find a way to prevent myself obsessing about Artie – about all that I had lost by casting him aside – I really would go mad. And though Donnagh was terrifying and predatory, losing my reason would be worse. Nothing was as scary as that.

I texted him back, and made plans to meet him in a bar – where I proceeded to get legless. As did he. Afterwards, we went to a club and did a few lines of coke, before returning to Donnagh's apartment to finish what we'd started. The sex was messy, drunken, dirty. High on drugs and drink, I didn't have any inhibitions so I sucked, caressed, kissed, bit and did whatever else Donnagh asked me to do with not a care in the world. It was only the next morning when I woke up in a tangled mess of sheets that reality hit me.

'Where are you going?'

I was tiptoeing out of the door when I heard Donnagh's voice boom after me.

'Eve?'

I turned to face him, blushing scarlet.

'Are you trying to escape?'

'No,' I said, feeling about eight.

'Then why are you carrying your handbag?'

'I don't know.' I hung my head.

'Come back to bed,' he said. 'I've got something I want to show you.' He pulled back the duvet to reveal a huge hard-on and I felt a sudden sensation of terror.

'I think I should be going,' I said, panicky now, not sure I could really go through with this.

Donnagh got out of bed, naked, walked over to where I was standing and took my handbag from me. 'Baby, you're going nowhere.'

Then he led me back to bed.

*

Afterwards, he rolled a joint and we smoked it together. The depression and anxiety that had been hovering over me since the Artie debacle were gradually receding.

'Do you smoke much?' I asked.

'Occasionally, but I try to keep it to a minimum. You?'

'The same.' Which was, of course, a lie.

'You're a sexy bitch, do you know that?' Donnagh was nibbling at my shoulder, and as he did so, I found myself touching his hair. I had expected it to be rough, but it was soft, like a baby's. Everything felt surreal.

And, oh, the temptation to blurt out everything. To tell him who I was. Would he still call me a 'sexy bitch' if he found out I was the fat little swot he had bullied for years? The girl he'd humiliated at the side of the swimming-pool. Yet something held me back from saying anything.

Self-destructive. That was what Janet had called me, a week before our big fight over Patrick. 'You've got so much going for you and you're throwing it all away, Evie,' she'd said. 'People would give their right arm for what you've got.'

'And what have I got?'

'I'm not going to spell it out for you.'

'Course you're not,' I sneered.

'Fine, be like that,' Janet had said. 'But the only person you're hurting with this behaviour is yourself. Nobody is going to swoop down from the sky and save you. You have to do that yourself.'

'You don't understand.' I'd felt wounded. 'You haven't lost your mother. You have a father who actually cares about you.'

'Evie,' she said, her voice softening, 'I know you've had

some terrible blows. But taking lots of drugs and shagging random men is not going to fix that. It's just going to make things worse. Why don't you see a counsellor? I can help you find one.'

I'd thought suddenly of the useless eejit in Trinity, her middle-class tweediness. I couldn't bear the thought of another person in open-toed sandals asking me to 'stay with the feelings'.

'Thanks for the offer,' I'd replied, 'but if I want to blow eighty quid on something utterly pointless I'll go to Harvey Nichols.'

'Christ, there's no reasoning with you, is there?' Janet had snapped, and stomped off to her room.

Now, in Donnagh's bedroom, I was getting dressed in the previous night's clothes, sparkly top and skinny jeans, when Donnagh came up behind me and put his arms around my waist. 'We should make this a regular thing, Eve, if you're up for it.'

'Hmm,' I said, still woozy from the joint we'd smoked. 'Why not?'

'I'll text you during the week, yeah? We can hook up at the weekend.'

'Sure,' I said, as breezy as someone who was having a careless fling.

Donnagh kissed me hard on the mouth. 'Stay beautiful,' he said, slapping me lightly across the backside. His phone began to ring at that exact moment, and he grabbed it from the bed: 'Donnagh Flood speaking.'

I watched him, his body drenched in light as the sun shone through the huge glass window. He looked like a sun god – beautiful and big and imposing.

I tried to say goodbye but he wasn't looking at me. He had turned his back and was lost in conversation. I doubted he even noticed me leave.

A pattern began to emerge. We would meet on a Saturday night, take quite a lot of drugs together (well, I would: Donnagh tended to stick to alcohol), then go back to his apartment and have sex. Then, on the Sunday, we would smoke a joint, have more sex, and I would go home. He didn't seem to suspect anything, and I was almost past caring. In a way, meeting Donnagh at the weekend was just an excellent way of passing the time. Since Janet had gone I'd been so lonely, and after the Artie fiasco I hated being alone with my thoughts. At least with Donnagh I was doing something: I wasn't getting stuck inside my own head.

Sometimes, a lightning flash of realism would surge through me and I would be jolted. It had happened earlier in the week when I'd been watching a programme on Amsterdam's red-light district. If Janet had been there, I'd have turned it over – women who slept with lots of different men were a bit too close to the bone for my liking – but instead I'd been glued to it, like some kind of voyeur.

'Many of the women are trafficked here from impoverished regions outside the EU,' an earnest Dutch academic was explaining. 'They come here thinking they are going to be dancers or performers, but instead are forced into the sex trade.' It cut to a shot of women in the familiar red windows, their flesh squeezed into leather hot pants, schoolgirl uniforms, sexy-secretary get-ups.

'Mostly I just feel numb,' a prostitute was explaining, in

Moldovan. 'I turn off my feelings. I take drugs. I try not to think.'

Her words hit me with the force of a brick. I thought of Donnagh, his huge thighs wrapped around me, pushing in deeper and deeper. It wasn't a violation because I allowed him to do it to me. Yet my body refused to respond. It was as if everything was frozen down there, as if I was a female Antarctica.

It wasn't Donnagh's fault. It was the same with every man I'd brought into my bed since I'd left Artie and Ireland. They could never bring me to the places he had. No matter how hard I tried, it was as if I couldn't get back there. All that was over now. That part of me was gone.

47.

It was the third Sunday in a row that we had done the clubbing/sex/joint in bed thing. I turned on the television and rolled myself a joint, feeling guilty about it, as I always did. But I promised myself I would cut down when the thing with Donnagh had run its course. Either that or I would finally wreak my revenge. I would tell him who I was, perhaps when he was tied to the bed wearing handcuffs, then leave him, naked and vulnerable.

Yes, that would be good.

Make him suffer.

Yet each time we met my grand plan failed to materialize. I would just go along with things. Party with him. Sleep with him. Almost as if I was grateful to be sleeping with him. Almost as if I wanted his approval.

'Come on, let's do something for the day,' Donnagh said, all clean and buffed from the shower.

'Like what?' I said. After that disastrous party, I was terrified of going anywhere with him.

'I dunno. Do you throw Frisbee?'

'Um, not really.'

'We could go to a football match?'

I made a face.

'Will we just get breakfast and see from there?'

'Sure,' I said, trying to sound nonchalant. It was just breakfast. How hard could that be?

Hard, was the answer.

Mick and Gemma Flaherty just happened to swing by.

'How did you know we were here?' I asked, faint with panic that they would properly sniff me out this time.

'Donnagh texted us to join you. Are we interrupting a romantic day or something?'

'No, no,' I blathered, turning puce. What the fuck was he up to?

'So, Eve, where did you say you were from again?'

'Leit–' I stopped myself. 'Clare,' I bumbled.

'Whereabouts in Clare?' continued Mick. 'I have relatives in Ennis.'

Darts of terror needled my innards. Where was I from? Think, think, think. 'I'm from Lisdoonvarna,' I said, trying to sound cool. I had been there once, on a geography trip to the Burren.

'Ah, Lisdoon,' Gemma said. 'Great craic for the Matchmaking Festival, isn't it?'

'Yeah, yeah,' I said, still suspicious of her, given the weird conversation we'd had in the Ladies.

'You must have spent your life in the Hydro.'

'Ah, yes, the Hydro.' I smiled weakly. I had no idea what the hell she was talking about.

'I don't know if I've mentioned this,' said Gemma, 'but you remind me of someone.'

'Oh?' I felt as if someone was squeezing my neck extremely tightly. 'Who's that?'

'Well, that's the thing. I don't know,' she continued. 'It's like I've met you before. But I can't have done, can I?'

'I don't think so,' I squeaked.

'Maybe it's someone famous,' she muttered.

'I think she looks a bit like Kate Winslet,' Donnagh interrupted.

'Who's she again?' said Mick, chomping a sausage.

'Jesus, Mick, where have you been living for the past fifteen years? The one who starred in *Titanic*. Kate fuckin' Winslet.'

'Oh, yeah, her.' He peered at me intently. 'I suppose you do a bit.'

I dropped my eyes to the floor, terrified I'd reveal myself if he held my gaze much longer.

'You look like Angelina Jolie,' I said suddenly to Gemma, hoping flattery would take the heat off me.

'Oh, go on out of that! I do not!' she said, patting her hair.

'You know Gemma won Miss Leitrim 2005?' Donnagh said, a smirk on his face.

'Oh, yes, of course,' I said, then stopped myself. How could I possibly know that? All three were staring at me now, clearly wondering the exact same thing. I felt a rivulet of sweat run down my back. Think again. Quickly. 'Um, this is kind of embarrassing but I googled you after I met you at the party.'

'Oh, yeah?' said Gemma. And the others started to laugh.

'You have a stalker on your hands there, Gem.'

Gemma's lips pursed.

'Yeah, sorry. It's the journalist in me. Anyway, there was a picture of you with your crown and sash and everything. You looked really beautiful.'

'Thanks,' she said, seeming to relax a little. 'But it feels like a lifetime ago now – before I had babies when I still had a waist.' She patted a non-existent tummy.

'Don't mind her, Eve,' said Mick. 'She's always been a stunner, and well she knows it. A bit like yourself, I'd say.'

'Not exactly,' I said, looking at the floor again, just praying this stupid brunch would end soon.

'Eve has hidden depths,' Donnagh said suddenly. 'She doesn't like talking about her past.'

I raised my eyes to meet his, but he was munching a piece of toast, as innocent as you like.

'It's because she's French, I reckon. She likes to add a bit of mystery. Isn't that right, Eve?'

'Hmm.' I began to tremble. Did he know something? Was he playing me? The awful truth was, I honestly couldn't tell.

Later, when I went to the loo, I noticed Gemma and Donnagh huddled outside, smoking. They both looked very tense, almost as if they were having a row. But they quickly reverted to normal as soon as they saw me.

Later, in the car, Donnagh told me Gemma thought Mick was having an affair.

'Is he really?' I asked, relieved the focus had been diverted from me.

'Maybe,' Donnagh said, not taking his eyes off the road. 'But I can't entirely blame him.'

'What are you talking about? Gemma's absolutely gorgeous. And she seems, um, nice, I suppose.'

Donnagh threw me a sideways glance. 'No, she doesn't, Eve. She's a pain in the butt.'

'Yeah, but it's still a pretty shitty thing to do. He must be a bit of an arsehole.'

Donnagh's face tightened. 'Hey, that's my best friend

you're talking about. And you've only just met him. It's not as simple as that.'

'I'm sorry,' I muttered, suitably rebuked. 'I just didn't warm to the guy, but if you say he's decent . . .'

For a moment, there was silence, then Donnagh glanced across again, a funny look on his face. 'Sometimes I wonder about you, Eve Durant.'

'You do?' I said, feeling my insides flip. By complaining about Mick, had I inadvertently revealed myself? 'What do you wonder?'

'I wonder what happened to you to make you so suspicious. You seem so wary sometimes, particularly of men.'

I was dumbstruck by the irony.

'Eve.'

'I'm not wary,' I said eventually. 'I just didn't warm to Mick, that's all.'

Donnagh sighed. 'Look, I admit he has his faults, and he can be a bit loud and brash sometimes, but Gemma is the real problem. She's the selfish and manipulative one.'

The harshness of his tone surprised me.

'She uses people. She takes what she wants.'

'Is that why you broke up with her?' I asked quietly.

'What?' Donnagh flicked his eyes to meet mine.

'When you were a kid. She told me you used to go out together.'

'Oh, right, yes, we did.' He changed gear in the car.

'Yeah, well, I realized what she was like years ago, but Mick, well, he wasn't quite so lucky.'

'What are you going to do?'

'Me?' said Donnagh, his voice rising a little. 'What can I do? If he's sleeping around, nothing I can do about it.'

'Will you cover for him if need be?'

Donnagh shrugged. 'I suppose so. As I said, the guy's my best friend.'

I was breathing deeply. I seemed to have got away with things for the moment, but this couldn't go on. It had to stop.

'But he will get caught,' said Donnagh.

'Why do you say that?' I stammered.

'Because everyone gets caught eventually,' he said. 'In fact, some people want to get caught.'

'That's not true.'

'Isn't it? The thing is, it's just a matter of when.'

48.

Rachel: day twelve, 3 p.m.

I had been seized by a depression so out of control I could barely breathe. Mammy was gone, Evie was teetering on the verge – and now Jacob, my beloved Jacob, had left my life too. Or, rather, I had pushed him away. Without him, I felt completely untethered. For the briefest moment, I toyed with the idea of jumping off Evie's balcony – joining Evie and Mammy in the dark ranks of unconsciousness.

But, of course, I did nothing of the sort.

Instead, after wallowing in self-pity for several hours, I'd finally got out of bed and tried to pick up my detective work where I'd left off, looking for clues around the apartment that I might have missed.

But my heart wasn't in it and after a while, with absolutely nothing to show for it, I finally abandoned my project and went to the same park Jacob and I had been in the previous day. I walked in circles until eventually I plonked myself down on a wet bench. In the distance, an old man, an artist, was painting the same horse-chestnut tree we'd stood under during the rainstorm. I watched him for a while, trying to come to terms with everything that had happened, that might happen.

Jacob and I were over. That much was clear. And as for

my detective work, that had come to a dead end too. I'd found nothing. Or nothing useful, at any rate. And even if I had done, what difference would it have made? Could it conjure Evie from her coma, like some runic spell?

Of course not.

After that I continued walking, tears plopping down my cheeks and onto my chin. I had tried hard. Too hard perhaps. And what had I to show for it? Nothing but a bunch of hurt, aggro and stress. Perhaps it would have been better if I hadn't tried. If I'd followed DI Ainsworth's advice at the beginning and left well enough alone.

At some point, I saw that the old man was packing up his easel and brushes and thought he was gesturing towards me – as if he was trying to say hello. All of a sudden I found myself walking in his direction, childhood thoughts coming back to me of my dad, of oils, of canvas, and then the man was backing away from me, clearly bewildered. 'I'm sorry,' I muttered, coming out of my trance, looking into his bemused eyes. 'I thought I knew you from somewhere.'

'No,' he said, shaking his head. 'No, we don't know each other from anywhere.'

Mortified, I hurried away, cheeks flaming, no idea why I had acted like such a complete and utter fool.

In a nearby café I nursed a cup of tea and tried to get a grip on myself. It was like I was losing my mind along with everything else, turning into some mad person who accosted strangers. But there had been something about the man, something that had reminded me . . .

He was an artist, Rachel, but he was troubled.

Out of nowhere, Mammy's voice rang out, clear as day. A memory of a conversation we'd had when she was dying. When she'd been talking about my father, what he'd been like.

'An artist,' I'd replied. 'You said he was a fisherman.'

'He was. But his real passion lay in art. He painted you as children, do you remember?' I shook my head, though I did vaguely recall something – me and Evie under an old oak tree, the warmth of the light streaming onto our skin.

'I have the sketchbooks somewhere. If only I could find them.' She'd tried to get out of bed then, attempting to throw off the sheets like a wilful child.

'Mammy,' I said, catching her by the shoulders, directing her gently back into bed. 'It doesn't matter about the sketchbooks or about Daddy.'

'But it does,' she wailed. 'It does. I got it all wrong, you see. I should have told you everything. I thought I was protecting you but I wasn't.'

I remained silent. What was she on about? What was this about protecting us? But then I reminded myself that these were just words. Ravings. She was on a lot of painkillers.

'It was the illness, not him,' she whispered. 'I know that now.'

There was a cold, hard feeling in the pit of my stomach, like a stone.

'He tried for so long, Rachel. Five years. But it was the eighties. There was no work. Then he slipped into a depression . . .'

'Depression?'

'Yes,' Mammy said. 'I suppose nowadays you might call

it bipolar. Some days he was in great form, full of plans, full of ambition, and other days . . .'

'Other days?' I couldn't contain my curiosity.

But Mammy's voice had trailed off, the morphine overtaking her.

Later that night, she had taken a turn for the worse, and the conversations about my father had stopped, so I never found out what he had done on those other days. I didn't really want to know. That way madness lay.

I paused, churning the memory in my head. Was that what Evie had too? Bipolar disorder? Could that explain the mood swings, the creativity, the alleged drug-taking and promiscuity that Janet had talked about?

I'd never for a moment thought Evie could suffer from something as serious as that. But suddenly I could see how it would all fit. And if it did, had Ainsworth been right all along? Had Evie been trying to kill herself?

I'd always rejected the simplistic idea that Evie had chosen to take Donnagh's car and crash it into a wall – but maybe I had to face up to the fact that it made sense. She'd had an illness; she was spiralling out of control. And it wasn't as if she hadn't tried before – back when she was twenty-one, at the end of her second year in college.

I thought of that time now too – Mammy on the phone to me in Australia, where I was working at the time, trying to bite back sobs as she explained that Evie had downed a cocktail of prescription drugs and vodka. Her flatmate had come back just in time to call an ambulance.

Stupid, stupid girl, I'd thought at the time, as I flew home, enraged by Evie's selfishness. But when I finally saw her, that gaunt, shivering thing, I knew I'd got the wrong end of the stick. The question wasn't why Evie had tried to kill herself, but how, through all her suffering, she'd stayed alive for so long.

I spent the rest of the evening googling bipolar disorder. As far as I could tell, there seemed to be numerous different permutations of the condition, ranging from mania and delusions to a version so mild that people often mistook it for high spirits.

I tried to tie some of what I had read to Evie. It often affected highly intelligent, creative people, so that fitted. Some believed it could be exacerbated by trauma, such as bereavement. Again, that would apply to Evie.

But at the same time I couldn't be sure. Did Evie experience racing thoughts, euphoria? As a kid she'd been highly energetic and disciplined – she often studied for five or six hours a night – and I knew she also experienced low moods. But did that make her bipolar? I had no idea.

I scrabbled around on the internet for a bit longer, finally landing on a list of famous people who'd suffered with the condition: Sylvia Plath, Virginia Woolf, Stephen Fry, Vincent Van Gogh, Michelangelo.

Van Gogh.

I remembered the *Starry Night* poster on Evie's desk at work. The postcard of the two children I'd found among her mail. He'd been an inspiration to Evie all her life, his work moving her to emotions she rarely liked to show. Once, after I'd received my first advance, I'd brought Evie to the Van Gogh museum in Amsterdam, and watched as she studied his paintings in tears.

'His story is very sad,' I'd said, wrapping my arms around her shoulders. 'Especially the last few paintings.'

'It's like he knew he was going to die.' She wasn't crying now, just looking past me, past everything.

At the time I hadn't thought much of it. Evie was a sensitive person, we all knew that. Now her words seemed to take on a different hue.

I thought back again to those two objects – the small poster in her office, the Van Gogh postcard she'd received from France. Was there a clue in there? Something to do with that artist? Nothing came to me, and the frustration made me feel like a fly bashing its wings against a windowpane. Where did the answer lie? Was there even an answer? Or was I deluding myself? No grand narrative. No conspiracy theory. Just me, refusing to see reality until, like the fly on the windowpane, I bashed myself apart.

49.

Following hours of such fruitless thought, I decided to go out and get something to eat. But in the end I never made it as far as the burger joint I'd planned to visit. Instead I found myself in a pub, knocking back tumblers of whiskey to deal with the twin emotions currently doing battle in my brain: depression and dread.

As I drank, I thought about Evie and our father. That he still hadn't responded to my voicemail (and probably never would – useless bastard) but, on a deeper level, how much damage he had inflicted on Evie and me by leaving us as kids. His abandonment had rendered Evie so insecure that she'd latched onto anything she could think of to give herself a sense of self-worth – exams and straight As as a teenager, drugs and one-night-stands as an adult. As for me, while my maternal instincts had never been strong, I'd cultivated a secret fear that I could turn out just like him, a disastrous parent. After the termination, I'd ruled out kids altogether. Best to make that decision when I was young and single before any more damage was done.

Eventually, after hours of drinking, I stumbled home to find Donnagh in the sitting room, laughing at something on the telly. He turned to look at me as I staggered through the door. 'Oh, Rachel, I was wondering where you'd got to. Had a good night?'

I stared at him, a funny feeling passing through me. I

didn't like the way he was sitting there, in Evie's blue armchair. So fucking comfortable. 'It was okay,' I slurred. 'You?'

'Just watching a bit of telly. Do you want to join me? You should – it's absolutely hilarious.'

That funny feeling rippled through me again, slowly, like a wave. 'No, thanks,' I said. 'In case you hadn't noticed, I'm not really in the mood for comedy, these days.'

'Rachel?' he said, glancing upwards. 'Have I said something wrong? Are you okay?'

'Okay?' I said. 'You're asking me if I'm okay?'

'Yes,' he said, stiffening a little, clearly regretting the question.

'Oh, I'm fine. Apart from the fact that my husband and I have separated, my sister is in a coma – oh, and the guy who swears blind he loves her is currently laughing his head off at *Mrs* fucking *Brown's Boys.*'

'It's Graham Norton, actually,' Donnagh said, making a feeble attempt at a joke.

I glared at him. 'You think this situation is funny, do you?'

'Of course I don't. I just think you're pissed. That maybe you need a glass of water.' He stood up.

'You're telling me what to do now?'

'Oh, for God's sake, Rachel, of course I'm not. I'm just concerned about you. You seem upset. Has something happened?'

I looked at him, the earnest way he was standing, and felt myself crumple. 'I'm sorry,' I said, collapsing onto the sofa. 'I shouldn't be having a go at you. It's not your fault. I'm just so scared.'

Donnagh walked over to the sink, turned on the tap and poured some water into a glass. Then he returned to where I was sitting and pressed it into my hand. 'Here, drink this. You'll feel better.'

I did as I was told, glad to have someone telling me what to do for a change.

When I was done, Donnagh sat down beside me – close but not touching. 'Rachel, I know you're terrified for Evie, just as I am.' He glanced up at me, and our eyes met. I could see worry in them and they were ringed with purple, as if he hadn't been getting much sleep. 'I know it seems callous, watching stupid TV shows when she's lying in hospital, but I don't know what else to do. I feel so impotent.'

I couldn't resist a watery smile. 'You? Impotent? Surely not!'

He shrugged, gave a half-smile back. 'You know what I mean, Rachel. I have money. I have contacts – well, to some extent, anyway – yet I can't do anything to save my girlfriend. To save the one person who actually means something to me.'

I sighed. I knew exactly how he felt.

'What are we going to do now?' he asked quietly.

'I don't know.'

We were silent for a little while until finally Donnagh stood up. 'Rachel, I meant to say, I'm due to go to Chicago again tomorrow – a brief trip – but I can cancel if you want me to stick around. If you'd prefer not to be alone.'

'It's okay,' I said. 'There's nothing you can do, and I can manage. I'll keep you posted – let you know if anything changes.'

'You're sure?'

'Yes,' I said. 'I'm sure.'

'Oh, and one other thing.'

I looked up from my glass.

'My apartment is nearly ready – I should be able to move in soon, probably when I get back from the trip.'

'What?' I was suddenly winded.

'They finished a little earlier than expected. Are you okay with that?'

'Of course. Why wouldn't I be?' I said.

'No, it's just . . .' Donnagh petered out, a faint blush spreading across his cheeks. 'Well, I'd better be off to bed. Early flight and all that.'

'Yes,' I mumbled. It was weird, but now that it was actually happening, I didn't want him to leave.

The truth was, I would miss him.

Perhaps it was a sense of impending loneliness, but after Donnagh went to bed, I continued to drink until I lapsed into complete unconsciousness. It was stupid, of course, but strangely cathartic. Now that reality had become officially unbearable, drink seemed as good an option as any. Sure, it was just temporary but who cared? At least it offered a momentary window of reprieve.

At some point in the night I vaguely recalled Donnagh coming back in, possibly to get a glass of water, possibly handing me one too. But perhaps I'm imagining that. And perhaps I also imagined trying to get off the couch, feeling wobbly. Falling backwards. Thinking, Fuck it, I can sleep here – right here on the floor.

Whatever, the next morning Donnagh was gone – with a note saying he'd be back in a week. And then it was just me, chronically hung-over, on the floor, nursing the worst headache I'd ever experienced in my life.

When I tried to remember the previous few hours, nothing would come. It wasn't so much that my memories were scattered. Quite the opposite. I had no memories at all.

It took almost four days for the toxic hangover to lift – during which time all kinds of weird shit ran through my head. In the end I put my suffering and memory loss down to the fact that, as well as drinking half a bottle of whiskey, I'd also contracted flu. That would explain the aches and pains. The lethargy. This strange mind fog I'd been experiencing ever since I'd got so stupendously drunk.

Eventually, though, the symptoms passed, and while the episode had left me rattled, I soon got back into my routine of visiting Evie, the days bleeding into one another until I could barely tell them apart.

We were nearly three weeks in now. I felt I was on the final countdown. If she didn't wake up within the next seven days, it was over. Okay, technically, Evie could wake up after that. But she would probably be brain-damaged or, at the very least, partially disabled. It would be virtually impossible for her to go back to leading a normal life.

In the evenings I arrived home to an empty flat and wished Donnagh was still there to keep me company. Yes, I'd mistrusted him at the beginning, but now I saw he had acted as an anchor, tethering me to real life, to the real world.

He'd texted me, saying he was staying longer than anticipated in Chicago, but that he'd be back as soon as he could. In the meantime, he was visiting a neurologist his uncle knew, asking for a second opinion. It all sounded very worthy, but I couldn't help feeling he was distancing himself, running away.

Quite frankly, I envied his ability to run.

Everything was losing its shape now. I couldn't tell what day or date it was. Seven days left to go, until we were into the dreaded month-long coma.

Sometimes when I got home I didn't eat. I just sat on Evie's beautiful blue armchair and rocked slowly back and forth, trying not to think about another funeral. About losing another person I loved. In those moments I thought of Jacob. And sometimes, when I did, everything that had happened between us seemed so stupid, so trivial. Who cared if he had (almost) slept with another woman or that we were at odds over children? Surely we could reach a compromise. Surely we could work something out. Yet every time I picked up the phone to reconcile, something stopped me. I wasn't sure what it was. Stubbornness? Stupidity? An inability to forgive?

But then it occurred to me, late one night as I sat smoking a cigarette on the balcony, I could not reignite my life while Evie's hung so precariously in the balance. Maybe I could move forward some day, when all of this was over, but for now I was waiting for my sister to wake up. To come back to me. Until that happened, nothing else could be done.

50

Evie

I'll admit things begin to get a bit hazy after brunch with Gemma and Mick. But as far as I know the following was what happened. There was a flood – a big one – in Donnagh's apartment block and he asked to move in with me for a little while. I think it was something to do with my flat being relatively close to his office in Canary Wharf. I can't be entirely sure.

Anyway, my further recollections suggest I let him.

What the fuck was I thinking? But you must remember I'm Irish and therefore in possession of extremely low self-esteem. It is literally embedded in my genes to be a people-pleaser. Saying no was not an option.

So he moved in – ostensibly for a few days. Well, five long days, actually, during which time I was forced to stash away all my books and paintings and photographs so that he wouldn't uncover my real identity and realize how much I had lied. Luckily, I had a hiding place – a legacy from the Second World War, which the estate agent had shown me when I'd first viewed the flat. At the time it had seemed like a quaint little folly – to be honest, I'd almost forgotten about it. Now it was a godsend – the shifty person's equivalent of a walk-in wardrobe.

Having said that, Donnagh didn't look like a man who had much time for sleuthing – he was gone by seven in the morning and not home till ten or eleven at night. In fact, by the time Friday afternoon rolled around, I was marvelling at how straightforward the whole thing had been, and was looking forward to seeing the back of him that evening. But another call at work put the kibosh on that.

'The repairs are going to take at least another fortnight, Eve. I'm really sorry to ask, but do you mind if I stay at yours a bit longer?'

I felt like slamming the phone hard against the wall. This guy had loads of money: he could afford any five-star hotel in London. Why was he insisting on staying with me?

'I can go to a hotel, if you'd prefer,' he said, but I could tell there wasn't much heft behind it.

'No, no,' I replied. 'It's fine. Of course you can stay with me.'

He'd thanked me profusely and promised to make it up to me that night.

Donnagh worked a half-day that Saturday, then col-lapsed on the couch and fell asleep, meaning we ended up staying in and getting a takeaway rather than going out on our usual hedonistic rampaging. As I tried to eat my sweet and sour chicken, I sneaked peeps at him out of the cor-ner of my eye. He was wearing a pair of tracksuit bottoms and a hoodie – more relaxed than I'd ever seen him – laughing at something on the telly. To the naked eye, he looked like a normal guy. A supremely good-looking, tanned guy, but a normal one nonetheless.

A thought struck me. Was he normal? Had he grown out of that evil teenage-boy phase and become a vaguely acceptable human being?

Hard though it was to admit, he'd been pretty decent to me over the past few weeks. There'd been countless bunches of flowers and numerous restaurant trips. And even though I hadn't expected it, on each of those occasions he'd made me laugh, treated me with courtesy . . .

Another thought struck me, disconcerting this time: was it wrong to be lying to him? Should I come clean about who I really was?

I gave myself a stern talking-to: there was no way I could reveal my true identity – not yet anyway. He'd think I was a lunatic, a psychopath. No, better to wait a while, see where this thing was going.

My breath caught. *This thing?* Had I taken leave of my senses? Was I honestly contemplating a relationship with Donnagh Flood? Did I actually think we had a future together?

I looked back to where he was sitting, my heart skipping a beat. He was still the most beautiful man I'd ever seen in my life.

'Eve, why do you keep staring at me?'

I nearly jumped out of my skin. 'I'm not staring. I'm . . .' I could feel myself blushing furiously.

'Can't believe what a handsome devil you've wound up with, is it?' He'd curled his mouth into a grin, showing perfect white teeth.

'Something like that,' I said, then turned my attention back to my takeaway.

It was hard to believe a leopard could change his spots. Did that ever happen? And, most importantly, did I even want to find out?

51.

The next day Donnagh declared he was all mine.

That was what I'd been afraid of. I'd hoped he would be working as usual, but when I asked him he shook his head. 'Nope. Man needs a break occasionally. I'm taking today off.'

My stomach heaved. The thought of seeing Mick and Gemma again was too much to bear.

'Why don't we go for a drive?' he suggested.

'Um, sorry, I have an article to finish,' I lied.

'On a Sunday?'

'Yes,' I said. 'It'll take me several hours.'

Donnagh's brow furrowed. 'Well, why don't you get up and finish it now? I was going to ravish you, but if you insist on working . . .'

I looked at him, at the grin on his face, and realized there was no point in arguing. He was going to bring me on a drive and that was the end of it. Might as well accept the inevitable.

An hour later, he popped his head into my 'study', which was Janet's old room. 'How are you getting on?'

'Fine,' I said, not making eye contact. I'd spent the last sixty minutes looking at the *Daily Mail* website, and watching videos of cats on YouTube.

'Will you be ready to go soon?'

I couldn't spend another hour fecking around,

pretending to work. Plus I felt jangly – there had been no drugs or drink that weekend – as if I was going to burst with anxiety. Maybe getting out was a good idea.

So off we went to Brighton. To walk the pier, and look at the sea and eat greasy fish and chips. As we walked, Donnagh held my hand. 'Which of us should go first?' he said, a half-smile playing on his face.

'Go first with what?'

'Talking about our childhood. I warn you, mine's more *Angela's Ashes* than *The Cosby Show*.'

'Why do you want to know about mine?'

Donnagh shrugged. 'Because it dawned on me we've been seeing each other for nearly seven weeks now, and I know next to nothing about you.' He smiled. 'Well, of course, some parts of you I know very well . . .'

I hit him with the side of my handbag.

'Oh, come on, Eve. Give me something. Sometimes I think you work for MI5, you're so secretive.'

'I'm not.'

'Oh, come on, you are.'

'What do you want to know? I've already told you I'm from Clare and my parents were French.'

'Are they still alive?'

'No,' I said quickly.

'Any brothers or sisters?'

'No,' I replied again, guilt enveloping me. It felt wrong, denying Rachel like that. But then again, it wasn't like I could tell him the truth.

Donnagh stopped walking. 'It feels like there's something you're not telling me.'

I froze. Had he discovered something? I'd been so

careful with my stuff, hiding it all away, but maybe I'd for-gotten something: a note, a photo? Had he hacked into my email?

'Jesus, Eve, don't worry, I'm only joking.'

I looked up into his face, into his huge brown eyes, and couldn't figure out what was happening. If he was taunt-ing me, I was damned if I'd go down without a fight. 'Donnagh, I –'

'Look, we've all got things from our past. Things maybe we're ashamed of or not ready to share. I get it. I didn't mean to push you.' He swept a tendril of hair away from my face. 'God, you're lovely, do you know that?' He was gazing into my eyes now, holding me around the waist.

I didn't know what to do.

'I have plenty of my own skeletons,' he said. 'Some day maybe I'll tell you about them.'

'Why not today?'

'Are you kidding?' he said. 'You want me to open up like I'm on *Oprah* but refuse to spill any beans yourself?'

'It's my right as a woman to be enigmatic.'

'Hmm,' he said. 'Pleading the fifth, as usual, I see. Well, okay, if you really want me to spill my guts, shall we sit down?' He pointed at the pebbles, gesturing for me to sit. He did likewise. 'Okay. If you insist, I'll tell you one secret. Just the one, mind. And you must promise to be very sympathetic.'

'I promise.'

'Okay,' he said, taking a deep breath. 'My secret is . . .'

I waited.

'I used to be married.'

'What?' I was genuinely shocked.

'Yes, back in the States. Her name was Maria and she was the most beautiful woman I'd ever met in my life. Before you, of course.'

'What happened?'

Donnagh shifted a little. 'I caught her in bed with the gardener.'

'Christ. That's rough.'

'Yeah, it wasn't the best, all right. Especially since I was twenty-two, hot-headed and crazy in love with her.'

'What did you do about it?'

Donnagh looked at me for a second. 'It wasn't pretty.'

'I don't imagine it was.'

'I got into a huge fight with the guy. Got my nose broken. Then she moved in with him, taking most of our savings and my car. We got divorced, and later they married.'

'Are they still together?'

'I believe so,' Donnagh said, his mouth drawn in a hard line. 'Needless to say, we're not exactly Facebook friends.'

We sat for a second, not saying anything. Then Donnagh faced me. 'Okay, so, your turn.'

'Donnagh, that wasn't part of the deal.'

'Oh, Eve. Give me something. I've bared my soul to you.'

He looked at me and I nearly opened my mouth to speak – but at the last moment I held back.

'Okay, if you're going to be like that, let me ask you something.'

I shrugged.

'You don't have to answer if you don't want to but let

me ask anyway.' He paused. 'Have you ever been in love?'

I gasped, shocked by the bluntness of his question. 'Um, yes, I guess I have,' I muttered. 'Hasn't everybody?'

'Tell me about it. What happened?'

I thought of Artie, the beauty of what we'd shared. 'It just didn't work out,' I said. 'I moved to England. We broke up. That's it. No big drama.'

'Right,' said Donnagh, nodding, deep in thought. 'And do you think you could ever love someone again?'

I looked at the golden flecks shimmering in his eyes. I didn't know what to say.

'The thing is,' he continued, 'after my wife left me, it made me hard, you know.' He was swirling patterns on my hand with his finger and I was letting him. 'I didn't think I could ever . . .' He stopped. Looked at me. For a moment it was as if everything stood still. 'It's not easy to love again, is it? Once you've had it and lost it.'

'No,' I said, and for once I agreed with him.

'But lately, I don't know . . .' He brushed his hand against my face.

A hard gust came in from the sea, buffeting us. 'Here, take this.' He removed his coat and wrapped it round me.

I found myself encased in the smell of his aftershave, a musky, heady scent. 'Donnagh, I . . .' But I didn't finish the sentence. In fact, I didn't even know what I was going to say.

He kissed my nose. 'We should get back.'

'We should.'

He laced his hand through mine and squeezed it.

We didn't say much on the return journey, didn't need

to. It was only later that I realized I'd been smiling the whole way.

Life went on. Donnagh continued to share the apartment with me and I decided that having him around wasn't so bad after all. He'd changed at least two light bulbs, and even unblocked the shower.

One Thursday evening I came home to find that he had cooked a meal for me. 'Hmm, smells nice,' I said. 'What's this in aid of?'

'Oh, you know,' Donnagh said, kissing me lightly on the forehead. 'Just treating my girlfriend to some home-cooked supper.'

'*Supper?* You're Irish, for God's sake. Would you ever cop on to yourself!' I scolded, but inwardly all I could think about was that he had just called me his girlfriend. And that I didn't necessarily hate the moniker.

Afterwards we lay on the couch and he stroked my hair. 'Did you enjoy the food?' he said, and I nodded. Even though I'd only had a glass and a half of wine I was in a strangely relaxed mood. At the beginning I'd been so stressed out about Donnagh moving in, about the big lie I was hiding, but as time had gone on things had got better. He was neat, he was easy to live with, and maybe it was my imagination but he seemed to have softened. These days, there was less swagger and he was kinder. Gentler, even.

'Hey, Eve. I just wanted to say thanks.'

'For what?'

'For taking me in, for making me feel so at home.'

'Don't worry about it. Anyone would have done the same.'

'No, they wouldn't. Most people aren't as nice as you.'

I tutted. 'I'm not nice. I'm just Irish. You should know that as a race we're incapable of saying no.'

He laughed. 'Suppose that's true, all right.'

We lay there for a little longer, Donnagh kissing my neck, then slowly moving his hands downwards until they were caressing my breasts. Normally when Donnagh and I had sex I was high or drunk or extremely hung-over. Almost-sober sex was a new experience.

I waited for the fear to swoop in – that sense of danger and disconnection I usually felt, not just with Donnagh but with all men. But the funny thing was, this time I didn't. Donnagh was taking his time, kissing me slowly, lingering over everything. And instead of fear I was beginning to feel desire – genuine, honest-to-God passion. It had been so long since I'd felt anything remotely like it. Years. True, I'd been no stranger to promiscuity since I'd arrived in London but I had felt no desire for any of those men. I'd slept with them so that I wouldn't feel.

'Will we move to the bedroom?' Donnagh said quietly, kissing my cheek.

'Okay,' I said, feeling a flood of nerves going through me. But it was the good sort of nerves. The first-datey kind.

Afterwards I lay looking at the ceiling, counting the shadows, listening to Donnagh beside me. I'd had sex with him lots of times, of course. But never like that. Never so . . . What was the word for it? It had been slow and sensual and I had come. For the first time in six years I'd had an orgasm.

Intimate. That was how I would describe it. Like we really knew each other.

Of course we did know each other. From all those years back. But this was different. As if we now shared a kindred experience.

I shook my head. It was so crazy. *Donnagh Flood.* My nemesis. My enemy. Except now it didn't feel like that. It was as if he was on my side. The truth was, he'd made me feel loved.

52.

Rachel: day twenty-one, 9.30 a.m.

I didn't know what else to do. Who else to turn to. Desperately clutching at straws, I researched alternative treatments for coma patients – mad shit involving Reiki and electromagnetic currents. I stayed up late, printing out reams of 'articles' by dodgy quacks claiming to have restored the comatose to consciousness. Red-eyed and unwashed, I shoved the sheaves of paper into Dr Bartlett's hands as she was doing her morning rounds, demanding that she take a look.

She sighed, then guided me into her office, gesturing for me to take a seat. 'Rachel, I'm so sorry, but the research you've done, well, I'm afraid it's all pretty pointless.'

'What?'

'First, there's no hard evidence that any of the therapies you've looked up actually works. Most of them are carried out by charlatans trying to make a fast buck.'

'Yes, but what if we struck lucky with one? Wouldn't it be worth it?'

Dr Bartlett sighed. 'You're more than welcome to try with the simpler ones – Reiki and aromatherapy and the like. But see this one here, the one that involves transferral to some clinic in Switzerland.' She was tapping one of the pages with her fingernail. 'It's out of the question.

Your sister could die in transit. I really mean that. She could die.'

I stared at Dr Bartlett, at her fine features, and promptly burst into tears. Then, before either of us could comment further, I jumped off my seat and ran out of the room.

After a few moments, rather sheepishly, I tapped on her office door again. 'I'm sorry,' I said. 'I overreacted.'

'No problem,' she said, walking towards the coat-stand and grabbing her jacket. 'Come on, let's get a coffee from the Costa place across the road. We can talk things through there.'

A little later, Dr Bartlett was sprinkling sugar into her flat white. Then she touched my hand gently. 'Rachel, I promise you, everything that can be done for your sister is being done.'

I already knew that. The alternative-treatments thing had been no more than a distraction.

'If you don't mind me saying so,' she continued, 'you're very pale.'

'Mmm,' I muttered. I hadn't slept properly since Jacob had left. Actually, I hadn't slept at all.

'Plus you've lost a lot of weight. Have you been eating?'

Food tasted like cardboard. I ate when I remembered, which wasn't often.

It was my turn to ask her a question. 'Why are you being so nice to me?'

'What?' said Dr Bartlett, and just for a second her unflappable demeanour seemed to fall away slightly.

'From what I know, consultants aren't generally known for their bedside manner. They certainly don't bring their patients out for coffee. Is it because you've read my books?'

'Your books?' Dr Bartlett said, furrowing her brow. 'Oh, yes, of course, you're a writer, aren't you? But, no, that's not the reason I'm trying to be helpful.'

I was mortified to have presumed such a thing. 'Why then?'

'Because, first, despite what you've heard, I regard it as my job to support families going through a major trauma such as this.'

Her blue eyes, wide and sparkling, made me think, suddenly, of sky. 'Yes, but you've gone above and beyond. You've been so kind to me.'

Dr Bartlett shrugged. 'Aren't doctors supposed to be kind?'

I laughed a little. 'They're not exactly renowned for it, no.'

She smiled. 'I suppose you're right.'

For a few seconds we sat in silence, sipping our coffee.

'Actually, you remind me of someone,' she continued quietly.

I looked at her, waiting for her to fill in the gap.

'My daughter, Annie,' she continued, in the same soft voice. 'She was so much like you.'

'Was?'

'She died three years ago, in a car crash.' Though Dr Bartlett imparted this information in a clear, matter-of-fact manner, I knew it was a performance. It was the same way I talked about Mammy – quick and clipped. No eye contact. 'I'm sorry,' I said.

She inclined her head a fraction. 'It's okay.'

I wanted to take it all back, my stupid portfolio of coma quacks. How I'd implied she wasn't doing enough to help Evie. But when I tried to say so, Dr Bartlett stopped me. 'You have nothing to be sorry for. You were just looking out for your sister. The thing you must remember, though, is that's exactly what I'm trying to do too.'

As we made our way back to the hospital I forced myself to ask the question I could barely bring myself to voice. 'Do you think Evie will ever wake up, Doctor?'

She looked at me straight on, her eyes less sparkly now than back in the coffee shop. 'I don't want to give you false hope, Rachel. All I can say is, don't give up just yet.'

'But it all seems so hopeless,' I spluttered. 'You already said those treatments I researched are useless. And it's not as if she's displayed any signs of improvement.'

'I'm not talking about treatments, Rachel. I mean believing in here.' She touched her heart. 'Are you religious?'

'No.'

'Didn't think so. Neither am I particularly. But I did find, after Annie died, some solace in the notion of a higher power. Not God necessarily. Just something. Something outside logic . . .' She stopped walking and looked at me. 'Don't tell any of my colleagues, though, will you? They're quite big on the whole logic thing.'

I raised my eyes to meet hers, returned her sad smile.

'I'd better head back in,' she said, returning to the calm, efficient Dr Bartlett I knew so well. 'Will you be okay on your own?'

I nodded. She touched me lightly on the shoulder and said something about 'keeping strong'. As she walked off, I was reminded of the first day I had met her. How, as she'd walked away, I'd said, 'Mammy,' in her wake. How it had made me think of war, battlefields, France.

That's what my mind was these days: a battlefield. Every day I went out armed with my weapons of logic and reason. And every day I came back battle-weary because those weapons hadn't worked. Perhaps it was time to leave the battlefield. As Dr Bartlett had said, some things were 'outside logic'.

Perhaps I could only fight with my heart now. Or perhaps it was bigger than that. Perhaps there was no point in fighting at all.

I spent the rest of the day by Evie's bedside, holding her hand, thinking of what Dr Bartlett had said. I understood now what I'd been trying to do in playing detective and researching madcap health remedies. On some subconscious level I'd believed that if I could find something logical – the reason Evie had crashed; a revolutionary therapy that would cure her – it would unlock everything. Evie would wake up, like Sleeping Beauty, and we could start again.

I'd been so stupid. Sure, it had kept me occupied for the past three weeks, but piecing together the jigsaw of Evie's last days wasn't miraculously going to resurrect her. As for a course of Reiki . . .

At some point, Dr Bartlett arrived.

'Anything to report?' I said, hoping against hope that there were some signs of recovery, but she shook her head slowly, then walked over to my side of the bed.

'Nothing so far, Rachel,' she said. 'Eveline remains heavily comatose.'

I emitted a kind of sob.

'Would you like me to arrange for the counsellor to see you, talk things through?'

I shook my head. If I signed up for that, I really was admitting defeat, I thought. And whatever shred of hope I still had for Evie, I needed to cling to it.

When she left I took Evie's hand and stroked it. 'Please wake up, Evie,' I whispered. 'Please, for the love of God, come back to me.'

For weeks I'd been able to deal with the nightmare by convincing myself I was some kind of super-sleuth detective and that there was more to this story than met the eye. Now, as I stared at Evie, at the tubes and ventilators keeping her alive, I saw that there was no mystery. My sister was in a coma. She would probably die. It was not a certainty, but the situation was looking increasingly hopeless.

I realized, with a thud, I had not been chasing leads so I could help Evie, so I could magic her out of her coma. I had been running around for myself. So I wouldn't have to think about her death.

53.

Another five days passed. I bumped into Dr Bartlett on one of her daily rounds, her face even less hopeful than when we'd had the chat in the coffee shop. I didn't bother to ask her if there was any sign of improvement. I knew the answer. There was not.

'Rachel,' she began, then faltered. She started again. 'How are you doing?'

I stared at her. *How do you think I'm doing?* 'Okay,' I muttered. 'I'm still hoping for a miracle.'

Dr Bartlett didn't say anything but I knew what she was thinking: *Don't.*

'Look, I know what happens after a month,' I said, just so she realized I wasn't completely deluded. 'You don't believe full recovery is possible. The person is likely to be brain-damaged or may never come out of their coma.'

'It's not an exact science,' she said, though her eyes betrayed her. Her eyes told me all I needed to know.

'What happens if . . .?' I couldn't finish the sentence.

'Rachel, I've still not given up hope of your sister emerging from this state.'

'But if she doesn't?'

'If she doesn't, I can sit down with you and go through the most likely outcomes. The options for care, how we can make her as comfortable as possible . . .'

A tremor went through me. 'Are you talking about Evie being in a permanent vegetative state?'

Dr Bartlett glanced away, as if adjusting something in her mind. Then she looked at me directly. 'Rachel, it hopefully won't come to that. But there may be a possibility your sister will not return to . . .'

'The person she once was?'

'Yes,' she said, averting her gaze again. 'I'm afraid that person may be gone.'

I didn't react. Not immediately. For hours after, I continued to act as if things were completely normal. As if I had never heard Dr Bartlett utter those words.

It wasn't until the middle of the night that it hit me. Like a tsunami. The Evie I remembered might be gone for good. Dr Bartlett had said that. She had made it clear I needed to prepare myself for the worst.

Without thinking, I got out of bed and threw on a battered pair of Evie's runners. It was probably inadvisable to wander through London in the middle of the night, but I didn't intend to walk. I intended to run.

In general I am no athlete, but this time everything felt different – as if I was being fuelled by a new type of energy: fear that I had not shown Evie how much I loved her when she'd been conscious; terror that it was now too late and she would never wake up.

As I ran, I could feel the sweat pouring down my back but I didn't care. It meant I was still alive. On the outside, at least. Inside, I felt dead.

On and on I ran. At times I felt weak and walked for a bit. But it was like my body was immune to normal discomforts. My lungs had grown in capacity; my feet had become strong and tough.

Finally, as dawn began to break, my body gave way and I collapsed onto some stone steps, not bothering to look up at where I was.

I lay there, attempting to get my breath back, watching the sun crack through the early-morning mist. It was so beautiful here. So peaceful. In an hour or so, the city would whirr back into action. I would be just another anonymous face lost among the throngs. But for now it was just me and the stillness, only a few taxis and buses and early-morning workers to disturb the silence.

When I sat up, a huge banner caught my eye: 'Van Gogh's *The Sunflowers* Exhibition 25 August–24 November'. It was only then I realized that I was sitting outside the National Gallery. What a strange coincidence: during my blind midnight run I had finished up in front of a sign for Evie's favourite artist. The source of all that was good and creative in her life.

If I were a more hippy-dippy person, I'd have come to the conclusion she was trying to tell me something – 'I'm not dead yet, Rachel. Please don't give up on me.'

I just sat there, gazing at Trafalgar Square and Nelson's Column, beneath a raspberry-pink sky. My eyes kept returning to the sign for the *Sunflowers* exhibition. I recalled again the weekend Evie and I had spent in Amsterdam at the Van Gogh museum. The poster at her work-station. The postcard she'd received from the elusive 'D' in France.

A ray of sunlight flashed over me, warming me, and it was as if something shifted in my brain. A thought. A connection.

But it couldn't be.

Could it?

I jumped up and ran to a taxi, suddenly stoked with adrenalin. Was this it – the missing piece of the puzzle?

It was a long shot, but I needed to test it.

Perhaps Evie had been guiding me, after all.

54

Evie

My memories of the days directly before the crash are little more than candyfloss. They're so delicate I can barely touch them, and when I do they disintegrate. I've tried and tried to piece them together logically, but each time they collapse, like a soufflé that's just come out of the oven.

So I grasp at little things. The whoosh of a train going through a tunnel, red wine, words being spoken in a foreign language. French, I think.

I can only surmise that, directly before the crash, Donnagh and I went to France. Perhaps Paris – I have a dim recollection of the Marais district, art galleries, walking around hand in hand. How did I let him persuade me to go there? Surely that would have spelled the end of everything. He'd have discovered I didn't speak French fluently and would have seen through my ruse. Had I known I was going to Paris, or did I think I was going somewhere else?

Fragments remain. The bitter taste of strong black coffee as it hit the back of my throat. A soft, warm wind. And then there's me in the Musée d'Orsay, staring at my favourite Van Gogh painting, *Two Children*, depicting two young girls, dressed in white bonnets, holding hands. The children are far from pretty but I love the way they seem so united; how the older one, holding a flower, seems to be reassuring the younger one – as if she's saying, 'Don't be afraid, little one. Things will be okay.'

It's not much of a leap to see that the painting reminds me of myself and Rachel. How close we once were . . .

Memories swirl, making me dizzy and discombobulated. But I know if I can only break through the fuzziness, I'll find the reason I'm in this coma.

I think I bought a postcard of *Two Children* – I bought some others too. I recall handing over money, putting a small paper bag into the side of my handbag.

After that, I can't remember a single thing. What happened in Paris? What did we do? Did I tell Donnagh the truth about who I was? I can't remember. And it's driving me insane.

I fall into an unsettled sleep. When I wake up, something else has come back to me, which convinces me I *was* in Paris with Donnagh. That it's not a false memory.

I recalled being on a waterbus with him, journeying down the Seine. Dusk was falling and the sky was a pink and orange haze – a pastel dream that reminded me of the Impressionist paintings I'd just been looking at in the Musée d'Orsay.

At the Eiffel Tower, Donnagh gently touched my shoulder. 'We're getting out here.' We took the lift up, my ears popping as we ascended. At the top, Donnagh arranged for a waiter to bring us two flutes of champagne, and then we stood there, taking in the panoramic view, marvelling at the carpet of beauty below.

After a little while, Donnagh reached for my hand. 'Eve, I brought you here because I want to tell you something.'

I looked up at him and was surprised to see that he was nervous. 'Okay,' I said, suddenly nervous too. Had he finally figured everything out? If so, then I was going to confess.

Donnagh took a slug of his champagne, then set it aside. 'These past few weeks you've been so good. So helpful and supportive.'

'It was nothing. Anyone would have done it.'

'No, you didn't have to, Eve. You really didn't. And since we've started living together, something else has dawned on me.'

'Oh?' I said, feeling butterflies in my stomach.

'I've realized that . . . I'm in love with you.'

I almost dropped my champagne glass. Did he really just say that? Was I imagining things?

It occurred to me that this was my final chance for revenge. I had achieved my goal – I'd made Donnagh fall hook, line and sinker for me – and now, if I wanted to, I could rub his nose in my victory. The fat girl he tormented for so long was now the chic woman he was in love with.

I'd won.

I'd finally beaten him.

But when I tried to utter a response, nothing came out. Donnagh was looking at me expectantly, almost as if he was holding his breath.

To this day, I don't know what made me do it. The sultry summer air, the pink sky, the fact that he used the word 'love'?

What came out of my mouth was not a victory speech or the revelation of my true identity. It wasn't even a sentence. It was just two words. So simple. So effective. And at that moment not entirely without truth.

'Me too.'

55.

Rachel: day twenty-six, 6.30 a.m.

I almost broke the door down in my impatience to get into Evie's apartment. Inside, I raced to her bedroom. I was damp with sweat and delirious from lack of sleep but I didn't care – not when something so significant had occurred to me.

I grabbed Evie's laptop from where it was sitting on her desk and fired it up. It took an age to get going but at last the password box appeared. Then I typed the seven letters I had thought of on the steps of the National Gallery.

VAN GOGH

The computer whirred, and I didn't move a muscle as I waited, prayed, begged for something to happen.

Finally, the pinwheel stopped spinning and a new screen opened: I was in.

'Yes!'

I opened Evie's email screen and began to search, starting with Donnagh's name. Unsurprisingly, there was quite a bit of correspondence between the two of them, but none seemed particularly noteworthy: most of the emails concerned restaurant bookings, silly jokes forwarded from the internet, the occasional soppy one, like 'Had such a great time last night', that kind of thing. Next, I moved on to my father's name, but there I drew a complete blank. There were no emails at all. Not that I was surprised – he was an elderly fisherman whom Evie hadn't seen in twelve years. He probably didn't even know how to use email.

Finally, I typed in Artie's name. I wasn't expecting much – they'd only met twice, after all – and was a little taken aback to see 'six results found' under his name. I clicked open the first thread of messages:

Eveline, it was so good to run into you the other night. And, yes, Shannon and I would love to meet up with you. How about dinner this Thursday night at our place? Would that suit?

He'd copied in someone called Shannon Curtis – the American fiancée I recalled him mentioning – and underneath was Evie's reply, saying she'd be delighted to, which prompted another email from Artie with an address and a map.

Okay, so Evie clearly had masochistic tendencies to inflict such torture on herself, but the exchange seemed pretty harmless. In any case, Artie had already told me about it, how they'd had a barbecue, how Evie and Shannon had got on. I clicked on the next email thread from Artie, expecting more of the same polite blandness. This time, Shannon had not been copied in.

Evie, I wanted to apologize one more time for what happened last night and say something I didn't have the guts to say to you last night. I feel from our last few encounters that you are sad at the moment. And I know what happened between us last night probably didn't help matters. But even though we can't be in

contact any more, I just want you to know how much I care for
you; what a huge effect you've had on my life. In another world,
things might have been different, but I'm with Shannon now, the
baby is on its way, and I know you will understand why I had to
say what I said last night. Please try not to be so down on yourself.
There are no words to describe how lovely you are. That guy you're
dating — he has won the lottery. I'm not just saying this, Evie. I
really mean it. Please promise me you will allow yourself to live a
happy life. You deserve it. You deserve everything. Artie

I stared at the computer screen — winded by the words in front of me. Sure the sentiment was beautiful, but what the hell was going on? Had I been right the first time? Were he and Evie having an affair?

I noticed Evie hadn't replied to this email. But then again, why would she? Being used like a piece of meat while Mr Perfect swanned back to his pregnant girlfriend. No wonder Evie had been so distracted in the run-up to the accident. No wonder Donnagh had thought she'd been cheating on him . . .

I clicked on a sixth and final email, dated 3 August: the same day as Evie's car crash.

Evie, I know you must be surprised I'm writing to you again,
after that last email I sent. But the truth is, I can't stop thinking
about you. Please will you agree to meet me? I was thinking
tomorrow night at the Horse and Hound in Lewisham. Around
8 p.m. if that suits you?

I stared at just one word: *Lewisham*. That was where Evie had crashed.

And what was all this 'I can't stop thinking about you' nonsense? What the fuck was Artie playing at?

Again Evie hadn't responded. Perhaps she hadn't even seen it. She'd have been on the way back from Paris with Donnagh, probably without internet access. But then again, could I really believe this email had had nothing to do with Evie's car crash? It seemed far too suspicious.

My hands were shaking but whether from fear or anger, I couldn't be sure. I reached for my phone, barely able to hold it properly, then dialled. 'You lying bastard,' I shouted, when he picked up.

'Woah, Rachel. Is that you? You do know it's not even seven a.m. yet?'

'Yes, it's me,' I snapped. 'Like to tell me what was going on between you and my sister? Why you lied to me?'

'What are you talking about?'

'Oh, for fuck sake, Artie. Quit the pretence. I've just found your email correspondence – yours and Evie's. You were obviously sleeping together. You met her the night she crashed.'

'No, I didn't.'

'Artie, I have the email.'

'What email?'

'Jesus Christ,' I said, tempted to slam the phone down.

At the other end of the line I could hear Artie mutter something – it sounded like 'Shannon'. Eventually he said, 'Where are you located?'

'What?'

'Evie's apartment. Where is it? Give me the address.'

'As if you don't know.'

'Rachel, just tell me.'

'Why?'

'Because I want to come over to you. I want to explain everything.'

'Can't you just do it now, over the phone?'

'No,' said Artie. 'I can't.'

I relented and gave him the details. Then, without saying goodbye, I hung up.

I paced Evie's apartment like a wild animal, my mind going one hundred miles a minute. Finally, unable to live with my thoughts for a second longer, I grabbed my jacket and walked down the stairs: a five-minute breather might help to settle me before Artie arrived. However, I was interrupted at the main entrance by a familiar face – the postman I'd seen a few weeks earlier.

'Ah, you're Eve Durant, aren't you?' he said, then rustled through his bag and thrust an envelope into my hand. I took it and watched as he placed the remaining letters in the other occupants' cubbyholes.

Back in the apartment, I stared at the letter in my hands, wondering what to do with it – it was white and thick with Greenwich College of Art and Design written on the front. Something triggered in my brain suddenly – the art course Evie had mentioned months earlier, the one I'd tried and failed to get any information on.

I ripped open the envelope and pulled out the letter.

Dear Ms Durant,

As you are a student on the Art Foundation Course (April intake), I am writing to inform you that your main art project is due shortly and I'm concerned that you haven't attended class for the past six weeks or confirmed the title of your project. From my

notes, I see that you were planning a short video installation, called
Sleep Walker (investigating if the sleepwalking you'd experienced
as a child had returned as an adult, which you believed to be the
case). You told me you were going to use a secret camera to
essentially 'spy' on yourself, see if you could get any footage, which
I felt was a clever, interesting idea, though your decision to involve
a male acquaintance in its installation did raise concerns. (I hope
you took my advice, and kept him out of it.) At any rate, can you
confirm that you still want to submit this project? If you think
you can make the deadline, we could look at ways for you to make
up the lectures you missed – possibly next term.

Best regards,
Ray Jones
Course Director

I stared at the piece of paper. I knew Evie had been doing an art course. But I couldn't remember her mentioning a video installation. I didn't even know she was into that kind of thing. And what was all this about sleepwalking? She'd suffered from it as a kid – chronically, in fact. But could it have returned after all these years?

My mind zigzagged in another direction.

I am watching you.

Those weird emails I'd had. The way they'd been so specific. Had they been connected to the camera Dr Jones was talking about?

I stared at the letter again, focusing particularly on one line: . . . *your decision to involve a male acquaintance in its installation did raise concerns.*

Jesus Christ, had someone helped Evie to set up the camera?

Had someone been in her bedroom?

Could this person be TBM?

In Evie's bedroom I ransacked everything – just as I had the first time – but now I wasn't looking for diaries or photographs or imaginary peepholes. I was looking for something specific.

I was looking for a spycam.

It took next to no time, now I knew what I was looking for. There it was, concealed on top of the curtain rail, trained directly over Evie's bed. I went into the hall, and found a second, perched high up, near the ceiling, partially concealed by the picture rail.

I had no idea what to do now. Should I ring the police and explain what I had just discovered? Or should I try to figure out what it meant?

I am watching you.

TBM flashed through my mind again.

I got out my phone and punched in Lorelei's number. Her reaction was swift and brutal. 'Jesus Christ, Rachel, how could you not have told me about this before? What the fuck were you thinking?'

I mumbled something incoherent.

'Okay. What you need to do now is pack your bags and go straight to the police.'

'I'm not leaving until I've found out who had access to these cameras.'

'There's one obvious culprit, isn't there?'

'You mean Donnagh?'

'Who else slept in your sister's bedroom? Who else had access to her flat?'

I thought of all the one-night stands Evie had allegedly been engaged in. The drugs. 'There could have been others. I'm not sure.'

'Rachel, listen to me. This is serious now. Whoever did this, we'll find them. But you need to check yourself into a hotel. You could be in danger.'

I felt a shiver run down my spine. 'Where are you, by the way?'

She seemed to hesitate. 'I'm interviewing Donnagh's ex-wife. Sounds like good timing, given what you've just found out.'

'I don't think Donnagh was involved with the spycam installation, Lorelei.'

'Why not?'

'Evie started the art course several months before she began dating him. So it must have been someone else who helped her install it.'

Lorelei went quiet, then concurred. 'I guess you have a point.' Finally she said, 'Look, take Evie's laptop and the cameras if you want to. But please get out of that apartment. Agreed?'

'Agreed,' I said, then hung up.

Except I didn't move out of the apartment. Rather, I stayed in front of Evie's computer, knowing I was standing on the precipice, the truth dangling in front of me. And I knew, without a shadow of doubt, that this time I was ready to jump.

My hands really were trembling now, but I forced myself to steady them, searching for relevant terms in Evie's inbox. 'Foundation art course' yielded no joy. Neither did 'Greenwich College of Art and Design'. But when I inserted the words 'webcam', an email immediately popped up on my screen.

I clicked it open quickly, then scanned through the contents.

Evie, of course I will help you choose and install the webcam for your project. Sounds really interesting! Would this Saturday suit?

Eve suggested eleven a.m. as a meeting time, and asked where she should go.

Eleven sounds perfect. As for where to go, why don't you swing by mine? We can have a coffee and a chat about the exact specifications of the project, then we can check out Dixons just round the corner from me — they have an amazing range of cameras.

To this end, the emailer had attached their home address.

As I stared at the name flashing up at me, I could hardly believe my eyes. This person claimed to care for Evie. To be her friend.

After that, everything I thought I knew began to crumble. I walked, as if I was in a dream, until half an hour later I was outside the culprit's door, praying this was some kind of sick joke.

I rang the doorbell a couple of times, but nothing. After that, I just pounded on the door. Finally, it opened, and a person looked out. A familiar face.

'Rachel.' That was all, and I wanted to hit them or scream or do something violent. Fuck them up for what they had done to my sister. To me.

'Can I come in?'

'Um?'

I pushed my way through anyway. 'Have you anything to say about this, you sick fucker?' I held one of the spy-cams up to the light.

But there was no response. No movement, even. All I could do was try to catch my breath and let my eyes adjust to the gloom.

56.

'So you are TBM,' I eventually spat, watching as the culprit's face turned whiter and whiter: Tom who had sympathized with me days earlier in Evie's office; the same Tom who had convinced me he knew nothing about her crash. Technically I should have been scared but I couldn't be intimidated by such a pathetic figure. He looked like a child who had been caught torturing the family cat.

'Answer me,' I bellowed, and he seemed to cower away from me.

Finally he whispered, 'Yes.'

'You helped Evie set up the cameras for her art course, didn't you?'

He nodded, unable to look at me.

'And you somehow hooked it up so you could watch the footage yourself.' I had no idea how that might work, probably something to do with the internet, but however he'd arranged it, he'd been able to spy on Evie, then on me. Creepy little shit.

'How did you do it?'

He was silent for a while. Then: 'Are you going to the police?'

'Yes, if you don't answer every single one of my questions, arsehole.'

'Please don't do that, Rachel.'

'Then answer my fucking questions,' I said, taking a step closer towards him.

'Okay, okay,' he said, holding up his hands. 'I hooked the camera up to her Wi-Fi. Got a live feed on my Mac.' He pointed at a computer nearby.

'Jesus Christ.' A wave of nausea overcame me. 'How could you have done something like that to her? How could she not have suspected you?'

'Because Eve and I were friends,' he said, in a defensive tone. 'She knew I'd never do anything to hurt her. Actually, we were more than friends.'

'Sorry?'

Tom raised his pale blue eyes to meet mine. 'We kissed once on a night out. It didn't go anywhere immediately – Eve said we were better off as mates – but I knew if I could just figure out the right approach, find the route to her heart, I'd win her over.'

'And your version of the right approach was to film her secretly?'

'Of course not. My plan was to help her with her project. I know I shouldn't have done the other thing but I couldn't help it. There was no malice to it.' He paused, as if he was concentrating hard on getting his point across. 'I was just having a sneak preview – before we got together. For real, I mean.'

I stared at him, utterly at a loss for words. He was so fucking delusional.

'And what about Donnagh? Didn't their relationship prove you'd got the wrong end of the stick? That Evie wasn't interested in you at all.'

Tom snorted. 'Donnagh meant nothing to her – he was

an arrogant tosser. I knew it wouldn't take her long to come to her senses. To realize she was supposed to be with me.'

A hollow laugh bubbled up from somewhere deep inside me. 'You're mad, you do know that, right? They have a name for what you do. Stalking.'

'Don't say that.' All of a sudden his tone had become harsher. 'Don't you ever speak to me like that again.'

'I'm sorry?' I said.

'How dare you question my motives? I'm telling you I love Eve. That I only want what's best for her.'

'Is that right?' I said, training my eyes on him. 'Well, if you're such a fucking gem, why have you been sending me those sick messages? Did you think that was also in Evie's best interests? Did you think that was going to help her wake up?'

Tom glanced downwards so he wouldn't have to meet my eye.

'Answer me,' I demanded.

Eventually he looked up. 'Fine. I sent them to you because I felt you deserved them.'

'You what?'

'For all that feminist propaganda you spout. For aborting your defenceless unborn child.'

'So you're one of the God Squad, are you?'

'No. I just think killing a child is wrong.'

'I did not kill a child. I had a legal termination.'

'Same difference. You hate families. You hate men.'

'I'm married to a man.'

'So you claim. Although I'm sure you'll dump him soon enough, if you haven't done so already.'

I must have flinched because something in Tom's face seemed to brighten.

'You've done it already, haven't you? Or maybe he's dumped you. Wouldn't blame the poor bastard. What did you do – chop off his balls as punishment?' He tittered.

I stared at him, his words spinning round and round in my head. Something was dawning on me very, very slowly. 'You're threatened by me, aren't you, Tom?' I said, in a low, quiet voice. 'You blame me and my "feminist propaganda" for how your life has turned out. For the fact that you're unmarried and alone – that Evie wouldn't go near you unless she was off her head.'

Tom shifted a little. 'I just think your type needs to be kept in check, is all.'

'My type?' I repeated.

'Filling women's heads with ideas – that it's okay to be a whore, to treat men like shit.'

'I've never encouraged women to treat men like shit. I simply campaign for equal rights.'

'Your idea of equal rights.' He snorted.

'So I'm to blame for the fact that you lead a sad little life and that Evie wouldn't give you the time of day. You think women like me are hampering your chances.'

'Well, aren't you?'

'How do you make that one out?'

'Without your type poisoning their minds against us, women like Eve would do what they've always done. They'd marry a normal man and raise a normal family. Instead, you fill them with bullshit about gender roles, about over-throwing the "patriarchy". Suddenly their regular lives aren't good enough any more and ordinary men like me, well, we're not good enough either.'

'Except you're not ordinary, are you, Tom?' I shot back. Something in his eyes flickered.

'I mean, ordinary men don't go around filming their female work colleagues behind their backs. They don't send pornographic images to women they hardly know.'

'You deserved that. You ruin people's lives.'

'Oh, for Chrissake, Tom, grow up. The only person ruining your life is you. Join a group or something – stop blaming all your pathetic problems on other people.'

I marched over to where his Mac Air was sitting on a table, open as if he'd just been using it. I tried not to think about what he'd been doing in front of it all this time. 'I take it this is where you watched your "live feed"? Do you have it all saved or downloaded or whatever the word is?'

Tom didn't say anything, a look of contempt in his eyes. But I was damned if I was going to be intimidated. Not by that pathetic, sick fuck.

'Are you the reason my sister is stuck in a coma?'

He wiped his nose with the back of his hand. 'Wouldn't you like to know?'

'Well, if you're not going to tell me, perhaps your computer will.' I picked up the Mac and its accompanying socket and placed it under my arm. Tom sprang into action and raced to the hall door. He got there before I did, blocking my exit.

'What do you think you're doing?'

'You can't leave with that computer, Rachel.'

'Are you intending to stop me?'

'Yes,' said Tom, but the word wobbled. I knew he

wanted to hurt me, but I could see he didn't have the stomach for it. That was when I took the opportunity to knee him hard in the balls, which forced him down onto the carpet.

'See how you like being violated, you little prick,' I said, then opened the door and pushed past him.

Out in the fresh air, I tucked the computer into my backpack, realizing I was shaking. But I was nearly there. Nearly at the truth. I'd been handed the keys to everything. Now I just needed to unlock the door.

57.

Once I was a safe distance away from Tom's apartment, I hopped into a taxi and directed the driver back to Evie's flat.

In her living room, I sat, cross-legged, on the carpet with a USB key and opened Tom's Mac. What disgusting secrets did it hold? Would I be able to access the files he'd been keeping on Evie? He had been using the computer when I'd taken it, so the screen immediately popped open when I hit the 'on' button – no password necessary. For someone supposed to be a mastermind cybercriminal, this seemed like a substantial oversight.

And, to my amazement, the very files I'd been hoping for were there, already open, in a folder marked 'E'. There were at least fifty videos, all with roughly the same run-time, three minutes. Tom had obviously been watching them before I'd burst in on him. I clicked on the first.

It was dated three months earlier, and was, as I suspected, footage from the spycam. There was Evie, changing into her nightie, getting into bed. In the process, she was revealing a quick flash of bum – no doubt the reason why pervert Tom had gone to the trouble of editing and saving it. I fought the urge to spew. And yet, despite the perverse nature of the footage, a part of me couldn't help feeling entranced as I observed a living, breathing Evie. It was as if she had suddenly come out of her coma and was a functioning human being again.

I clicked on another file, then another. Tom had obviously chosen his footage with care. Each clip was progressively racy. Evie's nightie became just a bra and knickers, then just a bra, building up to her being completely naked. I felt revulsion but also intense sadness. Would that beautiful body ever move again?

My phone rang but I ignored it. I was too focused on nailing Tom before he fled. Before it was too late.

I clicked through more files. In the early ones, Evie was sleeping alone but at some point Donnagh joined her. In the first clip, there was no funny business. They seemed to go to bed at different times, collapsing immediately into sleep. I wasn't even sure why Tom had bothered keeping the footage.

But the next one was very different: Evie and Donnagh were having sex.

I ran my fingers through my hair, engulfed by shame.

I shouldn't have been prying into my sister's life, raking over her most intimate moments. But something compelled me to keep going. A hunch. A gut feeling, a sense that I was getting closer to something, something big . . .

The phone continued to ring and I continued to ignore it. Whoever it was would just have to wait. I was so close now I could taste it. Part of me still thought that if I solved the puzzle, I could wake up my sister. I could break the spell.

On and on I clicked, through the remaining files. A picture was building up, an inadvertent mini-film. True, there was no sleepwalking, or if there was, Tom hadn't bothered to save the footage, but ironically he had done what

Evie herself had set out to do: to record her conscious and unconscious moments, a documentary.

I kept clicking. By accident I pressed one of the later files and was taken aback to see myself buck naked and straddling Jacob.

I jerked away from the computer. That was the day Jacob had arrived to visit Evie and we'd fallen into bed. Tom had probably wanked over us as he cut the footage, come noisily as he'd edited it into a neat three-minute clip.

At some point I remembered I could turn on audio and did so for the last few files. One of the final clips showed Evie sitting in her bedroom, clutching a pillow. Why had Tom bothered with this one? She wasn't naked or engaged in anything kinky. If anything, she just looked scared.

Out of shot I heard Donnagh asking her if she was okay, if she was nearly ready.

'Yeah, sure,' she'd replied, plastering on a smile. When he'd left the room she moved away from the camera, perhaps to lock the door, took a really deep breath and knelt quickly on the floor.

I pressed my face closer to the screen, trying to figure out what was unspooling in front of me. Evie was pushing back a corner of the rug and yanking at something underneath. I couldn't see it properly – the angle of the camera wasn't right – but I could only imagine it was a floorboard. A few seconds later, something gave way, and Evie seemed to plunge her arm deep into a hole. I couldn't see what was down there, but I understood what was going on. That must be where Evie had stashed things, her secret place.

She was removing her hand from the cavity now,

gripping something. It was small and book-like – her passport, perhaps? That would fit with the weekend she'd gone to Paris. And, if so, no wonder she was scared. I'd seen that passport and I knew why she'd want to keep it hidden. It featured a picture of her before she'd had the nose job. It showed her real name. Her real face.

The footage ended there, and for a second I just stared at the blank screen. Then, abandoning the computer, I tore into Evie's bedroom and pushed the rug aside, as Evie had done. Underneath it I identified the floorboard – it was a slightly different colour from the others. When I pulled, it came up, just as in the video footage.

Lying in front of me was a large dark hole, measuring perhaps one foot by three. A private bunker. Something Evie had never shown me.

For just a moment I stopped, a jolt of sheer adrenalin passing through me. Then I plunged my hand in, feeling my fingers connect with a variety of textures. I caught something and pulled it upwards into the light. It was a small framed picture of Evie and Mammy, Evie leaning towards Mammy, whispering something into her ear. The day was windy so wisps of Mammy's brown hair intermingled with Evie's blonde. I fingered the glass, feeling bereft. This was exactly how I remembered them.

So animated.

So alive.

I took a deep breath and rummaged some more. This time I pulled up three of Evie's watercolours, landscape paintings of Leitrim, books, the mug with her name on it, several official documents – her birth cert and the deeds for her flat – and finally what appeared to be letters, all addressed to our father. I was about to close the floorboard, go through all the correspondence, when I noticed something else shimmer up at me from the side of the bunker. A quick pat around the wall revealed a compartment I had overlooked, a hidden ledge. When I reached inside and tugged at the contents, I sensed immediately that I had hit upon the real treasure, Evie's diary, a small embroidered notebook with a purple and blue cover.

I sat back and began to flick through the pages. Evie had been contributing to her diary until a few days before her accident. That would have meant opening and replacing the floorboard without Donnagh noticing. Why had she gone to so much trouble? What had she so badly needed to get off her chest?

I began a cursory read of the entries, noticing that Donnagh's name cropped up again and again. *What am I doing?* she had written in an entry from two months earlier. And then a few weeks after: *Is he changing? Did I completely misjudge him? If so, how can I possibly tell him the truth?*

The days immediately before her crash were a blank white space. I sighed and pushed my fingers through my hair. It would take hours to go through all the diary entries. And I didn't have hours. I didn't have minutes, even. I needed to get to the police and report Tom. Why was I procrastinating? What was I looking for?

Something was nagging at me. The final spycam clip that I hadn't yet watched. Did it matter? They'd all been more or less the same – various shades of nakedness. The most important thing now was holding my nerve, reporting Tom to the police.

And yet that one file nagged at me – the final piece of

the puzzle. For some reason, I couldn't shake the feeling that I should watch it. Then I would have everything saved on my USB key, Tom's sordid documentary complete.

I carried the computer to the breakfast bar, sat on one of Evie's high stools, then pressed play. Almost immediately, I regretted it. There on the computer screen was a clear image of Donnagh and Evie: he was holding my sister by the hair, Evie appearing to give him head.

'Suck it, bitch,' he growled.

I was shocked by the strong language. But maybe they'd just been to see *Fifty Shades of Grey* together. Maybe this was why Tom had kept it: because it contained a new element for his repertoire – kink.

I was tempted to turn it off. I didn't want to watch any more. But I forced myself to stick with it. I wanted to record and remember every element of Tom's crime before I handed the computer to Ainsworth at the police station.

My phone beeped repeatedly, alerting me to a flurry of new messages. I stretched a hand for my jacket but couldn't reach it. In any case the video only had a minute or so left to play. I let it run.

Donnagh had released Evie's hair, and she was jerking her head away from him. She seemed to be making a noise, but it was extremely difficult to hear. I pushed the volume up as high as it could go, but still Evie's words remained muffled.

Next, Donnagh was pushing Evie down on the bed – roughly – catching her arms behind her head. 'You deserve to be punished, don't you, Eveline?'

His voice had the same aggressive tone as earlier but it

didn't look like role-play any more. Suddenly a lead weight seemed to be lying across my chest and droplets of sweat were forming on my skin.

Eveline? Had he really just called her that?

My phone beeped again, and this time I ran to my jacket and grabbed it out of the pocket. *Back in London. Apartment is finally ready. I'll be over shortly to pick up my stuff. D*

I was sweating now – real sweat, which was drenching my back and armpits. I was shallow-breathing, unable to get proper traction on my thoughts or movements, and feeling a wave of blood rush to my head.

Nothing was making sense, yet everything was. I clicked on another text – this time from Lorelei.

I tried to read it, but the words swam in front of me.

A sound from the door – a key in a lock.

I was trying to read but my eyes wouldn't focus. Finally I made out one word – short and to the point. I squinted. Strained to read it. It was three letters, clear and uncomplicated:

Run.

58.

Evie

It's come back to me, what happened before the crash. I'd arrived at my flat and I'd had an email from Artie, asking me to meet him. Although I knew I shouldn't, I desperately wanted to go to him. Because he was the man I was in love with, truly in love with. Those words I'd uttered to Donnagh at the top of the Eiffel Tower had not been a lie exactly, but neither had they been the truth. I was in love with the *idea* of Donnagh: a strong, authoritative man, who would tell me what to do, how to be. But now I knew I needed to do those things on my own. I needed to take control of my own life.

I packed away the last of my clothes and headed for the living room. I'd decided that I would finally come clean to Donnagh. However, as I approached my bedroom door, he was already standing there, almost as if he had been waiting for me.

'Where do you think you're going?' he said, straightening his arm across the door frame, blocking my exit.

'Um, I wanted to talk to you, Donnagh,' I said. 'We need to talk.'

'Uh-oh, sounds serious. How about we forget talking and do something else with our mouths?' He was wearing a lascivious grin but I was in no mood for sex. I couldn't keep up this ridiculous pretence. Not any more.

'Donnagh, listen, there's something important I've been meaning to tell you.'

'Really?'

'Yes. I probably should have waited until tomorrow night, when we're both less knackered, but –'

'I won't be here tomorrow night, Eve. Or the one after that.'

'You won't?' I said, and felt a prickling sensation, hot and scratchy.

'No, I won't.'

I raised my eyes to meet Donnagh's, and that was when I saw how his face had changed. Unlike at the top of the Eiffel Tower, when it had been all soft and yielding, it was now hard and angular. I hadn't seen that face in years. Not since his first day in secondary school when he'd called me 'Big Nose'. And on the day at the swimming-pool when he'd bared my breasts to all the other kids.

'Give it up, Eveline,' he whispered, just loud enough so I could hear him.

'What?' I replied, stumbling back a bit. Had he just called me Eveline?

Donnagh moved in closer now, bent down so that his lips were practically touching my ear. 'I know.'

The words hovered above us, begging for a response. But I was unable to provide one. Instead, I just stood there, all the blood rushing to my head.

'Don't you want to know *how* I know?' he asked *faux*-politely, the sides of his mouth curling into a smirk.

I shook my head, refusing to make eye contact. I didn't want to know anything.

'Truth is, I thought there was something familiar about

you from our very first meeting. An odour I recognized. A slightly rank smell . . .'

He was still smiling at me and I was struggling to remain upright. My legs had turned to jelly.

'Gemma agreed. We had a bet on – which of us could figure out who you were first. I obviously had the advantage.' He bared his teeth, perfect white pillars, and my breath quickened.

'Donnagh, I . . .' But nothing else would come. It was like my voice had simply given up, like a car battery. Conked out. Dead.

'You led me to it, actually. You were sleepwalking one night – do you know you do that? You bent down and started scratching at the rug near the bed. Weird, I thought. But then I took a closer look.' He stamped hard on the floor. I jumped.

'My favourite bit was finding your diary. That human drip Artie Columb was back on the scene. And I restored your orgasm!' He started to laugh.

Almost on cue, I began to cry: a racking sob coming from deep inside me. So this was the place they referred to so often in the Bible. This was Hell.

'Gemma.' My voice had returned, perhaps because I'd made my own connection now. 'You were having an affair with her, weren't you? And she was trying to end it.' It all made sense suddenly: why Donnagh had pursued me, then moved in. It hadn't been a bet: it was to make her jealous. That row I'd seen outside the restaurant. It wasn't Mick having the affair. It was them.

'So what if I was?' he snapped, sounding a little less in control now. 'But let me make one thing very clear, Eveline.

If you breathe one word of that to anyone, I will destroy you. Do you understand me?'

I nodded. I believed him. 'Why?' I found myself asking. 'Why go to the trouble of bringing me to Paris?'

He laughed then, a short, vicious grunt. 'Because it was fun. Watching the look on your face when you realized we were getting off the Eurostar at Gare du Nord, not Amsterdam. Your attempts at covering up your lack of French – pretending you had laryngitis. To be honest, the whole thing was absolutely priceless.'

He laughed again, but then he stopped and fixed me with a stare. 'Eveline, you should never play a player.' His face was hard as granite now, his eyes boring into me. 'Nobody ever beats me.'

Something inside me cracked. 'Your father did. He died, didn't he? And your ex-wife cheated on you. Or did she even exist?'

A spark of rage: 'Oh, she existed all right. Slutty little bitch. And she got the same punishment you're going to get.'

I felt a thrill of sheer terror run down my spine. Punishment? What the hell was he talking about?

'As for my father, if you ever speak about him again I'll throw you straight off that balcony.' He pointed towards the window. 'Do you understand me?'

'You don't frighten me,' I said, my voice rising a little.

'I should, Eveline. I really should.' A second later he had grabbed my arm and was pushing me backwards, inside the bedroom again.

'Get off me!' I screamed, struggling. But there was no way I could escape from his grip. Not a chance.

'Now that you're becoming hysterical we're going to have to shut that mouth up, aren't we?' He smiled a little, baring those perfect teeth again.

'Fuck you,' I spat, looking for a tiny bit of space to get past him. Every nerve in my body was alert.

I made a dart to the right of him, but he caught my hair. I yelped – the pain was breathtaking.

'Now, my lovely Eveline Darcy-Durant, as a finale to this happy weekend you're going to do something special for me.'

He yanked harder on my hair so that I was forced to look up. 'What?' I heard myself whisper.

'Press those lovely lips together,' he said, miming the action. 'Then blow.'

I screamed then – the fear coming as suddenly as the pain had. He yanked again, and this time the force knocked me to my knees. Donnagh repositioned himself so that my face was in front of his crotch. He unzipped his trousers and pulled out his dick. I pursed my mouth, refusing to make contact. Again and again he thrust my head at it, but I refused to open up. I wouldn't do it. He'd have to kill me first.

'Okay, Eveline, if you're not going to play ball, so to speak, we'll have to do this the old-fashioned way.' He pulled at my head again, forcing me upwards. Then he pushed me back towards the bed.

'No, Donnagh, please.' Terror surged through me, con-vulsing me. I began thrashing, using every bit of strength I possessed, but with one swift movement he had pulled my arms over my head. I could feel the sinews stretch as he held them. There was no escape now. Just submission. I began to cry again.

Quietly, almost softly, he spoke in my ear: 'You deserve this, Eveline. You tried to fuck me about, and you failed. Now I'm going to fuck you. Just accept it. Things will be easier if you do.'

He was hoicking up my dress with one hand — my spindly arms pinned in place by his single muscular one.

'Oh, and if you go to the police, who do you think they're going to believe? A fantasist who's been living a double life or a well-respected businessman, like me? And, by the way, I've asked around. Apparently the neighbours think you're a slut, Eveline. A complete and utter whore.'

He was lying on top of me now — his body so heavy I thought my pelvis was going to break. There was no talk any more — just the feel of his heavy breathing against my face, the smell of sweat, of animal musk, of my own fear.

It dawned on me now that he was right: there was no point fighting this. He had me like a caged animal, and he was going to do whatever he felt like. Would he kill me? It felt like he might.

There was just one problem. My leggings, the tight, shiny kind, weren't coming down easily, and I sensed Donnagh's frustration as he swiped at them with one hand, trying to rip them off. For an instant I felt the arm that was pinning me down slacken, and one of my own was suddenly free.

I seized this tiny window of opportunity and took my chance. I'd spotted a pair of nail scissors on my bedside locker a few moments earlier, and now I reached for them.

I plunged them deep into Donnagh's neck. Almost instantly, there was a scream, and Donnagh rolled off me. I could barely register what I had done. All I knew was that somehow I had managed to get out from under him.

I heard him scream: 'You fucking bitch, come back here now! Come back or I'll fucking kill you!' I believed him. I knew he would.

I needed to get out. My eyes landed on Donnagh's car keys lying on the hall table and I grabbed them, as much for weaponry as for transport, and then I grappled with the chain on the hall door, my fingers shaking so badly they kept slipping. Donnagh was coming up behind me. I could hear his steps heavy on the wooden flooring as he stormed towards me. If I didn't undo this fucking chain, he would grab me by the throat, drag me back into the bedroom and do – God knew what he'd do. In that moment, I felt such a bolt of terror that it paralysed me.

Then, out of nowhere, I heard something.

I'm with you, darling, a voice whispered. *Don't be scared.*

I steadied my hand and took a breath. Mammy? New energy filled my body. This time my fingers did not slip off the door chain. This time it slid off. Finally, there was a click. A pulling open. And suddenly I was out in the corridor – the faint smell of cooking. Then I was running. Down the stairs, out of the main door, the huge night sky above me. I was taking in panicky gulps of air as I went.

Out of the corner of my eye, I spotted Donnagh's gleaming Porsche, parked just a few feet away on the street. There was a bang from the main door, and when I turned around I saw him lurching towards me, one hand covering his injured neck.

He was like a demon, huge and terrifying, and it was the thought of him catching up with me that drove me to fumble with the car keys, insert them into the lock and get in.

I hadn't driven for years, not since Mammy had been ill, but somehow I made the engine start, and when I pushed my foot hard against the accelerator, the car took off, gravel flying out from underneath the tyres – a smell of burning rubber. It was as if the car had sensed my urgency and was propelling itself.

Even so, I continued to push down hard on the accelerator, sneaking a peek in the rear-view mirror at what was behind me. Donnagh was still there, but he was smaller now. A stick figure. A tiny, insignificant dot.

I wanted to pull over – my hands were shaking so badly on the wheel I could barely steer – but there was no way I was going to stop. If I did, Donnagh might catch up to rape and kill me. I pressed harder on the pedal.

As I drove, my thoughts collided against each other. How had I allowed this to happen?

Me too. The words I had spoken atop the Eiffel Tower came back to me in all their self-mocking glory and I wanted to die. Donnagh had humiliated me all through my teenage years, and now he had done it again. And I had let him.

I was still crying, still driving like a maniac. It was so dark. I used the back of my sleeve to wipe away the tears, but it was difficult: everything seemed so blurry.

I didn't know where I was going.

A dog ran out in front of me, and I swerved sharply to avoid it, narrowly missing it. I was going too fast. Way too fast. And suddenly the car wasn't under my control any more.

Everything slowed down then, the car careering towards the pavement, the stone wall coming closer and closer.

Images appeared suddenly in my brain: my dad holding me as a child; Artie and me with buckets in our hands, collecting blackberries; my mother making apple tarts in the kitchen. All of them spooled together, like a mixed-up reel of film, impossible to know where one ended and the next began.

It was a riot of technicolour and vivid imagery. I felt no fear. I accepted the inevitable.

In a way I was happy. I hadn't been right since Mammy had died. But maybe now, with this . . .

There was a sudden impact. I jolted forward, cracking my head against the windscreen.

There was no pain.

There was nothing.

Everything went white, quiet and peaceful.

And then all was still.

59.

Rachel: day twenty-six, 9 a.m.

He was inside the hall before I knew what to do with myself, and when I tried to click out of the clip I'd been watching, I inadvertently clicked 'play'.

As he walked into the living room the words 'Suck it, bitch,' rang out loud and clear. Donnagh dropped the bag he was carrying onto the carpet and stared at me. 'What's that you're watching, Rachel?' he said, though he must have recognized his own voice.

I couldn't say anything. I'd been rendered mute.

Donnagh made to move towards the computer, but I clamped it shut and hugged it to my chest.

'I asked you what you had there.'

I was trembling as Donnagh moved closer, more threatening. 'Tell me,' he said, clear and terrifying. 'Tell me what you've got here, Rachel.'

'It was you.' I couldn't keep my anger at bay any longer. 'Not Artie or Tom or some phantom third person . . .'

'Me what?'

'You who caused Evie to crash.'

He laughed, but in the quiet of the flat it sounded hollow. 'I didn't make your sister do anything.'

'You tried to rape her,' I said, loud and clear. 'I've seen it. You were recorded on camera.'

Donnagh flinched and his eyes seemed to darken. 'What?' he muttered, his voice wavering a little.

I wanted to scream at him, tell him he could knock off the innocent act, but this time I hung back – wary now.

'Just give me that computer and we'll say no more about this.' He was stretching his hands towards me, wearing a fake smile, as if to say, 'Let's put all this silly nonsense behind us.'

'No,' I said, still clutching the computer firmly against me, my eyes darting as I looked for an escape route.

'Just give me the fucking computer,' he repeated, moving towards me, forcing me back against the wall.

Donnagh was in my face now, speckles of spit hitting my cheeks.

'I don't know what you think you have on me, but let me reassure you, I had nothing to do with your sister's crash. She was the one concealing her identity, the one who stole my car.'

I remained mute, too scared to retaliate. I'd left it too long to escape – Donnagh had quite literally backed me into a corner and there was nowhere left to run. He wasn't touching me – yet – but I could feel his strength pulsating through his shirt, his hands just inches away, ready to grab me. To hurt me.

He moved his face closer now, ran a finger slowly down my cheek. As he did so, I felt the warmth of his breath on my skin. 'You're so beautiful, do you know that?' he whispered.

I was rigid – the hairs standing up on the back of my neck.

'I could have loved you.'

'What?'

'Oh, come on, Rachel, I've seen the way you look at me. That first night on the balcony when you couldn't take your eyes off me, then fucking your husband to make me jealous.'

'I don't know what you're talking about.'

'Knock it off, Rachel, of course you do. Why else do you think I've stayed here so long?' He half smiled at me. 'Because I knew you wanted me. And I wanted you too . . . wanted to fuck you . . .'

A tremor of horror ran down my spine. 'But you didn't, did you?' I taunted, with more force than was necessarily wise.

He continued to cast his creepy little smile at me.

'And what about Evie?' I spat. 'Wouldn't she have ruined everything if she'd woken up?'

'I thought she'd die,' Donnagh said. 'I still do.'

I looked into his eyes, trying to make sense of what he was saying, until it hit me with a terrifying *thunk*. He was crazy. He was a fucking psychopath. 'You said you loved her.' I forced myself to breathe, to keep looking at him.

'Yeah, right.' He snorted, the contempt audible. 'Of course I didn't love her. She was weak, unstable. You, on the other hand . . .' He traced a delicate line along my neck. 'Come away with me,' he murmured, so low I barely heard him.

'What?'

'Me and you. We could go away together – to Chicago, maybe. Or somewhere even further away.' His eyes were glistening like diamonds and, though we were still not touching, I knew he had me pinned. My back was now completely flush with the wall.

'Of course,' I said, forcing myself not to shake. 'We could go tonight. Leave England. Escape everything.'

He smiled at me. 'Somewhere we could be together. Properly.'

Maybe I could talk myself out of this, convince him I was desperately in love with him too.

'But first you must give me that computer.'

I felt my body sag. Donnagh was taking the piss, playing me. Of course he didn't love me: he just wanted to get the laptop. He knew exactly what it contained and that he needed to destroy it. He had his priorities straight.

I reacted swiftly, ducking under one of his arms, hoping to make a break for it across the living room and into the hall – towards freedom.

But he caught me – as one would a wayward toddler – forcing me back. 'Where do you think you're going?'

'Donnagh, please.' He was pinning one of my arms against the wall now; and I was clinging to the laptop with the other.

'Just give it to me, Rachel!' he shouted.

Out of nowhere, I felt something cold against my skin, and when I looked down I saw what it was. A knife: the one I'd used ages ago to cut open Evie's letters. He must have grabbed it off the countertop when I hadn't been looking.

'Rachel,' he said, pointing the tip of the blade to my neck. 'Make things easy on yourself and give me the computer.'

His voice was level, but I could see he was sweating – a drop landed on my left arm.

I stood there, knife against my artery – and it was like time stopped. Memories flashed in front of me: getting the call from Ainsworth; seeing Evie in hospital all wired up; running into Donnagh that first time. My gut had screamed that he was bad, but I had chosen to ignore it.

'Rachel, hand me the computer.'

I did so, no longer able to fight him.

'It's video footage, you say. Who gave it to you?'

I kept my mouth closed, but Donnagh pressed the tip of the knife so hard against me that I felt it pierce the skin. 'One of Evie's colleagues,' I muttered.

'His name?'

I shook my head, but Donnagh pressed the knife hard against me again.

'Tom. I don't know his second name.'

'Where does he live?'

I shook my head, but eventually Donnagh wangled this out of me too.

For a moment, there was complete silence, and then slowly – oh, so slowly – Donnagh removed the knife from my throat.

For a split second nothing happened. It was as if time stood still. I found myself gazing into his chocolate-brown eyes, taking in his beauty. He was hypnotic, if you let him be. But I wasn't going to let him. With that, I lunged at his face, sticking my fingers deep into his eyes, then made a desperate grab for the computer.

Donnagh staggered to one side, as I made a last dash for the door. But I knew he was gaining on me. A sensation from behind. After that, all I remember is pain and tumbling – a sea of blackness. Then nothing more.

I recall nothing about the next few hours. But here's what I know to be true. Artie, good as his word, came round to Evie's flat to explain everything about the emails. On finding the door open, he had come in and found me unconscious from the fall, blood dripping from my head. He'd called an ambulance and the police but because there were no witnesses it looked as if I'd had an accident. Artie repeatedly told them that Donnagh Flood should be sought out and questioned, but nobody could track him down. According to his PA, he was on a flight from Chicago to the UK, and his phone was ringing out.

Finally, after a number of hours, I regained consciousness. Artie was beside me, pale and unshaven. 'Oh, thank Christ, Rachel. You're awake. We've all been so worried about you.'

'Evie . . .'

'What about her?'

'You must protect her,' I whispered, but my voice was so faint I wasn't sure he heard me.

At that moment, a familiar figure entered the room. Dr Bartlett. 'Rachel Darcy, what the heck have you done to yourself?'

'Evie,' I whispered again. They needed to get to Evie. They needed to save her.

But Dr Bartlett was ignoring me, her eyes dancing. 'Your own coma must have unlocked your sister's,' she said, smiling widely.

'What?' I mumbled.

'Rachel, my dear, Eve is finally showing signs of waking up.'

'No!' I screamed. This time the word was definitely audible. 'Protect her. You must protect her.' Then I leaned over the side of my bed and was sick.

60.

Evie

I was awake – for the first time in four weeks, according to the nurses – and someone was leaning over the side of my bed, staring at me.

Him.

'Hello, Eveline,' he said, bending down, so I could feel his breath on my face. 'How are you feeling?'

I tried to respond but I couldn't – my voice wasn't working yet: all that came out was a moan.

'Brilliant to see you back in the land of the living. I just got a call to say you had woken up. They rang me when they couldn't get through to your sister.'

I didn't reply. All I felt was terror. What had he done to Rachel?

He walked away from me and proceeded to lock the door. 'I've put the "Do Not Enter" sign up,' he said, 'so we shouldn't be disturbed. In any case, I don't think any-body saw me come in here – it's still so early, isn't it?'

I felt my muscles sag. What was he going to do? Rape me? Kill me? It wasn't as if I could put up a fight.

'Donnagh,' I tried to say – but all that came out was another croak.

'Sorry, Eveline?' Donnagh said. 'Were you trying to say something?'

'Please . . .' Again the sound was unintelligible.

He laughed, a hollow, bitter sound. 'Are you pleading with me? Please don't hurt you? Don't put you back into a coma? What exactly do you think I'm going to do to you? What do you think I'm capable of?'

I was trembling. I knew perfectly well what he was capable of.

Donnagh pulled up a chair and took my hand. I tried to shake it away but I was too weak.

He didn't say anything and I felt myself hold my breath. All he needed to do was take a pillow and hold it over my face for about thirty seconds. I was so tired I wouldn't struggle, and he would be long gone before the doctors and nurses realized anything was wrong with me. It would be so easy. Such a simple plan.

'You remind me of my mother,' he said finally, and I turned my eyes towards him a fraction.

'She looked a bit like you. Before you had all the surgery. Pretty eyes. A big nose.'

He was smiling at me, but it was not affectionate. Deranged, more like.

'You know what my abiding memory of her is?'

His eyes found mine. I dropped my gaze.

'Eveline, look at me,' he said sharply, and slowly I did.

'Do you know what my abiding memory of my mother is?' he repeated.

I shook my head, or tried to.

'My father had come home from the pub, drunk as usual, and his dinner was cold. He shouted at my mother, said she was a stupid cow. She didn't contradict him, just whimpered a bit. Said she'd cook him something else.'

He was staring at me now – his eyes luminous.

'He dragged her away from the table by the hair. Grabbed one of her arms and pulled it behind her back. She screamed, told him she was sorry, but he kept pulling. I heard the bone snap. He broke her arm, Eveline.' He mimed snapping a twig. 'Just like that.'

I could feel my breath coming fast and hot now. What was he saying? That he was going to break me like a twig too?

'She was so weak,' he said, his eyes now enormous. 'And so were you.'

He wiped one eye with a sleeve. 'Why couldn't you have told me at school to fuck off? To leave you alone? Instead you just stood there and took it, like an abused dog. You made me do it, Eveline. You practically begged me to.'

I watched him, just inches away from me, and the terror was replaced by something else: disbelief.

Was he honestly saying it was my fault he'd become a rapist? Because I hadn't stood up to him when we were teenagers?

The colossal, unbelievable cheek of the man.

'Fuck you,' I said, and, to my total shock, those two words came out pretty clearly.

Donnagh's eyes flickered, as if he couldn't quite believe what he'd just heard. 'Say that again, Eveline.'

I tried a second time, but this time I wasn't quite so successful.

Donnagh laughed, then got up and stood over me.

This was it. I knew it. I'd tried everything – running away from him, stealing his car – but finally Donnagh Flood had cornered me. This time there was no fake identity to hide behind. No fast-moving Porsche. I didn't feel fear, just sadness. I'd had so many great people in my life: Rachel, Artie, Janet. But I hadn't realized it.

I saw Donnagh pick something up – a roll of something. I took a deep breath. Waited for the inevitable.

'It won't hurt, not for very long anyway. And the good news, for me anyway, is that suffocation is very difficult to prove, especially for someone with a fail-safe alibi . . .'

He smiled. 'Remember Gemma? Right at this very minute I'm enjoying breakfast at her house. Or, at least, that's what she's going to tell the police.'

With that he revealed the object he'd been holding earlier: a roll of masking tape.

'Just to make sure no fibres from the pillow are found in your mouth. I want to make it look like you slipped into cardiac arrest. Don't worry, Eveline, I've done my homework, planned this all along. It was just finding the opportunity that was the hard bit.'

He laughed. 'Funny how the moment you wake up, the doctors and nurses are nowhere to be seen. Where have they gone to, I wonder?' He pulled some of the masking tape away from the roll, then used a penknife to chop it. It made a horrible screeching sound.

Next he placed the tape over my mouth, gagging me. I tried to resist but it was so hard. Was this how it was going to end? After I had come so far and had been through so much?

'Nearly there.' He was holding a pillow over me now.

'Goodbye, Eveline,' he said, forcing it over my mouth. 'You fought a brave fight but you could never beat me. I warned you about that.'

Panic was taking over now, and I was struggling to stay conscious. Images swirled into my brain of Rachel, of Artie, of Mammy. Maybe things weren't so bad – maybe I'd get to see her again.

The thought soothed me.

The thought of Mammy.

But my reverie was interrupted by a loud bang.

For a second, I thought I'd been shot but then I felt the pressure of the pillow ease, and realized that Donnagh was no longer pressing it down.

Another loud bang followed, and next thing I knew there were voices in the room, people swarming all over me, removing the masking tape, telling me I was going to be okay.

'Donnagh Flood, you are under arrest. You do not have to say anything, but it may harm your defence if you do not mention when questioned something which you later rely on in court. Anything you do say may be given in evidence.'

Two policemen had grabbed Donnagh's arms and were restraining him.

Donnagh didn't put up a fight. I watched as they hand-cuffed him, then led him from my room.

Before he left, he stopped and looked back at me.

I wanted to look away but I held his gaze.

The police officer tugged on his handcuffs, but Don-nagh didn't move a muscle.

'It's like I told you that day in the car,' he said, a weird look on his face. 'Most people want to get caught.' He paused, staring at me. 'It's just a matter of when.'

61.

Rachel: day twenty-six, 5 p.m.

Later, one of the policemen told me everything. How Donnagh had got past the nurse on duty, an agency temp, who had been skiving off when she should have been on the desk. How he'd attempted to suffocate Evie.

'He what?' I spluttered.

'But we managed to apprehend him before he was able to carry out his plan. You can thank Dr Elizabeth Bartlett for that – she was the one who alerted us after the warning you gave her.'

'And is Evie okay? He didn't –'

'Your sister is unharmed. She will make a full recovery.'

A little later, when I was feeling strong enough to walk, I made my way into my sister's room. She appeared to be awake, staring up at the ceiling.

'Evie!' I shuffled over to her and kissed her a multitude of times. 'Can you hear me? Do you know who I am?'

She nodded, tears flowing down her cheeks, then attempted to say something, but I couldn't understand her. She seemed to be trying to point at me.

'Me?' I said, finally twigging what she was getting at. 'You're wondering how I am? Oh, I'm fine. Just a flesh wound.' This was basically true: when I'd fallen, my forehead had hit the door frame in the hall, meaning there'd been a lot of blood. But it was all superficial. I was going to be fine.

For a while we just sat there holding hands. Evie was still lapsing in and out of consciousness, but eventually she made a sound I thought I could identify: 'Sorry.'

'You have nothing to be sorry for.'

She shook her head, tears rolling down her cheeks.

We hugged then, for the longest time.

'How's about we forget everything, except that we're both alive and that we're both going to be okay?' I squeezed Evie's hand. 'Because things *are* going to be okay, kiddo, I promise you.'

She looked at me then – tears making her eyes glisten – and suddenly I felt pressure on my fingers. She was squeezing back. She was smiling at me.

It was the most beautiful thing I'd witnessed in a long, long time.

Shortly afterwards, I managed to talk to Lorelei properly.

'I'm so sorry about what happened to you, darling,' she said, and I could feel her voice choke with sadness and regret that she hadn't been able to prevent it. 'I'm so sorry I didn't get to warn you in time.'

'You did everything in your power, Lor. You couldn't have done anything more.'

Lorelei sighed. 'To be honest, it took way longer than it should have. Donnagh's record was so squeaky clean that it threw me for a while. But something about him bothered me – the way he just showed up in your life. The way he wouldn't leave.'

'What did you find out?'

'That ex-wife I spoke to,' she said quietly. 'Maria.'

'What about her?'

'She told me things.' Lorelei was silent for a minute. Then: 'She was terrified. She kept slamming the door in my face. Finally I screamed at her through her letterbox that two women in England were in danger. One was already in a coma and the other was living with Donnagh but had discovered a spycam. That was when she opened the door.'

'What did she say?'

Lorelei took a deep breath, as if to steady herself. 'For a long time she didn't say anything. She just cried. Eventually I got it out of her.'

'Got what, Lorelei? What are you trying to tell me?'

There was a pause.

'He raped her, Rachel,' Lorelei said quietly. 'Donnagh raped that girl.'

I felt myself go completely still.

'She said they had got married way too young. She'd realized very quickly that he was controlling and a bully. At some point, she met another man and fell in love.'

'Donnagh said his ex-wife had an affair.'

'Not exactly. Nothing had happened between them. She just told Donnagh straight that she wanted out of the marriage. That she wanted a divorce.'

'And his reaction was to brutalize her?'

'Exactly,' Lorelei said quietly. After a moment she continued, 'Maria's new boyfriend was from Mexico but, unlike her, he was illegal. Donnagh said if she went to the police he'd have the new guy kicked out of the US. It worked. She kept shtum.'

I stood there, phone in my hand, feeling as if some-body had punched me. How could he have got away with so much? How could he have been allowed to do almost the same thing to Evie?

'Maria thinks there might have been other victims. She suspects there was some incident back in Ireland when Donnagh was a teenager, hushed up by his rich uncle. That that was why he was taken out of the country so quickly, why his uncle took him under his wing in America.'

'So he's a serial sex offender?'

'Well, we can't know for sure. But there's anecdotal evi-dence to suggest he was.'

I slumped into a chair, completely winded. 'And no one ever reported him? No one ever found out?'

'No,' Lorelei said simply. 'He seems to have done a bril-liant job at covering it up.'

He had nearly done the same thing this time round. If he'd killed Evie he'd have shut her up for ever. As for me, there'd be no witnesses back there in the flat – plus he'd taken Tom's computer. Unless Tom had a back-up, which I imagined he'd already destroyed, it was his word against mine.

Later, as I shuffled back to my bed in the hospital, I bumped into DI Ainsworth, who flushed scarlet as soon as he saw me and began to deliver an excruciating apology. I held up my hand to halt him – too tired to feel angry.

Afterwards, in bed, I turned it all over in my mind. I still thought Ainsworth was an incompetent arsehole. But I'd been taken in by Donnagh just as much as he had. I'd allowed myself to be fooled by his beauty, attracted by his charm. I'd even bought into the whole sensitive, reformed-character act.

Yes, I'd had my suspicions. Yes, I'd done some research. But in the end I'd acted the same as everyone else who came within forty metres of Donnagh Flood.

I'd fallen just the tiniest bit in love with him.

And I'd forgotten the most important rule when it came to people who possessed both beauty and extreme cunning.

Watch your back.

62.

Evie

Once I knew Rachel was going to be okay, my own recovery was rapid. First my speech started to come back properly, so that I wasn't just uttering single indecipherable words: I was beginning to speak fluently, like a normal person. It didn't happen overnight – I had a lot of help from speech therapists – but slowly, the words trickled into my mouth.

It wasn't just my body the hospital experts focused on but also my mind. I spent a lot of time with a psychiatrist. And the early sessions really were awful. For the first couple, all I seemed to do was cry. But I was determined to stick with it because of what I'd put Rachel through. I'd meant it when I said sorry to her. I wanted to change. Become a better person.

The psychiatrist diagnosed me as being on the bipolar spectrum. 'Just like my father,' I said, as soon as I heard the diagnosis.

Rachel had filled me in on how she'd tried calling him when I was in the coma. How she believed he suffered from bipolar disorder too.

'Well, there is a genetic component to the illness,' the psychiatrist said softly. 'So if your father had it, you would be predisposed to it.'

'Does that mean I'll never be able to lead a normal life again?'

The doctor looked at me. 'Were you leading a normal life before?'

'Not exactly,' I admitted. 'There were a few incidents . . .'

We smiled wryly.

'Look,' the psychiatrist said, laying his palms flat on the desk. 'I'm not going to patronize you and pretend it will be easy. You already know it won't. But . . .' he paused '. . . there are ways of making things *easier*. I would recommend a mixture of medication and therapy – hopefully more of the latter than the former.'

I welled up – not because I hated what he was saying but the opposite: it was such a relief.

'You told me you love art. Is that right?'

'Yes,' I said. 'I do.'

'Bipolar and creativity have been linked. They theorize that the mania pushes people to levels of accomplishment and greatness others may never achieve.'

'Listen, I'm no Michelangelo.'

'Perhaps not. But during your recovery I want you to attend art therapy. I also want you to re-establish your link with art. For many people it's their salvation when dealing with mental-health issues. I sincerely hope it will be yours.'

As the weeks went by, people came to see me, most importantly Janet. We had a long conversation in which I apologized profusely for everything that had happened and we hugged a lot.

Some of my workmates came to visit too: George and Bob. Thankfully, Nigel didn't deign to join them, and neither did Tom – Rachel had already filled me in on his perverted stalking, how he was now barred from coming anywhere near me. It made me feel sick, but it also explained who the mysterious grunter had been when I'd been in the coma. It all suddenly made sense: it had been him.

Then someone else dropped by.

'Artie,' I said, barely able to believe he was standing in front of me. Apparently he'd been to see me briefly after the Donnagh incident, but I didn't remember it.

'I'm sorry I've been out of touch,' he said. 'Things have been kind of hectic.'

That day we didn't say much, but Artie kept coming every few days. I didn't press him for details of why things were hectic: I figured he'd tell me when he was good and ready.

Finally he did.

'I'm just back from America,' he explained. 'I was over with Shannon. She lost our baby a while ago.'

'God, I'm so sorry, Art,' I whispered.

'It was a ruptured uterus . . . and it happened around the time we shared that kiss.' Artie's cheeks flamed red. 'Shannon found the email I'd sent to you, telling you how great you were, and we had a massive argument. About two weeks later she had the miscarriage.'

'And she blamed you?'

'Yes,' he said. 'Which, in fairness, I think she had a right to. It was my fault.'

I frowned, and shook my head. The kiss had lasted little more than a millisecond, after which Artie had pulled away, like a frightened pony, declaring he needed to get back to

Shannon and saying sorry over and over again. If anyone was to blame it was me: I'd pushed myself onto him.

'What happened next?'

Artie shrugged. 'She left me. Went back to the States, warned me she'd use her father's shotgun on me if I attempted to follow her. So I stayed in London.' He dropped his head. 'I nearly went out of my head with the guilt.'

'Oh, Artie, I'm so sorry.'

A few minutes later he picked up where he had left off. 'Rachel contacted me around then, asking questions about you, but I couldn't face telling her everything that had happened. So I lied, told her me and Shannon were still together and denied anything had happened between the two of us.'

'Nothing did happen, Artie. It was one minuscule kiss.'

Artie shrugged. 'Yeah, I suppose.'

Something else occurred to me. 'Did you send me another email, the day of my crash? Something about meeting up?'

Artie raised his eyes. 'Rachel asked me that, too, and at the time it confused me because, genuinely, I hadn't sent any such email. But eventually I figured it out. It was Shannon.'

'What?'

'It happened shortly after the miscarriage when she was inconsolable with rage. She was trying to lure you to a pub to punish you for what had happened. But at the last minute she came to her senses. She explained it all to me when I went over to see her a few weeks ago.'

'Okay.' I was struggling to keep up.

'I went over to her shortly after you woke up, when it was confirmed you and Rachel were going to be okay.'

'And Shannon was willing to talk to you this time?'

'Yes, she was,' he said, taking a gulp from a bottle of water. 'Once she heard that you'd nearly died but that I still wanted to come to America, it was like a switch had flicked. She said she wanted to go ahead with the wedding. That she wanted to try for another baby straight away.'

Artie's eyes looked sad now. Really, really sad.

'And yet here you are.'

He bowed his head and nodded. 'We tried, for a few weeks. Took a trip out west, to California. We both wanted to make it work . . .'

I sat in my chair, watching him, struggling against the desire to reach my hand out towards him. To touch him. 'What happened?'

'We went to a big festival in the desert. We'd decided that before we started trying to get pregnant again we'd have one final blow-out. We ended up doing peyote – the drug you get from the cactus.'

I stared at Artie, my eyebrows raised. Artie never did drugs. He was always the sensible one.

'Anyway, on the morning we were due to leave, Shannon told me to go. I didn't understand what she was on about. I thought she meant go and get some breakfast or something, but that wasn't it.' His eyes were sparkling with tears. 'We loved each other. We still do. But, I don't know, it wasn't the same . . . It wasn't enough.'

I was confused. What was he talking about?

'She said, "Go to her." I thought it was the drugs talking. But . . .'

'Her?'

Artie was still babbling. 'She said she didn't resent me any more about the baby, that being in the desert had made her see she needed to let go of the bitterness, that she knew deep down it hadn't been my fault.'

I was still listening, aware that my breathing was becoming shallower.

'She said she admired my loyalty but she couldn't force me into a marriage I didn't really want. Especially given that I was clearly in love with someone else.'

He looked at me then.

'She said it was obvious from the first moment she'd seen the two of us together. That it suddenly made sense why I'd chosen to work in Greenwich – I'd been secretly hoping to bump into you.'

'Christ, Artie, you came looking for me?'

'I don't know,' he said. 'Not consciously. Not specifically. To be honest, I thought I'd never see you again.'

I found myself taking his hand. 'Artie, are you sure this is what you want? You know I can't offer you the same things Shannon could. I've been diagnosed as bipolar. There could still be side-effects from the coma.'

Artie put a finger to my lips. 'I don't want you to offer me anything, Evie. That's not what this is about.'

'But it is, Artie. You need to know the truth. You need to know that I'm damaged. Cracked.' I dipped my head so he couldn't see my face.

Artie put his hand under my chin, tilted it upwards. 'I know,' he said. 'Cracked right down the middle. That's how the light gets in.'

Epilogue

Rachel: day 298, nine and a half months later

While I was in hospital, the doctors told me something else I didn't know – that I was pregnant. That afternoon with Jacob, after the thunderstorm, we'd made a baby. He was visiting me in the wake of Donnagh's attack, but it had taken two consultants to convince him that the pregnancy was real.

'How did the baby survive the fall?' he'd asked, tears plopping down his cheeks.

'Strong little bugger obviously,' the consultant had said, smiling. 'Plus the abdomen wasn't damaged, luckily.'

'You are keeping it, aren't you?' Jacob had asked afterwards, and I'd nodded. This baby was unplanned but I wanted it. I wasn't quite sure why, but I did.

Now, eight months later, I'm finding it almost impossible to walk, waddling around, like some obese duck, willing the child out of me. I don't even have Erica Jong for company any more – I let Mrs Flanagan keep her. To be honest, she's better off there, given my state of near invalidism. I'm one week overdue and can barely move, except to shuffle around the house, take baths and think.

I've been doing a lot of thinking.

Three months ago, Donnagh's trial kicked off. Lorelei flew in, along with Maria, Donnagh's ex-wife, who took to the stand and testified against him, telling the court about his controlling nature, how he'd bullied her psychologically and raped her when she'd asked him for a divorce.

Tom was forced to give evidence, too. He admitted Donnagh had called over to his flat after my attack, threatening to slit his throat unless he handed over all back-ups of the camera footage. Tom had done as he'd been ordered – after all, it was in his interest to get rid of it, too – but the police had been able to retrieve some files deleted from his email. Apparently he'd been sharing some of his perverted documentary on the dark web. Not everything was there but it did include the file of Donnagh trying to rape Evie. It was likely to be the piece of evidence the case would rest on.

And, of course, we had other witnesses: the police officers, who'd found Donnagh in Evie's hospital room, after he'd put masking tape over her mouth; Evie's own account of how Donnagh had attacked her. Finally, there was the psychiatrist, Dr Kincaid, who testified that, while Donnagh could not be diagnosed as clinically insane, he appeared to display all the attributes of a sociopath, and symptoms of what he called 'narcissistic personality disorder'. He explained that people with that diagnosis tended to fear rejection and abandonment, often stemming from childhood, and that they often had extreme reactions to perceived slights or criticism. 'Other prominent features include anger, competitiveness, power struggles, and a tendency to externalize blame.'

At that point, Evie and I had shared a look. They didn't know the half of it.

I couldn't believe how remarkably well my sister was handling everything. She didn't seem fazed by the fact that she'd had to take the stand and testify against Donnagh, probably because she had Artie now – but also because she seemed so much more confident. She wasn't completely back to her old self – she needed more rest than normal and her concentration span was quite short – but Dr Bartlett was optimistic she would make a full recovery.

'She's a lucky girl,' she had said to me one afternoon, after I'd gone in to thank her for all she'd done. 'Most people don't survive an injury of that magnitude without some lasting legacy.'

'Oh, she has a lasting legacy, all right,' I said, meaning Donnagh and what he'd done to her. 'But we're working on that.'

I never heard a peep from our father. All that detective work linked to the postcard and it turned out Donnagh had sent it. He'd stolen it from Evie's handbag and paid some stranger in the Gare du Nord to post it for him, his idea of a sick joke. That person must have been on their way to Calais at the time and had sent it from there – nothing to do with our father at all.

As for the handwriting, that had been another con – Donnagh had simply mimicked a different script when he'd scribbled down that sentence for me in the flat. It was something he'd been doing since he was a child apparently: forging documents.

It had all come out at the trial. The first half of it, at any rate.

On the seventh day, a new person arrived at the court:

Donnagh's uncle from Chicago. There were rumours he had put off coming because he was so appalled by what Donnagh had done. But he came anyway. He told the court that Donnagh had been born into 'difficult circumstances' – his father an alcoholic, his mother suffering with severe postnatal depression. He cried when he described what a cute child Donnagh had been, how fearless, inquisitive and beautiful he was. He choked up several times. He said he'd done his best, tried to turn Donnagh's life around by bringing him to Chicago, where he had mentored him and offered him a partnership in the business.

I watched Donnagh's face then, intrigued by his reaction. Instead of looking at his uncle, or even keeping his head in his hands, he stared straight ahead. Unblinking. As if all the stuff his uncle was saying was going right over him. As if he didn't care.

The next day we realized Donnagh *had* cared. He had hanged himself in his cell overnight, using the tie he'd worn in court.

None of us, not Evie, myself, Jacob or Artie, knew how to react. We thought we should be relieved that he was out of our lives for good and would never again be able to wreak his particular brand of havoc on anyone else. Instead we felt empty.

Now I pace my house in Sandycove and I try to make sense of everything. Sometimes I sleep, and when I do, I dream of my father. That he is beside me, smiling at me, waiting for my baby to be born.

In the direct aftermath of everything, I went to a psychologist. I feared I might be suffering from post-traumatic stress disorder and that what I'd been through might affect the baby. I didn't feel traumatized, but something wasn't right. It was like I was fragmented: I needed to collect the pieces of myself and put them back together.

At some point I told the psychologist something I'd never told anyone. It was a memory of my father, Evie and me standing at the lake shore. We sisters would have been about five and three. My father was stuffing rocks into his pockets, encouraging Evie and me to do likewise. Then he took our hands, telling us we were going for a 'little swim'. I could remember the rough grasp of his fingers on mine as he coaxed me towards the water, the cold feel of it on my bare legs. Then, out of nowhere, I could see Mammy running – her hair blowing behind her in the breeze. When she finally caught up with us, she hit the back of my father's head with a stone, shouting at us to 'run like panthers' . . .

'I don't know if it's real or if I've imagined it,' I told the psychologist, who didn't say anything for a couple of minutes.

After a while she explained something about repressed memories: how we bury images in our unconscious that are too painful to acknowledge or talk about.

Now I think about this story, put my hand on my bump, allow it to rest there.

This is the only child I will ever have. I know that.

I didn't want to be a mother. But I want this child. This child saved me – saved me and Jacob – and I will love it with all my heart.

And yet . . .

Something creeps behind the surface of my brain; scuttles across it like an insect.

It's a memory of another night. Around nine months ago now, when I got so drunk I could hardly remember anything the next morning. I still recall the trampled-on feeling after I'd opened my eyes. Like I was no longer in my own skin. Like I'd been touched . . .

I feel my bump again. Rub it.

I could have a DNA test after the birth, just to be completely sure. But that would be paranoid.

That way madness lies.

I've never thought of confiding that to Evie, but I have debated telling her about my lakeside memory. Perhaps it would make her feel better if she knew about our father. That he hadn't abandoned us, like she thought. That he was just mentally unwell.

But then again, would it do her any good to know he'd tried to drown us?

I have my doubts.

The publishers want me to write the 'real story' of what happened on the night of Donnagh's assault – true crime meets feminism. But I'm taking a break from writing. From writing about myself, anyway.

Instead I'll wait here for my baby to be born, clutching my secrets to my heart, as I will my newborn.

Here's what I've learned over the past nine months.

Some secrets must be chased – held out to the light and examined – while others . . . they are different. With them, it's better that we never know.

Acknowledgements

It is hard to know where to start with all the thank-yous because so many people have helped to make this book happen, but anyway here goes.

Thank you, first, to Sheila Crowley, agent *extraordinaire* at Curtis Brown, who believed in me from the start and who gave me not just the title of this book but the kind of game-changing advice that made it publishable; to Rebecca Ritchie, of the same parish, whose helpfulness and enthusiasm never waned; also to freelance editor Sophie Wilson, whose early suggestions for this book were incredibly useful.

Thank you to everyone at Penguin Ireland: to my editors, Claire Pelly and Patricia Deevy, for seeing such possibility in *Sisters and Lies*; to Michael McLoughlin, Cliona Lewis, Brian Walker and Patricia McVeigh, for such a warm and wonderful introduction to the Penguin Ireland 'family'. To Lee Motley for the stunning cover and Hazel Orme and Keith Taylor for the meticulous copy-editing. Thank you all from the bottom of my heart.

To the amazing teachers I've had over the years: Kieran Tonra, whose early encouragement made me think perhaps I could write; to Mike McCormack and Adrian Frazier of NUI Galway, who did likewise. To the tutors at the Irish Writers' Centre – Conor Kostick, Claire Hennessy, Juliet Bressan and Mia Gallagher – for their unwavering belief. To the inspiring Vanessa O'Loughlin of Writing.ie. To the wonderful Orna Ross. Most especially, to Helen Bovaird-Ryan of Pen to Paper Writing Workshops, who set me on the path to creative writing as an adult and who threw in a husband while she was at it. (Helen, you should charge extra for that service.)

To my dear friends Tricia McAdoo, Aine Tierney and Joe Griffin, whose advice, good cheer and shared passion for fiction spurred me on to finish this book. To Lorraine Downey, who never stopped believing. To the Trinity, Whitespace and Galway gangs (all non-violent!), for the laughs and support. To Mairead Campbell and Amanda Kerr, for a host of memorable life experiences ☺

To my more recent writing pals: Gai Griffin, Marian Keyes, Mags McLoughlin and Clodagh Murphy. Gai, there are no words to adequately express my gratitude (you really are a little bit psychic). Marian, I am not worthy to touch the hem of your skirt. Thank you for being such a HUGE inspiration to me and for all your kindness. Clodagh, for the laughs, the dinner dates and the good advice. Mags – it's your turn next.

To all the wonderful writers I've met as a journalist and with whom I've shared writing classes down through the years – too many to mention: your support has been invaluable. Likewise, to all my colleagues at Zahra Media in Greystones, for demonstrating, every day, what it is to be creative.

To the staff at the Tyrone Guthrie Centre in Annaghmakerrig, County Monaghan, for everything. TG is where dreams become reality (and writers become fat because of all the fabulous food). Long may it continue.

To my extended family – particularly Raymond and Jerry Brogan for repeatedly asking if the 'fecking book' was finished yet – and to all the Mulligans and Brogans for being such a force for good in my life.

To cousin Claire Nicholl, for sharing the dream, reading early scribblings and generally being an inspiration.

To Clare and Ted Barrington, I couldn't have asked for lovelier parents-in-law. Thank you for your unwavering support.

To my brother David, for insightful advice on spycams (I will not ask how you know this stuff); to my sister Loraine, for always being my cheerleader; to Conor Power, for help when I really needed it; and to baby Sarah, for being adorable 100 per cent of the time.

To my father Brian and my mother Mary: for making me feel I could do anything I wanted to in life. To steal a quote from my sister: you are the breath in my lungs and the blood in my veins. I love you with all my heart.

And finally to Brian. I fell in love with your writing. And then I fell in love with you. Thank you for being the rock I build my life on. Here's to the next chapter.